To Jane (

3n May 2004

My story
Simon, ... -   *Marlis.*
...   *ne*

WHO WILL WATCH
OVER ME?

A CHILDHOOD MEMOIR

JEANNE IVALDI

First published in 2001 by
Cromwell Publishers
Suite 87
405 Kings Road
Chelsea
London SW10 0BB

E-mail: Info@CromwellPublishers.co.uk
Internet address: www.CromwellPublishers.co.uk

Paperback ISBN 1-901679-63-2

This is dedicated to my sister, Phyllis, and my brother, Andy, without whom I would not have been able to shape my stories, and who, I am sure, have stories of their own

"All of us will take to our graves a vast catalogue of memories that give us a picture of who we are and what we have been. Some of them are true and unadorned. Others, to put it kindly, are enhanced. A few are wholly false."

Richard Girling*

*"Unlocking Your Memory," by Richard Girling, THE SUNDAY TIMES, London, 1 February 1998, from "Total Recall", p.2.

ACKNOWLEDGEMENTS

I wish to thank:

- The Writers' Workshop of the American Women's Club of Geneva and the Geneva Writers' Group, Switzerland, for their combined wisdom and critiquing, especially **Yvonne Laverriere** and **Elaine Marejko** who read the first drafts of my manuscript.
- Susan Tiberghien, Wallis-Wilde Menozzi, Thomas E. Kennedy and Alexandra Johnson who have been both teachers and mentors, inspiring me to go on with writing.
- My husband, Giacomo, and our sons, Mark and Philip, who always wanted to know about my childhood and who gave me the courage to tell it.

PREFACE

Childhood memories recline in the corpuscles of my mind. They course through my veins unable to surface or escape. When friends show surprise at how much I can remember from an early age, I say,

"You must have had a happy childhood."

Why do certain childhood images remain so clear? It's hard to know. At times it is like traveling in a dream elevator. No matter what direction it takes the door opens onto a scene from the past. Can I ever be rid of them?

Years ago during Chinese painting lessons my 94 year-old teacher said to me, as she patiently ground the ink stick on the smooth stone, "There is no need to write down what I teach you. If you want to remember, listen to me, look at what I do, then do it. If you write it down, it is the paper that will remember it."

I hope that by writing down my story, it is the paper that will remember it.

Jeanne Ivaldi

PART ONE THE FIRST TEN YEARS

1945 - 1955

CHAPTERS

PART TWO　　THE HOME

1955 – 1963

CHAPTERS

Chapter One
The Christening Robe

Memory begins in the parlor. It is noisy and crowded and the blue walls reverberate with people's talk. I wade through a sea of legs, swim among serge trousers and plaid skirts. My brother, Andy, arrives in this world fourteen months after me and he's a December baby. How old am I when he is christened? Probably not more than two years. Christenings aren't put off for long in the mid-1940's.

Someone grabs me around the waist and stops me in mid-dive. "Who are you?" he asks. I wriggle and try to slip away, but hands criss-crossed with red hairs squeeze me. The man holds me up at arm's length and I laugh in spite of myself. I have a bird's-eye view above the bobbing heads. "Who do you belong to?" He drops me. "Whoops!" Then catches me quickly. His teeth flash white. I giggle in his arms. He nuzzles me, his red beard tickling the back of my neck. When he sets me down, I squirm away.

"Jeanne's ours, Big Red," Dad shouts above the din from across the room. He holds my new brother in his arms, a tiny bundle in a satin and lace gown with bonnet to match. His red face has a backside to match, too. I should know, I saw it.

"Isn't that your daughter over there?" He points to my seven-year-old sister, Phyllis, who is reading a book on someone's lap.

"That's our eldest."

"You mean you've had this daughter in between and we didn't know anything about it?"

"Yeah, well, this is to celebrate the two of them! Now leave her alone and get me another drink, will you?"

This is the first and only time we see him. Later on we hear about him while eavesdropping on our parents. Our ears perk up to things said in passing between them. Big Red. The name sticks probably because it is the first time we've meet anyone with a nickname. On this christening day, we are impressed with his booming voice, his confidence, his easy charm. I feel safe and important in his arms. Phyllis is enchanted by his storytelling. Later on Andy believes whatever we tell him about the man.

9

What is it that makes us want to create a hero out of him? He drops out of our lives as suddenly as he appears; yet we stoke the embers of his memory for as long as we can. When things go wrong and our world breaks apart, we debate about how we can get in touch with Big Red. "He might be able to help us," Andy suggests.

"He won't remember us," I say. He didn't come to see us after the christening, did he?"

Phyllis, who is older and usually knows everything, says, "We can't telephone him because we don't know his number. We can't write to him because we have no address."

Our hero fades from our midst, but memories of the christening are regularly revived. We use the blue wicker bassinet, from where my brother held court that day, to store our toys and books. Its rickety wheels squeak under the weight as we push it around the apartment like a trolley. We manoeuvre it from our bedroom to the parlor by way of the kitchen.

On rainy days, when we can't go out and Mom doesn't want us under her feet in the kitchen, we play in the bedrooms. We shut the adjoining door to the kitchen where she washes clothes at the sink within earshot of our games. Phyllis puts a finger to her lips and says, "Sshhh." Then she gets out the 'things we're not supposed to touch' like Mom's silver-blue powder puff music box that plays a tune when you open it. The powder has been used up long ago, but the puff smells sweet. On the lid there is a plastic dome that protects a crocheted silver star on top. Andy and I don't touch the box, but once the lid is raised, we are allowed to put a finger on a small lever that stops the music when it is held down. If we let it go, it tinkles out a tune.

The most important thing we aren't allowed to touch is the white cardboard box containing the christening robe. "You'll wear it out if you keep touching it," Mom says. But we can't resist it. This is our favorite thing we aren't allowed to touch. We lift the box out of Mom's top drawer and treat the robe like a holy relic, which, of course, it is. It has been to church, not once, but three times. We have all been christened in it. Its cocoon of tissue paper crinkles loud to our ears.

"What're you kids doing in there?" Mom yells from the kitchen. Because of the rain she hangs the still-wet wash on chairs and radiators and drapes our underpants over the icebox. "You better not be touching things you're not supposed to." Through the closed door she adds, her voice rising with every syllable, "It's only a shower. It'll probably stop soon so you can all go out. You hear me?"

Over the talking we get the robe laid out on the bed. The noisy tissue paper has not given us away. I count the tiny mother-of-pearl buttons down the back. Ten. I can't imagine myself small enough to wear the robe. None of us can. I hold the delicate bonnet in my hands and the ribbon ties snake down my arms. We find it hard to believe that these were handmade by Mom. Our equal shares in the robe unite us since we each wore it once. We are reverent before it. Phyllis whispers, "They light a candle, then pray. Then they put a white shawl around you, and pray some more. Then the man in charge rubs some sort of grease on your forehead. After another prayer, they chuck water all over you."

"But, what about the christening robe? That'd spoil it," Andy says.

"That's what the shawl is for, stupid!"

There are three small booklets at the bottom of the box beneath the tissue paper. Each one has our name on it. I take out mine. Phyllis reads out the words on the front page, "Baptismal Font". I can understand a few words from the inside, but guess they must be the instructions. On the last page, hand-written in black ink, is the word Methodist, a word I don't understand.

"Mom, what's Methodist? Does that mean christened?"

"In a way."

"In what way?"

"It means that you were baptized in the Methodist faith."

"What's faith?"

"It's your religion."

"You mean that everyone who has a christening robe has a religion?"

"Yes. But there are lots of religions."

"How many?"

"Oh, I don't know. Hundreds, maybe."

"Are we all the same religion in our family?"

"No... we aren't."

"Is that why we don't go to church?"

"Partly, yes."

11

"What part?"

"It's complicated."

"Other kids go to church."

I don't find out what the complications are until much later. We're Americans, but we're Russians, too. My grandparents on Dad's side came from Leningrad and their religion was Russian Orthodox. The other grandparents came from another part of Russia, and their religion was Islam. Mom told us that in New York City in the late 1930's neither church would marry them because they had different religions. The Methodists agreed to marry them, on one condition −they had to promise to baptize their children Methodists.

The box containing our christening robe surfaces as regularly as rainy days. We are drawn to its mystery and the ritual that surrounds it. We dress a teddy bear in the satin gown and tie his ears down with a rubber band so the bonnet will fit. We take turns being the parents and walk ourselves through the ceremony of an illusive faith, a faith that has been bestowed on us, for whatever reason, one that is proven, written in black ink in a booklet. It is important for us to know that we are Methodists. The world outside our apartment doors has made it clear that we've got to have a nationality, and we've got to have a religion. Luckily, we have both.

Chapter Two
Morality Matters

As we grow up we incubate under an umbrella of rules and regulations. Verbal codes of conduct are showered on us daily by our parents in the form of do's and don'ts. "Look after your sister. Don't steal from the candy store. Help your brother. Don't get into fights. No swearing. Don't keep secrets. Say you're sorry." Andy and I try hard to stick to the rules, but most of the time Phyllis does her best to ignore them.

"Do as I say, don't do as I do," is a phrase I hear many years later, but I already know how things are. Mom and Dad try to give us a moral education. "Don't steal. Don't lie. Don't talk about other people. Be nice, be good, have patience, be loyal, help one another," we are continually reminded; but the truth is, we hear them argue, swear, lie, and all the other don'ts in the book and draw our own conclusions.

"It doesn't take a genius to work out that what grown-ups tell you, what they expect you to do, doesn't amount to a hill of beans," Phyllis says. "You've got to figure it out for yourself." I try to, but get it wrong, even though Phyllis warns me. "No. Not now!" she hisses, but I can't help myself. While Dad changes a hot television tube, and there's a lull in the uproar he's making, I ask him why he's using certain words that we're not supposed to. He leaps forward and slaps me so hard with the back of his hand that bells ring in my ears.

"Go outside or I'll kill you!" he threatens. I see that "I told you so!" glint in Phyllis' eyes before I crash through the kitchen door with my hand over a smarting cheek on my way downstairs.

What is it like down there in the street, where religion, nationality and morals are so important? It's tough. All those do's and don'ts we've learned come in useful. Things I've heard at home and on the street automatically spring to mind. There's a boy who sits all day on the stoop across the street. He dribbles and drools a lot, but he's harmless. Once he gave me half a candy bar. If someone picks on him, I stick up for him now. "Hey you," I'll say. "Leave him alone. Wha'd ja go and do that for? Can't you see he's a Mongol idiot, you jerk? Get the hell outta here!" We need to protect the underdog.

New York City and Brooklyn, in particular, where we live, is a spicy blend of people from all over the world. Most of our neighbors are immigrants from both World Wars. Vagrants who sleep on park benches wander the streets picking through garbage cans. Recently-arrived refugees camp-out with relatives in apartments that are already bursting at the seams. And there are kids - lots of them - who run free in the streets.

"Oi, Joe, whatcha doin' out on the stoop?"

"My mudder kicked me out. Uncle Pete's got night shift. Needs ta sleep."

"Wanna go down the dump? See what we can find?"

We play together - skip rope, potsie, ball and jacks, marbles, checkers, stickball and tossing pennies; anyone can scrounge a couple of coins for a game. We stick together, forming a gang of ten, marching down the street singing our own lyrics to well-known songs like *Whistle While You Work*, our favorite from the movie *Snow White*.

> Whistle while you work.
> Hitler is a jerk!
> Mussolini is a weenie,
> But the Japs are worse!

We sharpen ice-lollipop sticks, getting a good point by scraping them back and forth on the rough sidewalks. "We want war! We want war!" we chant as the innocent sticks turn into weapons. Putting on our roller skates, we carefully tighten the metal clamps around the toes with our communal skate key, frightened a skate might loosen. It would be a disaster if one of us went down in front of the enemy. It's my job to look after the key that hangs around my neck on an old shoelace. The noise is deafening as eighty metal wheels hit the sidewalk at the same time. We head straight for another bunch of kids who skate towards us also chanting "We want war!"

It's nearly dark and our skates strike sparks on the granite sidewalks. We look for danger with fear on our breath. I'm so scared I can't control my legs and by the time I bring up the rear, the skirmish is over. The kids at the front have used their 'daggers' and the 'enemy' has dispersed. Since we are not allowed to cross the street at night, we continue skating around one square block, which will bring us back to our front stoop at 67 Wyckoff Avenue. Three quarters of the way around, in full darkness now, the biggest boy in our gang says, "I betch'a a dime none of youse guys will go up close to the shoemaker's store." We pull to a stop.

"The shoemaker's creepy. He talks weird and he's a cripple. Anyhow, you don't have no dime," a smaller boy says.

"You're nuttin' but a bunch'a scaredy cats."

"You know what happened the last time we banged on his window.

He came out with a rope and he might have hanged us," Phyllis reminds everyone.

"This time he's not even here. I saw him goin' down the subway about an hour ago," the big boy says. We sidle up to the plate glass window and press our noses to it. A breeze disturbs the street light and it makes crooked shadows dance inside the store. We see old shoes and boots, tools, laces, and a few boxes of nails.

"It's not one bit scary," I say.

"Look over there!" the smaller boy says. We follow a dirty, pointing finger. "It looks like someone is hanging by the neck!" We strain to see a vague shadow at the back of the store. Suddenly, a flashlight is illuminated from inside. Someone shrieks, and we skate away to the safety of our stoop. When our breath returns, and our skates are buckled together and slung over our shoulders, Andy says,

"It was only a hat and coat hanging there, wasn't it?"

"Ah, shuddup! Wha'd'you know, anyhow?" the bigger boy says slinking off home.

We are a bunch of kids trying to amuse ourselves and unintentionally upset our neighbors when we form a group and sing from our stoop. The trouble is, we can't really sing and we don't know many songs either. We start with "My Country 'Tis of Thee" and the national anthem which everyone ought to know from school. But we sing out of tune and mess up the words. We are only vaguely surprised when a bucket of water lands on our heads.

As a group we stem from a variety of nationalities, but are fundamentally the same - each and every one of us is prejudiced. We have names for everybody - Spicks, Reds, Yids, Niggers, Wops, Jews, Krauts, Polaks, Micks, Chinks, Dagos, and Nips – and we use them at will. Some of them I learned at home and others I picked up on the street. They stick like glue. Name-calling follows so swiftly in the wake of my nursery rhyme days that they slide off my tongue like butter melting in a pan.

Within the gang we do what everyone else does and act as one. When strangers wander into our neighborhood wearing yarmulkes and side curls, we heckle them. We shout names at people dressed differently from us and even throw things at them. We mimic people, ridiculing their speech, and imitating their disabilities. We hate hunchbacks and toothless old ladies, laugh at other people's expense and gain popularity for it, become defensive when challenged by authority. Compassion is still to be learned. We may like one another today, but we hate everyone else. Tomorrow we might not even like each other. Are we molded for life?

Chapter Three
A Mixture Of Minorities

Park benches under elm trees are boring places for most children, but this is where we find the only shade in our neighborhood in summer, three blocks away from home. I sit there and daydream while Phyllis and Andy splash in the wading pool. Men doze nearby in various versions of brown felt hats. Beside me a housewife knits a shawl, keeping time to an unheard tune while she rocks her baby carriage with the steady rhythm of one foot.

A change in light patterns on the tarmac path occurs whenever the breeze rustles treetops. Two men begin a silent game when a checkerboard appears on a bench opposite. One man puffs on a pipe, while the other rests his chin on a curved-handled cane. When one speaks, either through satisfaction or defeat, I hear a language from worlds away. Mom and Dad speak a foreign language when they don't want us to know what they're saying. "What's that language you were speaking?" I asked Mom.

"Russian and Polish."

"Why don't we talk like that?"

"Because you're American and you must speak English."

"Where did you learn it?"

"From my parents."

"The people who live next door speak Spanish, and I can't understand them."

"The Spicks? They bica, bica, meta, meta all day, drives me nuts."

"Why don't they speak like Americans?"

"Because they come from Puerto Rico. They just got off the boat. Don't worry, they'll learn quick enough when it comes to collecting welfare checks."

"I don't understand."

Everyone tries to speak English in public, but we live in a neighborhood where people come from all over the world, so it is only natural that we find out about them through the food they eat. In the evenings the smell of fried fish floats across the alleyway from the Puerto Ricans' apartments. Dad says they lived on a small island so fish was their main food. Our German neighbors have boiled potato dumplings, sausages and sauerkraut on Thursday nights making my mouth water on a weekly basis. We eat Russian food like blintzes, borsch and potato pancakes with sour cream. When Dad cooks his favorite - pigs' feet - it stinks to high heaven, but it tastes good. No one else I know eats it. Most of my friends eat spaghetti and goulash.

On our way home from the park we pass by a cellar where they make German pretzels. Metal doors lead down to an underground bakery. In winter, we warm ourselves by the ovens and feast on thick, doughy pretzels sprinkled with crusty salt crystals for only two cents apiece. The Danish bakery's window is crammed with apple squares, raisin crescents and cheesecakes three inches high and as light as a feather. At the German delicatessen salamis and strings of sausages hang from hooks on the ceiling. Cheeses as big around as a man's waist squat under the glass counter by the pickle barrel where I have fun chasing pickles in brine with a pair of wooden pincers. "I bought a pickle for a nickel," Dad sings from the song made popular by my favorite snack. "You're the only kid I know that would rather have a pickle than a candy bar!"

The neighborhood Italian restaurant is special, being more like someone's home than a public place. The brick wood-fired oven guarantees a cosy welcome on cold nights. The whole place smells like freshly baked bread. We order a family-size pizza that is so huge, it takes the three of us to carry it home. Our favorite dog, a German shepherd, lives there. While petting him and rubbing her fingers deep into his coat, Phyllis says, "Some day I'm going to have a dog and I'm going to call him Rex. That means King." We sit quiet for a while and watch a couple of kids do their homework at one of the tables in the corner covered with a red and white checked tablecloth. Chianti bottles substitute for candlesticks and I pick at layers of congealed wax stuck to the sides. We don't mind how long we have to wait for the pizza. The old man, who the kids call 'Nonno', takes our order. First he says, "So, how'sa your Mamma? and your Papa? You been gooda kids? I'ma sure, I'ma sure. How's abouta some moosica?" He starts up an old jukebox. A man's voice floats around the room.

"When the moon hits your eye like-a bigga pizza pie, that's amore..." After that another record slots onto the turntable. "Volare, oh, oh, oh, oh, Cantare, oh, oh, oh, oh...."

As the dog snores in his sleep and the logs shift in the oven, I begin to think I want to live here. But, "Here'sa your pizza," Nonno says, and we have to leave.

Dad's favorite food is Chinese. "Let's go to the Chinks tonight," he says and before he can change his mind Mom has us in hats and coats. To keep us quiet in the car on the way to the Peking Diner, Dad entertains us. "How do the Chinese get their names?"

"We dunno."

"After a baby is born someone throws a handful of silver spoons into the air. The sound the last one makes as it hits the floor is the name of the child - Ping, Pang, Pong, Ting, Tang, Tong." I believe it well into adulthood.

"You're making a general nuisance of yourselves," Mom says half-heartedly watching us spear one other with our chopsticks while waiting for the food to come.

"Don't leave anything on your plates," Dad advises.

"THINK OF ALL THOSE STARVING PEOPLE IN CHINA," we chorus. As if we would.

Unlike the relaxed family atmosphere of the Italian restaurant, at the Peking Diner there's a lot of frantic shuffling back and forth in slippered feet. The kitchen is all hustle and bustle. We hear waiters shout orders to cooks. The cooks shout at one another. "Aiiiiya!" Choppers bang on boards. Hot steam squeezes through the kitchen doors and when someone comes through them, it sounds like crockery is bouncing off the floor.

In the car on the way home, full of noodles and rice and a gallon of tea, I fall asleep and dream about the message in my fortune cookie, "You will live in a faraway country and visit many lands."

Chapter Four
Homes And Gardens

Summers are long for us. Mom wants peace and quiet, peace and quiet. Her plea echoes in our ears like the refrain of a song. "There's so much work. There's washing, there's cleaning… Stay out!" she pleads. "You're messing up the place."

Wash days are the problem. For some time there hasn't been enough money to spare for the launderette. "Even if we had it, it isn't convenient," she tells us, "and it's too far away." I remember it was a lot of trouble. To carry our dirty clothes over there, we had to stuff them into a shopping basket on wheels. Mom wouldn't waste money on the dryer, so we hauled the heavy, wet laundry back home again and hung it out to dry on the line. She says she'd rather wash everything at home in the deep sink beneath the wooden draining board on the left side of the kitchen sink. I sit at the kitchen table and play with clay while Mom spends the better part of the day up to her elbows in hot water. Soapy steam fills the kitchen as I watch the clothes float and swirl around the washboard. Her head down, she scrubs them hard on the corrugated metal surface and they moan - *bedove, bedove, bedove* - her sighs the only accompaniment to this lonely melody. Phyllis helps wring out the trousers and sheets. Holding one end while Mom grasps the other, they twist and pull at our blue jeans like home-made taffy.

The laundry hangs from a clothesline that's strung up on a pulley outside the parlor window. It's attached to a pole at the far end of the yard. Mom leans out of the window, pins, then pushes, pins, then pushes until there's a full line of clean clothes fluttering on a breezy day or sagging on a still one. In the middle of winter the clothes freeze into stiff imitations of our family. Mom pulls them through the window. "Be careful those jeans don't crack. They're your sister's only pair." We stand them up beside the radiators until they are sufficiently supple to bend them over the top. Soon the frozen clothes are steaming like dumplings.

Our building has three floors with two apartments on each floor. We are on the right side of the second floor and our landlady lives beneath us. We're supposed to be quiet especially when Dad's out of work and our rent isn't on time. Her grandson, who often stays with her, swaps comics with us when he can, but she makes him practice on the clarinet. His whistles and squeaks drive us crazy, but when he gets it right and plays a whole piece without stopping, his music smokes up the alleyway and spreads into our kitchen providing us with a private concert.

When she's finished hanging out the wash, Mom stands back and looks at the clothesline. She is about to smile in satisfaction, but cries, "Oh, no! My slip's fallen down in the yard."

"What are we gonna do, Mom?"

"You'll have to go and get it, Jeanne."

The yard is, and always has been, Out of Bounds. I have admired the rose bushes, flowers, a small square of lawn and all the other yards that stretch out as far as I can see from a second floor window. Our fire escape overlooks the yard and in the summer we have picnics on the landing outside the parlor window. Mom cuts up sandwiches into quarters and we dine off the pink plastic dishes from my doll's tea set. In the winter the fire escape is our icebox so we don't have to order ice in the winter.

"Who is it and whatcha' want?" the landlady queries through her keyhole when I ring the doorbell.

I shut my eyes tight and say through the closed door, "Mom says can I get her slip that fell in the yard...Please?" She opens the door and stands back to let me in. Her apartment smells of talcum powder and cats. It's exactly the same as ours only it's dark. Heavy curtains droop from the windows and don't let the light in like our venetian blinds.

"Hurry up. I haven't got all day," the landlady squawks. I run and get it and scoot out of the open front door as quickly as I can. In the hallway, sunlight streams through a window on the vestibule door. All the brassware gleams - on the doorknobs, mailboxes and stair carpet rods. There isn't a speck of dust anywhere, even the windows sparkle. Our landlady keeps the place spotless.

The front door to our apartment opens onto the kitchen. To the right are the two bedrooms, to the left, the rest of the kitchen, bathroom and parlor. I share a bedroom with my sister and we sleep in a double bed that has a smooth wooden headboard and footboard. The two bureau drawers, a tall one and a short one, are part of a matching set. Mom and Dad's room is next to ours, and they have to go through ours to get to it. There isn't a door, but an alcove separates our rooms. Andy sleeps in a crib in their room because there's nowhere else to put him.

Our parents' room faces the front street, so when cars pass by at night, their headlights make moving patterns on the walls. When the venetian blinds are not fully shut, stripes slide along the room through the slits. Their bed is a darker, glossier wood and the bureau drawers have a mirror on top. They also have a large chifforobe because there's no closet in their room.

I know this apartment well. It is the only place I have ever lived in, so it is the limit and the brink of my existence. I bounce from room to room confident of its dimensions and layout. There is order here. Sweaters lay in drawers with arms crossed, and coats hang on hooks behind my bedroom door. Groceries line kitchen shelves and the icebox bulges in summer. Daily routines, like brushing my teeth and taking a bath, meal times and bed times, structure my life.

We have chores to do, too. Phyllis takes out the garbage. Andy puts away the toys. I help Mom make the beds. I smooth my hands over the top and know that the candlewick bedspreads don't just cover the bed, they provide a dash of color that brightens the bedrooms on a dreary day. When I nap on top of the bed, a furry ridge is etched on my cheek.

It's the rare day I share in a treat, but a remembered one. The fruit and vegetable man's call is heard long before the clopping of his horse's hooves announces his arrival. "Shall we get some fruit today?" Mom asks me as the old man's warble reverberates around the block.

"Apples," I answer. "Red ones." We wave to him from the window and he acknowledges with a tilt of his head. "Whooa," he calls to the horse and tugs gently on the reins. The horse isn't Trigger. He's tired and worn out. His knees are knobby, his expression listless and hang-dog. Nor is the man Roy Rogers. His worn flannel shirt with patches on the sleeves and faded pants don't compare with Roy's fringed shirt and tight-fitting slacks that disappear into shiny cowboy boots. But he is kind, and while he weighs the potatoes, I am able to pet the horse before picking out the apples.

Back upstairs Mom peels them and long coils of the red-skinned mackintosh apples fall in one strip onto the enamel table. I claim them for my own, munching the spirals one by one, sucking them up between apple red lips until they are gone. Afterwards, the yellow flesh of the naked fruit is made into applesauce for everyone.

Chapter Five
The Closets

At night I dream I am being chased. I run as hard as I can but I am falling behind the others who are far ahead of me. Each time I look over my shoulder, the pursuer looms larger. It's a man. It's Frankenstein! With each step forward his heavy boots shake the earth. His advance is noiseless because the dream is silent and my screams are mute. I fall down, pretending to faint, hoping that he will pass by me for someone else. But he stops, bends down, and scoops me up in his stiff arms. He carries me to the closet in my bedroom, taking me through the open door and into the blackness.

The dream ends and I wake up. I open my eyes wide and am relieved to know that I am still in my bed. I hear the beat of the kitchen clock as it ricochets off the kitchen walls. Or is that my heart pounding? Phyllis is sound asleep next to me, but the dark lump of her back is so far away. I want to move closer to her but my legs and arms are paralyzed. The only movements I can make are to breathe and to blink my eyes. In the next room Dad coughs in his sleep then starts snoring. It's a low rumble at first, but crescendos until the venetian blinds begin to rattle. Mom prods him and he rolls over and is quiet again. I want to call out to them for help but can't; maybe I'm still dreaming? Am I?

The dream returns each night and I am afraid to sleep. I ask Phyllis to change places in the bed so she faces the closet and I can hide behind her back. I check that the closet door is shut tight before I go to bed, but in my dream the door is always open.

We have three closets in the apartment, one in our bedroom, one in the alcove outside my parents' bedroom and one off the parlor. We're not supposed to rummage through them, but occasionally Mom says, "Go and get me the galoshes out of your bedroom closet. I think it's going to snow," or "Stick these old clothes in the rag bag at the back of your closet," so we know what's in them.

The deepest and darkest closet is the one in my bedroom. We store a lot of junk in it like old clothes, boxes of crochet cotton, dress patterns, Christmas tree ornaments, sheets and blankets. After grandpa died, Dad wanted to put his father's stuff in our closet. But Mom objected.

"Put them in the cellar."

"No!"

"Throw the junk out."

"Stop telling me what to do! I want to keep them handy."

So there are pictures painted on black velvet, nice to the touch, but horrible to look at, in our closet beside old hats, broken boots and brown shoes without laces. Six large, dusty drawers full of nuts and bolts, odd pieces of glass, tools and spare parts for cars, are stored beneath our bed. Grandpa had been the janitor of his building, and the drawers were from his workshop shed. Whenever I roll over at night there's a clink or a clank from the stash under the bed. "It's enough to give you nightmares," I hear Mom tell Dad. "They're dead man's wares." Ooh. I shudder when I think of it.

My parents' closet is full of clothes like men's suits, women's dresses, high-heeled shoes, and handbags. Mom and Dad never wear them, but I know they used to because they have them on in the picture albums Mom keeps in the drawers under the mirror.

"You're not getting those old pictures out again, are you?" she moans.

"Just having a little look," I say meekly, afraid she'll tell me to put them away.

The black pages are dotted with black and white pictures of Dad posing in front of an airplane, and seated in a big old-fashioned car. Mom is with fashionably dressed friends at the seaside, standing in front of beautiful houses, or alone in a park. My parents look younger - Mom's hair is wavy and long, Dad's falls over his eyes. They are in another, happier life.

Mom brags about Dad always having had a car because he was so smart that he could fix any motor that broke down. She says that he had a part share in the airplane but I never asked her which part. There's one picture that makes me cry. It's one of Mom standing on a pier in front of a large white boat. The wind is fluttering her dress and she is rubbing her eye as the shutter clicks. When I ask her why she is crying she says, "Oh, that. I'm not crying, you silly. I have something in my eye." I look again. Yes, it could be true. But I feel sorry for her anyway. She's wearing a red and white polka-dot dress with a white collar. I know the color because the dress still hangs in her closet alongside another one with a small corsage of fake flowers on the lapel, but it's a bit squashed down and sad-looking from being in the closet for so long. I ask Mom why she never dresses up. "None of them fit me any more. I bought them with my own money, you know. Before I was married, I had a good job as a machinist in a clothing factory. I was lucky to get the job, too. Everyone was after it. The machine was a beauty and never let me down. It only needed some oil from time to time, which I did myself. It hummed like..."

"...a humming bird!" I say, finishing her sentence, fascinated with the idea of her going to work and having a machine that hummed.

The dresses she usually wears have been washed so often, the pattern has worn off, especially down the front. When I hand her the clothes to hang out on wash days, I see the inside facings and know that the gray dress used to be lilac with small purple flowers on it. The only time her other dresses come out of the closet is when Phyllis and I play dress-up, pretending we are on Fifth Avenue in the Easter Parade, when we also take liberties with her shoes and hats.

After we hang it all away, we pick over the boxes of books Mom has on the closet floor. She sees us and says with longing, "I used to be a great reader. Your Dad had to buy me eyeglasses when we were courting. I always had my nose in a book. But I don't have the time now." That isn't quite true. She sometimes slips away to the library on a Saturday morning when Dad is setting up my brother's Mecanno on the parlor floor. She returns with a heavy pile of books that smell of a place I've never been to. They have glossy photographs of the authors on the back and I can't wait until I am old enough to get books of my own from the public library.

Stuffed at the back of the closet are bags of knitting needles, crochet hooks and the start of projects she's begun but never finished like the stack of crocheted doilies under the picture albums. The maroon ones are nice, but I am partial to the dainty white ones that look like snowflakes. She promises to teach me how to crochet when I am older.

The closet off the parlor is 'Dad's Closet' because everything in there belongs to him. We have no reason to look in there except curiosity and every so often we peek into this wide but not very deep space. Long, thin boxes of piano rolls, stacked one on top of the other, take up most of the room. They are for the Pianola in the parlor. "I took that piano apart and put it back together again," Dad reminisces often. "Our neighbours moved out and said I could have it, rolls and all. The only trouble was, it was too big to fit through the front door, so I dismantled it."

It's just as well it's a Pianola and not an ordinary piano because none of us knows how to play the piano. With a Pianola you only need to have strong legs to get a tune out of it. Our favorite is the theme music from The Lone Ranger program that we watch on television. Phyllis says it's a duet, which means that four hands are playing. Andy and I had already figured as much by the amount of keys bobbing up and down when she pumps the pedals. Phyllis thinks that The Lone Ranger must be in the wrong box because The William Tell Overture is written on the label and we've never heard of it.

Dad rarely plays the accordion that sits on the floor of his closet. When he does, after much pestering from us, his fingers, roughened by manual work at the gas station, fumble for the buttons on the left while his right hand picks out a melody on the black and ivory keys. After he warms up and the wheezing becomes notes and chords, the room fills to the brim with music. He plays Russian folk music with skill and emotion, the sad songs making him melancholy. He sings low at first, in a soft baritone, almost bass, then crescendos and his voice matches the volume of the instrument. The song finished, he wipes a tear from his eye and smiles self-consciously as I hand him a cold beer. "At last, something to wet my whistle," he says swallowing in large gulps. "The name of that song, folks, was "Dark Eyes".

Dad's camera, tripod and studio lights are also in the closet. Mom often says what a good photographer he used to be as we pour over albums bursting with pictures that he took and developed himself. A few albums are devoted wholly to my sister when she was little. Andy and I are disappointed that there aren't any pictures recording our babyhood or childhood. We ask Mom why this is, and why he doesn't take any more pictures. Why doesn't he do something with the equipment?

"He's run out of steam," is her reply.

Chapter Six
It's Christmas, Isn't It?

I know it's nearly Christmas because there's snow on the ground. The days are dark and dull, but the snow throws up a light different from the sun and a white glow creeps inside.

Our friends on the block know what presents they're getting for Christmas and are forever talking about their 'list'. They have been to stores and pointed out what they wanted. A few made the trip to New York City where they sat on Santa Claus' knee on the golden throne at Macys' department store and read their lists out to him personally.

In our home we don't ask for Christmas presents. We've seen how it grieves Mom if we hint at any expectations. Instead, we mope around the apartment with disappointment rattling around in our heads like a pair of maracas. Only Dad manages to get into a festive mood. He's supposed to be looking for work, but says it's hard to get anything so close to Christmas. For weeks he's been coming home late at night after he's had drinks with friends in the bar.

"We're not waiting. Get the plates out, we're having supper now," Mom says, never sure what time he'll show up. After we've cleared the dishes, she sits at the kitchen table facing the door, drumming her fingers on its cool surface. Her eyes look far away in a face set like concrete. We're scribbling in our coloring books in the parlor when we hear him stamp his snow-covered boots in the hallway. He peers around the door and his sheepish grin dissolves into a scowl when he realizes that we didn't wait for him.

"I don't want anything to eat. I'm not hungry," he says peevishly, pulling out two bottles of beer from his coat pocket and setting them on the kitchen table. He flops down, not bothering to take his coat off, and he pours out two glasses. He passes one to Mom.

Dad sold our television to raise cash, leaving a big gap in our parlor and in our lives. We don't like imagining someone else watching our television as we switch on the old radio for company. Even the dim light has gone out on the yellow dial depriving us of its meager hint of warmth. As the nights close in, we listen to weather reports from different parts of the country, and sometimes from our own, if a blizzard from Canada threatens to come our way. By

Christmas eve we have lost all hope of a merry Christmas. Mom tells us to stop our hoping and get praying. By which she means that we better pray they don't cut off the electricity and gas because the bills haven't been paid. "It won't be much fun sitting around in the dark with no dinner on Christmas day," she warns.

How do I pray? I've only been to church once and that was at my christening. "Almighty God and Father..." Prayers on the radio on Sundays start like this, but is it appropriate to ask about the gas bill? Would cherubs or angels be interested in our electricity?

My sister is worried that her teacher might ask her class to write a composition called "What I Did on Christmas Day" on the first day back, like last year. "I'm sick to death of making things up. Last year I wrote about a thousand things I'd wished I'd got, only making out like I really got them, and the teacher whispered to me that I was lying. 'Now be a good girl,' she said, 'and tell us the truth. We don't mind if you only got something small. It's the thought that counts, you know. Just be honest.' So I had to write it all over again."

"What did you put?"

"I put in about Dad disappearing until the day after Christmas. I wrote about how he'd slipped on the ice and fallen down the subway stairs and broken his leg in three places. I left out that he'd been drinking, but put that he was unconscious in the hospital and they didn't know who he was until he woke up."

"Did you tell about the presents?"

"Yeah. I put that we never got nothing for Christmas."

"What'd the teacher say? Did she like the composition?"

"No! She said I'd make a good story-teller and to forget it for now."

It's late and Mom tells us to hang up the stockings. I'm the only one who wears knee-high socks that hold even more than one of Dad's. I run to the bureau drawers and choose a navy-blue one for Andy, a dark green one for Phyllis, and a red one for me. They hang from thumbtacks on the side of the parlor table. We bunch up together on the sofa and listen as Silent Night filters from the radio, staring at the limp socks which we hope by morning will be fat and bulging with candy, fruit and small gifts. Our thoughts are so far away that we are startled when Dad arrives. His coat and hat are powdered with snow, and his gloved hands are pulling a very large evergreen tree through the kitchen door. It's enormous and practically the length of the kitchen. Phyllis, Andy and I run to shift the sofa and armchairs to make room for it in the parlor as Mom and Dad pull the tree through the apartment. Dad stands it up in the corner and its top branches are bent down by the ceiling. I'm sad to see it like that. I suck in its special gift, the scent of the forest, pungent in the warmth of our apartment.

"Where did you get it?" Mom asks Dad in a whisper in the kitchen.

"Joe the bartender put me on to it."

"You didn't steal it?"

"Nah. I waited 'til it looked like business was over before I went up to him. The guy must've had a good day's takings because he said I could have it for nothing."

We don't hear any more because we're too busy fishing through my bedroom closet for the tree lights and ornaments. By the time we get everything out of the closet, find what we need, and then get it all back in again, Mom is in bed. Dad nails a few planks together as a base and nails the tree to it. He stands on a kitchen chair to cut off the top and we remind him to leave enough room for the star. He sways from side to side as he saws and the over-sized tree shivers. Pine needles stick to the ceiling and to the walls and tumble down to the floor. He curses under his breath but finishes the job. He steadies himself on my shoulder as he gets down then stumbles and as I straighten him, his sour breath envelops me. I can almost hear Mom say, "You smell like a brewery!" He makes it to the sofa and immediately falls asleep.

Phyllis takes charge. "Jeanne, get out the Christmas balls and, Andy, get out the tinsel. I'll do the star and the lights." She unwinds the lights from the cardboard as I take out our multicolored ornaments made of very thin glass in the shape of stars, balls and bells. Andy untangles the silver tinsel that we carefully preserve from year to year. We decorate the tree and, when we turn out the lamp, it sparkles like Cinderella on the way to the ball. Its magic transforms everything - even the dreary sofa with Dad sprawled out in his work overalls, and I don't feel sorry for the tree any more. For the final touch, Phyllis covers the planks and nails at the bottom of the tree with our white christening shawl, spreading it out over the base like a blanket of snow.

We squash up in one armchair to admire our work. It Came Upon a Midnight Clear is playing on the radio. As we drift into semi-sleep, a man tells the story of the first Christmas. He talks about a man and a woman expecting a baby. They take a trip through the desert and the baby is born in a stable and there are kings and shepherds and angels. But as I know that Christmas is really about getting presents and a Christmas tree, and not about a baby, I make a mental note to ask about it tomorrow.

Dad wakes up and shuffles off to bed. We rouse to turn in and my brother suddenly says, "It's crooked. The tree is crooked." Without really looking closely, we agree that maybe it is, just a bit, so he'll go to bed quietly.

I lay down and close my eyes, imagining the lights, the tinsel and the colorful decorations and I am glad I never gave up hoping that Christmas would come to us again.

Suddenly I am awake and sitting up. Phyllis jumps out of bed and turns on the light, blinding me. Mom and Dad run past our bed to the parlor. "Don't go in there without putting on your shoes," Mom says holding Phyllis back. I stand behind them and see our beautiful Cinderella Christmas tree on the floor. The lights are smashed and the decorations lay in a million pieces around it like broken eggshells.

"It's all your fault," Mom accuses Dad.

"I can't help it if the tree was too big for the stand."

"It would have been all right if you weren't drunk when you put it up!" It's the middle of the night. "You've woken up the neighbours." They bang on the ceiling and the walls. "You see what you've done!"

"Me? You're the one doing all the screaming! Shut up, will you?"

Dad slaps her and she shoves him. He falls on the floor and cuts himself on the shards of glass. He gets up, grabs his coat and goes out. Mom retreats to the bedroom, crying loudly into her pillow.

"You never heard the crash?" Phyllis says when we're back in bed.

"No," I say, shivering and pulling my pillow over my head to blot out Mom's crying. I feel something hard under my head and pull it out.

"What's this?"

"It's your present from me. It's Christmas, isn't it?"

Chapter Seven
Hot And Cold

Phyllis can always make me laugh even when I'm crying. She pulls a funny face or promises to tell me a story. When she's in a story-telling mood, I whisk a piece of paper in front of her and ask her to tell me about the princess. She squares off the paper like a comic book and draws a girl in a long gown with roses cascading down the front. "This story happened a long time ago," she begins, and crying is forgotten.

Mom says I cry a lot. She says that even as a baby I cried all the time. I don't like to hear this about myself any more than I like to cry, but I can't help it. I cry in winter when Mom sends us out to play in the snow. It is glorious at first to watch the snowflakes sailing down, transforming our gray street into a winter wonderland. When the snow piles up, we make snowmen, snowballs, and even cannonballs. We brave the cold for hours until our fingers and toes lose all sensation so that when the blood returns to them, they sting and throb. The pain is bitter - the wind is biting. We have to stay out until Mom calls for us from the front window.

Steaming cocoa and toasted cheese sandwiches revive us while we're inside at lunchtime, but the euphoria of warmth and comfort disappears when we are sent back out into the snowdrifts.

I beg Mom to let me stay in. "Please, I'll be good. I'll do coloring or read comics." But she won't give in and I cry because I think that it's unjust, and I begin to hate the snow I love. I try to hold back, moving in slow motion as I put on my snowsuit, which is deliciously warm because I dried it on a hot radiator during lunch. But my mittens and hat are wet and soggy and weigh twice what they ought.

By the time I wander downstairs, Phyllis and Andy are already out of sight and probably up at someone else's apartment by now watching television and eating their leftovers. Kids on wooden-slatted sleds sail past me down the middle of the street, their shrieks muffled by high snow banks deposited by snowplows during lunch. I watch them from the top step of the ice-covered stoop, jealous that they will not be forced to remain in the cold for longer than they can stand. With rising indignation, warm tears spill down into my woolen scarf as I quietly promise that I will never do this to my children when I grow up. I climb up a snow mountain and watch with envy as the sledders go back into their cosy apartments.

Everything around me is totally white - the contours of the street, the sidewalks and stoops, the cars, everything is hidden under a blanket of falling snow. Garbage cans look clean, almost pretty, in their new white coats. Car windscreens have little peek-a-boo eyes where the wipers have cleaned a space for the drivers to see out, and the chains wrapped around their tires *thump chink, thump chink, thump chink* down the street. I jump off my snow mountain onto carpet-smooth sidewalks and make snow angels, then resume my position to admire their perfection before footsteps trample them. When we are called back in, just before dark, I cry again, only this time from the pain of defrosting fingers, ears and toes.

Sometimes when I'm so cold that I can't play any more, I huddle in a corner by the front door and picture Mom alone upstairs. I'm watching her work as I often do. She's folding clothes and smoothing them out. Her reddened hands pass over them again and again as though they had a life of their own. Starting from the center and moving outwards, they cross with monotonous motions. Unseeing eyes stare straight ahead and who knows where her mind travels? Then she'll stop for no reason in particular, not stirring for a long time, even if I speak. She might replace a dark lock of stray hair behind her ear, then continue. She does this when we are alone, and I feel closer to her than ever before.

Shivering, my teeth chattering, and doing a jitterbug in my head, I try conjuring up summer, closing my eyes, as yellow sunlight floods in, almost warming me. I think of wearing shorts and swear to myself that I would rather broil to death on the baking sidewalks of Brooklyn than freeze to death in a snowdrift because freezing is such a cruel way to go.

In summer things aren't any better and I'm crying again. This time it is because I have to stay out and play in the heat all by myself as Phyllis and Andy have gone to a friend's house. The street in both directions is deserted. In this suffocating heat everyone else is either at the swimming pool or the beach or, at the very least, sitting under an electric fan inside. There's no shade and the granite stoop is so hot I need to stack a few comics underneath me before I can sit down. The sun burns my skin where my clothes don't reach.

I remember winter and picture myself holding a snowball against my burning face and begin to believe that dying of the cold isn't so bad, after all. Mom won't let me stay inside. She says that the fresh air does you good. She's upstairs reading a library book and putting her feet up. I only want to play in the cool of the parlor, or on the fire escape where I can feel a breeze come up from the back yard. If I could only chop off a sliver of ice from the icebox to suck on.

I skip rope for a while but the heat coming off the sidewalk sizzles through my sneakers. I'm out of breath before I can count to thirty-five. That's not even fifty, which is only half of my personal best - one hundred. Phyllis said the sidewalks are so hot in summer you can cook an egg on them, but I wouldn't eat eggs cooked on a sidewalk because it's dirty.

There's still no one out but me. I am bored, bored, BORED! I have a loose tooth so I work at loosening it further. If it falls out, I'll put it under my pillow and the tooth fairy will come. It's worth ten cents even with a hole in it. I'm wiggling it like mad when Dad drives up in our black car. He puts on the brakes and I run up and jump onto the wide running board. I scorch my arm as it brushes on the hot metal of the fat front fender. Dad looks sweaty and tired after working in the garage. He's wearing his dark blue work overalls with his name embroidered in red letters on the breast pocket - *Andy*. After fiddling with the knobs on the dashboard for a couple of minutes he gets out and rummages through the trunk. I sit on the running board in the patch of shade the car makes and wait. I want to sneak back upstairs with him, and maybe I'll tell him about my loose tooth. He slams shut the trunk and comes to the side of the car carrying his tool bag. "All by yourself out here?" he asks me.

"Yup. Look, my tooth is loose." I open my mouth and show him.

He drops his bag and wipes the grease off his hands with his red engineer's cloth.

"Where? I can't see anything. You'll have to open it much wider than that."

"Here," I say, pointing to it. I open my mouth so wide my eyes have to close to make room for it. Within a split second there's a yank, a crunch and a terrible pain. Through tears I see Dad holding up a tooth wedged between of a pair of greasy pliers. "Ha, ha, ha!" He laughs and hands me the tooth. "It looks like the tooth fairy will be coming." I can't say anything and more tears spurt to my rescue. Dad throws me the engineer's cloth and goes upstairs without me.

I choke on blood and phlegm, and sob into the cloth, remembering how we usually laugh when Dad uses these engineer's cloths for handkerchiefs and calls them his 'snot rags'. I gag on the gas fumes but need to blow my nose. The pain is going and I'm thinking about how I'll spend the ten cents from the tooth fairy, when somehow I drop the tooth. I hear it clink on the sewer grate near the curb before it falls down the drain, compounding my misery, and making me cry all over again.

When I am alone, I think about crying. I don't like to, but I feel better afterwards. Nobody forces me to cry, so I must cry because I can't help it, or because I want to. Crying helps me deal with the things I can't control. I must have a river of tears inside of me that are ready to slip down during the day, or to form pools on my pillow at night, when I cry silently.

Tears come easily and are familiar to me. They sit waiting on the ledges of my eyes and probably come from far down. They never dry up. If I try to force them back, my whole body shakes like the earth around a geyser before it blows – and they gush out anyway. I can save up tears, pushing the bad things out of my mind until night-time when everyone is asleep and I let myself remember. Crying soothes me.

My tears aren't only for me. I cry for others - for someone who falls over and hurts himself in the street, for my mother when she's sad, for people in love in the movies, for my sister when she gets a beating, for my brother when he's lost in the park, or when I win a prize or finish a good book. I never cry for nothing.

Chapter Eight
Making Money

All our friends share their candy, comic books and toys with us because my sister is the leader of a gang. When I ask how she got to be leader she says, "I'm bigger and smarter than them and they're scared of me." She's not scary, but for ten years old, she *is* big. She's taller and fatter than everyone else her age. She takes charge of things and loves to tell everyone else what to do. Andy and I are under her protection. Nobody picks on us. If they forget themselves and start a fight, she storms after them like a steam engine and they scatter. She's full of good ideas, too, especially about making money. "We can't rely on our parents to give us what they don't have. There are ways and means of making money," she says with a determined look. We don't usually have to wait long for her to come up with a scheme.

Christmas is over, and the neighborhood kids fly out of their apartments happy to be set free and to leave behind the stuffy warmth of grandparents' caresses. "We're sick of turkey," they groan.

"So are we," we lie, rolling our eyes and patting our stomachs to prove it, but secretly remembering the chicken wing and bit of white meat we got and how we wished there'd been more of that instead of bread and potatoes. Our friend, Jimmy, rolls out in the snow with a new Kodak camera slung around his neck. He lets us pose for him beside our snowman. "That's such a cool snowman. I wish we could've been allowed to come out instead of being cooped up with the relatives. You guys are so lucky." He lets Phyllis try the camera and she takes a few pictures of him. I can sense that she doesn't want to give it back. "You wanna do a swap?" she asks him casually.

"You kiddin'? My mother would kill me."

Not long afterwards, Phyllis reads an ad in a comic book about how we can get our own brand new Kodak camera for free. All we have to do is write to them and they'll send us fifty wall plaques to sell to our friends and neighbours. The money we earn goes back to them and in the return mail, we get a camera. We immediately write away for the plaques, and it seems like a long time before they arrive. When they finally do, we explain everything to Mom who eventually lets us sell them as long as we stick together and behave ourselves and don't traipse around the streets like Gypsies.

"We won't, Mom. See, they're religious plaques."

"Who wants those things? They're so garish."

"What's garish? Isn't that nice?"

"It means they're a bit bright, but the words are okay."

We take them to our bedroom and lay them out on the bed. The plaques are made of royal blue cardboard with sayings written in silver glitter - "Bless This House", "God is Love", "Count Your Blessings", "Do Unto Others As You Would Have Them Do Unto You", "Jesus Saves".

We think they're great, but our customers aren't so impressed. We walk miles of city streets and mount hundreds of flights of stairs to sell our plaques. We go down hallways knocking on doors with hope in our hearts, encountering all kinds of people, especially old ones. Some of them never go out - even their groceries are delivered. Others are so pleased to see us we're offered cookies and Kool-Aid. Doors are slammed in our faces and Phyllis gets disheartened. "We've only got six more to sell," I urge, wanting that camera more than my life is worth. We get lucky and sell the rest to a nice lady who says her husband is a minister of the word, whatever that means.

It's summer and we are impatient to get our camera. When it arrives, we realize we need some film. "It's a vicious circle," Mom warns when we ask her for the money. "When you get fancy things, you need money to keep them going. You will have to pay for the development, too. I know you're disappointed, but I can't help you just now." Though the camera remains in the box unused for a long time, we consider it a triumph – it's our very first earnings.

Sometimes there's nothing else to do except to ask Dad for money. "You ask him," Phyllis urges, "it's your turn."

"What do I say?"

"Just say, 'Please Daddy, can we have some money for candy?'"

"That's all? And then he'll give it to me?" I quietly practice what she tells me to say. When Dad comes home, I'm ready to ask him for some money. I'm scared of what he'll say, but we can't keep borrowing comics or roller skates from our friends if we have nothing to offer back. I think I'm going to be lucky because he's in a good mood. He's had work for nearly a whole week. He's also been at the Bar and Grill because he stinks of whiskey and cigarettes.

I ask him just like I was told, but I must say it wrong because he explodes. "Money? You're always asking for money. Not only does she," he points to Mom, "want money, now you kids are asking for it. The minute I walk in the door you're at me! All right then, here!" He puts his hand in his overall pocket and pulls out a handful of change. He holds it in his fist, looks at each of us then scatters the coins on the parlor floor. "If you want money so bad, go and run for it." At first we hesitate; then Phyllis makes a dive for it and we jump in after her.

Pennies, nickels and dimes roll under the sofa and slide under the Pianola. Dad mocks us. "Wait until tomorrow. I'll show you how to get all the money you want." We don't hear it all because before he finishes, we are on our way to the candy store.

I'm ashamed I ran after the money. Phyllis says, "So what? We got the money, didn't we? Look a quarter!" She's happy. I'm miserable.

The next night Dad comes home early. And sober. He's carrying a large paper bag and we watch as he empties it out in front of us. He's bought us a wooden shoe-shining box with a compartment on either side of the central handle containing four brushes, two round tins of polish, and two soft polishing clothes. "If you want money, you're going to have to learn how to earn it. I started off shining shoes so I don't see why you can't."

We like the idea and after supper practice what Dad has shown us on our own shoes. I sniff deeply into a newly opened can of polish, my nostrils twitching at the heady smell and slide a finger along the top of it. "Look at this!" From the black can we make a set of our fingerprints on a piece of cardboard.

"That's enough," Phyllis says. "We're not going to waste the stuff playing police with it. Tomorrow after school I'll take you to the park. There are lots of old men sitting around that'll make perfect customers. I think we should charge 10 cents a shine. That's sounds right, doesn't it?"

The first day we do well. "Ten cents a shine, ten cents a shine," we sing out and get six customers. They seem to think it's cute for two girls and a boy to be out shining shoes. Afterwards we spend everything on ice cream, chewing gum and pretzels. "You're the best polisher," Phyllis says to me between licks on her cone. "So you can shine the shoes. Andy can carry the box, and I'll find the customers." And that's what we do.

One afternoon, Mom calls to us as we head out the door. "On your way home, go to the bar and get your father. I don't want him staying there all night making a damn fool of himself." We don't like to do this. We're not supposed to go into bars; we're too young.

We sit on a bench to count our weekly earnings when we've finished doing the rounds. "Six dollars!" Phyllis says finally. "Let's go and buy the Viewmaster! We've got enough for it, plus a Hershey bar each. What d'ya say?"

The Viewmaster is a toy we want very badly. Everybody has one. It's like binoculars that you hold up to the light and look through. Round story cards, with a series of small pictures on them, are inserted into a slot at the top. When you press a lever, it moves it to the next picture. Sometimes the cards contain cartoons or real pictures from the movies. We decide to buy it when I remember that we're supposed to get Dad on the way home. "You'll have to do it," Phyllis says. "We don't have time to do both. We'll buy the Viewmaster and see you at home. Take the shoeshine box. It's too far for us to carry it." I trudge on to the bar because if Dad doesn't come home, Mom will be mad at all of us.

Harry's Bar and Grill, Lounge and Entertainment (Nightly), as the sign says outside, is a dark place that always smells of beer and stale cigarettes. My stomach heaves when I step inside, but I squelch down my nausea and look for Dad. It takes a while for my eyes to adjust to the dim light. I see him propped up on a stool at the bar, talking about the airplane that he used to own. A woman with frizzy yellow hair leans against him. She laughs at everything he says.

I tug lightly at his jacket and he lurches. "What're you doing here?"

"Mom says to come home."

"Tell her to come and get me herself."

Everyone laughs, except the woman this time. "Don't be like that. This your kid?" she asks. He nods and turns his back to me. "Cute."

I stare at his back for a while. He tells me to wait and gives me a dime to try out the pinball machine by the window near the door. I put the dime in the slot and the panel at the end lights up in a thousand colors. I slide the silver disk down to the end. The machine *bings* and *whirrs* and lights flash whenever I score. When it's over, it's quiet again and I don't know what else to do so I sit on the windowsill with my shoebox on my lap and wait. Dad calls to the bartender, "Gimme another whiskey and beer chaser, Harry."

Someone puts money in the jukebox beside the bar and a couple gets up to dance a slow, sad dance. It's beginning to get dark and I'm hungry. A man comes out of the toilet. He adjusts his trousers and burps out loud, thinking no one can see him. He leans slightly to the right and heads straight for the street door, but stops when he sees me. I smile up at him. "Hello there, little girl. Whatcha got there?"

"It's a shoeshine box, Mister."

"Now, ain't that cute. I could do with a shine."

"Yes Sir!"

He puts his foot on the windowsill while I polish his shoes. He loses his balance a couple of times, but I do a nice job. "That's great!" He spins around and shouts, "Hey Harry. Look at this. Ain't it cute, a little girl shining shoes?" Harry doesn't hear him, but my Dad does. He turns around, giving me a quizzical look, then throws his head back and takes his whiskey in one gulp.

"You done a good job. Here's a quarter and it's worth every penny of it. S'long." As my customer goes out the door, a wedge of evening light and a waft of fresh air land on George Washington's face on my silver quarter. It's hard to believe that anyone would give a quarter for a shoeshine. I guess after coughing up for drinks all the time a quarter seems like nothing.

"Let's go," Dad says. I quickly pocket the coin.

At home, Phyllis and Andy are already fighting over the Viewmaster, but they let me have a quick try at it before supper. In bed Phyllis confides that she's been asked to join a gang that doesn't usually take girls. They want her because she's already a gang leader. They say Andy can join, too, and she wants to know what I think. "It's a great idea. Go and join," I say, because I know it's what she wants.

"It means we have to give up the shoe shining business. We're nearly out of polish, anyway."

"We could still make good money, even better than before. I know, because today I...."

"We're sick of it. It's gonna get cold soon and we won't find customers so easy. I hear this new gang has good ways of making money."

"I'll buy more polish and do the shoe shining by myself if I can't join the gang."

"Okay by me."

From now on, when Phyllis and Andy go off with the new gang, I go shoe shining up at Harry's Bar and Grill and ask a quarter for every shine. I only go inside when it's freezing cold, otherwise I wait outside. When someone comes out, I say, "Wanna shine, Mister?"

Chapter Nine
The Grandparents

I know about death. It means you aren't living and you aren't breathing. "It means you're not going to walk back through that door because you can't," Mom says. "When Mamma died I was sixteen years old. I was the eldest of her four daughters. She was only 38 years old, not much older than I am now." I tell her it sounds old to me, but she says not. "We had a brother who died when he was a baby." I frown. "It was like that then." This means I have three aunts. "After she was gone I looked after my sisters. I cooked for them and did all the housework, too. Papa worked and the girls were still at school. Someone had to do it."

"What did Grandma die of?"

"Consumption. Her cough made her so weak that she had to hold onto a kitchen chair or the sink for support. Then she collapsed and was taken to the hospital. Later on they brought her home in a large wicker basket, turning up on our doorstep with her dead and we didn't know what to do. Papa was at work. So they set her down on the kitchen table and left. We grieved over her among the pots and pans. I guess that was as good a place as any to say good-bye. Mamma spent most of her life in the kitchen. She was so thin and white…like a fragile China doll - her hair was jet black." Mom cries into the palms of her hands and her own jet-black hair slides forward covering them. I don't like this talk about death and slip away to count my marbles.

I never met this Grandma whose name was Mary. She was dead years before I was born. So was Dad's mother, also named Mary, though he never talks about her. When I ask him if I have any aunts or uncles on his side of the family, he says, "I was an only child." At first this sounds wonderful to me. Then I think he must have been lonely.

Both my grandfathers are alive. Dad's father, Andrew, is the janitor of the building that he lives in. This gives him special privileges like lower rent and tips from the neighbours at Christmas. When he visits, he tells stories about the people who live in his building. "There's a lady with a little white poodle dog that she treats like a person. It has a waterproof coat to wear in the rain! You wouldn't believe how she feeds him. She gives him chocolates for dinner. The man on the top floor has a bakery down the street. Every night he brings me the unsold bread. Such an angel he is to me. I am so lucky." Grandpa promises to show me around and introduce me to them when I am bigger.

Two policemen arrive one evening in late October with bad news. They tell Dad that his father hadn't been seen for a few days. Some of the tenants were worried so broke into his apartment and found him dead. The policeman waits a moment before saying, "The coroner reckons his demise took place on or about the 21st of October...."

"That was on my fifth birthday," I blurt out.

"Is that so, young lady? Sir, would you care to accompany us to the apartment for verification of the contents? You understand, there was a break in...."

"Sure. You want to come along, too, birthday girl?" dad says and winks at me. "You'll get a chance to see the old place." The building is bigger and older than our building and run down. The entrance hall is wide and the steps on the marble stairs leading to the upper floors have been worn smooth down the middle. Bits are missing from the fancy brass banisters. Grandpa's apartment is near the entrance. The front door has the number "1" and the word Janitor written on it. The rooms are large and the ceiling is high. The place is cluttered with furniture that he saved from the garbage. He told me that he kept anything good that was thrown away and sold it later. "I made some money on the side. All legal and correct, too."

While the policemen show Dad around the apartment, I wander into the kitchen. There aren't any colorful things like dishcloths, a kitchen clock, potholders, jars of crayons and pencils, like we have in ours. Scattered around are the brooms, buckets and mops that he must have used for cleaning the building. As I lean in the kitchen doorway by the parlor, I see that the Sunday comics are strewn over the kitchen floor so I bend down to read them. As I shift from one foot to the other, I feel something lumpy under my sneakers. I sneak a quick look underneath at some dried-up crunchy stuff, a bit like slush turned to ice on the sidewalks in winter, only it's brown.

"Put that down!" a policeman shouts, running in from the bedroom. I nearly jump out of my skin.

"It's all right, Missy. You weren't to know," the other policeman says. "Now be a good girl and sit on the couch." He motions Dad over and lifts up the newspapers. "This, Sir, is where they found him in a pool of blood. We guess he had a brain hemorrhage and died on this spot."

Over supper that night, Mom and Dad discuss funeral arrangements. "What's a funeral parlor?" I ask, picturing rows of coffins in our parlor. "Not now. It's time for bed."

We get the day off school because of Grandpa's funeral. I am not very pleased because my class is in the middle of making Halloween decorations and I'll miss it. Mom squeezes into one of her old dresses. "The last time this dress saw the light of day was about six years ago." Dad wrestles with a white shirt and his tie is black. We have to look presentable. I comb Andy's stick-um-up hair flat against his head with so much water that it drips down his face like tears all the way there in the car.

The inside of the funeral home is quiet, like being under water. The gray carpets are so thick that our footsteps sound far away like when I am hiding in Mom's closet with the door shut and my head is buried in Dad's trousers. Phyllis makes a false fart with her hands and we giggle. Mom shoves her forward but doesn't say anything. We go in a room at the end of a lot of closed doors. "Sit down in the front row," Dad whispers and points to chairs set up in rows like a school auditorium. Mom and Dad bend over the gray coffin that rests on pedestals at the front. He unfolds a clean snot rag and blows hard into it. Mom puts her hand on his arm.

"Go pay your respects to Grandpa," she tells us. We don't move. "Go on up to the coffin. He won't bite you!" she urges, but not even my sister is keen to look a dead person in the face. Mom pinches me. "Think of your father."

Grandpa is clean-shaven and wears a new suit. The coffin is satin-lined and there's a white satin pillow under his head and a satin blanket halfway up his chest. No sign of any blood. He looks okay. Better than usual. Comfortable, too. Tears prick the corners of my eyes. I hear Mom's words, *'he's not coming back through that door'* - that kitchen door, his apartment door, the coffin door.... I feel a clicking in my throat. I put my hand over my mouth and look at Dad. He carries me to the room next door. "Look at all the lovely flowers, Jeanne. Aren't they beautiful?" He makes me sniff the white lilies and carnations. The room is full of bouquets and wreathes. All the flowers are white. "Isn't she something?" he asks me, leaning into a white coffin. I look inside it, brave now. There's a dark-haired lady in a white lace wedding dress. Her bright red lips are shaped like a heart.

"She looks like a sleeping princess," I whisper. Dad agrees. "We can go now. I'm okay," I say pulling on his sleeve.

"I saw her yesterday and can't help wondering what she was like when she was alive."

"Come on, Dad."

People are arriving with bouquets of flowers and hankies. We are taken out by a lady before anything starts. She treats us to a soda and a movie. It's dark when we go back to the funeral parlor. Grandpa's coffin is gone. So are the flowers and the people. The room is empty except for Mom. Dad is in the room with the woman in white. He has a white carnation in his hand and his cheeks shine with tears. I take his hand and we go out to the car together.

My other grandpa, Alexander, dies too. "He's got sugar diabetes," my cousin Alex informs us. It's a sunny day and all our aunts are at the hospital because Mom's father is very sick. Children aren't allowed inside so we gather in the hospital gardens.

Aunt Helen, Mom's youngest sister, was living with Grandpa in a small apartment. He's always in bed when we visit. She says she won't marry Uncle Bob until Grandpa dies. When we ask her why not, she says, "Who else will look after him?"

Grandpa does die - in the hospital. There is no gray funeral home and coffin. He's inside a long shiny black box with the lid down in the middle of a hall in a basement. A red cloth with a crescent moon and star on it covers the coffin. Phyllis says it's different because Mom's family is Muslim. We aren't sad at this funeral because women in long black dresses and headscarves pass around warm rolls and other food, while another bunch of ladies, total strangers, are paid to cry beside the coffin.

We miss them. Our grandfather, Andrew, used to bring us treats from his friend's bakery like a cheesecake or a cherry pie. He'd say,

"My friend tells me it's for you. 'Go on, take it for your grandchildren,' he says 'and God Bless Them.' So, who wants a piece of pie?"

The dusty old drawers full of Grandpa Andrew's washers, screws, chains, and bits of glass under my bed are my only reminder of him. Nothing else is left. Mom told Dad to throw out Grandpa's old suits because there was no room in the closets. Mom bundled them up with other old clothes that she had put aside for the ragman.

The ragman's place is a warehouse full to the brim with old clothes. There are piles of shirts on the floor, suits and coats on racks, tables covered with hats and boxes of buttons scattered around. Socks and gloves lounge in baskets by the door. A few old women are picking through the stacks, holding up articles to the light for inspection, throwing aside anything with moth holes. A wizened old man tackles a newly arrived pile of women's clothes taller than he is. He throws woolen sweaters to one side and cotton skirts to the other with the speed and dexterity of a baseball pitcher avoiding the bat. In a quiet corner, two youths try on shoes. The ragman piles our load onto a weighing scale that is large enough to weigh our whole family at once. We get fifty cents per pound of rags.

Mom is in a good mood on the way home and asks if we want spaghetti and meatballs for supper. "We'll get a pound of chop meat at the butcher's. And you better remember your grandfather for it," she adds. I do, and I have other things to remember Grandpa for.

It was around last Easter and everyone in the neighborhood was excited. They were going to the Easter Parade on Fifth Avenue in Manhattan. People turned out for it from all over the city. Young girls in Easter bonnets, white gloves and shiny patent leather shoes smiled alongside boys in bow ties with hair slicked down like strips of licorice. Streets were cleared and bands with booming drums headed up the parade. Crowds lined the sidewalks waving flags and cheering. The kids on our block who couldn't go to that parade imitated them, happily falling in with their own celebration and strolled down the street in new Easter outfits.

Anyone like me who couldn't look nice on Easter day, might as well stay inside and sit by Mom's bedroom window and watch the parade from there. My sister and brother had something to wear. Mrs. Bowler, our upstairs neighbor, had recently given Phyllis a dress.

"Our girl outgrew it before she could wear it twice. It's practically new," she said. Andy had a hand-me-down suit that had belonged to the landlady's grandson. I tried to squeeze into last year's dress but the waistband was under my armpits, constricting my movements like a straight jacket. Mom agreed it wouldn't do.

"There's nothing I can do to fix it and there's nothing else to wear. I'm sorry, Jeanne," she said, sighing, leaving me to struggle out of it.

I told Grandpa about it on Saturday when he came for his visit.

"You shouldn't have to worry about things like that. Especially not on Easter Sunday, such an important day."

After he left, Mom told me to stop feeling sorry for myself; there was always next year. As if a four year old could wait that long.

After lunch on Easter Day, Mom and Dad retreated to the parlor with the Sunday papers. I sat by the front window and watched Phyllis and Andy fade into the crowd in the street. The doorbell rang and I answered it, surprised to see Grandpa. He took his hat off, and, smiling, held out a brown paper bag. "Open it," he said. "It is for you." Inside was a chocolate Easter bunny. "So who needs to go out and show off when there's a whole chocolate rabbit to eat?" he chided. There were tears in his eyes.

Not long after that I was rummaging through Mom's bureau drawers for loose photographs that had fallen out of albums and noticed an envelope containing our birth certificates. My sister's and brother's had their names on them, but mine said Female where the name should be. On the back was stamped, "This is to certify that the child's name is," and on the line provided, written in ink – JEANNE. It was dated two months after I was born. I showed Grandpa the paper and he laughed. He called me, 'Jeannie-boy'.

"Do you know what? I named you. Your Mom and Dad were so sure you were going to be a boy, they couldn't think of a girl's name. The lady at the registration office told us she had to put down 'female' because the law says you must register the birth before six weeks. She said to come down later and add the name. We couldn't call you 'baby' forever, so I named you after that movie star, Jeanne Crane. And since you were supposed to be a boy, I nick-named you Jeannie-boy."

Now that Grandpa's gone no one calls me Jeannie-boy anymore.

Chapter Ten
From The Window

It's late August. There's been a shower and the evening air is still. From the front window, Mom and I watch cars ride by on the rain-washed street below. We play a made-up game called "My car, Your car." As we sit and talk, the first one to say "my car" as one comes along gets a point. It is best played as darkness falls because we can spot the cars with their headlights on sooner. Some cars go by with only one headlight, and we call them 'piddidellies'. Phyllis coined this word and it sounds right for a one-eyed, lopsided car.

We're waiting at the window for Dad to come home. Working as a car mechanic, his hours aren't regular. It depends on how much work he's got at the garage. His job is a dirty one. He doesn't wear a suit or carry a newspaper under his arm like some Dads I see coming home from work. He wears rough pants and a flannel shirt underneath his dark blue garage overalls with metal buttons down the front. He carries with him the smell of gas fumes and engine oil. A layer of black grime remains underneath his fingernails no matter how much he scrubs them. They remind me of the lima beans with the black edges that we buy at the grocer's. Mom says Dad's a genius, a mechanical genius. He can fix any make of car. She says, laughing, "I think he's got cars in the blood. He buys a broken-down jalopy and in no time gets it running. We're lucky in some things. If nothing else, at least we've got transport." This is true. There are only two cars on the entire street and ours has a running board.

Dad's jobs never last long. He works for a couple of days, or maybe weeks, then comes home one afternoon and says he's quit. Mom thinks it's because ever since he lost his own business, he can't work for anyone else. "It all has to do with the war. No one was bothered about fixing cars once the war started and he lost his car parts store. He went to work in the Brooklyn shipyards fixing warships. When the war was over, we didn't have enough money to start up another store. You were born then and your brother came along the next year."

With a faraway look in her eyes, she tells me that Dad learned to drink whiskey when he worked in the shipyards. "He only drank milk when we got married, if you can believe it. After his shift, he'd go out with the guys for a drink. He's had too many disappointments. Things just get worse."

"My car!" I blurt out. That's ten to me." Mom has been talking and not looking. I'm winning tonight. I watch the car slow to a halt at the traffic lights. As they change from stop to go, a red and green trail is displayed on the slick tarmac. They are brand new, only installed last week.

When the lights finally went up, Mrs. Bowler from upstairs said, "Humph! It's about time. We've been asking for them lights for ages. Now it's too late for some." By this she means it's too late for Tommy from across the street. Last month he was run over by a car right in front of our building. We heard a loud screech and then a thud and stopped in the middle of making ham and cheese sandwiches and ran to the front window. Tommy was lying very still in the middle of the street. A gray car, with its doors open, was stopped in front of him. People milled around; some too scared to get close were straining their necks to see from a distance. A man shouted, "Would someone please call an ambulance?" Then I heard, "We need blankets!" Phyllis ran to our bedroom and stripped off the blue candlewick bedspread. She tumbled down the stairs with it and flew out into the street. An old woman helped her fold it in two and they neatly tucked it around Tommy. He could have been asleep under that bedspread. He looked peaceful, like he was having a nap. It was hard to believe he was injured.

Traffic piled up in both directions. When the police arrived, they directed all cars down another street. I couldn't take my eyes off Tommy. He was there for so long that people began to drift away. We were all waiting for the ambulance. Mom came in and looked out of the window. From over my shoulder she said, "It's disgraceful how long it takes an ambulance to arrive in this city." Tommy's mother knelt beside him the whole time. She asked his name over and over. "Tommy? Tommy? Tommy?" as if she wasn't sure it was him.

Andy and I got tired of watching and left to have our sandwiches. Mom kept a vigil by the window while we ate. "The ambulance is here. My God," she said checking the kitchen clock, "it's taken them over an hour."

Phyllis came back upstairs a long time after Tommy was taken away by the ambulance. She hung around the street with several others, waiting for news. When she at last came up, she was carrying the rolled up bedspread in her arms like a baby. "Tommy was dead when he got to the hospital," she said. "I just heard it. I don't want my sandwich. Give it to someone else. I'm going to lay down." She slept all afternoon with the bedspread cradled in her arms.

Everyone wanted the traffic lights after that. As Mrs. Bowler said, "Who needs to go to New York City to be murdered when you can get killed on your own front doorstep? No one." A week later we got them.

From our second-story window I have a good view of the American flag at the top of elementary school, P.S. 123 a couple of blocks away. It flaps fiercely in the wind, its raggedy edges grabbing at the air. I'm lonely when Phyllis goes to school. She's been going since I was born, so I should be used to it, but I'm not. The flag marks the spot where she is and where I want to be. I want a school bag like hers, and pencils. I want notebooks, textbooks, and crayons. I have pumped enough information out of her to know everything that happens in school. I am so obsessed I force Andy to play school with me. He hates it because I'm always the teacher, but he's too dumb to teach me anything, so we wind up fighting. Now he runs away and hides in the closet whenever I get out my paper and pencils no matter how sweet I am to him.

It's boring at home. I help Mom wring out the wash, practice ironing small things, and wash the dishes. In desperation I fish out a half-finished crocheted doily, a ball of cotton and crochet hook from Mom's closet. "Can you show me how to do this?"

"It isn't that easy. You're too young. Put them away." I bring her needles and yarn and ask her to teach me how to knit, but she says, "Keep out of my closet!" She finishes wiping the black and white kitchen floor on her knees; backing herself into the parlor and wiping that floor until, as the light bounces off the wet surface, the blue linoleum printed with red roses on it looks like an ice-skating rink.

There's chaos in the kitchen on my first day of school. Mom is preparing breakfast and braiding my hair at the same time. She reaches for the milk, then the cereal, and my head is yanked from east to west.

"We'll never make it on time," she complains. "I'm not even dressed yet."

"I'll take her," Phyllis offers. When we get there she drops me off outside the kindergarten classroom. "Good luck, kid," she says and leaves me to go in. The noise is deafening. There's a kid crying in every corner. I recognize one or two and wave, but they don't see me. There are almost as many parents as there are children. I sit down at a table and open up a box of crayons, running my fingertips over the new points and sucking in the smell of the wax. Our crayons at home are either stubs or lumps. The stubs are less than an inch long and the lumps are ones we've melted down on radiators and sculpted into animal shapes. I take a large piece of paper from a stack on the table and draw. I finish my third picture and look up. The parents are gone and the children are seated at the tables. The teacher closes the door and takes attendance. Then she says, "It's time for Activities. Who would like to go in the Playhouse?"

Hands fly into the air and five of us are chosen. The Playhouse is made of wood and it has a real door and windows, as well as furniture. In the kitchen there are plates and knives and forks, like a real house. While I'm preparing dinner, a boy wets himself. He's supposed to be helping me, but instead, makes a puddle on the floor between the stove and the sink.

After school I sit at the window and look at the flag. It flutters in its usual place. I can situate it now. The flag is attached to the roof of the school. The roof is attached to the walls. The walls hold up the windows from the top of the building to the bottom where my classroom sits, empty now that we have all gone home. Mom's hand is on my shoulder. "How was your first day at school?" she asks.

"Okay, but we only draw and play. We're not going to learn how to read and write until the first grade. The teacher said so when I asked her. What am I going to do?" Mom shrugs and pats my head.

51

Chapter Eleven
Small Crimes

From the very beginning, my first grade teacher at P.S.123 gives me extra responsibilities. It's my job to see that the classroom is tidy during the day, and I empty the wastepaper basket before we go home. Teachers are like mothers. They tell you what to do and when you do it they praise you. If you don't, they shout from the rooftops and punish you. I find out that it's one thing to be smacked at home and sent to bed with no supper, but another when you do something wrong at school because you're put to shame in front of the whole class.

On the day before Christmas vacation starts, it is as though a magic wand is waved and misses me because everyone in the class arrives with a present for the teacher except me. If I had known about it, I would have nagged Mom. She might have come up with something – anything. When the rest of the class closes around her desk to watch her open the gifts, I hang back in the shadows. I hear *ooh* and *aah* as she opens them, one after the other. "Who brought this lovely one?" she coos, slipping the red ribbon off the silver paper. "You, Johnny Thorn? Why I thank you and your parents." Johnny blushes proudly next to her.

In my boredom I spy a piece of chalk on the blackboard ledge. The golden rule flashes through my brain - Nobody is allowed to touch the chalk or write on the blackboard except the teacher. But since my teacher is busy and has her back to me, I figure it's all right just this once. I've been dying to try out the chalk and the blackboard. I draw a couple of small lines, then, for want of anything else to write, I print my name - J E A N N E. Chalk dust dribbles onto the ledge. I test it, rubbing it between my index finger and thumb and draw a line beneath my name. As I do so, the teacher is about to open Rosa de Marco's huge present and there is a reverent hush. The chalk squeaks. "Jeanne's writing on the blackboard!" Rudy Finkel shouts from behind me. I turn around and freeze.

"What?" the teacher squawks, leaping out of her seat suddenly, her head jutting above the pupils like an ostrich on the prowl. She stretches indignantly to full height, a tall, thin woman with gray hair in a white blouse and straight skirt. "Of all the people...I never thought that you could so blatantly break the rules. How dare you write on the blackboard? What have you got to say for yourself?" I look down at my feet holding back tears. "If you've got nothing to say, you can stand in the corner. T...T...Turn around. Turn your back to us. We don't want to look at you." This is a mercy because I don't want anyone to see my tears or me.

I don't mention what happened at home. I broke the rule and got punished. The trick is not to get caught. That's what's so good about brothers and sisters, most of the time they don't tell. The three of us do a lot of things we're not supposed to, like lying, cheating and stealing. If we get away with anything, the next time it gets easier. We tell ourselves that if we had all the things we wanted through regular channels, we wouldn't resort to stealing them. Comics and baseball cards are the hottest things to have and the easiest to acquire. Alongside money, we covet these most. They can be swapped or used as currency. We already own a few comics and cards, but Phyllis tells us her idea of how we can increase our stash. "We call in some kid that's not too smart, but has a lot of comics," she says. "We say to him, 'If you wanna swap, you gotta come and sit on our hall stairs'."

"Why not swap out on the stoop like usual?"

"Because there's a rug by the bottom step."

"So what?"

"When there's a comic I want, I'll hand it to you and say, 'Look at this one, Jeanne'. I'll keep him busy. When you get the chance, slide it under the rug." I'm scared of getting caught so we get Andy to be the lookout on the stoop. If anyone tries to come in, he can warn us. Phyllis agrees, but I'm still not convinced. "Look," she says exasperated with me, "the kid's got thousands! He's not going to miss one or two." By the time it comes for the swap, I'm sweating bullets. Phyllis gives me the nod four times and she's right, he doesn't have a clue that we're robbing him. Our pile of comics is so high we're sure that we have more than anybody else in the neighborhood. Our stack of baseball cards is too heavy to carry around. Andy has duplicates and triplicates of his favorite players. Now he can legitimately swap them for bubble gum, candy or money.

We are always hungry and our success keeps us busy thinking up new ways of filling our growling stomachs. At mealtimes, we've begun to fight over the thick end-slice of bread that we used to think was too tough to chew, because there's more on it than an ordinary slice. After breakfast one Saturday morning my sister whispers that someone at school told her that sandwiches were being offered free to anyone who wanted them. "The nuns are giving out cheese sandwiches at the Roman Catholic Church. You know, the one over by the park near the school with the tall iron gates."

"Are the sandwiches only for Catholics?" Andy asks. We're scared to death of nuns, Catholics, priests and anyone who wears black clothes and talks about God. Nuns have shaved heads and moustaches, too, but the temptation of getting hold of free sandwiches is greater than our worst fears. We discuss the pro's and con's of getting the free food outside on the stoop so that Mom can't hear us. We decide to go for the sandwiches. It's my job to hold Andy's hand in case they want to kidnap him. Mom would kill us if anything happened to him, especially since we're supposed to keep away from Catholics.

The church isn't far away. We once went to the Catholic school's summer fair when they blocked off the whole street and put up stands along both sides of the curb. It was on all day long, and after dark they lit hundreds of paper lanterns and hung them above the stands where they swung in the evening breeze. They had great food like home-made pizzas and 4-inch high slices of cake as well as games with prizes. I won a goldfish by throwing a ping pong ball at a table full of goldfish in bowls of water. I got to keep the one my ball landed in.

When we get there the Catholic school gates are wide open and a nun greets us. "Good morning to you. Now what'll we be having here? Brothers and sisters are we?" We nod. "I suppose you've come for the catechism. It's just through there." She points to an open door across the courtyard. I squeeze hard on Andy's hand and we run into the church through a back door.

"Where are the sandwiches?" Andy asks as we take our seats.

"Sshhh!" we say looking over our shoulders to make sure no one's heard. Kids we've never seen before squeeze up next to us on the benches. The nun shuts the door and walks to the front. I suddenly have to go to the toilet.

"You'll have to wait," Phyllis says between clenched teeth.

"Today I'm going to talk to you about Jesus, Mary and Joseph," the nun says. She tells us the story we heard on the radio at Christmas. After half an hour, she says, "Before you go, tell me, how many of you know the difference between right and wrong?" No one budges. "Come on, don't be shy." We slowly raise our hands with the others. "Good. We'll talk about that next week. Now run along for refreshments."

An arched wooden side door squeaks open and a young nun carries in a tray about the size of our kitchen table stacked high with sandwiches. Following everyone else, we take one in each hand. My teeth bite down on the soft white bread, sinking first to the level of the butter and then resting a moment on the thick slice of cheese in the middle. Do I eat them fast and fill my stomach, or slowly and savor every bite? I decide on fast. The tray comes around again and we help ourselves as before. It's eleven o'clock on a Saturday morning and we're eating cheese sandwiches - Catholic cheese sandwiches!

Back to the safety of our street, we offer around a few of the sandwiches that we had stuffed into our pockets when the nuns weren't looking. Our friends won't touch them. "They're filthy Catholic sandwiches. We wouldn't eat them if we were starving. If you eat them you're gonna go to hell!"

"Ah, shuddup! What d'you know, you dimwits!" That night I get stomach cramps and I am convinced it's because I've eaten Catholic sandwiches. I solemnly vow between clenched teeth not to eat them again. But the next day I am fine and we agree that neither nuns nor Catholics scare us any more. On Saturday mornings, when Mom and Dad think we're on the swings in the park, we scramble for a seat on the benches in the big, gloomy church. "Be ye grateful that the Good Lord in His generosity provides," the nun says. And we gratefully gobble up His cheese sandwiches.

Phyllis has started going to Mass with a girlfriend on Sunday mornings and she's very mysterious about it. I pester her to let me come, too. She is supposed to be looking after me, but instead makes me sit alone in the park. When I threaten to tell Mom and Dad on her she reluctantly gives in and lets me tag along. We split up outside the church; Phyllis and her friend sit up front and I head for the back. The Mass starts when a bell rings and the priest walks in. I can't understand a word he's saying. The people stand, then they sit, then they kneel, then they sit, then they stand, until I lose track, and stay sitting. The priest bangs a smoking brass ball against a chain and the white smoke smells sweet but a few people cough anyhow. A lady near me fingers a string of glass beads with a cross dangling from it. She mouths words, her fingers deftly slipping from one shiny bead to the other. People fumble in pockets and purses for a money collection. I hear *chink, chink* as coins hit the bottom of a plate. By the time it reaches the back of the church, it's overflowing with silver coins and dollar bills. I am surprised to see that Phyllis and her friend are collecting the money.

We are on the way home and a few blocks away from the church when Phyllis holds up a ten-dollar bill. The two friends laugh. I go hot and cold all over. She looks at me and says, "If you say a word to anyone, I'll kill you!" When I start to cry she says, "We're going to have ice-cream sundaes 'cause it's Sunday! That's a joke. Laugh, you dummy."

"I don't want no ice-cream sundae. I wanna go home," I protest. But they persuade me to come and sit with them anyway. The scent of vanilla, chocolate and strawberry reaches my nostrils. In no time I'm choosing between a hot-fudge sundae with nuts and a banana split.

Late that afternoon when I am alone playing checkers on the front stoop and just about to king myself a red, I remember what the nun said about knowing the difference between right and wrong. I didn't steal the money, but I enjoyed the ice cream, so I might as well have. I can't make things right now. I can't tell on them because I'd be telling on myself. There's something else bothering me, though. It's what the nun said just before we had our refreshments. She said, "Remember, my children, God sees and knows everything we do. We can't keep secrets from Him." My parents won't like it if they find out. We'll get a beating. It's happened before and even when we weren't guilty.

It was the time when Jerry from across the street showed Phyllis a ten-dollar bill and said that his mother gave it to him to buy candy for his friends. Taking charge as usual, she rounded up his friends, ourselves included, and spent the ten dollars on ice-cream cones, lollipops, tootsie rolls, chewing gum, licorice, orange slices and M & M's. About an hour later, when a hint of chocolate was still on our lips, his father rang our doorbell and told Dad that we'd spent his son's money. That's when we got the beating. Dad's ears were deaf to us, because we had shamed him and he had to pay back the ten dollars. It turned out that Jerry had taken it from the kitchen table without permission in the first place.

Dad's leather belt ripped into our backsides and legs. They throbbed all night, which was long, because we were sent to bed at the crazy hour of 3 o'clock in the afternoon. Sunshine danced around our bedroom, mocking us, and we shut our eyes to its jollity. Dad's words as his belt whacked my buttocks rang in my ears. "Don't you ever learn anything?" I learned that day that the strap hurts more if you are innocent than if you are guilty.

I am bored with my game of checkers and about to give up when Dad drives up. His black Studebaker is full of watermelons! The nose of the car is pointing towards the edge of the sidewalk. Suddenly it jerks and jumps the curb, missing the fire hydrant by two inches. The engine dies in front of the apartment building next to ours. Dad stumbles out and yanks open the back door. He pulls out a couple of watermelons that are probably ten pounds apiece and balances one on each shoulder. "Looka' wha' I ga' fr ya'," he mutters, looking at me. His right foot goes up to mount the curb but misses it. One of the watermelons slips loose from his grip and smashes on the sidewalk.

"Ah, shit," he swears and swings back to the car for another one.

Curiosity compels some of our neighbours out of their apartments. They watch Dad with amusement through narrow eyes. A man leans against the front door with a hand on his hip, another casually scratches the back of his head and looks around. They are waiting for something to happen. Dad waves his free arm. "Com' on, youse guys. Com' and ge' a wata'melon. They're free." If something's going for nothing, people aren't shy and don't even care if you're drunk. The men come forward and pass watermelons from hand to hand until our car is empty. Dad sways at the bottom of our stoop, his feet mashing the splattered watermelon. He conducts the watermelon-takers with both elbows, because of the watermelons on his shoulders. "Jest help yourselves, g'won."

Hearing the ruckus, Mom leans out of the upstairs window. "For God's sake," she shouts at him, "get up here you drunken bum! You're shaming us in front of the whole neighborhood." Then she turns to Phyllis beside her, "Go down and clean up that mess. And where's your sister?" she calls after her and slams the window shut with a bang. Dad's face is pinched and angry as he pushes past me on his way upstairs.

Mom gives him hell in the parlor. We listen from the kitchen. Argue, argue, argue. "Eat that watermelon or else…" Dad tells us. We do, but don't enjoy it. We wonder what our neighbours think. Are they laughing at us? Most of them are from Puerto Rico and only speak Spanish. "Maybe they don't understand what's going on," I suggest to Phyllis who shakes her head.

"Maybe they think we're loco, you know, CRAZY!" She screws up her face and crosses her eyes, making me laugh in spite of everything.

Uneaten triangles of watermelon stand lonely on the kitchen table. Pink and green sailboats in a sea of juice and pits, I think to myself. Phyllis puts them away in the icebox. I wipe the table clean. She lifts Andy up to turn out the kitchen light and we shuffle off to bed. In the dark I close my eyes and try to blot out the sound of Mom and Dad arguing in the parlor.

Chapter Twelve
Illnesses And Injuries

Mom's cure for everything is a regular enema. Phyllis and I try to hide when she spreads out her old towels on the kitchen table. "Okay, who's first?" she asks. Andy volunteers, happy to be first in line for something for once, having forgotten since the last time what it's all about. "Hop up here," she says cheerfully and pats the thick layers. She fills the orange, pear-shaped enema with warm soapy water and squirts the contents into his rectum. It's an awful sensation, but not painful. The worst part is having to sit on the towel-covered chair near the toilet door, desperately wanting to go, but waiting until she says we can.

We're not allowed to miss school unless we're sick with something serious like chickenpox or measles. Slight fevers, headaches, colds – it doesn't matter - we're sent to school. "You'd better not get sick again," she said to me, the only time I remember the doctor visiting us. "We can't afford it. His cure for tonsillitis is having them out. You heard what he said. Do you want that?"

Whenever we lose a milk tooth, it's got a hole in it. But since we can't afford to see a dentist, we are reminded morning and night how to brush our teeth. "You're wasting toothpowder," Mom complains. "First you sprinkle some into your left hand, then you wet your toothbrush in your right hand and scoop it up. If you shake the powder onto the brush directly from the can, it'll get all over the place."

I don't want to flunk out of the first grade because of rotten teeth, but I might. I brought home a letter from school saying that no one can pass Gym unless they've been to see a dentist. We need a dentist's note saying that we've had a check-up and that our teeth are okay. Mom says it is out of the question; we don't have the money, plain and simple. She says they can't enforce it, but looks worried anyhow. Phyllis is already in the fifth grade and swears the disgrace would kill her. In the end Mom gets the letters for each of us - somehow. Even though we have never opened our mouths to him, the dentist helps us to pass Gym and we move up to the next class.

My second grade teacher says I'm a hard worker. Whenever she asks me to do something, I jump to it. I don't mind what it is - stacking books, cleaning blackboards, or checking out books in the library. It is easier than the jobs I do at home like washing clothes, sweeping the kitchen, peeling potatoes and ironing. On top of that, everything I do is appreciated.

I have a lot of friends now who ask me over to play. I join them straight after school to avoid going home. Mom doesn't mind; she says that at least I won't be under her feet all afternoon. But I'm not so sure because lately she has been relying on me to help her with the housework. She saves things up for me and I start ironing or cooking as soon as I get in because she's lying down on my bed near the kitchen. Her eyes are shut, her shoes are off - one arm covers her forehead, the other is at her side, lifeless. "After you empty the garbage, Jeanne, I'll tell you how to make lima bean soup," she says through dry lips.

Each afternoon when the school bell rings at three o'clock, I leave the world of learning that I love. I put behind me ideas of achievement and creativity, praise and encouragement and return to a place where I try to survive with the least amount of conflict. Each day I wonder to myself, Will I get through today without a scene or a beating? At home, instead of practising the piano or the clarinet, like some of my friends do, I practice other skills. I cut off the bottoms of dresses and hem them to fit me, trim my brother's hair and convince the grocer to extend our credit for another week. The world works on different levels and I am caught between several. I strive hard to do well in everything by trying to please my teachers at school, keeping pace with my friends, wanting peace within my family, and making it easier for my mother at home. The challenge proves too much and I begin having migraine headaches. My head feels like it is splitting in two and I want to vomit so forego any supper. The next day it's gone and I don't bother to tell Mom about the pains in my head. Sometimes I get headaches that don't go away.

One day at school my head hurts so bad I can't see the blackboard. The teacher puts her cool hand on my forehead and exclaims, "You're burning up!" She writes Mom a note telling her I have to stay home until my fever is gone. My headache is bigger than my head by the time Mom sees me. "Open your mouth," she says. "I thought so. It's those tonsils again." And after administering an enema, she puts me to bed for a week.

My headaches are so painful that I skip supper, crashing asleep on the bed as soon as I hit the pillow. I might hear voices in the distant background, and try to, but can't, get up. The next morning I've still got my school clothes on. Mom watches me quizzically, making me tea and toast for breakfast, but I'm not hungry. "What happened to you last night? You slept right through supper. Have you been working too hard at school?" I find it difficult to speak and my eyeballs smart from the glare of the kitchen light bulb.

The school nurse thinks I have too many headaches for a young girl and asks me if I have ever fallen on my head. "No, I don't think so, but I was hit in the head with a baseball bat last summer," I tell her, remembering the episode and wincing inwardly. We attended summer school, not because we failed something and had to make it up, but because it was free and it kept us off the streets and out of Mom's hair. She always signed us up early to make sure we got places. It wasn't really 'school' since we mostly listened to stories, drew pictures and played games. At lunchtime, while the others were watching a baseball game, Phyllis and I played catch over by the side of the schoolyard. I dropped the ball and she shouted to me between cupped hands, "Run for it!" I leaped up, ran and bent to pick it up. As I straightened up the baseball player swung for the ball and hit me with the bat. The boy hadn't seen me heading straight for him because I came from behind. I got knocked out cold. Phyllis was scared that I was dead because I didn't move for a long time. When I finally opened my eyes, she helped me to me feet. I never said a word. She and Andy walked me home.

I don't remember how it happened and they had to tell me that later, but I do remember my sister ringing the doorbell and Mom opening the kitchen door, screaming and putting her hand over her mouth. "What in God's name happened to you? Is this the way you look after them?" Mom shouted, turning to Phyllis. Andy was already crying with fright. "Look at her! Oh, my God! What am I going to do? Mrs. Bowler, Mrs. Bowler." Our upstairs neighbor ran down the stairs. She took one look at me and ran back up to get her husband. He grabbed me by the arm and said he was taking me to the hospital right now and Mom had to come, too. His car had been sitting in the sun and the hot plastic seats scorched the back of my legs below my shorts. Mom wanted to know if my head hurt. "No, just my legs." She looked at me now more worried than ever.

Dad yelled at everyone that night. "You're grounded," he said to me, "for the rest of the summer! You're not to budge from the front stoop until I say so." I was a sight. White bandages were wound around my head like a turban gone mad. They covered my right eye and cupped me under the chin. These came off the following week and were replaced by a thick white patch and long strips of surgical tape to hold it in place. Andy laughed at me, calling me a pirate. While they were changing the bandages, I had a chance to see my injury. I couldn't say I recognized the face staring at me from the mirror on the hospital wall. My right eye was completely closed. The dark slit in the middle of a purple mound might have been where my eye was supposed to be. The whole right side of my face was swollen and colored blue and purple. Over the summer it changed to blue and red, and then to pink and yellow. The school nurse listening to my story remarked, "You're lucky you didn't lose your eye!" She frowns and gives me a couple of aspirins for my headache in a white paper cup and another paper cup of water. I try to swallow them but because of my perpetually swollen tonsils, I gag and cough them back up. She swaps them for two pieces of Aspergum that look like Chiclets chewing gum, only they are not and taste nasty once the outside sugar has dissolved.

When it's Andy's turn to go to the hospital, it's all my fault. I'm doing a jigsaw puzzle in the bedroom and he's being a real pain in the butt. He's leaning on the bed and making the pieces fall on the floor. I tell him to stop it and he doesn't, so I hit him and he hits me back. I whack him one hard and stomp off to the kitchen, disgusted, giving up the idea of a quiet game on my own. He chases after me and pounds his fists into my back. Pain ripples through my body and I scream out loud. Mom is in the parlor hanging out the wash. "Quit it!" she shouts through a mouthful of clothespins. This stops me for a second. Andy takes advantage and throws a few more punches. I dash away to the bathroom with him at my heels and slam the door shut, locking it in triumph at having escaped his blows. I hear a blood-curdling scream outside the door. "Now what is it? Mom yells on the warpath.

I'm on the bathroom floor wedged between the linen basket and the bathtub in the dark with my knees scrunched up to my chest, my eyes shut tight, and my hands over my ears to shut out the hullabaloo on the other side of the door. Phyllis bangs. "Open up! You're gonna get killed for this!" Her words pour over me like molten lead. I'm trapped. I've run to the safety of the only room in the apartment with a lock on the door with the thought of shutting them out, not locking myself in.

Then the kitchen door slams and suddenly it's quiet and I can hear the bathtub faucet drip. It's sound gets louder and louder until it forces me to my feet. I'm scared, really scared. I switch on the bathroom light but it doesn't help. I'm better in the dark. Still nothing. Turning the key in the lock and opening the door a crack confirms my suspicions. They have gone and left me alone. I stick out my head and hear the kitchen clock ticking cheerily on the shelf. Minutes pass before I can leave the bathroom. There's blood on the floor by the bathroom door and on towels beside the kitchen sink. I stare at it and warm pee trickles down my legs. I creep back to the bathroom and lock myself in. Welcoming the darkness, I curl up on the bathmat and fall asleep.

"You'd better get out of there and face up to what you've done," Mom's deadpan voice filters through the wooden door jolting me awake. "You can't stay in there. Someone's gonna have to go to the toilet sooner or later." The lock clicks loud and I poke my head out. Mom grabs me by the hair and slaps me around the head and face. My arms fly up to protect myself. "What (Smack) the (Slam) hell (Crack) did (Crunch) you (Punch) think (Shove) you (Pummel) were (Shake) doing? (Fling)." There's screaming in my ears - it's mine.

Compared with the dreadful wait, the smart of the slaps is almost comforting. The anticipation of punishment has a special pain of it's own. "He punched me so I ran to the toilet and locked the door." I blurt out still not sure of what I did.

"It's your fault he's in the hospital. You squashed his finger in the door and nearly took it off." Shit, I think, with a capital 'S'. "Wait till your father gets home. Then you're gonna get it! Go lay on your bed and stay there until I say you can get off." My scalp throbs where

Mom yanked me by the hair as she dragged me through the kitchen. I pat my swollen lip with the corner of my tee shirt.

Dad hears everything in an excited rush as Mom prepares to leave for the hospital. "I'll deal with her first," he says filling the doorway of my bedroom with his great shadow. "When are you kids going to start behaving yourselves?" He asks the air. "You're going to drive your mother nuts, if you don't stop it." I say nothing in my defense. He'll twist my words if I do. No explanation will lighten my punishment. Dad hesitates a moment, interpreting my silence as defiance. I know that anything I say will fuel his anger. "Roll over on your stomach and pull your pants down," he says as a doctor would order a patient. I hear his leather belt slither through the loops of his pants. I picture him folding it in half like I've seen him do before. My heart leaps as I bite hard into the blue candlewick bedspread. For a second I visualize my sister being beaten - not me. She gets a thrashing whenever we get in trouble because she's the oldest and should know better. I wince when his belt slashes her bare buttocks and cry because of her pain, because I am glad it's not my punishment and because I am ashamed that I am glad. Now it's my turn. I want to be brave like her and not even whimper. Is she listening? Will she cry for me even though she won't cry for herself?

When it's over and my sobs slow to a hiccup, I pull my pants up. It's the second time in one day that I've been left alone and that is more fearful than the beating.

Andy returns home a few days later full of stories about the hospital. He's better and doesn't bear me a grudge. His left pinky finger is still bandaged but he's able to do everything with it, except pick his nose. When the bandage is removed entirely, his little finger is bent at an angle and the nail is gone. When the nail grows back, that's crooked, too. The sight of his crippled little finger is my daily reminder of what happened that day.

Chapter Thirteen
Mysteries

Dad's turn

Most parents don't get ill enough to stay in bed like their children. Maybe it's because there's no one to look after them. They soldier on and show up at work wearing their coughs and colds like badges of courage. When Mom gets a cold, she sniffles a lot especially when she washes the clothes because her hands are under water and it's impossible to get her hanky out of her apron pocket. Dad gets what he calls 'head colds', meaning his head is packed full of phlegm. He blows hard into one of his red engineer's cloth, or his 'snot rags', then wipes it several times across the bottom of his nose in the space above his moustache. Afterwards he balls it up and sticks it in the back pocket of his overalls. He fills up several snot rags a day. In addition to this his racking smoker's cough lets fly and the whole place shakes and rattles with his congestion. Aside from colds, my parents suffer from other illnesses, but I'm not exactly sure what's wrong with them. It's a mystery.

One Christmas Eve Dad doesn't come home and our lengthy vigil by the bedroom window goes unrewarded. "I betcha' he's drunk somewhere. He'll probably sleep it off and show first thing in the morning," Mom says, comforting us, so we don't lose hope of getting the presents he's promised to bring home. We spend all of Christmas Day looking out the front window for him, but he doesn't show up. We peer down at the top of his car that is gradually disappearing into the mountain of snow around it. "I'm going to work by subway today. I'm not risking getting stuck in this snow," he told Mom that morning. "My tires are nearly bald."

"What's that mean?" I ask Phyllis.

"What'd'ya think? There ain't no hair on them! Ha, ha!" She guffaws and we giggle over it. Our neighbors probably think we're having a great time. Christmas is awful. There is no tree, no presents and for Christmas dinner we have canned spaghetti. Mom doesn't want to cook the plump chicken sitting on a dish in the tin 'ice box' that's wired to the windowsill in the alleyway off the kitchen in case Dad comes home. It wouldn't be right if we ate it without him.

The day after Christmas our landlady knocks on the door. "There's a message come over the telephone box for your mother."

"Yeah?" Phyllis says, waiting for her to tell it.

"I'll tell her direct, if you don't mind," she says with a sniff, rubbing her parchmenty fingers together like two dry sticks about to burst into flames.

"Mom!" Phyllis shouts in the direction of the bedroom where Mom is dusting the venetian blinds. "The landlady's got a message for you." Mom tells us later that Dad has fallen down a flight of stairs at a subway station and broken his leg in three places. He has been in a hospital in New York City since Christmas eve and that an ambulance is supposed to be bringing him home tomorrow. She seems relieved, even manages a smile.

The two ambulance men in white coats have a struggle getting him up the stairs. Once they install him in the bedroom and shut the kitchen door, Mom listens carefully to what they have to say. "Give him one of each of these medicines three times a day," she is told. "To avoid any adverse reaction, he's not to have any alcohol whatsoever. He needs plenty of rest. It will be a while before he's able to get up, but when he does, he will need to use these crutches." Two tall wooden crutches with red rubber tips and red rubber underarm rests stand, one each side of the kitchen door, like sentinels to the misery we have to endure the following weeks before Dad is able to get up and use them.

Through the closed door he complains so loud half the neighborhood probably stops what they are doing, "I'm fed up to my teeth with all this shit!" We rush in and find him tangled up in the sheets. His eyes blaze with fire and dark circles surround them on his white face. Added to this, he hasn't shaved for days and his beard has begun to sprout.

"Shut up and stop flapping. Here, take your medicine," Mom scolds.

"I don't want it. Get me a drink. I need a drink!" And he shouts the house down again as we scurry away to the safety of the parlor. At first we think it's funny that Dad acts like a baby and Mom has to tell him off. We listen to his childish outbursts from the parlor and giggle out loud and behind our hands. He says he's bored and hates staying in bed. Can't he even have one little, one insy-tinsy little drink? We're not even allowed to talk like that. But, as Mom points out when she catches us chortling over his inane requests, it isn't long before we are laughing on the other side of our faces. His moods go from black to very black as he orders us around. "Andy, get me a snot rag! Jeanne, go buy me a newspaper! Phyllis, empty my piss-pot! Fay, where the hell're my cigarettes?"

Dad's leg is in a cast from his ankle to his groin. It's horrible to look at, white and leg-shaped like a missing part of a mummy's body. He says it weighs a ton. "I can't lift it off the bed or move it. That medicine makes me so weak." He has to pee in a potty, just like a baby. It stinks and we have to empty it. The whole bedroom stinks.

"You're smoking like a Trojan," Mom says. "You're gonna smoke yourself to death." We open the window a crack.

"It's too draughty!" he whines, so we shut it. We adjust the venetian blinds a dozen times a day. "The light's in my eyes! It's too dark in here." Some of his pills put him to sleep and when he finally gives in, he falls asleep flat on his back because he can't roll over on his side or stomach. Then he snores loud enough to beat the band. "Come and empty this piss-pot!" he calls when he wakes up. As it's my turn, I go in, hold my breath, pick it up and just as I'm about to leave, he shifts his good leg a couple of inches off the bed and farts loudly in my direction. "Go chase that one around the corner," he says, laughing when he sees the expression on my face. I run like hell for the toilet.

Mom says staying in bed all day gives him gas and he can't help it, plus the medicine makes his urine stink. "Go and talk to him, get his mind off his leg." We take it in turns to entertain him, to keep the peace, to have a few moments of calm.

After his fourth day in bed, there's a change, something's not right. It's as though he has a fever. His pillow is soaked with sweat and we watch in the bedroom doorway as he shakes and tosses on the bed, throwing his head repeatedly from side to side, apparently not seeing Mom or us or anything. His breakfast coffee is untouched and still sitting by the bed. "Keep an eye on him," Mom orders Phyllis. "I'm going to the store for some eggs. He likes a fried egg." She sounds worried. Maybe she's changed her mind about him and the things she said last night.

Dad had taken one of his sedatives and was out cold. In her relief and exhaustion, she started working her way through a large bottle of beer and confided in us. "He's nothing but a lousy drunk," she said waving a cigarette in one hand, and balancing her beer glass on her knee with the other. "Do you want to know what happened to your Christmas presents? He lost them! He had them, all right, but on the way home, he stopped for a drink. As usual he had one too many and slipped on the stairs at Canal Street. He got knocked out. Someone saw an old tramp pick up your Christmas presents and do a runner. Your Dad was unconscious in the hospital for a couple of days, that's why we never heard anything." Before she goes out to the store we remind Mom that we're out of bread.

No sooner is she out of the door than Andy notices a noise from the bedroom. It's Dad. Afraid to enter the bedroom, we watch him from a distance. He's having some sort of a fit, talking gibberish and thrashing hard in the bed like a stranded fish. Suddenly he sits up ramrod straight, no longer mindful of the weight and the pain of his leg and points at the wall opposite. "Snakes!" he shouts. "Millions of them." Fright fills his wild eyes. "Don't you see them? Ahhhh. They're coming for me." He throws the covers over his head, shivering violently, and the bed rattles beneath him.

"I'm going for Mom," Phyllis says, her voice cracking. "You two go and sit in the parlor."

A couple of hours later when Mom is talking to the doctor in the kitchen, we listen in from the parlor. "I'm afraid he's in a bad way," the tall doctor with the shock of white hair on his head as well as on his hands says to Mom. "How much alcohol does he consume on a daily basis?" We strain but can't hear Mom's answer. "What we have here is a case of the DT's. That is, delirium tremens, a severe psychotic condition that occurs as a result of chronic alcoholism. In simple terms, he's like this because he's been off the liquor for several days. He's going through what we call 'cold turkey'. He ought to seek help or it will kill him."

When Christmas vacation is over we are so glad to get back to school that we run all the way there. We can't join in when our friends brag about their Christmas presents, nor do we breathe a word about Dad's recent confinement. Being in ordinary company again makes our sad time seem sadder.

To give Mom a break, one by one, we keep Dad amused. After the first day back at school, it's my turn. He asks me how was school and I mumble, "Okay." I can't bring myself to say what's on the tip of my tongue - how miserable our life is and how different from everyone else's.

"What's the matter?" he asks. I stare at my feet. "Look at me when I speak to you! I have told you often enough - you've got to look a person in the eye. Never let anyone stare you down. Don't show your fear."

I look him in the eye. I look deep into the soul of this man who is my father and of whom I am afraid. I stare into pupils like deep black pools and I see my own eyes there. Can he read my thoughts? I blink and turn away. "I can recite a poem I learned at school today."

"Okay? Let's hear it."

It's called *The Owl and the Pussy Cat*. "The owl and the pussy cat went to sea in a beautiful pea-green boat..." When I finish it he comments, "You're my smart little one, aren't you? How's about a dance for your Daddy?"

He knows I like to dance because he sees us practising for our family 'shows'. When Mom and Dad are playing a game of rummy in the parlor and listening to the radio, we sit in the kitchen and have pretend talent contests. We are either announcer, performer or audience. The 'performer' stands on a chair opposite the kitchen table where the audience sits. "Ladies and Gentlemen," we start, standing next to the stove which is still warm from supper. "Tonight we present..." and we introduce our act. Andy has only one act. He hugs his teddy bear and sings, "Me and My Teddy Bear."

Me and my teddy bear have no worries, have no cares.

Me and my teddy bear just play and play all day.

He is working on "Rudolph the Red-Nosed Reindeer", but he doesn't like it when we tell him we don't want to hear it in the middle of summer. Sometimes we try a duo-act - Phyllis sings while I dance. "Look at the little Miss Fancy Pants" Dad teases me. "Such a glamour girl." I'm quietly annoyed. I don't want to be no fancy pants, glamour girl. I like learning songs, twirling the words and notes around my tongue. Knowing songs, stories, poems or dances, is like knowing what 'treasure' means.

"What's she got a face on for?" Dad asks Mom. "And what's he doing with a teddy bear? He's too old for that thing, gimme here." At five years old a boy gets rid of his baby toys, Dad informs us. But we know Andy loves his teddy bear. There's no harm in him keeping it. We snatch it away from him and hide it out of Dad's sight until Andy goes to bed.

Finally Dad gets out of bed. He washes and shaves off his beard, looking better, but his mood hasn't improved. He lurches awkwardly around the apartment on the crutches, but won't be able to manage the flight of stairs to go out. When he stumbles or stubs his toe, he curses to hell, but looks up when he says it. Then he snarls at Phyllis. "I've run out of cigarettes. Go to the store and get me two packets of Pall Mall's. Well, what are you waiting for?"

"The money."

"Ask him for credit. Tell him I'm laid up in bed, and can't work."

She looks at Mom for approval. Mom nods. "It's okay, we've been on credit for a while. Pick up a quart of milk and some frankfurters for supper. We've got enough potatoes for now."

Non-stop smoking calms him. He sits in an armchair with his leg propped up on the hassock. "I'll skip supper. Give me another cup of coffee." He can't get comfortable. "This damn leg is starting to itch. It'll kill me, yet," he complains, clawing uselessly at the cast with his fingernails. He pulls at the armchair cushion and pulls out Andy's teddy bear which was hidden underneath. "What the hell...?" He struggles up on one crutch, drags himself and his bad leg to the window. He opens it, throws the teddy out as far as he can, then shuts it with a bang. "That takes care of that!"

My heart bangs furiously against my ribcage. The frankfurter and mashed potatoes stick in my throat. Swallowing hard, I go up to him and look him straight in the eye. "Can I please go out in the yard and get it?" He looks away and pretends he can't hear me. I repeat it.

"Get outta here or I'll whack you from here to kingdom come! That kid's gotta grow up some time." I peek out and see it in the Puerto Ricans' yard - a small dark dent on top of the crusty snow, and decide that when the time is right, I'm going to retrieve it. The next morning I get up before anyone else and look out, but it's gone. There are footprints all around the spot where it landed. The small ones are cats', the large are humans'.

We distract Andy during the day but he is disturbed at night because there is no substitute for his teddy bear. Nightmares start and bed-wetting is frequent so that he receives new punishments for old. A change comes over me as I watch my father through half-closed eyes. Inside of me a small knot of mistrust boils up then hardens like the colorful candies we suck on that last for ages.

Mom's turn

One minute my shoes fit and the next time I wear them, they are too small. Does it happen overnight? "Don't be stupid, stupid. It happens gradually. You just don't notice it, that's all," Phyllis reassures me. It's the same with Mom. One minute she can juggle breakfast, comb my hair, tie Andy's shoelaces and give orders to Phyllis all at the same time. The next minute, she's in bed, barely able to whisper to us where our socks are.

"It's Dad's fault," Phyllis decides. Since he recovered from his accident, he doesn't keep regular hours and might not come home at night, showing up late the following afternoon. We watch him stagger, like some wayward stranger, through the front door, past the kitchen and drop down asleep on the parlor floor without a 'by your leave, or thank you'. He snores without constraint and raucous honking noises, whistles and snorts punctuate our after-school hours until it's time for bed. It is hard to do our homework or listen to the radio with a body stretched out on the floor like a dead man, only he's noisy enough to wake the dead. He hasn't shaved for days, and his thinning hair stands straight up. His overalls are stiff with grease and he reeks of engine oil, gasoline, cigarettes and whiskey. "It's enough to make you gag," Mom says, stepping over him on her way to the sofa, trying to make like he's not there. Then she goes quiet and still, like the air on a too-hot summer's day before a storm blows, and stares ahead without blinking.

Suddenly I'm awake and it's the middle of the night. Mom and Dad are shouting from the top of their lungs and swearing at one another in the parlor. Mom screams out in pain. "He's hit her," Phyllis whispers, her lips close to my ear as we listen huddled together in the middle of the bed. There's a crash and the sound of broken glass. They are running towards us. We stare at our closed door, the only thing separating us from the fight. It bursts open and Mom lands on top of us screaming, her snot and blood smearing our sheets and pyjamas. Dad grabs her by the hair pulling her backwards to her feet. She struggles away, striking out with pummeling fists. Dad turns on the lights, blinding and exposing us at the same time. "Stop it!' I hear myself scream with an abandon I didn't know I had. Dad is slapping Mom's face from side to side and she's kicking him, throwing punches, blind to everything but fury.

Andy is out of his crib and in the doorway. "Mommy, Mommy!" he cries. We try to untangle ourselves from our parents but can't. Someone is ringing the doorbell and pounding on the front door.

"Open up. Open up in there." The bed slats give way and it collapses, but doesn't have far to go because grandpa's draws and Dad's tools are propping it up from underneath. I crawl away to answer the door and am on my feet when I see Andy holding a hammer above Dad's head. "Stop it! Stop it!" He's saying and before I can do anything, he hits Dad. "Don't kill her, don't kill Mommy," he sobs, frightened. Phyllis grabs the hammer from him and throws it back under the bed.

At the front door two uniformed policemen hold back a small crowd of angry neighbors. The kitchen clock says it's a quarter to three when we let them in. While Mom and Dad are with them in the parlor we heat up a cup of cocoa for Andy and afterwards take him in bed with us. He shivers and jerks in his sleep until he eventually falls in with the rhythm of Phyllis's breathing.

I lay awake beside them, my body rigid under the covers. More than anything else I want to curl up and fall asleep into deep nothingness. Instead I stare wide-eyed at the ceiling. After a while, I relax and my feelings of dread lift. I feel myself floating up to the corner of the room. Up and up. I'm high up and touching the ceiling and I'm not scared. I can see all three of us asleep in the bed. I hang there all night and watch over us, light and airy and free.

In the morning Dad gets up. Without speaking to anyone, he goes through his morning routines and leaves, slamming the door behind him. Mom stays in bed and we get ready for school by ourselves. Our breakfast things are on the kitchen table when we return from school and Mom is in her night-gown asleep in our bed. An ashtray overflows with butt ends and empty beer bottles litter the floor beside the bed. We do our best to clean up the mess, including the broken lamp in the parlor. When it gets dark, I shake Mom, who hasn't stirred yet, and ask her what's for supper. "Tell Phyllis to do it. I can't," she says, rolling over and going back to sleep. Her eye is black and blue and closed tight. A cut on her lip has crusted over with dried blood.

Mom stays in bed over the next few days, saying little and eating less. She sends us to the grocer's for more beer and cigarettes which we have to get on credit. Her hands tremble when she lights up and I offer to do it for her thinking she might start a fire when we're not there.

She and Dad are talking again, but they shut the door, so we can't hear. He tells us that we have to do the housework now because he works all day so how can he help out at home? Then one morning, like sunshine that follows up a storm, Mom gets better. Breakfast is on the table and the beds are made before we leave for school. When we come back, clean clothes flutter on the line, and there's a stew simmering on the stove.

Mom's recovery doesn't last long and every couple of months, Phyllis and I are back in charge. It's always the same, out of the blue she doesn't get up one morning. She lays in bed for a week or more, half-drunk on beer. When she's better and we're back to normal, we always think this is the last time, but it never is. We call it "Mom's spells". Housework is hard and we all hate it. "I'm sick of doing this shit," Phyllis moans one afternoon. "I'm losing friends because I've got to stay home and clean up the mess you guys make."

"She won't be in bed forever," I say half-heartedly.

"If you're so sure, you can sweep the kitchen floor, I'm going out." She flies out of the door taking Andy with her.

"Where have they gone?" Mom calls from our bedroom.

"Nowhere. Out."

"There's a marrow bone in the icebox. Get it out," she says sighing. "You can learn how to make lima bean soup." Mom instructs me from the bed, calling out what to do, and I need to push a chair up to the stove and stand on it so I can see into the soup pot.

During Mom's spells Phyllis cooks most of the meals, picking up the groceries from the store on the corner after school. Andy sets and clears the table and carries down the garbage. I wash the clothes and hang them out. What we do is never enough. Dirt piles up behind the sofas and under the beds. The blinds are streaked with grime and we have cockroaches in the kitchen. We slaughter the one or two we see during the day, but at night, if we have to get up and turn on the kitchen light, thousands of them scatter in every direction. "It's the Puerto Ricans," Mom says when we tell her about them. "They brought them over on the boat. Everyone knows that. They come from across the alleyway." After that I envision cargoes of cockroaches arriving in New York, and armies of them marching up the walls, crossing the great divide of apartments buildings, the alleyways, and settling into our cracks and corners.

Our personal hygiene suffers. A note from the school nurse says that I have nits and can't go back until I've had treatment. The only treatment Mom has is to yank a fine-tooth comb through my hair and rake out the tiny eggs. I sit on the edge of her bed while she combs out the 'cooties'. She vents her anger at our neighbours. "That's the second thing the Spicks have brought over (cockroaches are the first) - lice. I don't see any jumping around. One must have landed on your head and laid a million eggs." She snaps one dead between two fingernails. The ivory-colored comb is so fine it feels like my hair is being pulled from my head strand by strand. I bite my lip and hold my neck taut, watching balls of hair mount up on the bed beside Mom as she cleans the comb.

Mom never seems to notice the housework that we have been doing while she lolls in bed. Her standards, the pressure of the work, its burdens and responsibilities have fallen to us and she doesn't see it or care about it. She calls us in to her speaking to us in a slow, monotonous voice about things from her past or else she shouts and complains about the neighbours. "Those sons of bitches are always nosing into our business!" She scares us with her new agitated energy and violent hatred of everyone. If she's up and on her feet, she paces the room and shouts at the windows with her fists raised to the ceiling. Spit flies from the corners of her mouth when she speaks, and her curses fill up the room, my ears, fall about her rumpled sheets. She parts the venetian blinds, yelling swear words down the alleyway and curses and damns to hell everyone she knows. We pray that no one will hear her. We beg her to get back in bed, plead with her to eat something or go to sleep. She refuses all food, even sandwiches, but is eventually enticed to calmness with a chilled bottle of beer.

"I wonder what she does during the day when we're not here," I say to Phyllis. "Does she open the window and curse at people in the street?"

"She probably sleeps most of the time. We'd know if she did anything else."

Dad won't be coaxed into talking about Mom's behavior. We don't think he knows exactly what is going on himself. Like us he's relieved when Mom gets out of bed and things start back to normal. We never know which way the wind blows with him and have been keeping out of his way in case he gets mad when he's drunk and comes after us. We move in the shadows and are grateful when he pays off our credit bill at the grocer's. Sometimes he sends us out for a pizza, which we eat straight out of the box . Mom would die if she found out. She expects us to eat off of plates.

"Mom's up," Phyllis whispers to me early one morning. "I can hear her in the kitchen." I open my eyes wide. It's Spring and a warm sun sifts through our bedroom from the alley window. "It's been over two weeks this time."

"It's a mystery to me why she goes like that. It's the same with Dad's visions when he broke his leg. What was that all about?"

Phyllis doesn't answer me. She's thinking about something else. "Remember when you sat and talked to him, you know, when he was in bed with the leg. Did he touch you in a funny place?" she asks.

"What do you mean by funny?"

"Here," she says pointing to her chest.

"NO! And if he ever does, I'll tell him a thing or two."

Chapter Fourteen
Traveling

All of life isn't a disaster. There are enjoyable times when we are carefree and happy, days when it seems that summer will last forever. There's no need to ask us, but Dad does anyhow, just to see our reactions. "Who wants to go on a picnic?" Pandemonium reigns temporarily as we fly in different directions and rake through closets for the necessaries. I fill an old school bag to the brim with empty glass jars for lake specimens, a kite, a bathing suit, a tennis ball, and a battered New York Yankees baseball cap for a day's outing in the country. Mom hauls down the green metal gallon thermos and makes cherry-flavored Kool-Aid, adding large chunks of ice she's picked off from the block in the icebox. Phyllis shakes the dust off a rickety straw picnic basket that has languished in our junk closet since last summer.

"We're gonna have peanut butter and jelly sandwiches, aren't we, Mom?" Andy asks, holding up a jar of Welch's grape jelly in one hand and Skippy Peanut butter in the other.

It's a long drive. Like Mom says, we're luckier than most people are because we have a car, only I get carsick. The minute I slide in the back seat and smell the fumes, I feel a headache coming on. Dad goes around a couple of corners and I am reeling. My head's splitting and I'm queasy. "I'm gonna throw up!" I cry. He slams on the brakes, aiding and abetting my churning stomach, and I throw up undigested corn flakes all over the back seat. "Look! They're still good," Phyllis says. Maybe you better eat them again." Mom tells her to shut up and me to sit in the front seat with the window open from now on.

At the park we head for our favorite spot through the woods and far away from the parking lot. Andy and I run ahead to stake our claim on a spot on the crest of a hill. We drop our bags under a tree and race to the edge of the slope and roll down the hill. We tumble over and over, hands and arms pressed to our sides, and the sense of freedom that we feel as we abandon ourselves to the force of gravity is exhilarating. I clutch a clump of grass in each hand to anchor me when I stop. The sky spins out of control and I am giddy until the earth lines up with the sky.

Everybody suffers when there's a heat wave in New York City. It's impossible to cool off and you feel like you want to jump out of your own skin. There's isn't a hint of a breeze. The air is thick enough to slice and mosquitoes are the only ones keeping busy. Some daring soul might slip out with a wrench and open the fire hydrant that's just outside our front door. It's against the law to waste the city's water like that, and no one ever knows who does it, but that doesn't stop us all from running out in shorts and bathing suits and frolicking in the fat, welcoming geyser. The street goes from deserted to Grand Central Station within minutes as the precious water gushes over the sidewalk and into the gutters. Laughter peels along the scorching windowpanes and bare-armed men and women lean on windowsills to watch the spectacle, laughing out loud, and would join in if they didn't have babies to nurse or wives to criticize. A playful fight breaks out among the teenagers who want to get in front of the spray, and further down the street, toddlers splash and jump in swirling eddies. The high-pitched whine of a police siren headed our way is as good a warning as a school bell. By the time they arrive, a stray dog is the only one they can interrogate before the tongue of water that had flowed from the hydrant is silenced.

Dad takes the day off and drives us to Long Beach to cool off. We've been to Coney Island, Brighton Beach, Rockaway and Canarsie with Mom on the subways and busses, but Dad says that anyone living in New York City can do that. Public transport doesn't go as far as Long Beach from Brooklyn so you've got to have a car to beat the crowds. "God, it's beautiful. I love this place," he says, flexing his arms and sucking in a long, deep breath. "We better get a place in the shade otherwise we'll be like lobsters by tonight judging by that sun."

"Last one to the beach is a rotten egg!" Phyllis shouts, leaving us behind. The sand is burning hot and we hop from one foot to the other until our parents choose a spot and our scorched feet can sink gratefully into the cool sand under the boardwalk. Mom spreads out the old blanket that, during the day, will serve as tablecloth as well as bed, and repository for shells, seaweed and sand crabs. She passes out tin cups of home-made lemonade and the ice chinks on the side of the cup as we sip. The chilled liquid etches a path down our parched throats.

Before lunch Dad takes us to the water's edge. As usual, the swell of the ocean and the roar of the waves as they crash ferociously close, tugging at our ankles, sucking at our feet, excite and frighten at the same time. Dad is a good swimmer. We watch mesmerized as his powerful arms and long legs propel him towards the horizon and he's far away from us in a matter of minutes. After lunch when he's stretched out asleep on a towel, Mom tells us a story from the past. "He saved a woman from drowning when he was young, you know. We were sitting on the beach like this when he suddenly sat up and said he heard someone shouting for help. I said it must've been them over there playing with the beach ball. No, he said pointing at the ocean, look over there. I looked again and saw what might have been a person, but it was too far away to be sure. Dad ran to the water and swam as fast as he could. By this time I was scared stiff because he'd gone so far out I couldn't see anything. I waited by the water quite a while and a crowd built up. Finally, we could see two heads slowly coming our way. He brought back a woman, half drowned she was and wild with fear. She said she'd got cramp and couldn't swim back and spoke with an accent. Maybe she was French."

There are a million questions I want answered, but ask, "What's cramp?"

"It's when your legs won't move. You get it if you swim too soon after you've eaten. That's why you've got to wait an hour." We don't want cramp, so we wander off and collect shells for making necklaces when we get home. We pass the rest of the time making sandcastles and hunting for sand crabs.

Phyllis and Andy sunburn easily and develop painful water blisters that burst, leaving ugly dangly bits of white skin. My skin turns browner as the day passes and Phyllis nicknames me 'Beans' because, she says, it rhymes with Jeanne and I am the color of a bean. I don't care much, except that, somehow, "Beans" sticks, and at home she calls to me down the street, " Beans, it's time for supper." I run inside as fast as I can, so that no one else will catch on and start calling me 'Beans' as well.

We take turns riding the waves inside an inflated inner tube that's slicker and blacker than licorice when it's wet. Dad grips tightly to the rope wound around it so we aren't dragged away. The rest of us hang onto him in the water, clasping his arm or straddling his back for dear life. "Hold on tight!" he shouts. The undertow is strong and you could be swept away on a current and never come back. "Look out, here comes a big one!"

The breeze drops to nothing in the parking lot. I take one last look at the beach as the sun dips towards the ocean. "Why can't we sleep on the beach?" I whine, wanting to stay there longer, and dreading the hot city, the sultry nights.

"It's hotter than hell in this car!" Mom exclaims.

"Open the windows and stop lallygaging or we're never gonna get outta here!" Dad shouts, finding his New York City voice again. "There'll be a breeze as soon as we get moving. Get in the car, all of you." A large black patch has already formed on the back of his shirt by the time he gets behind the wheel.

For the rest of the summer, when Dad's not home and Mom's having one of her spells, we're left on our own. For amusement, we spend the day riding the subways. The underground tunnels stretch from one end of New York City to the other. For the price of a fifteen-cent token each, we travel the length and breadth of Brooklyn, cross over into Queens and venture as far away as the northern end of Manhattan Island or the southern tip of Brooklyn at Rockaway Beach. The subways touch on all the boroughs except Staten Island. All day and much of the night, trains snake their way along tunnels beneath our street because we live directly above the BMT Line. Through the subway ventilation shaft on the sidewalk in front of the apartment, we hear the roar of trains passing by underneath.

The shaft is deep and the grate that covers the opening is made of sturdy metal. We lay down with our stomachs flat against the grate, shielding our eyes as we peer into the darkness. Six feet down there is a ledge. Chewing gum, cigarette butts, soda bottle tops and other objects small enough to slip through the one-inch square holes in the grate have been deposited there over a period of time. "There's money down there!" Phyllis says, straining hard to see. "At least two dimes and a nickel. Or is that a bit of silver paper?"

We're over the moon. We've found money. Only how do we get it out? Phyllis, as usual, has an idea. A while later we have a long piece of string with a small stone tied to the end of it. A blob of soft, chewed-up bubble gum that we stole straight out of Andy's mouth, is stuck to the bottom of the stone. Phyllis gives it to me. "This is a two-man job; you get over there and fish the coins out. I'll help from the other side." I ease the stone through one of the holes and press my face against the grate. "More to the right," she directs. "To the RIGHT!"

I swing the string between two tense fingers, making an arc a foot too wide. "It feels like the stone's gonna fall off."

"Never mind that, when it slows down, drop it on the nickel." We only have the one piece of gum. I must concentrate. If it falls off, we've lost the coins. I'm sweating. The sun is burning the backs of my legs below my shorts. What if someone else gets the money instead?

"It's nearly on top," I report from my angle. Then I feel a slight vibration. The train is coming. I lower the string an inch and the arc narrows. The rumbling in the distance increases.

"You can lower it any second now," Phyllis coaches. The ground shudders. Musty air rushes up my nose. Dirt, dust and candy wrappers dance above the ledge. The train is passing beneath me with a deafening roar. My hair flies straight up and air billows up my cotton blouse like a balloon. I will my eyes to stay open until the stone is above the nickel, but the swirling dirt gets in them. I blink, give up, and let go of the gum-covered stone.

"Hooray! You've done it," Phyllis cries. "Haul it up. E.aa.ss.y, don't let it fall off."

Over lunch Phyllis fingers the coins. "This money comes from the subway, so it's only right we use it on the subway. Tomorrow, we're going traveling."

"But it's all dark down there. What's the use of traveling if we don't see nothing?" Andy asks her.

"There is plenty to see. There are the stations... plus we go outside on the El train, and the train goes above ground before Coney Island," I tell him. Perhaps like me he is scared of getting lost or left behind. But I am curious about what we'll see, how far we'll go. We never get out at any of the stations. For fifteen cents each, we can go anywhere, and back, provided we don't exit. That would mean having the return fare, and leaving the neighborhood, which, strictly speaking, we're not allowed to do.

The platform is long and draughty with slot machines, litter bins and a couple of benches pushed up against the white-tiled walls. Bare light bulbs hang from the ceiling throwing out brackish light that barely illuminates the station's name written in a mosaic of dark-blue tiles. I stay close to the wall, knowing that if you got anywhere near the rails, you'd be electrocuted "It's coming," Phyllis says, holding out her hand. "Come on."

"In a second," I say, my hand still touching the tiled wall. I wait for the screech of the wheels, the blinding light, and when the train stops and the automatic doors open, I run for her hand and hop on. We pull away with the bare backs of our legs already sticking to the seats of yellow woven cane.

Sometimes the doors open on an empty platform. A man gets off looking like a lonely sailor on a deserted beach. We change to an express train that flies past stations like a speeding bullet. At large junctions we change for another line. People mill around like ants. They turn right, then left, stop dead in their tracks, hop on or off trains, run up and down stairs, and so do we.

Suddenly Andy is hungry. He notices that all the stations have cigarette and candy machines. "I want some candy," he whines. We get off at a quiet stop and wait for the train to leave and the people to go out before we pull out all the slots, push the buttons and are rewarded with a candy bar and someone's forgotten change.

When we get bored we play a people-watching game. Phyllis picks out someone and without saying a word, nudges us and uses her head and eyes to tell us which person we're supposed to look at. After they've left the train, she imitates them, the way they talk or nod, frown or smile.

People travel alone, in pairs or in bunches. At the 42nd Street and Lexington Avenue station, near the United Nations, distinguished-looking Africans wearing brightly colored floor-length robes stand in groups on the platform. Indian women in silver-threaded saris with bare midriffs get on and sit down beside New Yorkers in shorts and sneakers. We stare at everyone, but everyone else looks straight ahead paying no attention to the rest of the passengers. Classy women struggle through the doors at Fifth Avenue with shopping bags from Macys'. At Wall Street Station, gentlemen in pinstriped suits come on and reading newspapers while standing up, their eyes dart back and forth behind very small eyeglasses.

The Brighton line train we are on suddenly pops out into the open like a whale surfacing from the deep. Coney Island, our destination, is at the end of this line. We get out to change platforms and go straight back. While waiting for the next train, if we stretch our necks, we can see a corner of the giant Ferris wheel. The station smells like the sea and the sea air smells like fish. It's hot out and we would love to stroll along the shore. A slight breeze carries screams from the roller coaster. We have already seen the freak shows on the way to the beach. Signs advertising The Bearded Lady, The Strongest Man in the World, The Fattest Lady in the World, The Two-Headed Calf, The Fire-Eater, Siamese Twins, with lurid descriptions and gory hand-drawn pictures, are designed to entice people of all ages.

My stomach growls on cue, remembering the long row of food stalls outside the subway entrance. "I smell popcorn," Andy says, breaking into my thoughts.

"I smell Nathan's foot-long hot-dogs," I add, mimicking him.

"Me, too," Phyllis chimes. "If you had a hot dog, what would you have on it, sauerkraut or mustard?"

"Both," we say together.

Chapter Fifteen
Our One-And-Only Family Affair

For all our traveling on the subways, when it comes to going anywhere
in particular, we walk. Andy and I have almost no sense of direction.
We know what's around the block, where the park is, the subway, our
school and the movies, but anywhere else is a blur. Wherever Phyllis
leads we follow like a pair of puppy dogs, even when we go to see
Mom's sisters when Mom isn't well enough to come.

Whenever she does walk us over to see them, Dad scolds her.
"Why do you have to go and pester them? Don't they have enough to
worry about without hearing all our problems?" He's afraid they'll find
out what he's really like, but he's wrong. Mom doesn't discuss her
problems. She never complains or talks about Dad's drinking. She
makes sure, too, that she doesn't have a black eye when she goes. The
sisters talk about things in general, and the old days. Mom, whose
name is really Fanny, but likes to be called Fay, is the eldest of four.
After her come Aunt Sophie, Aunt Rose and Aunt Helen.

We have to play with our cousins who are okay except it's obvious
that we're the poor relations. They look at our clothes, which don't fit
too well, and are patched and a little misshapen. Our shoes (and
there's no doubt about it) are dilapidated. I've had mine for two years
and my toes and heels are trying to escape from both ends at the same
time. My cheeks burn whenever the cousins give us the once over. It's
worse for my sister. Lately, she has pulled and tugged at her clothes
like she'd prefer to rip them off and start again. But how and with
what? She whines, "How can I have a personality when I have to wear
clothes like these? Even the ragman doesn't want them!" She's twelve
years old going on thirteen. It means more to her than to me - I'm only
eight. Aunt Rose comments that my sister is nearly as tall as our Dad.
Mom agrees, "She's growing up fast."

Aunt Rose's husband, Uncle Victor, is an Italian and a barber. His
barbershop is on the ground floor below their apartment. We pass by
Uncle Victor's barber shop on the way up and he taps Andy on the
shoulder. "How about a haircut, young man?" Phyllis goes upstairs
with Aunt Rose but I hang back and watch as Uncle Victor escorts
Andy to a chair. He drapes a large white cloth around him and ties it at

the back of his neck. My brother looks like a young prince about to prepare for a feast. He glances at the mirror, sees me watching him, and manages a tentative, nervous smile.

Uncle Victor daintily picks up his comb and scissors and quietly contemplates Andy's head before raising his arms to shoulder height and cutting. He has a limp, but it doesn't slow him down. It's just the opposite. He hops around the chair with the energetic movements of a dancer. Clad in heavy brown shoes, his feet swirl the cut hair beneath them. The silver scissors glint in his right hand, while he waves the narrow black comb in his left. Snip! Snip! For every four snips of the scissors he cuts at one bit of hair. The rest of the snips clip the air. Snip! Snip! Snip! Snip! Hair flies. It floats in the air and lands on the floor. His dexterity is art. What is it like, I wonder, to be a barber?

Our uncle removes the white cloth with a flourish, a snap cracking the air as he shakes off the hair. He turns the chair around and announces, "That's it, son, all finished!" The thing we like most about Uncle Victor is that he never stints with us. He gives Andy the full treatment, including the final application of the talcum-powdered brush, even though it's a free haircut.

I'm so pleased that Andy has finally had a haircut, that I smile from ear to ear as he comes towards me. However, I quickly hide my rising shame when I see how dirty his neck is now that his hair is short and no longer covering it.

Upstairs Aunt Rose has already made a stack of salami sandwiches that are waiting for us on the kitchen countertop. We eat our sandwiches in front of their larger-than-we've-ever-seen television and watch the Seal Test Circus and the Howdy Dowdy Show. Mom says, "Go and play with your cousins now that you're finished," but we don't budge. We'd rather watch television.

In our opinion they're spoiled because they have more toys, clothes, food, and even more space, than anyone we know. The gap between what they've got and what we haven't is too big to understand. To put it simply, we're jealous of them. They've got their own, large bedrooms with thick, soft carpets and curtains with matching bedspreads. "Their rooms are like private toy shops," I whisper to Phyllis. "I know I'd want to steal something if I went in there. So what's the use?" We polish off the salami sandwiches, having been conditioned not to leave anything on our plates, drink a couple of glasses of chocolate milk and sit in front of the television. We manage to get through the visit without being punished or shaming ourselves.

A few months later when Mom is in bed again and we're sick to death of each others' company, Phyllis brings the conversation around to Aunt Rose and how Andy needs another haircut. "It's so far away," I complain, "almost in the country. We don't really know where it is either."

"It's on Fresh Pond Road, near Metropolitan Avenue in Maspeth. I found it on the map."

Aunt Rose is surprised to see us without Mom whose spells we make a point of not telling her about. We expect our aunt to throw us out, but she says to come in and she'll make some salami sandwiches. "What a shame. Your cousins have gone out for the day." We look sad, but we're not sorry because we only came for the haircut, the sandwiches, and the reassurance that we wouldn't be turned away.

The worse things get at home, the further we reach out elsewhere for comfort and for company. We try not to spoil our chances of a welcome by becoming nuisances, so spread our visits to Mom's sisters evenly over the months. One mid-December morning, we start out before the snowplows have had a chance to clear the street and reach Aunt Rose's frozen to the bone because of the deep snow and our inadequate clothing and footwear. Between her surprised look when she opens the door and the - 'How's your mother? You must be excited about Christmas. Come in and see our tree.''- I think to myself, she could never guess it, but we have given up on Christmas.

Their impressive Christmas tree sags under the weight of the enormous amount of decorations hanging on it, plus the twinkling white lights that resemble tiny stars. Instead of using common silver tinsel they have garnished it with angel hair, the latest thing in tree decorations. The pearly wisps are spun around the tree like white cotton candy making it and the whole thing about Christmas seem as remote to us as the North Pole. We spend the day soaking up as much of the atmosphere as we can stand, and hoping that the aura will last before the snow melts on our galoshes in the hall back home.

Aunt Rose surprises us by giving us each a present on our way out. "Don't open them 'til Christmas," she makes us promise. At the barber shop entrance, she and Uncle Victor wave us off. "Good-bye for now," they say. "Watch out how you cross the street. And be good kids to your Mom. Merry Christmas."

As soon as we are out of sight, we rip the presents open. We've all got tartan-plaid slippers. We've never owned slippers. I notice tears running down Phyllis' face. She wipes them away with her coat sleeve. "Would you look at that?" she says. "The cold is making my eyes water."

Our Aunt Sophie married Uncle Alex before World War II. During the war, while she was expecting their first baby, Uncle Alex went missing in action. Mom says Aunt Sophie went to pieces when she heard the news. When he came back, a year later, Mom says she went to pieces even more.

Aunt Sophie is a slender, pretty woman who always looks nice in a way that I'd call prissy and neat. She has Mom's black hair, and would have the same eyebrows only she shaved them off when she was young and they never grew back. Since then every morning of her life she sharpens her eyebrow pencil and draws on new ones. Aunt Sophie keeps her apartment as neat as a pin. She's a bit strict, frightening us a little whenever we step a foot out of place. Everyone in her family jumps to attention when she speaks. She's the sort of person who has the dinner on the table at the same time every night, the shirts ironed and the floor swept - and that's okay by us because it's more than we get at home.

Aunt Helen is our favorite aunt. Her long engagement (due to the fact that she wouldn't get married while she was still looking after her father) to Uncle Bob, is nearly over and they are getting married soon. We've been invited to the wedding. She is so kind and always remembers to bring us a little something whenever she comes to see us. On our birthdays she and Uncle Bob take the birthday child and, often one other, out for the day, buying them a present, like a blouse or a sweater. Unlike her sisters who have dark hair, Aunt Helen's hair is a lustrous strawberry blonde that she wears in a pageboy like Veronica Lake.

The four sisters get together occasionally and one time they and their families converged on our place and the women cooked potato dumplings for everyone. They all peeled the potatoes which were then boiled and mashed. Aunt Rose fried onions, which were added to the potatoes. Aunt Helen and Aunt Sophie made flour and water dough and kneaded it on the enamel kitchen table. They rolled out the pastry and filled dough circles with the potato mixture. These were folded over and pinched at the edges with a fork. Mom dropped them into a large pot of boiling water and as the dumplings rose to the surface, she scooped them out and buttered them. I remember Dad reminiscing in the parlor about his mother's dumplings and how they were the best when Mom handed him a huge steaming plate of the sisters' dumplings. He stopped talking there and then, polishing it off without any complaints.

When Aunt Helen and Uncle Bob's wedding invitation arrived, Dad warned, "Don't get your hopes up."

"We have to go. It's my baby sister's wedding and we can't miss it. We'd be the only ones," Mom said, sounding disappointed.

"Well, I'll see what we can do."

We run our fingers over the embossed writing on the invitation so many times that we practically wear it out. "We have the Honor of inviting you... "Your Presence is Requested at the Reception..." We ask Aunt Helen to tell us about her wedding dress.

"It is ballerina length with Chantilly lace over a taffeta bodice and skirt. The sleeves are long, to the wrist with satin-covered buttons up to here," she says indicating half way to her elbow. "The neckline is scooped with scalloped lace along the top." Phyllis and I are enchanted. It will be our first ever wedding.

Aunt Helen's wedding was months away but Mom and Dad argued about it all the time. Mom had saved up some money for a present. "Hand over the money. I'll look after it," Dad said.

"The hell you will. It's mine. No one's touching it."

"You know, if I'm lucky, I could double it."

"Leave off," Mom said, dismissing the subject.

Dad had been better. He hadn't come home drunk every night and he liked his new job. They celebrated the day he got it, sitting at the kitchen table drinking a dozen bottles of beer between them. We were disgusted at both of them. "They're going to be useless tomorrow. We'll have to do everything ourselves," Phyllis said loudly.

"Sshhh. They'll hear you."

"Well, I don't give a shit."

"You're gonna get it now," I warned.

Phyllis is scared of nothing. She has been nasty to Mom left, right and center and Dad was next on her list. The more she answered back, the more she got beaten. The next day Dad got up at noon while Phyllis was making ham and cheese sandwiches for our lunch. He dressed and left without a word to anyone. When he came home, he had a strange look on his face like he had a joke on us. "So, what's up?" Mom asked. She was still in her bathrobe since getting up in the morning.

"Nothing," Dad said, standing by the table and watching us eat, trying hard not to smile.

"Well, you can at least take your coat off if you're going to stand around doing nothing."

Andy saw it first. "What's that?" he asked through a mouth full of mashed potatoes. He was pointing at Dad's coat pocket.

"What's what?"

"That...what's moving in your pocket."

"What? There's nothing. I swear," Dad laughed. Dad kept up the charade for a while but Andy jumped up and slid his hand in Dad's coat pocket. A little puppy with teeth as sharp as needles poked his head out. Andy held it first and when it peed down the front of his shirt, he dropped it and it scurried under the table.

We've always wanted a dog. We had begged for one for so long that we'd given up on it. Now, out of the blue, our dreams came true. "Is it a he or a she?" "What'll we call it?" "What kind of dog is it?"

Rex turned out to be a male mongrel. Mom said it was funny to see three kids walk a puppy down the street with one leash. Everyone came out to see our new dog. Could they pet him? No. Could they walk him? No. Could they brush him? No. "Dad, Mom - Rex is so smart. He did everything in the gutter when we took him out!" Andy bragged, proud of his new, smart pet.

"Well, he'd better," Mom said, smiling for the first time since he arrived. "I'm sure as hell not cleaning up after him."

Phyllis was like a new person with Rex, too busy to get into trouble or complain when she had a dog to train. She spent the afternoons with Rex teaching him to catch a ball, to fetch a stick, to roll over. "You're the smartest dog in the world," I heard her say one afternoon after a training session on the sidewalk.

"He's just a mutt," some guy in the street said when she wouldn't let him take the leash and play with him. Before he had a chance to defend himself, Phyllis lunged at him, knocking him down to the ground. Then, straddling his chest and brandishing a clenched fist in his face she said,

"You shut your mouth, you hear? No one says that about my dog."

Rex obeyed all our commands. He performed tricks and ran faster than anyone. His black, brown and beige coat was glossy and we never minded brushing it, fighting, even, over who would do it. Mom said he slept all day but he jumped for joy when we came home from school. He didn't like it when anybody shouted – he would hide in our bedroom and shiver.

"What's that dog doing in your bed?" Dad bellowed, waking up the whole neighborhood one night. We'd been asleep for ages, but he and Mom have to pass through our bedroom to get to theirs and he saw Rex asleep at the foot of our bed. "Get off of there. Off!" Rex slunk away from the warmth of our bed to his place under the kitchen sink. "If you keep doing what I tell you not to, I'm gonna get rid of that dog!" Dad picked on Rex. When he was in a bad mood he said, "God, that dog eats more than I do."

Nowadays we hide Rex in the evenings, and keep him out of Dad's way. There is tension between Mom and Dad and it electrifies the air. The tiniest spark sets off an explosion in one way or another because of the wedding. The day is getting nearer and Mom is in a panic. Finally she announces, "We're not going to the wedding." Phyllis, Andy and I stiffen, looking at Mom for the rest of the story. "We don't have enough money for a present and for clothes for all of us."

"That doesn't matter. We can go in the clothes we wore at Easter," Phyllis offers.

"It's the wrong season. They don't fit anymore, and look at your shoes. They're a disgrace!" Mom says, wringing her hands.

Phyllis, who has a special rapport with Aunt Helen and wants to go to the wedding more than anyone else, suggests, "Why don't you and Dad go, you know, by yourselves. I can take the kids out for a pizza."

"No. We're going as a family, or we're not going at all," she answers, a touch of pride creeping into her voice, before turning away from us.

In bed that night we overhear Mom and Dad talking heatedly.

"What's the old man up to now?" Phyllis asks, rolling over in my direction. She's been facing the other way and hasn't heard them clearly. I poke her in the ribs. "He'll kill you if he hears you call him 'the old man'. They're talking about Aunt Helen's wedding."

"Well?"

"I think Mom's giving him the money she's saved up. Dad says he can easily double it. How can he do it?"

"Go back to sleep. We'll find out tomorrow," she says, pulling the pillow over her head.

"Do you think maybe we can borrow some clothes?"

"Yeah, like from who? The fairy godmother? Go to sleep!"

Talk of money and the lack of it, of who's got it, and who doesn't, bounces off the walls of the apartment like a ping pong ball in a tournament. Once more the police are at the door in the middle of the night. "Open up!" Neighbors shout from above and below us. "Stop that noise!" Someone angry and annoyed bangs on the heating pipes adding to the cacophony. Mom and Dad have woken up the neighborhood again.

I am having bad headaches. I sit at my school desk pressing my fingers against the side of my temples, trying to push the pounding beat - boom, boom – back into my veins where it belongs. The sound of my heartbeat bangs so loud in my ears, I can no longer hear the teacher's words. I feel nauseous and everything on the blackboard slurs into a jittery blur. My head sinks into the crook of my arm beneath the weight of the pain and the noise. "Is it the police, the pipes, the front door?" I spend the rest of the afternoon in the school infirmary where the nurse lays a cold compress on my forehead and I drift off into a tormented doze.

I crash down on the bed in my clothes as soon as I get home. I can hear Phyllis and Andy arguing over a comic book in the parlor and

Mom asking from the doorway what I've been doing at school. I want to answer her but can't open my eyes or move anything, not even my lips. I wake up the next morning feeling as though I've been run over by a bus, and find it hard to talk or focus my eyes. Mom lets me stay home and I sleep fitfully most of the day. In bed that night Phyllis wakes me up, rocking my shoulder, causing me to jump. "What are you crying about?" she moans, annoyed.

"I don't know. Was I crying? Nothing, I guess."

"Well, shut up and go to sleep or I'll give you something to cry about!"

I'm wide-awake now. I hear Dad's gentle snores rippling the air in the adjoining room and I lay still, not daring to move, for fear of disturbing Phyllis. I listen to his even breathing. It doesn't seem possible that not so long ago screamed curses, accusations, promises to maim and kill rang out in the now tranquil rooms. My wide-open eyes strain in the dark for the familiar spot where the wall meets the ceiling and I float up to it, drifting out of myself. Anchored there, I look over all of us in bed, keeping watch in my place of vigil. I am okay once more and can glide away to sleep.

We know for certain now that we're not going to the wedding. No one has told Aunt Helen yet because Mom can't bring herself to and Dad has washed his hands of everything. "Maybe Aunt Helen will be too busy to notice we're not there," I say, trying to be helpful.

"Oh, just shut up, all of you!" Mom shouts, squinting hard as she blows out a thick stream of cigarette smoke before stubbing the cigarette out into the already overflowing ashtray. Suddenly, fat tears fall down her cheeks. Trying to light up another Pall Mall, she says through pursed lips, "That father of yours is nothing but a fucking son of a bitch bastard! I HATE HIM!" The unlit cigarette drops onto her lap, then rolls to the floor. She bends down for it, her words rattling in the kitchen sink like broken glass, before clinking down the drain.

"I thought she was going to do something horrible," Phyllis confides to me later in the parlor when all is quiet. Mom has gone to lie down and we are sifting through some recently acquired comics.

"Me, too," I agree.

"It's the wedding tomorrow and Dad's gambled and lost her money."

"You mean he played cards, like rummy...?"

"No, he played the horses – you know…"

"What horses? I don't get it."

"Forget it. He lost the money, that's all."

The next morning, Mom and Dad are talking in the kitchen. We hear him apologize to her, he's sorry, but Mom doesn't think that helps matters. She wants to know what her sister is going to think of her. With his arm around her, he says that she'll understand once Mom explains everything. But Mom doesn't answer. She's too busy crying into his blue flannel shirt.

"Look," he says, wiping her eyes with a clean snot rag. "I've got one dollar to my name. Here, take it. It's yours. Treat yourself and the kids to the movies. It'll get your mind off the wedding. By the time you come home, it will all be over." We look at one another, then cross fingers, hoping that Mom will agree. At twenty-five cents a piece, we four could enjoy an afternoon out. It would be a relief to be out of the apartment.

We walk the twenty blocks to the Paramount Movie Theater in silence, each of us involved in our own thoughts. The one-and-only family affair we are ever likely to get invited to, we can't attend. Beyond the shame of not going because we couldn't afford it, the sadness for Mom's loyalty to her sisters and their now forgotten dependence on her for things she'd done for them in the past, beyond all these things, I see in a bright light Aunt Helen in her lace wedding gown. She's radiant, smiling up at Uncle Bob, handsome in a new suit, dark against the strawberry blonde hair and fair skin, the white veil, pearly satin under dress and white satin sandals of the bride. The wedding cake, three tiers, no doubt, with edible sugar roses in palest pink cascading from the top and trailing down the sides, a miniature bride and groom peeking out from a silken arbor on the top, dominates a table groaning under the weight of food for all the wedding guests.

Mom scrounges at the bottom of her purse and comes up with a dime and we share a box of buttered popcorn and watch a cowboy film in the half-empty theater. The crackle of the guns, tramping of the horses' hooves, loud and excited music, drives out the picture of Dad looking like death warmed over as he shut the kitchen door behind us.

He should have come too, cowboy movies are his favorite, but a dollar wouldn't stretch to it.

The evening streets are wet when we get out, the air fresh and cool after a shower. We dodge and jump small puddles. Cars shush by, their headlights temporarily blinding us after being in the dark for so long. The apartment is in total darkness and Dad and Rex are gone. "He can't have gone out drinking; he's bust. He gave me his last dollar," Mom sighs. "All right, kids, get ready for bed. It's late."

The popcorn I enjoyed a few hours ago churns in the pit of my stomach as I lay in bed mulling over the day's events. Something isn't right. Where is Dad and where is our precious dog, Rex? I shut my eyes and hug my pillow. Fear sidles up, fear of the unknown mixed with intuition. I want to pray so bad, pray that whatever it is, won't happen, will pass us by. I don't know how to pray, but repeat to myself part of a prayer overheard at school. "Now I lay me down to sleep, now I lay me down to sleep, now I lay me..."

Nobody hears Dad come in. This is because he doesn't stagger through our bedroom, turning on the lights, and waking us up like usual. Instead he creeps in and goes to sleep on the sofa in the parlor.

"Where's Rex?" Phyllis' voice pierces the air and I sit bolt upright in the bed. "Where's Rex? Where is he?" She is shaking Dad awake. Andy flies past my bed and joins her. I jump out and follow.

"None of your business," Dad says sitting up. "Get me an ashtray, will you, Andy," he says looking right through her and lighting a cigarette as he coughs up the phlegm from yesterday's smoking. He is trying to take control of the situation, but looks so ridiculous with his hair standing up instead of lying flat against his head. He hasn't shaved for days and since he slept in his clothes, the best that can be said for him is that he resembles a bum from the Bowery. I almost want to burst out laughing, except I have a gnawing feeling that something isn't right.

Phyllis won't give up. "Just tell us where he is," she says less aggressively. "I'll go and get him."

"You can't," Dad tells her point-blank, sitting up and attempting to put on his shoes. "He's gone."

"Gone where?"

"I sold him."

"You're joking," she says, half laughing, darting a desperate look at us, and waiting a moment for him to say it is all a joke. "Okay," she says finally, "Where's the money?"

"Yeah, show us the money if you sold him," Andy chimes in.

"I don't have it," he shouts, throwing his shoe at my sister. It hits her square in the mouth. Her hands fly to her face. "I sold him to a man at Harry's Bar." Then he says hurriedly, "We couldn't afford to feed him, you know."

Phyllis suddenly pounces on Dad like a wildcat, beating him around the head with her fists. All the bad words that we have ever heard in the whole wide world spill from her, dropping around us like so many rotten apples, mounting so high that we are stuck and cannot move.

Dad, fully alert now, manages to stagger to his feet and with the force of a baseball player at bat, wallops Phyllis on the side of the head, knocking her flying. Andy and I scurry out of his way to the bedrooms

"You've gone too far this time, madam." He grabs her by the scruff of the neck and drags her to the front door and throws her out on the landing. "YOU STAY OUT!" He slams the front door, locks it and turns to us. "You better not let her in. You hear me?" He is shaking and exhales through his nose and mouth in thick, angry waves; his words fly like bullets. We nod. "I'll kill the first person who opens that door and lets her in."

Phyllis, who is slumped against the front door, cries in the hallway for hours. She is probably hurt. What can we do? For the rest of the day Dad lies half-awake and half-asleep in the parlor. Mom, on hearing the commotion earlier, sank back under the covers and remained in bed. Because there is nowhere else to go, Andy and I sit at the kitchen table, a couple of feet away from the front door where Phyllis is crying on the other side, and scratching on it from time to time. "Jeanne," she says, "let me in. Please. It's cold out here." Then, "Jeanne, let me in. I've got to go to the toilet." Or, "Give me something to eat, I'm starving." By evening she has changed her tune. "Beans, I'll kill you if you don't let me in, I swear it. Just you wait. Tomorrow you're dead."

94

This is not the first time I've been 'dead if I do and dead if I don't'. I've been put on the spot before where I have had to take sides whether I liked it or not. It is impossible to be neutral. I have to make a decision. I wait until I hear Dad's snores in the parlor before I slip the lock and let her in.

I have stalled my mourning for the loss of Rex the entire day. I got the breakfast, lunch and supper. I made the bed, ironed some clothes, swept the kitchen floor, played with Andy, looked in at Mom, emptied the garbage, found clean clothes for Dad and let my sister in.

Phyllis's face is so swollen that she winces when she speaks. "I'll kill that goddamn bastard if it's the last thing I do," she says in a low, determined voice, the strong words curling her lips in an ugly way.

"I saved you some soup. I'll make you a baloney sandwich," I say, coaxing her to the table, and off the subject.

"He sold Rex for a drink. That dog was way better than him."

Through her pain the worm of disbelief finally eats its way into me. But her loss is greater than mine because I hadn't allowed myself to love Rex the way she did. I held back, keeping a small part of me intact. I had conditioned myself against any loss, so if it came, I could bear it.

"Let's go and look for him tomorrow. You never know, maybe we'll be able to buy him back," she says hopefully. I nod, doubtful of it.

During the night Andy cries out in his sleep. "Rex!"

Chapter Sixteen
Bigger Crimes

It's Spring. Sporadic brightness from a peek-a-boo sun lights up the bedroom where Mom lays in a sleep-tousled bed. During the day she dozes on and off. When she's awake, she sits alone cradling a glass of beer, looking into space at nothing in particular. If anyone stirs nearby or makes a noise in the kitchen or parlor, she becomes agitated. If things were normal, she'd be bothered by the dust on the venetian blinds, the streaks down the windows, and the dirty, crumpled sheets which lay beneath her. She doesn't notice anything like that anymore. The bedroom is rank with the smell of her unwashed body mixed with the odor of overflowing ashtrays and empty beer bottles. "Jeanne," she calls out one afternoon when we are alone, "is that you in the kitchen?"

"Yeah."

"What are you doing?"

"I'm washing some clothes, that's all."

"Come here when I talk to you."

I climb off the kitchen chair, annoyed to be interrupted at my work, and take my time about getting there. "What?" I say in as deadpan a voice as I can muster from my stance in her bedroom doorway because I'm mad. I'm boiling over because it is up to me, a nine-year-old, to keep the place in order. Andy and Phyllis have given up. They race out of the apartment whenever they can.

"Get that look off your face right now," she hisses. I want her to know that I don't approve of her. She ought to know how angry I am, and how hard it is to stay angry. But I can. I'm just like Superman in the comics. I can crush my anger like a lump of coal, making it into a sparkling diamond. I like the feel of its cool, hard surface.

"Go to the store and get some more beer," Mom orders. She reaches to pick up a couple of bottles but instead knocks them over. "Take those back. There's a deposit on them," she says with the wave of an arm.

"We're out of money, you know. We've had beer and groceries on credit for too long," I bark back.

"I don't care. Get me three more bottles."

Often Dad comes home with money jangling in his pockets and we are flush for a while. Our credit is taken care of at the grocer's, there's meat for supper, and we have money for the movies. We've had none of these luxuries for a while and I have almost forgotten what it was like to chew on a piece of licorice.

The empties fill up a whole paper bag. The bottles *chink* and *clink* against my chest. Rising up, their beery smell stuffs my nostrils to overfull and I'm sick of beer and all it stands for. At the store I struggle with the door and the grocer comes around the counter to help. He wants to know where Phyllis and Andy are. "Out somewhere. Can I have three more bottles, please?" I blurt out, getting it over with quick. He never asks, but he must know that Mom is having a drinking binge again. "Can I have cold ones?"

He re-uses my brown sack. "I'll put it on your bill. It's getting a bit high," he says, adding without looking up. Shame spreads through me like a fever. "Here's something for you. On the house," he adds smiling, and throws in a couple of packets of bubble-gum.

I open the first bottle and pour Mom a glass. She winces at its iciness, then sips while I straighten the bed. As I pick up her bathrobe from the floor, she asks angrily, "What do you think you're doing?"

"Cleaning up."

"Well, I don't want you to. Get out of here." I look at her unable to believe my ears. "You heard what I said, get out of here! Now!" I throw the bathrobe back on the floor, stomp out and slam the kitchen door. "Who do you think you are, Miss La-Di-Da?" She shouts through the door. "Place not clean enough for you? If you don't like it you can kiss my ass! Hey! Miss Prissy Pants! There's dust under my bed. Why don't you come and lick it up?"

Her words buzz in my brain as I rub our underwear up and down the washboard. She is trying to make me look ridiculous. Maybe I am ridiculous. But I can't turn my back on chaos even if she can. Anything can be done if you want it to be done, I tell myself. All you have to do is roll up your sleeves and do it. It's only work - anyone can work, can't they?

By the time she has gone quiet and probably dozed off, the water is cold and the suds are gone. I stare at the gray water, my arms in deep past the elbow, wondering vaguely to myself how Andy's socks can float on the top even though they are full of holes. While I stay like that humiliation creeps up on me like a breeze through an open window. Fat tears splat onto the dirty water. Snot drips down my chin. I wipe it away with my arm, hiccuping and shuddering until I am through.

When Mom first took to her bed, she used to shout and rave about the neighbors, picking on their every idiosyncrasy, racial trait, or habit, imagining personal slights and slanders, continuing arguments never begun. With her fists flying and her head stretching to the height limit of her neck, she would begin her tirade, her monologue to the window, to the ceiling, or the front door. Now she picks on us, finding fault in whatever we do, starting arguments, raking up past sins, shaming us in front of each other. It's the drink, it's her nerves and it's hell. Then suddenly, she begins to make sense again. She calls Phyllis and me in for a chat, asking us if we want to know where babies come from, and about the facts of life. I'm not exactly sure what she means so I decline and quickly absent myself from the room, leaving her on her own with Phyllis.

Phyllis has a ten-dollar bill. "I found it in the gutter," she says all excited. "I had to look hard for it, though. Next time I go looking, do you want to come?" Of course I do because for the entire week we have ice cream every day.

We have to keep it a secret even though I mention to Phyllis that Mom could do with the money for groceries. Phyllis says Mom and Dad would never believe us in a million years if we said we'd found money in the street. We might get beaten for it. Whenever we do something we are not supposed to, Dad beats us, no questions asked. Sometimes I think only mind-readers get it right all the time. We do something new wrong every day. Phyllis takes the brunt of it because she's the oldest and should know better; she's supposed to keep us out of trouble. She must have skin like leather. Dad's belt leaves welts on her butt, back and legs, and she hardly ever cries.

The first time Phyllis takes me searching for money, I find a five-dollar bill swirling in the gutter after an April shower. "I knew you'd find it," she says excitedly, quickly whipping the wet money out of my hands. "Let's get some candy with it."

All the money we find in the gutter turns out to be stolen. On Sunday morning Dad sends Phyllis to the grocer's for some rolls and milk. When she gets back, she returns Mom's purse to the kitchen where it's kept by the alarm clock. "Jeanne, get me my purse," Mom shouts from the bedroom. She looks inside. "There's money missing. There should be three one-dollar bills in here."

"Maybe I dropped it." I run back to the kitchen to look, getting Andy to help me. We check everywhere, under the table, behind the clock, by the sofa, under the armchairs, beneath the piano stool. Mom and Dad are at the kitchen table questioning Phyllis. Her head is down and her chin is resting on her chest. "It must've got lost," I tell them. "Should I go back to the store and look for it?"

"Shut up, you," Phyllis snaps.

Dad grabs hold of her arm and twists it. "We know you stole it. And it's not the first time, either. You've stooped too low this time. You stole from your own mother. You ought to be ashamed of yourself!" He hits her hard several times, his arm flying rapidly up to the ceiling and back. The smacks smart against her flesh. I run and hide in the parlor. "Don't you hide," he shouts after me. "You're next!"

A stab goes through me. I'm guilty, too, but what of? I sit in the armchair and wait. I've been here before. First, I concentrate, closing in on myself, hiding inside a compartment in my mind. Then I take my mind and put it somewhere else - anywhere - in the icebox, in a closet, in the toe of a shoe under the bed. My punishment won't hurt me because it won't happen to me. I won't be there.

Phyllis is crying on the landing outside the apartment where Dad has thrown her out again. His footfall is heavy as it nears the parlor threshold. He looks me in the eye and questions me. I tell him, no, I have never stolen from Mom's purse; no, I didn't know Phyllis was doing that; and, yes, I did have ice cream every day. I'm lucky. He lets me off the hook.

I know that there is no such thing as luck. I am a gullible fool, easily duped. If I were lucky, I'd never find money in the gutter. Somewhere else, maybe? Perhaps. But I'll be looking on my own from now on.

I have to wait up to let Phyllis back into the apartment. I know she'll beat me if I don't. She has already done it. She pummeled my head, slapped my face, punched my back, pulled my hair, pinched me and poked me in the ribs. The last time I unlocked the door and let her in, it was too soon, and Dad threw her out again. I got a few hard slaps for that. It will be safer to open the door when everyone has gone to bed.

Phyllis hates me having so many friends at school. She's jealous. She gives me the third degree every time I go to a friend's house. "What did you do today? What's your friend's name? Are her parents rich? What's their place like? Do they live in a house? Can I come over? Why don't you bring me something?" When she finds out that they've offered me a sandwich or cookies and milk she orders me to bring something, anything, back for her. Each day she waits for me and gets angry when I come home with nothing. She says that if I don't bring her something, she'll beat me up. "Steal it if they won't give it to you." I can't ignore her much longer. After school she pinches my arm hard and says under her breath, "If you're going over to a friend's you'd better bring me back something today or else."

After we have our snack at my friend's house, the plates are cleared from the table. I slip off my chair and wander into the kitchen. My friend's mother says, "Are you still hungry?"

"No. Err... Can I help with the dishes?"

"I'm afraid there's nothing left to eat."

"That's okay."

I glance around quickly before she *shoos* me out into the parlor. I'm in a sweat because I'm afraid to go home without anything. We play checkers for a while and I pretend I have to go to the bathroom. I sneak into the kitchen while her mother is in the bedroom. I open some drawers. I find a Hershey bar. The clothes I'm wearing don't have any pockets and I don't know what to do except stuff the bar of chocolate down my underpants. I cross my arms below my waist and press down on it to hold it in place.

I saunter as nonchalantly as I can into the parlor and tell my friend I have to go home now. I'm just about to leave when her mother comes out to say good-bye. "You're such a nice girl. You can come and play anytime you like. Would you mind doing me a small favor and take this milk bottle downstairs on your way out? Leave it by the front door with the others."

As I reach out to take it the candy bar slips down and lands on the big toe of my right foot. I'm too panic-stricken to look down.

"Here," she says bending to pick it up, "this must be yours."

Phyllis gets what she wants and I know I can never go back to my friend's house again. By now they have found out I stole their candy bar. I feel sick when Phyllis offers me a piece, shaking my head, unable to entertain the idea of putting it in my mouth. Next time, maybe I'll go for the beating.

Summer arrives and we get off school for ten weeks. We always used to hang out together but lately, if I want to be alone, Phyllis lets me. She and Andy go around with other kids and I read a book, or jump rope on my own.

Sometimes Dad takes Phyllis to work with him. They leave around 4 o'clock in the afternoon and don't get back until I am already asleep. I wonder where they go, but resist asking her because I'm relieved she's away and off my back. The only problem is, with her gone I have to watch Andy. I run up and down the street for him trying to keep the peace. "He stole my baseball cards!" "He promised me candy if I let him read my comic, but he's got none." "He lost my caps." The squabbles are small, but many and a nuisance.

I ask Phyllis when she returns one night what she does the whole time she is working with Dad. She says, "Shut up and leave me alone," then rolls on her stomach and goes to sleep. One day they leave as usual but are back within an hour. Dad is in a bad mood and Phyllis has been crying. He sends her to bed with no supper, taking Andy with him instead. I wonder why he hasn't asked me.

As summer wears on Mom makes no effort to get out of bed. I have almost forgotten what she looks like when she is dressed up for an outing. Whether we went to Coney Island, or made a trip to the butcher's, or to the movies, or shopped to buy us a pair or shoes, she used to care about her appearance. She would slip a freshly laundered blue polka dot dress, still warm and smelling of the iron, over a pale pink slip - the dress's crisp white collar starched and pristine against her ivory neck. I would follow her around the apartment as she dashed from the bedroom to the bathroom and back again in the unaccustomed rush to go out. I sat next to her on the toilet seat lid as she stood in front of the bathroom mirror to powder her nose, and looked with detachment at the person reflected back. I admired the transformation as she dabbed a spot of rouge on each cheek, bringing a speck of sunshine into her expression. Flecks of face powder dribbled onto the sink and I ran a finger along the white porcelain scooping up a bit to pat on the end of my nose. Unsheathing a bright red lipstick she carefully outlined her lips, then filled them in, running the lipstick back and forth until her mouth stood out luscious and ripe as a mackintosh apple skin. Blotting came next. Folding a tissue carefully in half, she made a carbon copy of her lips by pressing on the tissue between them to remove any excess. She let me have the tissue to throw away, but I admired the heart-shaped kiss so much that I hid it under my pillow, keeping it for a long time afterwards, until my sister found it one morning and blew her nose in it.

We went to the beauty parlor once. Mom and I were walking, on our way to Aunt Sophie's, when she suddenly stopped and said, "I don't want to visit anybody today. I think I'll have my hair cut instead." We had already walked a considerable way, and were under the El train. Mom slowed down at the first Beauty Parlor sign we came to. A blinking pink neon arrow indicted that it was one flight up on the second floor.

The beautician washed and cut Mom's hair as I kept tally of the trains swinging by on the curved subway tracks just outside the window. "What do you think?" she asked me. "The lady says I would look nice with a permanent wave." Not sure what she was talking about, I nodded and smiled, and watched as the beautician rolled Mom's short, straight hair into metal curlers. When she was finished, and Mom looked like someone from outer space, she hooked up the curlers to The Electric Permanent Wave Machine.

"Just relax. I'll be back when it's ready," the beautician told Mom, who had been looking at her uncertainly. The machine's clock-timer ticked loudly. "How about a magazine?" The permanent wave stank to high heavens, but the result was amazing. Mom shook her head, now a mass of tiny curls, glad to be free of the cumbersome Machine. "Your hair is so fine! It took the curl real good," the beautician said beaming.

Mom's permanent wave looked nice at the Beauty Parlor, but she doesn't bother to look after it. Her hair has become the texture of cotton candy. She gives up halfway through whenever she combs it. "I can't. I haven't got the strength to comb my own hair," she sighs. So I take the comb and try to undo the knots without hurting her. Her hair is as soft as a baby's. It is also natty at the back where her head rubs the pillow, straight where the new hair comes out from the roots and crinkled on the ends.

The dark bags under Mom's eyes rest on puffy cheeks and jowls. She's gotten fat and looks shapeless in her old night-gown and the faded chenille bathrobe she has taken to wearing all the time. We don't know how she could have put on any weight because she eats practically nothing. She drinks plenty of beer, though. Whenever she talks to us, which isn't often, her speech is slurred like she was speaking under water. The only time she gets up is to go to the toilet. Sometimes she stands in the shadows outside the parlor and watches us for a while. Once she asked us what we were doing, as if she couldn't see for herself.

We usually have the same old boring routine of not making any noise when we come home from school to avoid disturbing Mom who is asleep or resting in her bedroom. But we invited Phyllis's friend over and to make sure everything is ship-shape, we sweep the parlor, pick up the comics, put away the piano rolls, empty the garbage, then wash, dry and put away the breakfast dishes. Everything looks wonderful and for the finishing touch, I sneak into Mom's room while she is asleep and take out a dozen of her white crocheted doilies. I distribute them on the arms of the dark-blue sofa, lay a few across the backs of the armchairs, and spread the rest over the table and piano.

I must have disturbed her while rummaging in her room because she is suddenly behind me on her way to the toilet. She stands in the doorway of the parlor and surveys the room for a moment. Then she shouts. "What the hell is this supposed to be? Where did you get those doilies? It looks like a whore-house in here!" She flies to the sofa, the armchairs, the piano, grabbing up the doilies in fistfuls. Spit sprays from her mouth. "If I want these spread around the place, I'll do it myself." She looks at us, but her eyes can't focus and her head wobbles. "I want to know who did this."

"I did," Phyllis says quickly, owning up before I have a chance to. Mom leans over and I gasp as she slaps Phyllis right across the face. Then Mom throws the handfuls of doilies at her and they fall like giant snowflakes around my sister, landing on her face, shoulders and at her feet.

"Put them back where they came from!" Mom shouts and slams the door on her way out.

"Sneak back in there and put these away in her closet, Beans," Phyllis says handing me the stack of doilies as she rubs her swollen cheek. "I'm going down to tell Jimmy he can't come over today." By the time she comes back, the light in the parlor has grown dim and Andy and I are listening to the radio turned down low. Phyllis joins us, plopping down on the sofa with more weight than usual. Sadness falls among us like a cloak. There's no need to say it - Mom is getting worse.

We open a can of vegetable soup and have it with a cheese sandwich, eating our supper in the cleaned-up parlor. Andy drops his sandwich in his soup and is about to cry. Unable to withstand another drama, I giggle to divert him. Phyllis jumps in and grunts like a pig. We all laugh until we can't stop. Then we tell old jokes and have a 'who can make the worst face?' contest. As usual, Phyllis is champion, distorting her nose, eyes and mouth into unbelievable contortions. I sing "Yankee Doodle", a song which Andy loves. Phyllis stands to attention and says, "And now, Ladies and Gentlemen, for the highlight of our show tonight...." and she does an imitation of Mom getting mad about the doilies.

She starts off in the doorway, then staggers across the room. Andy and I are in stitches, tears stream from our eyes. Phyllis has the imaginary doilies in her hand and mimics Mom, word for word, killing us all the more.

Suddenly, like an apparition, Mom is there at the door. Stunned, Andy and I can't move to warn Phyllis who has her back to the door. We stop laughing and Phyllis spins around. She sees Mom who knows exactly what is going on. The sick woman who can't find the strength to comb her own hair suddenly hurls herself at my sister like a locomotive on the run, striking several hard and fast blows to Phyllis' face, neck and head. Andy and I try to pull Mom off, but she swings at us, loses her balance and falls down of her own accord. "Get away from me! Don't touch me!" With an effort she hoists herself up with the help of the sofa. Her chest heaves in her struggle to breathe. "If it's the last thing I do," she gasps, "I'll kill you for that!"

"Go to bed, Mom, please," I plead. "We saved some soup for you and there's one more beer in the icebox. Should I get it?"

"Go to Hell."

I hold a chunk of ice wrapped up in a dishtowel over Phyllis' black eye. She's swears to me that she's going to run away. "Where to?" I ask.

"Aunt Helen's, maybe."

"She's expecting a baby. She'll be too busy."

"I could help her. I wonder what happened to Big Red? That guy that came to Andy's christening? He might be able to help us."

"Why don't we tell Dad?"

"What can he do? He's worse. He's nothing but a stinking criminal himself. There's some things I know that you don't."

"Like what?"

"Like what he does when we go to work with him that he can go to prison for."

"I wouldn't know. He never asks me."

"That's because he's scared of you. Scared of what you might say. Anyway, he's got this deal, see, where he parks the car outside a bar. It's usually somewhere near the railroad tracks or some woods, or a deserted spot. I have to sit quiet on the back seat while we wait. He turns off the engine and the lights and waits in a dark corner of the parking lot until someone parks a nice-looking car. Once the man is in the bar, Dad gets to work."

"What's he doing out there in the dark?"

"Let me finish, will you? He slides under the car and takes out the fuel pump. In its place he puts a broken one. He comes back to the car, dumps the fuel pump with me in the back seat and goes into the bar. It's my job to shine up the man's fuel pump, you know, to make it like new.

105

"When the man comes out and his car won't start, he goes back to the bar for help because there's nowhere else to go. 'I happen to be a mechanic', Dad tells the man when they are in the parking lot. Dad looks under the hood and tries to start the car. He tells the man that he thinks it's the fuel pump. 'You're lucky. I have a new one in my car,' he says. 'Wait here a minute.' He comes over and gets the pump that I've been cleaning up."

"But that's the man's pump!"

"Precisely. He sells the man his own pump. He puts it back and charges him for it. The man is so grateful, he even gives Dad a tip!"

"You think he could go to jail for that?"

"Sure, if he got caught. It's against the law."

"Why can't he just get a regular job like everyone else?"

"You've heard him. He's always saying he can't work for anyone. He's funny in the head."

"He's a no-good-sonofabitch, if you ask me."

"You see. That's why he won't take you on a job. He's scared you'll split on him."

"You know what? He's right."

Chapter Seventeen
Over The Rainbow

When the August heat waves break and cooler air streams through the apartment in early September, Mom gets up and comes with us for a walk in the park. She wears dark sunglasses and is unsteady on her feet, but the fact that she's out of the apartment encourages us.

I am glad to be back in school. From nine to three there's order in my life. I have the feeling of going forward instead of sinking into the mire of life at home. At school I think about the State of New York, George Washington and America and fractions now that I'm in the fourth grade.

I join the Mobile Library, a van that travels between schools and parks outside P.S.123 every Tuesday afternoon from three to four o'clock. Anyone who's got a school library card can select three books a week. The van is often empty, except for the librarian and the driver, and I can choose from all the books by myself. I keep a close guard on the ones I borrow. There's hell to pay if I lose one of them. The trouble is, they regularly go missing at home. I might find one on the floor holding the kitchen door open for a breeze or all three under the bed to prop it up after one of the slats has broken.

After school, Phyllis and Andy roam the streets with friends, but I'd rather say inside and read a book. This way I can stick close to Mom and keep an eye on her. I watch her cook and sometimes she explains things to me, urging me to put to memory her recipes for lima bean soup and meatballs. She has rekindled her interest in knitting and as I sit nearby with a book in my lap, she unravels an orange woolen sweater she knitted way back she says, 'in the Middle Ages'. She asks me to help her by rolling the yarn into a ball as she pulls the stitches out. "Wind it tight so the wrinkles flatten out."

"What are you going to make with it?"

"Mittens."

"For your three little kittens?" I ask, smiling up at her.

I pick through her bag of knitting needles and crochet hooks and pull out a pair of number 8's. She knits fast, without a pattern, and often without looking at her hands. Her fingers work a miracle and the large balls of yarn shrink as the mittens take shape in her hands.

Phyllis claims the first pair of mittens. Andy gets the second. I don't mind waiting for mine. I enjoy watching Mom knit. It gives me a good excuse to sit with her as she works on them. "It doesn't look like I'm going to have enough to finish yours," Mom says sadly.

"Does that mean I won't get any?"

"I've got other balls of yarn. I could add another color somewhere. Is that okay?"

The next day the finished mittens are ready on the kitchen table when I return from school. They have green thumbs! "What's the matter? Don't you like them?"

"They're great. Will you show me how to knit?"

"Soon."

But Mom's recovery doesn't last long. We find her camping out in our bedroom one afternoon. She lays there in her old night-gown and ragged chenille bathrobe, hunched over a glass of beer, in a cloud of cigarette smoke thick enough to choke a horse and leaving it's aroma forever on our bed and in our clothes in the bureau drawers. It doesn't take long before chaos takes over from order. The kitchen floor gets dirty and becomes filthy. Cockroaches leap across the alleyway and without Mom's persistent slapping at them with the fly swatter or the broom, they take up residence in every nook and cranny. Some of their hiding places must be overbooked because at night when we switch on the kitchen light on the way to the bathroom, millions scatter helter-skelter.

Andy and I are sent home from school with the nits. It's Chinese torture having to endure the fine-tooth comb again. Mom leaves her bed to treat us. Throwing her legs over the side of the mattress like two blocks of solid wood, she struggles up and staggers to the kitchen. Seated on a kitchen chair, she wedges me between her knees. As she runs the ivory-colored comb through my tangled hair, I keep my neck taut and bite my lower lip to stop myself from screaming out loud, letting the tears flow over my cheeks and into my ears. I know how hard it is for her to get up, and I also don't want to slow down the process by giving in to pain. It isn't so bad for Andy. His hair is short, but he still squeals like a pig when it's his turn.

"You probably got the nits from those Spicks next door. They bring them over on the boat along with the 'cookarachas'." She means our Puerto Rican neighbors. "They've all got big families and write to their relatives to come and live with them. You saw how they knocked through the walls of the apartments next door. The whole building is one big family. They squeezed in the whole kit n' caboodle - cousins, grandparents, aunt and uncles, you name it."

I don't know about the nits and cockroaches, but she's right about the big family. On the whole they don't bother us. In the summer they like to congregate on their stoop and everyone talks at the same time in Spanish. It's easy to think that they are talking about us because we don't understand. They say something, then laugh behind their hands, black eyes dancing in all directions. They could be laughing at anyone, anything. They have openly laughed at Dad, and seen him up to his tricks more than once. "Who cares?" I ask, not wanting to stir up trouble and thinking about how we have enough trouble of our own.

"We do," Phyllis answers. "Why should they speak a foreign language when we don't understand a word they say? We ought to make up our own language."

"What about Pig Latin?"

"It takes too long to learn it. We'll just have to invent a language."

We play around with a few sounds and come up with gi and gwi, adding one syllable at the end of each word. If Phyllis wants to say, 'Should we go to the store now?', she adds a gi at the end of every word. When I reply, 'Okay, let's go', I add a gwi onto each word. Spoken fast, it sounds like a foreign language. We try it out on Andy. "What's up with you guys? I can't understand a word you're saying." Satisfied, we sit on the stoop and talk in louder-than-ordinary voices. Our neighbors look puzzled. It's a language they have never heard before. We're happy now - we're equal.

Winter arrives and so long as we don't get into fights and chase one another, Mom lets us stay inside to do our homework. She has rejoined the library and brings home several hardcover books at a time. When she isn't looking, I pick them up and run my hands along the thick spines. I turn them over and look at the authors' photographs on the back. I can't wait until I am old enough to read books like these. Reading makes Mom more subdued, but she might as well be sleeping because now she reads all day and still doesn't have time for the housework or us.

There is a growing mountain of ironing to do because we only iron things as we need them, usually first thing in the morning. To avoid a traffic jam on the breakfast table, which serves as our ironing board, I make up my mind to iron everything when I come home from school. I spread out the stack of old blankets and piece of white sheeting over the table, smoothing out the lumps and bumps. Ironing is not easy and I seem to iron more wrinkles into the clothes than I do out. The iron is heavy and my wrist aches. I keep forgetting to stand the iron up and scorch marks appear on the white cover. As I am finishing up, I somehow touch my right forearm with the flat of the iron. The smell my burned flesh registers just before I feel the pain. Phyllis blows hard on it, and rubs a quarter pound stick of butter over it. I want to show Mom but Phyllis says to leave her alone, she has enough to worry about, and wraps it in a white bandage. A blister forms and bursts. My arm oozes water, pus and blood. She puts on another bandage that gets stuck to the scab, which comes off, and the cycle is repeated. The scar it leaves looks like a white caterpillar resting on my right forearm.

The school year passes and Mom's bad spells come more often and last longer. Dad is almost never home and when he is, he is almost never sober. Apart from leaving us money to buy groceries and to pay the rent, we have nothing to do with him. Sometimes we are surprised to find him asleep, out cold, in the middle of the parlor floor when we return from school. Phyllis has lost all respect for him, calling him 'the old man' out loud whenever she refers to Dad. He would kill her if he heard her because despite the way he acts, he still wants us to be respectful to him.

Phyllis is a big girl and already the same height as Dad, five-foot ten inches tall. She can now look him straight in the eye; she doesn't have to look up to him. At only fourteen years of age she is the biggest kid on the block. She defies him every chance she gets, deriding him when he is drunk and vomits on the kitchen floor, scolding him when he misses meals, forgets to pick up his clothes, acting like his mother instead of his daughter. It used to be Mom who nagged and told him off. Arguments strike up between them and Dad lashes out at Phyllis's weak points. He gets nasty with her, calling her a 'fat, overgrown pig' and 'lard ass' right in front of everyone. Her biggest complaint at the moment is that he won't allow her to wear make-up. He says she looks like a whore with it on. Once he stopped her in the street in front of all her friends and wiped off her lipstick with the back of his hand.

By mid-August we realize that we have practically gotten through the summer without any major incidents. Mom hasn't been out of bed for nearly a month and Dad has sobered up some over this. He has been coming home more regularly and takes Andy with him to work so we don't have to look after him all the time.

"Keep an eye on Mom," Dad says as they are leaving one morning. "And don't go too far. She's not looking so good today."

Phyllis and I are cleaning up in the kitchen when we hear Mom move from her bed to ours. She is having her first glass of beer and it's just after nine o'clock in the morning. She seems calm enough, and when we tell her that we want to go to the park, she nods, so we leave.

We come back home at noon and make ourselves some sandwiches. When we ask her if she wants anything, she shakes her head and says without looking up, "Maybe later." A few minutes later she calls us. "Come here, you two." As we sit on the edge of the bed, waiting for her to say something, we don't quite know what, she sighs and lays her head back on the pillow. Her dry, cracked lips hardly moving, she manages to say in a little voice, "I'm sorry I'm like this. I don't want to be useless, but I can't help it. All my strength has drained right out of me."

"It's all right," I mumble, breaking the silence, unused to apologies of this or any kind.

"Why don't you girls go to the movies today. Take a couple of dollars out of my purse. Didn't I hear you say "The Wizard of Oz" is on at the Paramount again?"

It promises to be a hot afternoon and we welcome the chance to sit in an air-conditioned theater. "Okay," Phyllis agrees taking the initiative. "We'll make some sandwiches for you and leave them in the icebox. Don't forget to have some lunch."

The movie theater is packed. A couple of hundred kids jump up and down in their seats, talking, laughing and shouting to one another during the news and for most of the second feature. But when Judy Garland appears as Dorothy, everyone sits down ready to be transported to Kansas and the Land of Oz. Jaws slacken to munch popcorn and all eyes look straight ahead. I make myself comfortable by slinking low into my seat. My sneakered feet rest on wads of discarded chewing gum that have, over the years, altered the surface of the floor.

When the main feature is over we watch the news and the cartoons again before we decide we've had enough. In the street the air is torpid and the strong sunlight dazzles us after four hours of subterranean conditions in the movies. The walk from the Paramount movie theatre is twenty city blocks, about a mile long, and we work up a thirst on the way home. Before we go upstairs to check on Mom, we spend the rest of our money on a couple of ice-cold Coca-Cola's, sipping them slowly on the stoop. The street is empty. It's past five o'clock, and still too hot to sit out for long in the sun.

When we open the kitchen door we realize immediately that something isn't right. "What the heck...?" Phyllis says pointing to a loaf of bread and a carton of milk. We don't use those brands. What's going on?"

"She hasn't touched her sandwiches. They're still in the icebox," I say shutting it. "Mom?" I call out opening the door of the bathroom, and swinging a look over the parlor.

"She's not in the bedrooms, either," Phyllis says, her face flushed, her eyes filling up. She's gone! Let's check the fire-escape." The window is locked from the inside.

"Where could she have gone to? At lunchtime she didn't have the strength to lift her head off the pillow, she can't have gone out." I hear my voice tremble, rise and get stuck in my throat. We were supposed to be looking after her. Dad will kill us for leaving her alone when he comes home. She told us to go to the movies, but he won't listen to explanations. Where is she? Where is she?

We run down the street shouting "Mom!" to the heat-soaked streets. "Mom!" bounces back from the broiling window panes. Like worried parents seeking a lost child we chant for her around the entire block until we are hoarse with panic. A neighbor nursing a baby pokes her head out of the window out of curiosity but quickly withdraws it. On the verge of tears and wondering what to do next, we see a Puerto

112

Rican man whom we recognize from next door. He moves shyly towards us. "Pleese," he says. "Are you looking for your madre?"

"Yes. Have you seen our mother?"

"She's een there." He points to a second-floor window in his building.

"What's she doing in there?"

"I do not know. You go look."

We charge up the flight of stairs and knock on the door. "Mom? Are you in there?" Phyllis shouts through the closed door.

"Go away." Mom answers in a small voice that travels from way beyond the door. We hear her pleading with someone. "Please, Mister. I don't want anything to do with them. Help me. Someone protect me, please. Don't open the door. Please, have pity on me. Don't open the door." By now Phyllis and I are pounding with our fists to open up. A shadow appears behind the frosted glass of the door and we stand back ready to fly in when it opens. It cracks open a chink and we get a two-second glimpse of Mom sitting in their parlor before it shuts tight again.

We don't want to believe our eyes that see Mom in a pink satin night-gown with thin straps that we have never seen before. She lounges on their sofa smoking a cigarette, her legs crossed, as if she were sitting in a bar. Her feet are bare.

"Oh my God! We've got to get her out of there," Phyllis shouts at me as though I were across the street. She pulls me downstairs with her. Cupping her hands around her mouth she screams for Mom with all her might. "MOM! COME HOME!" Little, big, young and old family members lean out of the windows and everyone is talking at once. "Is that half-naked woman your mother?" "It's a disgrace." "Who is that woman?" "What is she doing in there?"

"She called us from the window. She said she was hungry," explain two small children, a boy and a girl, standing next to us on the pavement.

"What are you talking about?" Phyllis asks alert to important information.

"That lady yelled from that window," the young girl says pointing to Mom's bedroom window. "She said that she was being held a prisoner and that she was starving."

"It's not true!" I argue.

"It is true," the boy says. "We were playing a game by the stoop and she called us over and told us she had no food for days and days."

"It's not true! We left sandwiches for her in the icebox."

"Anyhow, we brought her over some bread, milk and ham."

"How did you get in?"

"She opened the door. You can ask her." They both nod. I notice that the orange halter-top dress the girl is wearing is mine as well as the blue shorts on the boy.

"Where did you get those clothes?"

"She gave them to us. We did not steal them, if that is what you are thinking. She gave us them in exchange for the food."

"Other things, too?"

"A couple of things."

Phyllis yells up to Mom again but the window remains blank.

"Let's go upstairs and see what's left of our belongings," she says and I follow behind, glad to be off the street and out of the line of prying eyes. In our worry over the loss of Mom, we hadn't noticed that the bureau drawers had been ransacked. Clothes dangle lifelessly over the sides of the partially opened drawers. While I try to straighten things up in the bedrooms, Phyllis reports that Mom's purse is gone from its place on the kitchen shelf.

"Jeanne, come here quick!" she calls out suddenly. I see her pointing her finger at Mom through the alleyway window. "Look!" The kitchen window of the apartment Mom is in is directly opposite our kitchen window. She has moved to their kitchen table and is drinking a glass of beer. Two skinny men with thin moustaches steady her as she begins to slide off the chair. Their dark hands clasp her hard and their fingers sink into the white flesh of her upper arms. We call out to her and bang on the window, but she won't look our way.

"I'm going down in the yard. Maybe I can get in from the fire escape window off their parlor," I say and leave without waiting for Phyllis's reaction.

"Beans!" I hear her shout from the parlor window, but I don't answer because I'm already in the yard and I'm scared. This is the forbidden yard. The yard I have looked down on for the past nine years and have scarcely stepped a foot in. Looking up from this angle,

114

our fire escape landing seems like it's miles away. I feel like I have broken away from everything up there where Dad cools his boiled pig's feet on the fire escape in winter. Last summer we sat there in the shade and made perfume from roses that we'd stolen from gardens all over the neighborhood. We pounded the petals until they were mashed to a pulp, added water and filled soda bottles with it before selling it to friends.

I run up to the fence and easily leap over it as though my legs were on springs. Their fire escape is stacked with a bunch of garbage like car tires, broken baby carriages and cardboard boxes full of empty jars and rags. I squeeze past them and make it to the second floor. Pressing my nose to the window I see Mom. She has her back to me. I scratch gently on the glass not wanting to alarm her. I just want to get her attention for a second. But she is talking and the men are laughing at something she is saying so I resort to tapping on the window. "Mom!" Spanish music, something like a cha-cha with bongo drums, beats above me from an open window. "Mom, please come out." I think I am begging. A Spanish tenor's vocal chords spring to life and I am drowned out.

I think I see one of the men telling her to turn around. "Jeanne?" she mouths. I manage a smile and boldly slide the window up. "Mom, come home, please. We've been looking for you." She puts down her glass of beer and walks unsteadily towards me. The satin night-gown clings to her body. Her loose breasts swing heavily from side to side as she closes in on me. Then she stops as if she's forgotten something. A man with a pencil-thin moustache, the sleeves of his white shirt rolled up to reveal a pair of stringy arms, runs forward to accompany her.

"Hi, Mom. It's me, Jeanne. Let's go home."

She continues towards me staring wide-eyed. I am on my knees on the windowsill. As she gets closer I look into her black eyes. They are wild. She doesn't recognize me. "What do you want?" she asks me like a complete stranger. "Have you come to threaten me? Because if you have, you know where you can go."

"No, I've come to take you home," I say surprised.

"I have no home. These kind people have taken me in. I'm not leaving."

"No! You mustn't. You can't." I reach out and touch her. She shrinks from me.

"Get out of here. You hear me? GET OUT OF HERE!"

"MOM, YOU'VE GOTTA COME HOME NOW!" I'm not expecting her to slap me, so when she does, I lose my balance, falling backwards and hitting my head with a bang on the metal bars of the fire escape. The window is pulled down and the curtains drawn shut by the time I get up. My left cheek is scalding.

Phyllis has had no success in getting into the neighbors' apartment through the front door and since we both feel soiled by the invasion of the strangers into our space, we set to clearing away the milk container and loaf of bread and any other traces that we've had of visitors. We make the bed where Mom had been sleeping, clean the brimming ashtray with its stale cigarette butts and put away the empty beer bottles. Taking her bathrobe and shoes with us, we sit out on the front stoop and wait for something to happen. We have reached a stalemate because the Puerto Ricans think they are protecting her. They believe what she tells them. How could they know that she's making it all up?

The empty street is bathed in the orange glow of an August sunset. We have lost the power to help our own mother. She stepped over some invisible line and stepped out of our care at the same time. We continue to wait for something to happen. Phyllis, sitting next to me with Mom's bathrobe draped across her knees, is numbed into silence. The fingers of her right hand at her lips, she bites her fingernails until they bleed. I shield my wet eyes from the sinking sun.

An ambulance pulls up and a couple of men in starched white coats get out. "Hi!" One says cheerfully to us and smiles. "You wouldn't happen to know where we could find the lady who is wandering around in her night-gown?"

We point. He nods. They wear white shoes that make no noise on the steps as they go up.

We hold hands and wait.

The whole Puerto Rican apartment building empties out to see Mom leave. The sight of the men in white coats sobers them. The music has been silenced. No babies cry. Old women sniffle into hankies. The young men look older.

116

Mom's hair has been combed and her face rinsed. She walks towards the ambulance between the two men, passing by us without a glance. They each open a door at the back of the vehicle and guide Mom through. Phyllis gives them her bathrobe and shoes. "Where are you taking her?"

"Bellevue Hospital."

I feel the weight of the crowd behind us, yet no sound is made. When the ambulance disappears, we turn around. Dark pairs of eyes find interest in the palms of their hands, feet shuffle on the sidewalk, mothers pat the tops of children's heads. Neighbors quietly peel away into the building and we hear their front door shut with a click.

Shadows lengthen, creep over the sidewalk, sidle up to us on the stone stoop, hugging our shoulders while we wait for Dad and Andy to come home. Dad will say 'You shouldn't have left her alone.'

When Dad eventually drives up, he's in a good mood and happy to see that we are waiting for him. His expression crumbles as our words tumble out like stones in a landslide. We unburden everything on him and he's not even mad at us. He listens fully for once to what we have to say. When we come to the end of our explanations, excuses and details, he says, "I'd better get up to the hospital and see what's what."

It's a lovely night, one full of stars, and cooler outside than in so we scatter our blankets on the fire escape and lay down side by side, looking up at the heavens. Down in someone's yard several houses away people are laughing. A cat meows. Music trips lightly from a radio. Someone turns up the volume and Judy Garland is singing.

> Somewhere over the rainbow
> Bluebirds fly.
> Birds fly over the rainbow
> Why then, oh why
> Can't I?

Phyllis is telling Andy about *The Wizard of Oz*, filling his ears and mind with a tale of good versus evil. How easy it is to push past the parameters of our day and wander into the realm of make believe.

I've seen rainbows up in the sky and in puddles where oil has been. I have even seen them in bubbles. But I've never seen bluebirds. Maybe when I understand about them I'll be able to fly over the rainbow and far away from here.

Chapter Eighteen
We're On Our Own

Summer peters out and we start back to school. We don't talk about Mom and if the subject comes up for some reason, we don't speculate either. 'No one knows what the future holds,' was one of Mom's favorite refrains whenever we tried to get the smallest glimpse of later on or tomorrow out of her. She is being looked after. There is no need to worry about her. She is safe. Dad has seen her several times.

"They've got her all doped up. It's no good going all the way up there. Kids aren't allowed anyhow," he says, and goes alone. Her stay at Bellevue Hospital in New York City isn't long and they transfer her to a state mental hospital on Long Island. The following Saturday morning Dad announces that we're going to visit Mom.

"Is she coming home?" hope asks. Only it's me saying the words to thin air.

We've made a special effort to look presentable so Mom won't be ashamed of us or worried that we can't take care of ourselves. Phyllis even dots her lips with tangerine colored lipstick, just enough to notice, but not enough for Dad to get worked up over. Andy's too-long hair is plastered against his head with Dad's hair cream and I've got clean socks on under my open-toed sandals. The drive is around two hours long with me sitting up front because of my car sickness. We pass through unfamiliar neighborhoods, eventually joining a tree-lined highway, gliding by people walking dogs, pushing baby carriages, and helping small children onto bicycles. I want to shout from the window, 'We're going to see our mother today!' But I swallow my words, letting only my heart leap up from time to time at the thought, as we slip by the landscape like admiring tourists on a bus.

Houses and streets disappear and we are among cornfields. Cows huddle in the shade of trees near white wooden farmhouses and stout red barns. "Have we got far to go?" Phyllis asks from her seat at the back. "It's hot."

The car finally tilts to the right and we enter a long, wide drive. A modest white sign with black letters says - Kings Park State Hospital. Shamrock green lawns stretch on either side of the drive. Low redbrick buildings dot the parkland at intervals. Dad slows down to read the names of the buildings and stops outside one. There are a few other cars circulating under the hot sun, but nobody is walking around in the grounds. All is quiet but for the sound of crickets hidden among the bushes.

Dad makes inquiries and a nurse directs us to a large waiting room with honey-colored wooden floors. Metal fold-up chairs are set out in rows with an aisle down the center like a school auditorium. The windows reach from the floor to the ceiling, letting in strong sunlight that heats up the floor in patches. Vending machines line the walls between the windows offering cigarettes, candy, soda, and chewing gum. We are tempted to juggle the levers for stray coins but keep to our best behavior with our hands folded in our laps. We wait with impatience showing only in the swinging legs beneath our seats. Dad checks the clock on the wall. "What time is visiting?" I ask him.

"Two." It's only a quarter to 2. I watch the second hand drizzle past the minutes, going down to the six and up towards the twelve. A couple of visitors trickle in and sit down on the other side of the room. Nobody talks. What do we say to Mom? How is she going to look? Will she cry? Will I?

"Mr. Andrew Kliarsky? Will you please come this way, sir?" Dad gets up and follows the nurse out. At the door, he turns and says in a loud whisper, "I'll come for you later."

On the dot of 2 o'clock the door swings open and a string of women stroll in. At first they appear to be together, but they soon disperse around the room. A few sit down with visitors, but the rest continue to wander around, staring at us, pointing and giggling. Phyllis nudges me in the ribs. "They're from here!" she whispers, excited. "A bunch of weirdo-loonies!"

An old woman with gray, drab hair is fiercely arguing a point with an imaginary partner. Another one, around Mom's age though taller and a blonde, rocks back and forth on a chair. Her arms hug bony knees to her chest and she chants the same words over and over. One very small lady with shaky hands approaches a vending machine and pushes the coin release button. Nothing comes out so she bangs on it with her fists and yanks at all the pulls. She tries the next machine, and the next, until she gets to the last one. Her hope of getting anything dashed, she flies into a rage, throttling the metal machine with her

119

hands and feet and head. A nurse rushes in and puts her arms firmly around the woman. "What's the matter, Peggy? No chewing gum today? Maybe you'll get lucky tomorrow. Come along now."

We are too stunned to move. We haven't seen anything this good since a small kid in the park got into a fit and smacked his screaming mother in the face. The rest of the strange ladies leave when the visitors go. It's three o'clock. Phyllis pulls out a couple of cough drops from her pocket. "Here, you guys." We jump at them. Bits of fluff are stuck to them, but we're not particular. We haven't eaten since breakfast and we're hungry enough to eat pocket fluff and anything else edible that might happen our way. Ever since Mom left, we have filled ourselves up on canned soups, canned spaghetti and canned corned beef hash.

Andy and I play marbles on the floor. The sun has changed sides of the room since we've been here and long rectangles of light stretch across the yellow wood. "When are we gonna get to see Mom?" he whines. "I'm hungry. When are we gonna eat.....?" He stops in mid-sentence. "Look! It's Mom!" We throw our heads over our shoulders and see her face framed in the small square window of the side door. One glimpse tells us that she has lost weight. Her hair is combed down tight against her head, the frizz controlled. Her eyes are deep, dark pools that show no light. She turns to go and we run to the door. It's locked! Our heads together in the pane, Phyllis and I watch her walk away.

"Where did she get those clothes?" Phyllis asks.

"They're not hers," I say, realizing that I, too, had expected to see Mom in the pink satin night-gown she wore on the afternoon she was taken away in the ambulance. "Someone must've lent them to her."

"I wanna see, too," Andy cries. We lift him up to look but she's already gone. He buries his face in Phyllis's shoulder, pummeling her angrily with clenched fists, the long wait and disappointment having taken their toll on him. "I want Mommy. I want my Mommy. I'm hungry." Phyllis wipes his nose on her skirt. She says things to him that Mom might have said. "Shhh. It's okay. She's probably too sick to see us today. We'll see her, maybe, next time, you know. Don't let her hear you cry. It'll only make her worse. That's it. Enough for now." Her words silence him but do little to comfort me. I wish I could believe them, but I don't, not any more. I don't think Mom cares about us. She doesn't want to see us, or talk to us, or ask us how we are. Why can't she tell us not to worry, that she'll be home soon and things will be like before.

"She can't see you today," Dad says when he returns. "She has to go back to the ward. Maybe next time she'll come out and talk to you. Come on, you kids, get in the car." We don't move. "Well come on. What are you waiting for? She's gone back to the ward. We have to go home," he says without looking at us.

I want to scream, to stand in the middle of the waiting room, open my mouth wide and scream loud enough to break the sound barrier. Then I won't hear Dad. I won't hear Andy crying that he's hungry or Phyllis muttering curses under her breath. As I scream, my eyes will screw shut tight and I won't see the empty window on the hospital door. I won't see Mom's retreating back. But I never get the chance. Dad shoves me from behind and I catapult through the exit door into the lengthening shadows of late afternoon.

Our stomachs growl on the way home. We pester Dad to stop and get us something to eat. "I don't have any money. I spent it on gas," he says through tight lips. We groan. Then he stops the car by the side of the road under a tree. "I'll tell you what. If you're so hungry, you can go and pick some corn." Is he joking? I don't believe him. Does he expect us to just go and take corn from the fields? "The farmer won't miss a couple of ears. Go on," he urges. "Run in there. You'll be hidden among the stalks. They're so tall, no one will see you. Look how far off the house is – it's miles away. By the time you grab the corn and run back to the car, they'll never know the difference." He grins widely, but we still don't move. "It's that or no supper at all," he snaps, his voice irritable now. "Just get out there and pick some corn!" Then in a milder tone, "I'll keep the engine running. Go on. Go on!" Phyllis and Andy jump off the back seat together and run into the field. Dad leans over me, opens the door and pushes me out. "Quick. Run or you'll lose them."

My heart thumping loudly in my ears, my breath stabbing my chest, I try to catch up with them. I steal my way through the maze of stalks, following in their footsteps, not sure where I am going. The corn towers above me and the rough stalks scratch my bare arms and legs.

"Where are you, Phyllis? What am I supposed to do?" I listen for an answer. On hearing nothing, I take a closer look at the corn. I've only seen corn-on-the-cob in the grocery store. Where is it on the stalks?

Then I catch a glimpse of the others. Andy is holding his arms out to receive the picked corn as Phyllis steadies the stalk with one hand and plucks off an ear with the other. So that's it. This one's empty. Oh, God! I can't go back empty-handed. He'll kill me. Try another. Yes! There's two on it. No, one. The other is rotten. Phyllis and Andy are already headed back. I must get a couple more. I look at the farmhouse from the corner of my eye. It's much nearer than I thought. I'm practically on top of it! Sweat rolls down into my eyes. As I wipe my forehead with my shirt sleeve, the corn I'm cradling falls to the ground, scattering in all directions. I bend down to pick it up and hear a rustling noise coming from the direction of the house. *Woof! Woof!* A dog. No. Two dogs are after me.

I gather up the corn and dart back with the brown and white hounds crashing madly through the stalks, gaining ground behind me. I can almost feel their hot breath on the back of my legs. "Who's there?" A man shouts from the farmhouse, sending bristles down my spine. Careless of the rough stalks, I sprint towards the road. In my recurrent nightmare, where a man chases me and my legs won't work, flashes through my mind. In my dream my legs feel like lead, but now they are weightless and spin like dynamos. I can't even feel them beneath me as I speed ahead.

"Get in, for Christ's sake," Dad hisses as the car lurches onto the road before I have a chance to shut the door. I hug the corn, sinking my head into its golden silk. My shallow breaths suck up its sweetened ripeness and my skin luxuriates in its autumnal warmth.

In the kitchen Dad peels back the husks and picks away the corn silk. One by one he slides them into the boiling water of a great big pot used for boiling chickens and pigs' feet. From time to time he prods them with a fork to check their tenderness as they change from pale gold to bright yellow. "There's nothing better than eating corn picked straight from the field. Think how good it is for you," Dad brags, forgetting we had to steal that freshly-picked corn.

Hungry as I am, I have already made up my mind that I won't eat the corn under any circumstance. The pot bubbles and spits for an eternity. It takes so long for it to cook that my resolve begins to weaken. Condensation drips from the ceiling above the stove. Steam fills the kitchen and spreads the aroma of corn throughout the apartment. I get up and go into the parlor to escape it, but no matter where I go, the smell chases me, like the dogs did. My stomach growls tunes, melodies, then whole symphonies, as my mouth waters. Phyllis sets the table for four. I say with as much conviction as I can muster, "Don't bother setting a place for me. I'm not having any."

"Of course you are. You must be starving. We all are."

"Nope. I'm not eating no stolen corn."

"Ah, forget it. It's in the pot already. They'll never come looking for it here. Look, here's a nice juicy one with plenty of butter and salt on it." I shake my head and squeeze shut my eyes.

"Okay. Suit yourself. Supper's ready!" she calls out the window to Dad and Andy who are now cleaning corn silk and husks off the car seats.

At the table Dad asks, "Where's Jeanne?" Phyllis shrugs without saying anything and looks towards me in the parlor. He comes over and pulls the comic I am reading out of my hands. "Well?"

"I'm not hungry."

He drags me to the table by one arm and sits me down with a thump. "Put some corn on her plate. Now you butter and salt that and eat it. That's an order."

My mouth waters like a sprinkling can at the sight of the buttered corn. I stare at it.

"PICK IT UP AND EAT IT!"

It's not exactly a punishment to eat corn-on-the-cob that is smothered in butter when you've not eaten anything but a bowl of oatmeal and a cough drop all day. Sniveling and hiccuping I sink my teeth into the flesh and separate out a couple of rows that I eat systematically from one end to the other. In between swallows of his corn Andy says, "My teacher says it was the Indians that showed us how to eat corn."

The kernels slide down and I feel them hit bottom and begin to fill up my empty stomach. I'm on my second piece when there's a sharp pain in my mouth and I crunch down onto something hard. I spit it out and a tooth falls onto my plate. "Jeanne's lost a tooth! Her tooth's come out. You're lucky you didn't swallow it. You'll get something from the tooth fairy. Isn't that right Dad?" Andy asks excited. Dad holds out his hand to have a look at it and I drop the tiny tooth into it, the side with the big brown hole facing upwards.

"It's lucky it came out before it gave you a toothache," Phyllis remarks.

"Put it under your pillow, anyway. It's got to be worth something," Andy adds. "And don't forget to make a wish."

My tongue automatically probes the hole left by the tooth as I lay in bed. A wish. I have to make a wish. Nothing comes to mind. Everything I have ever wished for hasn't come true. I have lost hope in wishes. I roll over and go to sleep, but am awakened in the middle of the night by a noise. I open one eye and see Phyllis standing by the open window in the darkness. She throws something into the alleyway and slips back quickly under the covers. I pretend to be asleep and wait until her breathing is steady before I slide my hand under my pillow. My fingers close around a dime.

We travel back to the hospital the next week, but wait as we did before without seeing Mom. We spend the time watching the crazy ladies acting up and thinking about our supper. Dad has already told us about his plan to send us into the fields to pick eggplants. He explained that while he was waiting for us to 'get our asses back to the car' last time, he saw the dark purple vegetables in a field on the other side of the road. I am anxious again because eggplants grow low to the ground and, unlike the tall corn stalks, there is nothing to cover us.

I listen carefully as he recites the final instructions. Once on the job I forget my futile protest against stealing and hunger helps me to ignore my fear of getting caught. The stem of the smooth, almost slippery vegetable is prickly and so tough that it needs to be twisted around several times before it yields and comes off.

When Dad slices the eggplant into rounds and then dips them in egg and breadcrumbs before frying them in butter, I am quick to take my place at the table with everyone else.

It is only a month since school started and six weeks since Mom was taken away, but it is already impossible to keep up with the housework. With so much homework to do we don't have time for washing the clothes, ironing or cleaning the bathroom and kitchen. It's hard enough to remember to empty out the water from the icebox. We have forgotten it so often that the cockroaches regularly drown in their nests underneath it.

We quickly run out of ideas of what to cook for supper and wind up eating baked beans and spaghetti straight out of the can. Dad hasn't been coming home regularly, often missing 3 or 4 days in a week, so we have to fend for ourselves. Regular mealtimes no longer exist. We eat whenever we are hungry, which is most of the time. We live off of credit at the grocery store. Dad tells us to make a list of what we buy and he'll pay the bill when he can. We do this for a while then Phyllis gets an idea. "Let's buy things that we like and make up a list of what we're supposed to get," she suggests and we go along with it. Thereafter we buy and consume cupcakes, ice cream, peanut butter and canned fruit like it is going out of style. Meanwhile we make up shopping lists of eggs, cereal, butter, cheese, making sure the total is exactly the total we spent, which is all that is shown on the grocer's books.

We could never afford desserts before. Now we buy nothing but desserts. After school one day we are sitting on the edge of our bed feasting on canned peaches. We have opened three cans, one for each of us, and are scooping them straight out of the can and into our mouths with large tablespoons. Juice dribbles down our chins, our mouths are crammed with the fruit as we giggle and laugh over funny things that happened at school. Suddenly we freeze as we hear Dad's key in the lock. We stash all three cans and tablespoons underneath the bed among grandpa's hardware and tools and quickly wipe our mouths on the candlewick bedspread. A close call I think as we run to meet Dad with sugar-sated peach breaths.

Dad has been on the booze and falls asleep on the sofa within minutes of getting home. He wouldn't have noticed anything unusual if he hadn't asked us what are we having for supper when he gets up. Phyllis tells him we're not very hungry. We'll have whatever he wants. "That's not an answer. Do you want spaghetti, or hot dogs or meat loaf?" We can't tell him that we aren't hungry because we've just finished off the three giant-sized cans of peaches while he slept.

"Campbell's soup," Andy says. "Let's have Campbell's soup."

"That's not enough for supper."

Dad smells a rat by now and chases up our reluctance to eat like a dog after a bone. He suddenly gives in. "Okay. You want Campbell's soup. You'll get Campbell's soup!"

He comes back from the grocer's with several different kinds of soups and puts them all together in the same pot. Split pea and ham and cream of chicken, tomato and chicken noodle merge to create an unappetizing gray concoction. To this he adds chili powder, ketchup, mustard and horseradish from half-empty jars in the kitchen. "You asked for it, now you got it!" he says as he slams the soup into three bowls and sets one in front of each of us. "You've been up to something. I don't know what, but all I know is, you're gonna eat this!"

He sits down heavily at the table and waits, his blood-shot eyes straining to keep open. The soup tastes disgusting, and the smell is worse. The stink competes with Dad's filthy clothes that have been slept in for days, maybe weeks. We tentatively sip the soup but it's so awful that we can't eat it. "What's the matter? You wanted soup so bad. You'd better eat every last drop of it. You're not leaving this table until you've eaten it. Have it while it's hot! Ha, ha!"

It's the middle of the night by the time he gives up his vigil and falls asleep, fully clothed, on his bed. We have sat at the table for over six hours and stared into plates of congealed soup, with additions. We quietly tip our bowls into the sink and wash our dishes before we go to bed.

It is already mid-October and Mom's absence creates a void that no one can fill. The apartment no longer echoes with her reminders or reprimands. There is plenty of ' Mom says' exchanged between us, though. And, strange as it may seem, we have been on our best behavior and hardly ever fight among ourselves.

I am already ten years old and in the fifth grade. My class is working on a project called "Who Am I?" and we are all bringing in things that prove our nationality, religion and age. Phyllis says I can't take in the christening robe or the shawl, but lets me have my little booklet, the Baptismal Font, which says I'm a Methodist and a copy of my birth certificate which shows my nationality and my age.

We are having fun seeing where everyone comes from and finding out what their birthdays are. Each child stands up and reads out the information and the teacher marks it on a chart on the blackboard. My turn is coming up as soon as mid-morning milk break is over. We are putting away the bottles and straws when the school principal knocks and comes in. Our teacher signals the class to stand up.

"Thank you class," the principal says. "You may sit down." He whispers to the teacher who then looks at the class and calls me up to her desk. I accompany him into the hallway where he says, "This lady would like to speak with you." Then, resting his hand on my shoulder for a moment, says, "Good-bye, Jeanne. Good luck."

The lady introduces herself as a social worker and comes directly to the point. "It has been reported that you and your brother and sister have been living on your own for a while. Your father is unable to look after you so the Welfare Department has decided that each of you shall stay with one of your aunts. You will be staying with your Aunt Sophie. Your aunts will be paid a State allowance for this. Do you have any questions?"

"Where's Andy? He's not used to being on his own. He'll be scared."

"He's already been taken to your Aunt Rose's. Your sister is on her way to your Aunt Helen's. If there are no other questions, we'll go."

"I need to get my things from the classroom."

In the social worker's car, I watch the neighborhood go by not knowing, but suspecting that, I am leaving it forever. We don't go past 67 Wyckoff Avenue so there is no chance to run up the flight of stairs and get something I might want. The lump in my throat feels like I swallowed a wad of very dry paper. "Ahem. Ahem." I try to clear it. My eyes water.

"You'll be all right. Don't worry," the social worker says, passing me back a box of tissues.

I look straight ahead, fingering in my lap the only things I own now – a tattered notebook, a pencil, the copy of my birth certificate and the Baptismal Font.

Chapter Nineteen
Betrayal

Aunt Sophie takes one look at me and frowns. When the social worker goes she vents her displeasure. "You're filthy. Don't you ever wash? Get in there and take a bath. After that we're going to buy you some clothes. These rags are going straight in the garbage can. You can wear a pair of the boys' blue jeans and I'll find you a shirt."

I close the bathroom door behind me and as soon as the water gushes out of the faucet, I begin to cry. I bite into the washcloth and use it to cover my face, muffling my misery until Aunt Sophie bangs on the door. "Don't spend all day in there. We have things to do." When I come out she looks me up and down. "What's the matter with your eyes? They're all red and puffy?"

"I got soap in them."

"Well, be more careful next time. Put these on."

I'm glad my cousins, Alex and Michael, are at school and Uncle Alex is at work. Everything happened so fast that I haven't had time to think. I don't know what to say, what not to say, or how to act. Aunt Sophie keeps me so busy that I can't think straight. On the way to the clothing store she says, "They've given me a clothing allowance for you. I think, if we're careful how we spend it, we can afford three school dresses plus a blouse and slacks for after school, and some underwear, of course, plus a pair of pyjamas. Tomorrow I'll show you the way to school. It's a short walk from here."

"Why can't I go to my old school?"

"Because it's too far away. Stop asking questions. Just do as I tell you."

At the store Aunt Sophie rushes to the racks, scrapes back the hangers one after the other and picks out some dresses. I can't get enthusiastic about any of it even though it is a dream come true, a wish granted – new clothes. Maybe I'm bewildered because Aunt Sophie can't help pointing out my faults. "The dresses are too tight for her," she tells the saleswoman. "I realize she's fat around the middle, but the larger sizes are too big all over. Haven't you got anything in the chubby line?"

Looking in the mirror I expect to see a blush rising to my cheeks because they are burning hot, but my sallow skin camouflages my embarrassment and doesn't give me away. Reflected behind me in my blue flowered cotton dress with the buttons down the back and the large bow tied behind, is Aunt Sophie admiring herself, straightening her long, tight skirt over her slim hips. I didn't know until now that I was fat. Maybe this is because I had never been to a store and stood in front of a large mirror to try on new clothes. My clothes always fit me because they were hand-me-downs from my sister, and were probably always too big for me anyhow. I knew my sister was fat because she was always talking about it, and anyone could tell you that my brother was as skinny as a stick. I'd always fallen somewhere in between, accepting my middle size as easily as I did my middle place in the order in which I arrived in the world.

"It's all right, dear," I hear the saleslady say to me quietly amid the din of words whirring among the images in my brain. "It's only puppy fat. You'll grow out of it. Why, I've seen hundreds of girls like you turn from ugly ducklings into lovely swans."

"Can you wrap them up?" Aunt Sophie interrupts, dismissing the woman.

On the way home Aunt Sophie says to me, "You'll wear each dress for two days. After day one, you must change into your slacks and blouse after school. After day two, you may keep the dress on until you go to bed. Do you understand?"

"Yeah."

"Yes, what?"

"Yes, Aunt Sophie."

The first couple of days are crazy ones for me. It's hard trying to get used to living with strangers. Visiting your aunts and cousins for an afternoon is a whole lot different from staying with them permanently. On the first day, when night falls and I am still there, my situation slowly dawns on me. Although people surround me, I feel completely alone. There is no telephone, no way I can communicate with Andy or Phyllis. I realize how much I have depended on them for their reactions and their opinions. I don't want to consult my aunt or uncle or my cousins. They wouldn't understand anyhow, so I keep quiet and don't speak to anyone.

Phyllis is lucky. She is staying with Aunt Helen who understands her and all of us. They get on well. Andy is probably getting another free haircut from Uncle Victor and between watching their television, eating an endless supply of salami sandwiches and swilling gallons of Sealtest chocolate milk, he'll be fine.

That leaves me being bossed around by grumpy Aunt Sophie. She can't let go of a thing once she starts. Whenever she picks an argument with Uncle Alex or criticizes my cousins, they put their heads down and keep quiet. They figure there's no use in arguing, that they'll never win. They don't fight back in their family like we do. We have always voiced our complaints and given our opinions. We might get slapped for it, but at least we have had our say and no one carries a grudge.

At Aunt Sophie's we eat at exactly the same time every day. We change our clothes according to schedule. We watch a limited amount of supervised television, and go to bed. There's nothing extra - no frills, no laughs, no tears, no nothing. It makes the home I left seem rough and tumble, disorganized; but there was room for games, 'live shows', outings, creativity, even if it meant melting our wax crayons on the radiators and shaping animals out of them.

I like my new school not only because it gets me out of Aunt Sophie's way. The teacher continually praises my work and lets me have extra privileges like delivering messages to other teachers and watching the class when she goes out. I can't say anything about this at home since my cousins are having trouble at school. Every night their parents have to go over their homework with them. They sit in the kitchen and pour over each page. The boys have to practice their penmanship over and over. I sit with a book in the parlor and pity them.

My teacher has asked me to design and paint the backdrop for the school play. It had to be ten feet high by twenty feet wide. I had no trouble drawing it and five other kids helped me paint it. On my 11th birthday, she bought me a big box of cookies to pass around the class, a school tradition. I was so touched because my birthday would have passed by unnoticed since I couldn't bring anything to share with the class. Aunt Sophie wasn't planning on recognizing my birthday. All she could say was, "Humph," when I told her about the cookies at school. "Well, by coincidence the social security check arrived today,"

Aunt Sophie informs me, "for your winter coat. Don't look so puzzled. I told them you had no coat and they sent some money. We'll go right now. No time like the present."

My very first winter coat. We stop in front of a window displaying several styles of coats for young ladies. Pointing to a pale-gray woolen one with a fitted waist and shoal collar, I say, "I like that one."

"Don't be so stupid! You're too fat for anything like that. That one is better for you." She indicates a blue and green checked coat, box-shaped and with white buttons. I feel as though I've been stung. I HATE IT! I want the other one. In the store she tells the woman I want to try it on.

"What's the matter, dear? Don't you like it?" The saleslady says taking one look at my miserable face.

"We'll take it," Aunt Sophie says drawing the money out of her purse. "The buttons will have to be adjusted. She'll have to learn how to sew on buttons if she's going to have a stomach like that." I hate the coat, but hate myself more for being fat and ungrateful.

Christmas is getting close and I still haven't seen or heard from Phyllis or Andy. I never thought I would miss them so much. I even miss home. I miss having the run of the place, the familiar sounds of Puerto Rican music and language drifting over the alleyway, the smell of Mrs. Bowler's sauerkraut, the polished brass mailboxes, the carpeted staircase. I miss eating when I am hungry, cooking something for myself, and having the freedom to come and go up or down the stairs and out the front door. I miss not knowing what is going to happen from one day to the next. I miss using my imagination, getting creative with food, clothes and managing the household. I don't miss the beatings, the contradictions, the worrying about Mom and Dad, my sister's bullying, having to look after my brother; but if that's part of it, well, then I guess I miss that too. We share so many in-jokes and have been through so much together that we only need to look at or nudge one another to communicate something.

My cousins are okay, but I am so lonely. For recreation in the evenings we lay on the rag rug in front of the television and watch the Mickey Mouse Show under the watchful eye of Aunt Sophie. When she is busy in the kitchen and isn't watching us like a hawk, I find myself wandering into the boys' bedroom where my makeshift bed is

131

set up at the foot of theirs and stand by the window, craving a little privacy to think for a moment. I peek through the venetian blind at the wet night and watch the traffic going by. I often did this at home, only Aunt Sophie's apartment is on the ground floor and the view is different, but the sound of cars passing by is the same on the wet streets here as it is over there.

"WHAT ARE YOU DOING?" Aunt Sophie shouts, creeping up and scaring the living daylights out of me.

"Nothing, Aunt Sophie. Just looking out of the window," I hear myself say in a voice that is scared and small.

"I heard you sighing. What have you got to sigh about?"

"Nothing."

"Nothing, what?"

"Nothing, Aunt Sophie."

Had I been sighing? What's wrong with sighing? I have tried to be brave and not give in to crying. I know that it would be interpreted as being ungrateful. I ought to be grateful to have a bed to sleep in, food to eat, a roof over my head. I am. But what about Mom? Is she better? Is she worse? Where's Dad? Does he know where we are? Why doesn't anyone get in touch with me? I need to know the answers to the questions roiling around in my head, but I can't ask Aunt Sophie. She'll only ball me out, and I never get to see Uncle Alex alone. He is usually so sympathetic.

It's Christmas next week and I imagine Andy has been decorating Aunt Rose's tree, maybe even putting on the angel hair. Aunt Sophie has asked me what I want for Christmas. When I told her knitting needles and wool, she said, surprised, "Wouldn't you rather have a doll?" I shook my head, not wanting to go into detail about learning how to knit because I left behind the orange mittens with the green thumbs that Mom had made especially for me and wanted to knit another pair.

I unwrap my present on Christmas morning and a rubber doll with curly hair that grows out of the roots as you comb it is smiling up at me. She's very pretty and nearly the size of a real baby. My biggest and best surprise is seeing Phyllis the day after Christmas. Aunt Sophie knew she was coming but didn't tell me. She makes sure, too, that we don't have any time together on our own; however, when she goes to the toilet, we talk about Andy.

"Andy's loving it at Aunt Rose's. He can play with all their toys. He has put on weight, too," she assures me. "How do you like your doll?"

"It's great. How did you know I got a doll for Christmas?"

"I bought it for you. I gave it to Aunt Sophie when she came over to Aunt Helen's last week. Didn't she tell you she saw me?"

"No," I say and quickly change the subject. "I like your new clothes," and openly admire her from top to bottom.

"They got me a bunch of things. You should have seen me in the store. I even have two bras!" Phyllis looks grown up. In the couple of months she has been at Aunt Helen's she has transformed. Her hair is clean and cut in a pageboy style. She is wearing stockings and a pair of black flats. Her new pale woolen overcoat is long and makes her look tall and slimmer. "Another girl from school and I go out together. We're having so much fun. Aunt Helen gives me an allowance out of the social security money so I'm not stealing any more. How are things with you?"

"Okay. What's happening with Dad? What did he do when he found out we were all gone?"

"Haven't you heard? He's been evicted!"

"Oh, God. Not that."

"He had it coming to him. Come on, quit crying, Beans. Shush. Aunt Sophie's coming."

"It'll be dark soon. Isn't it time you went back?" Aunt Sophie suggests on her return. Phyllis shoots me a quick glance and gets up to leave. At the door she fills me in. "He didn't pay the rent and wasn't living there, so they threw everything out in the street. I went to see Mrs. Bowler who told me that a bunch of men came and cleared the apartment out. They lined up everything on the sidewalk. They just left it there and walked away. During the night most of it disappeared. The next morning the garbage men cleared away the rest. There is nothing left - no furniture, clothes, toys, dishes or photographs – nothing. Everything is gone."

You can lose a tooth, or a friend, or a dime; and now I can see how you can also lose your childhood. All you need to do is get evicted. I can't get to sleep and when I finally do I dream about the player piano. It is parked near the curb in the snow where Dad used to leave his car. Beside it piano rolls in broken boxes sag in the dampness. Night is falling and looking into a lighted window from outside I see Dad's photographic lamps on bedside tables illuminating a dingy apartment. Mom's white crocheted doilies are spread on backs of sofas like delinquent snowflakes. Someone is sleeping in my bed and my brother's crib squats alone against a wall, empty but for a teddy bear. Back in the street the ragman is picking through the contents of the junk closet. He drags a large burlap sack over to Mom's dresses and fluffs up a fake-flower corsage, smiling, before stuffing all her clothes into it. As I watch him shuffle down the street, dragging his booty behind him, old photographs of Mom and Dad, enjoying themselves in another season, twirl by on a wind keen to file them away in icy gutters.

All through the Christmas vacation I daydream about the eviction. I don't talk to anyone about it because maybe I'm not supposed to know about it. I sigh heavily, despite Aunt Sophie's sharp ears, as the lifeblood of my childhood trickles away like the pieces of furniture and articles of clothing that once defined it and held it together.

"You're quiet," Aunt Sophie says looking hard at me.

I am at my happiest when I'm at school. There I can be myself, no matter where I come from. And I can enjoy small successes. We perform the class play in early January and the backdrop I painted with the help of classmates turns out to be a great success. It wasn't much of a picture, just a landscape scene containing a house with a smoking chimney in the distance. I enlarged it from a small sketch I made in art class. "We must make more use of your talents," the principal said to me at the end of the performance, patting me on the head. "Fancy being able to draw that to scale without a grid." I didn't know what he was talking about but enjoyed the praise I got for doing something so simple.

A few weeks later while going down the stairs with my teacher to the lunch room, she admires my yellow dress. "Let's call it daffodil yellow. Spring is just around the corner," she says placing her arm around my shoulder. Before we reach the bottom of the stairs a school monitor tells me I'm wanted in the office.

"I'm afraid you can no longer stay with your aunt," a tall woman in a dark suit carrying a leather briefcase tells me in front of the principal. "We'll be taking you to a temporary shelter for now. Run along and get your coat."

I fly up the stairs in a blind panic with my blood pumping fiercely in my veins. My knees nearly buckle beneath me as I reach the empty classroom. I unhook my coat with trembling hands and look around the room where I have been my happiest over the past few months. The sketch of my backdrop is pinned to the back wall. Maps of Asia Minor and North America line the walls opposite the windows, and the blackboard is covered in long division problems. I head for the stairs and bump into my teacher who has been looking all over for me. When I tell her my news she says, "I'm going to miss you, Jeanne. We all are. I'll get your new address and will write to you."

My sadness at parting is turned to joy when I see Andy sitting on the back seat of the car. "Did I forget to mention it? Andy is coming with you."

Once we're on our way, I ask the social worker, "Is Phyllis coming, too?"

"No. Phyllis is too old to go into a children's home. The age limit for admissions is thirteen and she is already fifteen. She'll stay with your Aunt Helen."

A children's home? Has it already been decided? If Aunt Helen can keep Phyllis why can't Aunt Sophie and Aunt Rose keep Andy and me? Why are we being sent away? What have we done to be sent away?

"Are we stopping to get my clothes and things?"

"No. They have everything there that you will need."

As the car speeds through new neighborhoods, Andy and I hold hands. "I bet Aunt Sophie knew they were going to come for me. Why didn't she tell me? Did Aunt Rose say anything to you about leaving today?" I whisper to Andy. He shakes his head, looking worried. I squeeze his hand. "It's okay," I tell him.

But it's not okay I tell myself. My anger mounts, pressing me in on all sides, convincing me that we have been betrayed. We are like coins sent spinning on our edges. We pirouette and move away, twirling around and around, until we slow and stop. We have no control once set in motion, doing what we are told, going where we are told, unable to question our destiny.

The sun suddenly pierces the edge of a dark cloud and I put up a hand to shield my eyes. In doing so I feel its warmth and let my hand slide back to my lap and welcome the sun, letting it fall over me and warm my spirit and resolve.

I can't forgive my mother's family for having us put in a home without a word of good-bye, or sign of regret. There was no apology or word of good luck, or 'see you soon'. Taking into consideration how I feel about this, I know that I will never underestimate the depth of understanding and feelings of a child.

"They wouldn't let me go back for any of my Christmas presents or clothes," Andy whines next to me, bringing me back to today. "I only have this crappy school bag and a couple of broken pencils."

"We're supposed to be getting everything we need at the new place," I reassure him with little conviction and not really caring because I know now that the most coveted possession is not what I can hold in my hand, but what I can keep in my heart.

Chapter Twenty
Temporary Accommodation

After a day in the children's shelter, I no longer believe that the neighborhood I grew up in was rough. The most serious weapons we carried were sharpened ice-lollipop sticks, handmade 'guns' made from a thick stick of wood, a nail, a rubber band and lots of one-inch squares of linoleum, water balloons, and cap guns (which were only meant to frighten the enemy). I had never seen a switchblade knife before, or the deep scars on a switchblade-knife-owner's face either. My first day and my first sight of one of these knives close-up scared me more than Frankenstein, the Mummy and Dracula put together and will probably give me worse nightmares.

Three boys running down the stairs knocked me over on the girls' staircase as I was making my way up to the recreation room to meet Andy. You'd think I was invisible. "Get out of the way, bitch," one of them said. He slid his hand in his pants pocket and pulled out a slim piece of metal. Holding it at arm's length, he pressed a button on the handle. With a click a blade as thin as a one-dollar bill leaped out. He admired it for a second, turning it until the sharp edge glinted, then thrust it at me. "You want this in your belly?" They didn't wait for a reply.

Andy and I are separated most of the time because one side of the building is for boys and the other is for girls. The only time we see each other is at mealtimes or at recreation. Adults supervise the dining room which is also segregated, but during recreation, which is after supper and until the bed time bell, we are free to mix. It is only because I want to be with Andy that I dare go up there. Big kids rule at recreation - the loud mouths, the ones with exaggerated walks and clothing statements, like wearing hats and scarves, even though they are inside. Their amusement is to pick on the little ones, the 'punks'.

Andy has been edgy. We are both nervous of this place full of rules and regulations, bullies and gangs. A temporary home for children who are waiting placement in children's homes, foster homes, or delinquent centers, the kids hang in limbo, anxious and uncertain.

Many of them have already been separated from their brothers and sisters. Only a few are lucky enough to be together.

When we arrived everyone was in the playground for morning break. The social worker parked the car outside the metal gates and a supervisor unlocked them from the inside and let us in. We walked through a narrow crack in a wall of children who, on seeing us, immediately stopped their chasing, jumping and running to crowd us and to size us up. "Return to your games," the supervisor said shooing them away with the wave of his hand like pesky flies on carrion. A loud bell sounded as we left the office and were led down into the dining room for lunch.

In the girls' dormitory dozens of narrow white-painted beds are laid out in rows like a hospital ward. Off the stairwell on this floor is a small entrance hall which leads to the dormitory, a supervisor's cubicle, the bathrooms and toilets, and a wardrobe room. "It's lights-out in a couple of minutes," the girl in the bed next to mine says. "Where are your things? You can take a locker for them." I can see that she is surprised when I tell her that I don't have anything else besides a coat and the clothes I'm wearing, but she doesn't ask any questions. "Come with me." I follow her to the wardrobe room where she picks out a clean towel and a pair of flannel pyjamas for me. "You'd better chose some clothes for tomorrow. There's such a mad rush in the morning, you'll wind up wearing God knows what. Everything in this room has been donated. What we do, see, is throw our dirty clothes in the basket, and they wind up back here after they're washed and ironed. You can put in that yellow dress you're wearing and it'll be here tomorrow afternoon. But once it's washed I'd fold it up and hide it in my locker if I was you. You don't want it to go walking, do you?"

Clothes are stacked to the ceiling in cubby-holes that look like open letterboxes. I pick out underpants, an undershirt, pants and a sweater. After washing, I hang my towel on a hook and return to the dormitory where I slip under the covers like everyone else. The sheets are sparkling white and smell of detergent.

All the lights go out at the same time and we are suddenly in pitch black darkness. It takes a while for my eyes to adjust to it and I see the red bulb over the emergency exit first, then a slit of light under the door and approaching car lights peeping through the roller blinds at the windows. There are noises, too, coughing, muttering, muffled giggles, and in the distance, probably on the boys' side, shouts echoing down the corridor, up the stairwell and under the crack of our door.

I keep my hands under the covers and fold my arms across my chest. But as tired as I am, sleep won't come. My mind drifts and kids me into thinking that I'm still at Aunt Sophie's. Any minute Alex or Michael will say something funny, and we'll have to cover our faces with our pillows to stifle our laughter so their mother won't hear. I will my eyes shut, but they won't stay closed for more than a couple of minutes. They keep popping open. Everyone else is asleep. I sit up and look around. My pupils are wide enough to make out the humped bodies of girls asleep in the other beds. Do my cousins know what's happened to me. Do they know where I am? Are they worried?

A loud bell like a siren roars across the beds and dozens of pairs of feet hit the floor at the same time as the supervisor switches on the lights and shouts. "Everybody up. Line-up for breakfast in ten minutes."

"My name's Geraldine," the girl that helped me last night says as we get in line by the staircase. "Geraldine Bennett. That's my big sister, Marianne," she adds, pointing to a tall, pretty girl with long blonde, curly hair, "and my little sister, Linda. We've got a brother, Michael, on the boys' side. We've been here a couple of weeks already and we're hoping to be placed together. We heard that the homes are all full. Some of the kids have been here for months and months."

"NO TALKING IN LINE!" the supervisor shouts, glaring at us. Another bell roars, this time above our heads. "Lead on," she nods to the girl at the front of the line and we march downstairs.

"Is everything done by the bell here?" I ask Geraldine. She nods.

I am assigned to a classroom, one of two classes, grouped according to age – the five to nine-year olds are in one class and the ten to sixteen-year olds in the other. The teacher hands out babyish workbooks and we fill in the empty spaces with worn down pencils. The rest of the time we play games like Which Group Can Pass the Basketball to the End of the Row Fastest? And, Hands Behind Backs and Pass the Sheet of Paper Between You With Straws. School finishes at lunchtime. In the afternoons, we have Religion.

My escapades into the Roman Catholic Church and my two grandfathers' funerals, one Islamic, and the other Russian Orthodox, are no help to me. I am interviewed by two women and everything starts out nice and sweet. "Sit down, please, dear, will you? What's your name? Do you have any brothers and sisters? Where are your parents? Do you have any other relatives?" When they ask me about religion I tell them, "I'm a Methodist."

"How nice, dear. Can you say The Lord's Prayer for us, dear? You must know it. 'Our father…'"

"No."

"How about the Apostle's Creed?"

"Who's Greed?"

"Em…You must know the Glory Be…"

"No."

"You mustn't be nervous, dear. Say any prayers you can remember."

"I can't remember any."

"You MUST! Our records show that you and your brother are Christians. You have been baptized?"

"Does that mean christened?"

"Yes, but…Doris, do you think we have the right information here?"

"She's just another little heathen," Doris says looking at me, flustered.

"I just remembered one!"

"Go ahead."

'Now I lay me down to sleep, I pray the Lord my soul to keep. If I should die before I wake, I pray the Lord my soul to take.'

"That's it?" Doris squeaks.

"I'm afraid there's been a mistake…"

"I've got a religion," I blurt out, waving at them the envelope with the copy of my birth certificate and the Baptismal Font in it, which have been safely hidden in the deep pockets of the coat that Aunt Sophie bought me.

"You may go and join the others, dear."

During 'Religion' everyone in the shelter must attend, boys and girls together. Someone reads from the Bible and talks about God and prophets and sins, and we sing hymns.

As the days roll by kids leave and new ones arrive. Just as I am beginning to get used to things, Geraldine and her sisters and brother are taken into a children's home together, leaving a gap in my life as wide as a missing front tooth.

There are outings on the weekends for those of us without parents or relatives to look after us. We line up in the playground and march down the street in pairs with one supervisor at the front, and another one at the back. We go as far as the nearest grocery store to stock up on comic books and candy and walk back in a freezing February wind.

When it's too cold to go outside Andy and I sit in a corner of the recreation room and talk about getting in touch with our family. But how can we? None of them has a telephone and we don't have any money. No one has contacted us. Maybe no one knows where we are.

Finally it's announced that we're having visitors. Everyone has been told to put coats on and gather in the playground. We are lined up in front of the iron gates and left there to wait in silence staring at the empty street. The sun is weak and the air icy, but we are fired with excitement. We hear a hum and cars begin to pull up outside the gates. Andy and I crane our necks to see if there's anybody we know. The visitors stand on the sidewalk and peer through the bars at us. A middle-aged couple points to a small blonde girl with dimples. A supervisor appears, opens the gate and lets her pass through. She gets into their car and rides off. Someone else points to a boy and he goes out the same way. "What's going on?" I whisper to the boy next to me.

"They're choosin' kids to take home for a day. You know, like, to treat them to stuff like candy, toys and maybe even new clothes."

"We don't even know them. I don't want to be picked."

"Sure you do. What's the matter? You too proud or something? Man, that's a cool way to get extras we *never* get! Smile! Come on, come on! A BIG smile. Your chances are better then." More children disappear through the gate. I don't want to get in a car with strangers, but I don't want to be left out either. I smile a wide, bright smile and my face is about to crack when a lady with reddish hair beams back at

141

me. I've been picked. I've been chosen for the day. I look around for Andy, but he has already been chosen.

I'm still smiling, almost giggling, as I pass through the gate. It's like being a prize at a shooting gallery at Coney Island. Only instead of winning the prize, I am the prize. "What's your name, child?"

"Jeanne."

"You look like a happy girl, Jeannie. Come on. My car is over there." As I step off the curb, I look over my shoulder at the kids standing behind the gate. They are no longer smiling. They haven't been chosen and will spend the rest of the day inside and bored out of their minds. Among them is the boy who told me to smile.

The lady and her husband have no children, but they have a dog. They let me play with him in their yard and I can't help wondering about Rex. After lunch we go shopping and they buy me a pale blue cotton dress with tiny red roses in the pattern. The dress has white lace down the front and ties in a large bow at the back. My smiles are genuine now; being with strangers is better than with my own family.

Andy is waiting in the recreation room when I return, anxious to show me his new toy dump truck. He runs it along his thighs, up the leg of the table and over the polished top. "*Vroom. Vroom.* The kids who were left behind went on the rampage after lunch. They broke windows and smashed dining room chairs," he says, running his hands along the truck's wheels and making them spin wildly.

That night I go to sleep with my new dress tucked safely under my pillow. When the lights are out I feel the need to say a prayer - I don't want to say the Lord's Prayer or the Creed – I need to talk to someone in regular words about how I feel. I make sure no one is watching as I press my palms together. "Dear God and Heavenly Father..." I whisper. Then pause, stuck for what to say next.

"*Thank you's come first,*" the Religion teacher had told us. "*Then you can ask for things.*" "Thank you for letting me get chosen." No. I can't say that. A lot of kids didn't get chosen. "Dear God," I press on. "Thank you for my new dress. Please can you get me out of here? Amen."

PART TWO THE HOME
1955 - 1963

Chapter Twenty-One
New Arrivals

A lump of brown sugar and a pat of butter sink beneath my spoon into a steamy bowl of cream of wheat. I am lost in the buttery swirl but am quickly brought back when a hand touches my shoulder. "Go straight to the office after breakfast. Bring your brother, too," a supervisor says. I turn to nod 'yes' but he's already gone. I scan the faces of dozens of sleepyheads hunched over their breakfast bowls for Andy. I spy him on the other side of the room scooping hot cereal into his mouth faster than he can swallow it, his cheeks bulging like a chipmunk's.

News travels so fast in the children's shelter that everyone knows our business before we do. "Hey. Did ja hear that? They're leaving today!" the boy next to me says out loud.

"You lucky sticks! How long have you been here? I've been waiting to hear for six months," the girl across from me says.

"Six weeks," I say, but quickly add, "but he never said anything about leaving," because I don't want to get my hopes up for nothing.

"We know what it means when they come for you at breakfast. I'll bet you a social worker is waiting in the office. It happens all the time," she replies, looking down with renewed interest in her cereal bowl.

What luck if we are leaving after only six weeks.

Everyone, including this girl, is afraid of waiting for more than six months. It means you are either going into a delinquent home or a detention center, which is a kind of children's prison. If you can't be placed it means that no one wants you. The only thing worse than this is to end up in a psychiatric hospital.

The office is warm and smells of coffee. "Go and pack," we're told. "You two are going to a children's home. You leave in five minutes."

Our good-bye to the Shelter is a backward glance as the iron gates shut with a slam behind us. Before we are spirited away, I notice a few of last autumn's leaves inside the wire fence. Frost and snow have blackened them and they are pressed hard against the fence by an icy March wind that has no intention of letting them out.

Andy and I sit still on the back seat. He stares out the window with his paper sack limp in his lap. It contains whatever he has managed to salvage from the hound dogs in the shelter. I, too, have little to call my own except the new dress with the roses on it that I took the precaution of wearing since I got it, and carry my yellow dress in a bag.

The car stops and my heart skips a beat in front of a square redbrick building on the corner of 4th Avenue and Ridge Boulevard in the Bay Ridge area of Brooklyn. The giant home sits proud on top of a hill and smooth lawns lead up to shrubs that screen the ground floor windows. A sign on the lawn reads: KALLMAN HOME FOR CHILDREN, 85-15 Ridge Boulevard. Great big houses squat comfortably on large lawns all the way down the street. Some neighborhood, I think, as Andy and I nudge each other's elbows in silent agreement while we mount the steps to the main entrance.

Inside the main entrance the walls are lined with the same dark marble as the floors. Light bounces off them and each footstep echoes down the long corridor. No one is in the office because it isn't nine o'clock yet. Andy whispers, "What's happening through there?" He points across the hall to doors leading to a balcony. We go over and see a flight of stairs going down to a basketball court, a playground and a gravel yard with swings.

A loud bell suddenly sounds above our heads, making us jump. In the distance there is a faint rumbling that gets louder as kids fly out into the playground. Footsteps pound on the landing stairs to the right and to the left of us.

On a door near the office a sign reads, Mr. Fred Persiko, Director. It opens abruptly. "Good morning," a medium-sized man with gray hair says cheerily, and shakes the social worker's hand, smiling at us at the same time. "You must be Andy and Jeanne." He waits for us to say something, but when we don't, he says, "Follow me. There's plenty of time for us to get to know one another." Our social worker hands over our files to the home's social worker who has just arrived and is busy

144

sorting papers in his small office. We are handed over to Mrs. Persiko, the director's wife, who gives us a tour and introduces us to most of the staff.

Our tour of the Kallman Home for Children makes me realize how enormous the place really is. An imaginary line runs down the middle of the building separating it into two equal halves. Only a pair of swinging doors divides the boys' dorms from the girls' dorms on the top floor. The main floor, which is in the middle of the building, houses the administration offices, the infirmary, the main kitchen, the director's apartment, the auditorium, the library, and a storeroom. Below, on the ground floor, are the large playrooms, one on each side, plus on the boys' side there is a woodwork shop and on the girls' side, a laundry and ironing room. Between the playrooms there is common territory – the dining hall, which has a small kitchen behind it, and a walk-in refrigerator and various storerooms nearby.

Afterwards, Mrs. Persiko takes us to a clothing storeroom and when she finds out that we've come with practically nothing, we are each given a stack of brand new undershirts, underpants, socks, pants, shirts, a pair of shoes and sneakers, plus flannel pajamas. "Anything else you need, you can get from the grab bag. That's a large closet in the dorms full of clean clothes that belong to everyone. Your house parents will assign you a bed. They will tell you anything else you need to know."

The dorms are empty now because everyone has left for school. Only my housemother, "Binnie" as she is known by everyone, is in her room in the outside corridor. She shows me to my dormitory and gives me clean sheets to make my bed. Standing over me while I shake out the tightly folded, starched and pressed linens, she instructs me on the making of perfect hospital corners, taking over when I fumble and get it wrong. "You'll soon get the hang of it. Bed linen changes are every Wednesday morning. The girls will tell you what to do." She turns to leave, but smiles and pats my shoulder first. She stops to adjust a couple of wisps of pure white hair that have fallen loose over her silver-rimmed spectacles using a tortoiseshell hair comb that she plucks from the depths of her large bun. "Put your things away in this drawer and I'll come back for you later," she says smoothing the white apron that she wears over her flowered cotton dress with a white lace collar. The room is so quiet, yet I can feel the presence of the other 19 girls who live here. My eyes fall on a pair of pink furry slippers, some small nail scissors, a Spanish doll in a lavish costume propped up by a pillow, a jar of Noxzema face cream, a tube of toothpaste. Of the twelve windows that surround three of the four walls, the ones that face the boys' side are made of frosted glass, probably so that the boys can't see in if the girls forget to pull the curtains when they undress. Through the other windows I can see the steep drive at the back of the building, the tops of shrubs and trees, a good portion of the lawn and the black iron fence surrounding the place as well as buildings across the street.

I fold my new clothes, putting them into a neat stack before stowing them away in my drawer. Not knowing what to do next I sit on the edge of my bed in the eerie silence and look around. Beside each bed is a narrow bedside table with three small drawers. Some of the girls have jewel boxes on top, or transistor radios, matching comb and brush sets, nail polish and Holy Bibles. I open the one beside me. All the drawers are empty. I have nothing to put into them except a broken, dirty comb and the papers I have carried with me ever since I left home. I slide everything into the bottom drawer and lay down on top of the bed. What is Andy doing on the boys' side, I wonder?

"You're as quiet as a mouse," Binnie says at the door. "Come long with me. It's nearly time for lunch and the children in P.S.185 will be coming home soon. Look through that far window over there, and across the street. That's the school where you will be going tomorrow. Our social worker will take you to the principal's office in the morning to introduce you."

The kids are noisy and excited when they come home. They rush to the toilets and, washing their hands, splash around at the sinks. Then they line up outside the dining hall, boys on one side, girls on the other. A houseparent heads up each line and checks hands, first one side then the other. The girl in front of me in the line turns around to say something and it's Geraldine! My friend from the children's temporary shelter. I can't believe it. She hooks her arm through mine and we stand for a few moments side by side, our bodies falling against each other as naturally as two sisters. "One behind the other down there, please," the housemother says pointing at us. We separate

146

immediately, but Geraldine has her hands behind her back and I place mine in hers until we reach the doors.

Over baloney sandwiches, glasses of cold, frothy milk and a crisp apple, Geraldine tells me that her whole family is together. "Mine, too," I say, "I mean, Andy's here, too. I don't know where my sister is. I haven't heard from her."

"That's okay," Geraldine reassures me. "You've got us now."

It takes a while before I can go around the home without getting lost. One hundred and twenty kids live here, which is about as many as they can squeeze in. The 20 beds in each of the three girls' rooms – the young, the middle and the seniors – are lined up along the walls like mackerels in a can with the obligatory 18 inches apart strictly observed. Each girl has hanging space in a wardrobe and a large drawer, plus a locker in the playroom for coats and books.

An electric bell rings to wake us up at 6.30 a.m.; another one tells us when to go to breakfast and to supper. Lights are turned out at the same time every night at 9 o'clock. No one is allowed to hang around the dorms during the day. We must stay in the playrooms or the playground after school until suppertime. When that's over we line up to go to the auditorium for Chapel. Afterwards, we are released to the dorms to do any further homework, or watch t.v., listen to music, read and take baths.

The back entrance to the building, which is where deliveries are made, or where visitors might arrive with cars, or a bus comes to take us to church or on an outing, is off the playground and leads down to 4th Avenue. We always use this entrance, climbing up and down the steep drive to go to school, catch a public bus, or walk a few blocks to the subway. We never use the main entrance unless we are new arrivals, with relatives or social workers or, if we are leaving the Home for good.

P.S. 185 is an elementary school and, as I am only in the 5th grade, I join the other young ones and walk across the street every day. The Junior High School kids need to take a public bus to get to school and anyone in High School might be going anywhere in the city, depending on what course they are taking.

There is an 'on the grounds' curfew imposed on all of us, no matter who you are. No one is allowed to leave the home after six o'clock.

This is especially hard for the older kids who want to socialize with friends outside the Home. One of the first things I learn is that there's a lot of sneaking off and covering up going on, but as it doesn't concern me, I keep out of it.

During the first week at the new home a nickname is slapped on me that stays with me until I leave – Pear Shape. I have no idea where or who it comes from, but it is my tag, used liberally by everyone whenever I fall out of favor. It gets shouted out for not scoring during a volleyball game. "What's the matter, Pear Shape, all fingers and thumbs?" But almost everyone else has a nickname so the sting is only bittersweet. I laugh to myself when I call someone else 'lard ass', 'buck-tooth', 'big ears' and other names.

My nickname distinguishes me from someone else called 'fatty' Geraldine explained to me that night because though I am big around the middle, I've got skinny arms and legs. Binnie, on hearing me called Pear Shape, smiles slightly when she assures me I'll outgrow the name because I'll probably get taller and my middle will stretch to normal. "You're just short. You're sure to grow. Look at the size of your feet! You've got to grow to fit them sooner or later." I am eleven years old going on twelve and self-consciousness is falling on me like a ton of bricks. I hadn't noticed anything until Aunt Sophie bought me that square box of a coat because I couldn't fit into the one I loved with the tapered waistline. I remember Aunt Rose coming to my defense once when they were discussing my pros and cons. "It's just puppy fat, Sophie," Rose said. "Leave her alone. She'll outgrow it." Ever since then I wanted to stretch, or to change shape altogether.

Every so often we have head checks. We line up outside the infirmary to see the nurse who inspects 120 heads in an afternoon. We watch anxiously as she studiously parts each girl's hair with a brand new pair of sterilized sticks, everyone of us hoping not to hear the dreaded words, "This one's got nits!" Two seconds after I feel the sticks on my scalp she says it. Upstairs the housemother is waiting at the ready with a bottle of A-200. The orange-colored, lice-killing liquid is rubbed into my hair and scalp and has to be kept on for a couple of hours. We are obliged to sit still on chairs lined up along the walls of the bathrooms. Later on the medicine is washed out and a fine-tooth comb pulled through the hair to remove the dead eggs.

To add further to my misery, I now have dandruff. In a desperate attempt to solve the problem someone gets the idea of covering my head in Vaseline Petroleum Jelly. The whole jar is massaged into my scalp. Aside from not having cured the problem, it proves impossible to wash out. My hair is plastered to my head. I fly into a screaming fit when I see myself in the mirror, refusing to go into the dining hall or be seen in public. I am kept in the infirmary in isolation for a week, sleeping with a towel on my pillow so I don't ruin the sheets. My hair is washed every day until it is finally grease-free.

It is while I am waiting for my hair to get back to normal that my tonsillitis returns. "Your tonsils are so swollen, there's hardly room for you to breathe!" the nurse exclaims. After the doctor examines me, I overhear him tell her that I'll have to have them out.

A whole year passes before they are surgically removed. I am at times delirious, with fevers as high as 105 degrees. Andy has also missed school because of infected tonsils. So one Spring morning, we are taken together to the hospital.

The surgeon is a portly, bearded man. His green operating coat is stretched tight across his belly. I am not scared until he puts a mask over my face and tells me to lie back on the hard table beneath me. As he holds the metal mask firmly over my face, I hear the loud hissing of gas, and I struggle to run away. He speaks soothing words and tells me to count backwards from ten. I get to six.

I wake up in a strange bed with bars around it like a baby's crib. The pain in my throat is bigger than I am. It is a red-hot searing pain that stops me from speaking or calling out. Then I remember everything. "Andy? Andy? Andy!" *Where is he? I need him.*"

A nurse says, "Andy is over here. Wait just a minute." She pushes over another baby crib like the one I'm in; it looks more like a large cage. Andy is asleep. "That's better, now, isn't it?" the nurse asks me and leaves the room.

I slip my left hand through the bars and tap him on the shoulder. He stirs, struggling to rise to the surface of consciousness. By the time he opens his eyes I am already crying with relief.

Chapter Twenty-Two
"Gimme That Ol' Time Religion"

When I asked Geraldine at supper the first night in the Home what 'Chapel' was all about, I guessed it was something like we had in the Shelter, only hoping it wasn't. "You know, religion and that," she said and quickly changed the subject to nail polish colors.

We have Religion, with a capital 'R' at the Kallman Home for Children. Mostly the Baptist Religion with the Salvation Army thrown in. Our routines revolve around religion. We say grace together before we sit down to eat; we have prayers before we go to bed; we pray in Chapel, have Bible studies and sing at religious summer camps, perform concerts with the Salvation Army band and make pilgrimages to Madison Square Garden to hear Billy Graham preach. We are quoted at from the Bible, starting with "Thou shalt not," when we do something wrong and ending with "…the Lord taketh away," when we are punished and have our privileges and belongings confiscated.

Chapel is held in the auditorium, a large room with a raised stage at the end on which an upright piano is hidden by maroon velvet curtains. There are polished wood floors, rows of metal folding chairs with an aisle in between separating the boys on the right from the girls on the left.

At the center stands a lectern where the visiting preacher places his notes and Bible. I pick a seat up front where I can get a good look at his Bible. There is usually no need for him to use it because he can recite whole passages by heart. But while he's talking the Bible is caressed, slapped upon, pointed at, held close to the chest or high above his head for emphasis, or he might hold it out to us by the spine so that the pages flap open like the ends of a large baloney sandwich.

The preachers' Bibles are not like the ones issued to us when we arrive. Ours are cheap and stiff with red around the edges that wears off quickly, leaving our fingers pink as though they were smeared with lipstick. Theirs are bound in black leather that has become as smooth as silk from the constant referral and use and the edges are gilded. They have extras like cut-out indexes naming the books, just like an address book, and so many explanatory notes and cross-references at the back that their Bibles are twice the size of a normal Bible. I watch as they confidently flip through the tissue-thin pages, effortlessly finding the place they require.

We often have 'Who can find the Bible verse the fastest?" contests and I can open to Psalms, Proverbs or Revelations in a split-second with a thumbnail. I am ashamed to admit this but I covet the preacher's wife's Bible. I love its creamy white cover with the title in gold letters on the front (it is even personalized with her own name on it). There is also a cream ribbon bookmark resting between the color pictures inside. She lets me look at it after Chapel and it feels good in my hands. Its femininity appeals to me – it is so much smaller than her husband's Bible. Passages special to her are marked in pen and by thin bookmarks depicting praying hands and crosses with lilies. I wouldn't mind a Bible like that. In no time I'd know all the books of the Bible in order, starting with Genesis and ending with Revelations. Even now I can find a Bible verse faster than anyone else in the Home and have memorized many of the Psalms.

Preachers come in all sizes and shapes. Sometimes they are women, but usually they are serious men in dark suits who are smiling, calm and self-assured when they come in, but during the sermon they often change. They become angry, passionate and tearful. Their message is becoming familiar - *"Have Faith, Hope and Charity, That's the way to live successfully. How do I know? The Bible tells me so."* The words to the song ring in my ears and I read the Bible through twice. There are a lot of 'begats' in the Old Testament which tell who was who's father or mother and Revelations doesn't reveal much because it is much too complicated to understand. Most of all, the book is filled with people and their stories that are repeated to us so often, we think they are part of our own history like the Pilgrims and the Indians in our American history books at school. I have been in the Home a year when a contest is announced. Bible passages are listed on a blackboard in Chapel and we are told that the first four kids to learn them all will win a trip to Niagara Falls. Right there on the spot I find the chapter and verse and start to read the first passage, I Corinthians, 13. I run my finger along the first line: "Though I speak with the tongues of men and of angels…" I don't stop to listen to our speaker, Joey. Joey is probably a man, but it is hard to tell how old he really is. He is a grown-up spastic boy who walks up to the lectern with difficulty. His knees point one way, his feet point another; his head jerks from side to side; he has trouble keeping his arms at his sides and his Bible from flying out of control. He begins falteringly. "Boys...and....girls..." The first time I saw him I nearly burst out laughing. I thought he was joking.

"He talks through his stomach," Geraldine whispered. "He makes himself burp and a sound comes out. He hasn't got a voice box. Whenever I've tried it, it doesn't work." Whenever he talks to us, I strain to understand his words, in awe of Joey, the living proof of miracles, as told to us many times.

During the weeks that follow the announcement of the contest my hand shoots up in Chapel every time the director asks for someone to recite the memorized Bible passages. When the final tally is made, Beverly, Marie, Harry and I are the winners of the four-day trip. It takes two days to drive there and back and we will have two days to visit Niagara Falls. Don Arbiter, the boys' housefather, is taking us in the Home van. There's only one problem - the name of the Home is written in bold letters on both doors. We beg him to do something about it and are glad when we see there's a square of brown paper taped over the words that would have labeled us from New York to Canada as inmates of THE KALLMAN HOME FOR CHILDREN.

Geraldine takes a picture of us that morning as we stand together beside the van. When she gives it to me later I hate what I look like so much that I take a piece of scotch tape and rip it repeatedly over my face until it is obliterated. This has nothing to do with the trip. It is because the day before our departure permission was given to a school of hairdressers to practice doing permanent waves on some of the girls' hair with the new ammonia solution. I didn't want a permanent, remembering how Mom's hair frizzed under the Electric Wave Machine, but they said I had to, and I was furious and hated it, especially since I was going on the trip the next day.

When we get to Niagara Falls the next evening, Beverly, Marie and I share a room in a brand new motel. Harry rooms with Don. After breakfast we have our first sight of Niagara Falls. Nothing could have prepared me for the size or the sound of the waterfall. Water from an innocent river crashes down at the point where the land abruptly gives out. The falling water seems in a permanent state of shock as it slides down hundreds of feet, spitting spray, resisting gravity momentarily, before tumbling to the bottom, where it furiously boils and churns until it continues its journey along another waiting river below.

We hire yellow slickers, waterproof boots and hats and walk through a series of damp tunnels before emerging under a canopy of water so dense, fast-moving and powerful that I am grinning, smiling, laughing – giddy with it all. Ice cold spray hits us from all directions and water drips down our faces forming a rivulet by our chins. We try to talk to one another, but have to use sign language because we can't even hear our own voices. We shout from the top of our lungs and still cannot hear ourselves above the roar of the wall of water passing in front of us. The sensation is breathtaking. At the motel, showered and dry, I sit on the sofa with my Bible in my lap thinking for a while that I understand what the Power and the Glory of God is, and why this place was chosen as our prize.

At night the Falls are floodlit with colored lights turning the waterfall into a giant rainbow, a dazzling sight for a 12-year old. "If you think this is great, Jeanne," Don says, "wait 'til you hear about the surprise I have in store for us." While we were showering, Don had bought tickets to see *The Ten Commandments*, the film that everyone was dying to see. It was being shown on Broadway but had not yet reached the neighborhood theaters. "Wait till my brother hears about this," Harry says grinning.

Chapel is dull without a contest in progress. A regular stream of preachers, including Salvation Army officers and Baptist ministers, come to teach us about the 'living word', the Bible. Hymn singing takes up a lot of time and we can ask for favorites. If the preacher doesn't have a wife who plays the piano, we sing without music.

Once a visiting lady preacher/piano player from northern Canada came and stayed at the Home for a while. She had once played honky-tonk piano for a living and we liked her version of the hymns. She pounded the keys so enthusiastically that it could have been three people playing. She played to a private tempo, her hands a blur as they flew with abandon over the keyboard. "Gimme that ol' time religion, *Gimme that ol' time religion, Gimme that ol' time religion, It's good enough for me.*" Her speed was so amazing that we found it hard to keep up with her. The harder her hands hit the keys, the higher her bottom lifted off the piano stool. She finished every song with a flourish, using her thumbs to give us a run of the keys, even at the end of the sad hymns. We crowded around her after chapel and she told us about her hometown in Canada where she was the only piano player available and always in demand. Winters were long and she entertained for ten months out of the year.

"I've played so darned much my fingers are fair worn down. Why the tips are so callused I've completely lost my fingerprints," she confessed one evening, splaying out the long fingers of her right hand like an octopus. Some of the older boys thought it was extremely interesting, reckoning that crime might pay with no fingerprints to prove guilt, and they began to speculate about taking up the piano.

On the nights that we don't have a preacher we spend Chapel time rehearsing for the show we put on for the governing board. We take part in an annual Salvation Army concert. Many of the kids are in the band and play trumpet, coronet, trombone and the tuba. Andy, Geraldine and I are in the choir, along with another forty or so kids. It is organized by the director's wife and we learn songs from *Oklahoma!* and *The Sound of Music*. In addition to this we are learning Norwegian folks songs and dances which we hate. Not a single one of us is Norwegian and never shall be. The colored girls aren't very convincing as Norwegians even though they, like the rest of us, are fitted out in genuine Norwegian national costumes. It takes place in an enormous concert hall that is packed right to the back seats. We try hard and perform well because we know that a portion of the money we help to raise is going to come back to us in the Home. It will go towards supplying us with sports equipment like basketballs, a new volleyball net, ping pong bats and balls and baseball mitts.

The pressure of Religion is off during concert season, but we are still expected to go to church and Sunday school on Sundays. We were bussed to the Baptist Temple in another part of Brooklyn, about 45 minutes' drive away. A yellow school bus picked us up just after 8 a.m. on Sunday mornings. I have trouble riding in the front of a car for half an hour without getting carsick, and it took only a couple of minutes at the back of the bouncing bus for me to shout "I'm gonna be sick!" The driver asked if I could be allowed to stay home after I made several messes on his bus.

The bussing stopped and we walk to the local Baptist church on our own. The Church of Galilee, a fifteen blocks' walk away, is not at all like the tall, brick-built Temple. The Temple had red velvet upholstered seats like they have in movie theaters and its crenellated exterior drew attention to itself from far away. This building has a plain and simple message - to come together and worship in its serene surroundings. So it sits low down on the ground and it's undecorated, plain exterior is painted pure white. The pale blue carpeted interior has matching pale blue velvet fabric on the seats. Painted across the entire front wall is a watery scene. It shows an empty, grassy bank beside the Sea of Galilee. There are no people in it. It must be the calm time, the time either before or after the faithful have been dunked in one by one during their baptism by immersion.

I am living in the calm time. My life has been like the river above Niagara Falls. It flowed innocently along until the bottom suddenly fell out from under me. I bobbed up and down in the turmoil, swallowing a lot, but keeping afloat. Now that the churning has ceased, I glide with the current into another stream, at a different level. With Religion sustaining me as the river banks support and guide the water, I, too, can follow my destiny.

Chapter Twenty-Three
Camp Joy

"What do you think camp is like?" Andy asks as we sit on the swings two days before departure. We feel low now that school is out and summer has officially begun. It means more changes for us. We've gotten used to our new school and the Home and even learned the names of most of the kids that live here. "Someone said that the boys have got to have their heads shaved because we'll be in camp for nine weeks."

"We'll have to see," is all I can think of to say.

The yellow school bus that will take us to upstate New York zooms up the hill at 7 a.m. parking at an angle in the courtyard. Everyone twelve years old and under piles in with raggedy suitcases bursting with a whole summer's worth of pyjamas, shorts, bathing suits and underwear. The older kids wave us off from the dormitory windows. They will leave for Camp Jubilee tomorrow and are still packing, sitting on their suitcase lids in the hope of making room for yet another pair of pedal pushers. From what I hear, they have horse riding, more freedom and less religion to look forward to than we do. The bus door slams shut and as the driver pulls away, we quickly lose sight of the imposing institution on the hill I've called home for the past three months. We're headed north, to the Catskills, and to Camp Joy.

We pass a few kids gathering to play stickball in the street. They plan to make the most of empty, early-morning sidewalks and traffic-free streets while the rest of Brooklyn sleeps. I have an urge to jump out and join them, not wanting to face another new place and more upheaval. But my hands continue to grip the seat in front of me. I press my nose against the window, eyes glued to the city streaking by, and the bus bounces over potholes. The mosaic of washing lines strung between tenement buildings in Harlem yields to lone houses in flower-filled yards. When these thin out, the countryside opens up and signs of habitation fall away.

I love the wide open spaces, but miss the embrace of the city where I feel secure among the stores and shoppers, subway stations, and buses. The flat landscape of Kings County concedes to rolling hills with mountains behind. Everything is green.

It will take nearly five hours to reach Camp Joy, the farthest I have ever been from home. At the back of the bus a bunch of noisy, excited boys, Andy among them, have forgotten their 'baldy' haircuts and have begun to enjoy the trip. Once we leave the highway, the bus winds along a dirt road, hugging the side of the mountains. Deep in the woods the cool air cradles bird songs and chirping crickets welcome us. My hankering for the city fades when the bus's engines slow and the driver pulls to a stop at the camp.

We are separated into groups of boys and girls according to age and are assigned cabins. I'm in the group called 'Sparrows'. Our wooden cabin holds ten bunk beds and I notice right away that its three windows have screens instead of glass. Our counselor, Beth, has a room of her own near the entrance door. We don't have any toilets in the cabins. They are in a separate building up the hill under the trees and are shared by everyone. Our cabins form part of a quadrangle and face a central flagpole. The dining hall, the largest building in camp, takes up one whole side of the quadrangle. The Chapel is a short walk from the cabins.

Beth gives us all sheets and assigns us beds, which we hurriedly make, before our first meeting on the lawn outside the cabin. As she talks, I notice that she holds a clipboard in her right hand and her left hand dangles at her side. When she greeted us I noticed her freckled face framed by short, curly brown hair that wiggled when she spoke. I wondered how long she'd been at Camp Joy because the smooth legs below her red shorts were already tanned the color of toast. Now I can't take my eyes off her lifeless hand. It looks babyish and unused. The fingernails splay out like claws that cannot grip. She gives instructions about curfews, dining hall manners, Chapel times, roll call, reverie, sports, swimming and rainy day routines. Winding up her talk she says, "I know that some of you are wondering about my hand." I blush because I know she is talking about me. "Well, I have been unlucky. I've had polio."

Beth has courage. She also has a knack of swinging her body back and forth so that the affected arm lifts high enough to be grasped by her right hand. She can fold her arms, or put her left arm in her pocket and stand naturally.

157

Beth is our leader in all things. "Come on, Sparrows. We're going to the pond," she says after breakfast, and takes us down a dark path to a sun-splashed opening in the trees. The pond is more like a lake. Dragonflies and frogs swim on top, or laze on lily pads in the shade. I've never been so close to a frog before and now I'm swimming beside one. There is mud between my toes.

Kids jump off the jetty - "Geronimo!" If I could swim, my feet wouldn't have to touch the slimy bottom. But, during swimming lessons when the instructor shouts, "Get your face down in the water," I begin to think more kindly about the mud.

I'm good at archery, bee-bee guns, leather crafts, and memorizing things like Bible verses, hymns and camp songs. I would pass up five-mile hikes and sleeping overnight on the ground, if I could. I especially don't like hearing scary stories around a campfire. During the night stones under my sleeping bag and ghosts compete to keep me awake.

There's danger everywhere. We study charts about poison ivy, poison sumac, and poison oak. We have to know how to identify their leaves. If not, we're likely to step into a patch and have an itchy rash for the rest of the summer. During a hike in the woods, Andy sat on an old log that unfortunately had a beehive inside it. He was in the infirmary for a week and had twenty stings removed from his butt. And there are skunks! Those cute and cuddly black and white animals that waddle aimlessly in the woods can spray you with a smell so bad that you can never wear your clothes again. You either have to burn them or bury them. How can people say it isn't safe in the city?

The heart of Camp Joy is the Chapel. We have a service and a pep talk in the morning before activities and another, longer service, in the evenings after supper. These are led by the camp director who is also our religious leader. We form two long lines outside - boys in one, girls in the other. When we are ready and standing stiff at attention, a rickety upright piano at the front of the hall coughs into life and we march into Chapel singing Camp Joy's theme song, *Onward Christian Soldiers*:

> *Onward Christian soldiers,*
> *Marching as to war,*
> *With the cross of Jesus,*

We keep time along the dusty path and take our places among the rows of wooden benches until the Chapel is full. After the service, which is mainly hymn singing, Bible readings and a sermon, we slither into the darkness like two long snakes half-singing, half-yawning *Onward Christian Soldiers* towards our cabins.

Before we go to sleep, Beth leads us in devotions. This usually begins with her reading a passage from the Bible. Then we have a chance to talk over problems or events of the day. We end with a prayer. On one occasion, Beth handed out pamphlets about the facts of life and we read it over together. What I heard surprised me, but when someone mentioned it the next day, I pretended I knew about it all along.

My headaches, which are never very far away, return early one morning. "Your pulse is racing," Beth says looking at her watch and holding my wrist with her good hand. You'd better go back to bed." She drapes a wet washcloth on my forehead and tucks my sheet tight around me as I drift back to sleep. When I wake up later, everyone has already gotten dressed and gone out to their activities. I hear a scuffling noise on the windowsill. I get up to see what it is and a mouse has given birth to four squirming, pink and hairless babies that are suckling her.

Since I've been to camp, I've learned not to be afraid of animals, I know where babies come from and I have begun to notice boys.

When we got off the bus together, Geraldine and I were thrilled to be in the same cabin and decided to share a bunk bed. We have also paired up as 'buddies' meaning we are supposed to stick together and be responsible for one another. But, ever since we arrived, she has spent a lot of her time in the toilets. The toilets are in an unsupervised area because our counselors are with us most of the time. Geraldine meets her boyfriend behind the toilets. "Get yourself a boyfriend so we can go together," she says to me when I complain of being left alone. "Tony's sort of interested in you, if you could fix yourself up." She knows so much more about boys than I do even though she's a couple of months younger than I am.

Taking her advice to heart, I get out my red, short-sleeved sweater with the white trim on the collar that I am sure will improve my appearance. There's only one problem. It is a little tight on me and won't look right if I don't wear a bra. I'm almost twelve and dying to own a bra. The housemother wouldn't let me have one to take to camp, because she said I'll need one soon enough, and there was no need to rush into things, so I borrowed someone else's from the laundry room. I hunted frantically in a stack of unsorted underwear for a Maidenform bra. I had seen one of the older girls wearing one and admired it from a distance. I liked the way the even stitches spiraled around the padded cups that came to a sharp point in the center. But I only managed to untangle a tatty, worn-out relic of a bra before hearing the housemother's footsteps approach. I haven't tried it on yet.

I need to work out how to put it on before taking off my undershirt. Slipping my arms through the straps, I try to fasten it at the back, but the ends won't meet. The hooks and eyes won't come together. *You've got to be a contortionist to get into this thing.* I slip it off, wrap it around my waist and fasten it at the front. *Success.* I turn it around so that the cups are at the front and yank it up. Crooking each arm in turn I slip them through the strap and settle the bra over my chest. It's tight around the back. *I must remember not to take any deep breaths.*

I'm sweating by now and look down before I put the sweater on. My breasts don't fill the cups, so I stuff a tissue down each one to smooth out the wrinkles. My arms above my head, I am about to pull the sweater down over my face when the bra snaps - the hooks have ripped off. *What do I do now?* My hands are already trembling when I remove the safety pin from my pyjama bottoms, where I'd lost a button, and pin the ends of the bra together. I'm sweating like mad now and begin to think that the red sweater is no longer worth the trouble, but it's late, so I press on, dressing quickly, not bothering to examine myself in the mirror before I leave.

Boys buzz around like flies whenever Geraldine is around. I'm excited to be included in her circle. A few minutes after I turn up, a girl in the group whispers to her friend, loud enough for me to hear, "Jeanne's wearing a bra!" My cheeks heat up but I pretend I haven't heard and lean towards Tony who is telling a joke. I laugh like everyone else when he finishes, but still feel uncomfortable about wearing the bra. Maybe I'd better go before Tony notices it. I ought to sneak away but the chat continues. Tony is telling us how he made an apple-pie bed for a new arrival and we all laugh. He looks at me with sparkling eyes, flashes his white teeth. I'm in heaven. Then something awful happens. The safety pin holding the bra together breaks open and releases the two rounded contours that the bra had created. I look down at what looks like a crumpled up newspaper underneath my sweater.

I break my own record running across the quadrangle, flying for cover in the woods. When I stop to catch my breath, I bend over to retch but only the dry heaves oblige. Resting on a sawn-off tree trunk, I stare for a long time into a forest of fluttering leaves. It is so calm in the woods. Bugs and spiders, small animals and birds are busy as usual so only I notice the piano playing *Onward Christian Soldiers* in the distance, marking the start of evening Chapel.

I slip to the ground and use the tree stump as a backrest. A shaft of sunlight pierces through the trees and stabs the ground in front of me. The sunbeam looks strong enough to step on. I'd like to do that. I'd like to step on it, walk up and disappear right up into the sky.

I can hear them singing *Jesus, He Wants Me For a Sunbeam* in the Chapel. Sitting here beside a real sunbeam, I think someone is sending me a message. It almost makes me want to pray. Not like we do in Chapel when the preacher says, "Let us pray", and sends up a plea from all earth's sinners below. I know I can talk to someone who is listening.

Afterwards, I dust off my knees, remove the bra that sags below my breasts, and throw it into the undergrowth. Making my way towards the Chapel, the opening words to the final hymn reach me, loud and clear, in the still evening air:

> *What a friend we have in Jesus,*
> *All our sins and griefs to bear.*
> *What a privilege to carry,*
> *Everything to God in prayer.*

Chapter Twenty-Four
Cocoa And Cookies

From the moment I heard about the SP, or special classes, I set my heart on winning a place. So when my sixth grade teacher wanted a show of hands from those who would like to take the test for the SP classes in junior high school, mine shoots up with the rest. Anyone who passes the test, enters seventh grade in an accelerated class and goes from there straight into ninth grade, finishing school a year ahead of everyone else.

My fifth grade teacher had been very encouraging, and so was my sixth grade teacher, so I was surprised when I approached her desk that she motioned to me to stay behind. As soon as the door clicks shut behind the others, she turns to me. "I don't think you understand, Jeanne. Those children are trying out for the SP classes. Do you know what that means?" I nod, gaining control of a lump rising to my throat. "I see. You are one of the 'Home' children, aren't you?" I blink assent. "I don't think there is any need for you to apply for the SP class. Run along and finish your apron. There's a good girl."

We've been working on our aprons in preparation for next year when we will have domestic science. Aprons and matching caps are required in this class and all sixth-grade girls are busily sewing them by hand, preparing for the future. I go back to the cherry red bias binding I had been stitching with so much pleasure a few moments ago, but it twists and tangles between my fumbling fingers. My disappointment is bitter and I sigh at the thought of another dream dashed. I think I could have accepted it if I would have failed, but cannot understand why I have been denied the chance to try for it.

When I joined P.S. 185, in the middle of the fifth grade, the girls in my class had already paired off. Not having a special friend to spend time with gave me the chance to catch up with the others. The teacher said I was making great strides. I began to feel good about myself. The harder I worked, the more praise I got. I decided that this was where I would try to excel. School is neutral territory for me. I don't think about my family or the Home here. All I need to do is show up, behave, do my homework, and get good grades. It's simple, and that's what I like about it.

Continuing to stitch the binding on my apron, I hide the raw edges beneath the bias tape tucking them in along with my frustrations. As I look around the room at my remaining classmates, I wonder if I am among those content to take a back seat for the rest of their lives. I don't want to be counted among them. If I can't break the mold here, there must be something else I can try for that will guarantee the challenges I crave.

Two weeks later I get the chance during the try-outs for the Glee Club at McKinley Junior High School where I will be attending. I scramble with the others in the rush to the music room. The audition takes place over lunch hour so my teacher doesn't stop me from going. Each pupil has to sing *ahh* to the scales that the music teacher plays on the piano, reaching some very high notes and some very low ones – and this in front of all the others. When it's my turn, I am so nervous I hear only the piano, not my voice. Convinced that I've flubbed it, I turn to go, but the teacher calls me back. "Don't you want this letter for your parents saying that you're in the school choir?" I turn back to take the letter, surprised at the news. "You're a first soprano."

My apron is nearly finished. While sewing, I hum to myself. Ever since I became a Glee Club member, I've been more aware of my voice. I have done a lot of singing lately. Throughout summer camp we sang hymns in the chapel, folk songs around the campfire, and patriotic songs on the quadrangle during flag raising and lowering. We are always learning new hymns in the Home chapel in the evenings and popular show songs for our concerts with the Salvation Army. The last stitch done, I press the apron and cap, putting them away until September when, I am sure, I will find my chance to shine.

After chores on Saturday mornings, there isn't a lot to do in the Home for the rest of the weekend. Since most of the kids leave to go home with relatives, activities aren't planned by the staff for the few stragglers left behind. If it's too cold or wet to go outside, I mooch around the playroom for something to do. I usually wind up alone and stretched out on the hard bench by the window all day with my nose stuck in a book.

On one such Saturday morning, Mr. Persiko, the director, calls me to his office. "Jeanne," he says, after I have knocked and entered, "I want you to meet Mr. and Mrs. de Rosa." He beams a smile at the couple seated in front of his desk. "This is John and Rose." They look up at me. I look back, not sure what this is leading up to. "They'd like you to go home with them on the weekends. Would you like that?"

"Yes." I smile now, with confidence, thinking back to my new dress occasion in the temporary shelter when spending time with 'real' people, not directors or houseparents, meant special treats, personal attention and new clothes. "Can my brother, Andy, come too?"

"Not this time. Let's see how it works out first. Why don't you pack your toothbrush and pajamas and come back when you are ready." I fly upstairs to the empty dormitories and pull out a tattered overnight case from a pile in the communal closet. I throw in a change of clothes, some underwear and a couple of books, as well.

Rose de Rosa and her husband, John, a policeman, live in a duplex. Their big parlor is at the front, next to it is a separate dining room that leads to a bright, yellow kitchen. The two large bedrooms and bathroom are at the back. Rose is a tall, slender woman with light brown hair. She is gentle and kind and smiles more than she frowns, which is hardly ever. John is big. Tall and wide, and quiet but jolly at the same time. They have no children and spoil me, often giving me things I don't even ask for. While we watch television in the evening, Rose makes us ice-cream sundaes, even though it seems like we have been eating all day. I eat everything offered in case she thinks I don't like it. John laughs, patting his stomach when she hands him the ice cream saying he doesn't need it, but he enjoys it anyhow.

All weekend I am careful to be on my best behavior, speaking only when spoken to, washing my hands after I go to the bathroom, straightening out the towel before I turn out the lights, going to bed on time at night, and making my bed as soon as I get up.

Being spoiled is a novelty. Sometimes I don't know how to handle it, but I luxuriate in it anyway, every weekend until the sixth grade is over and I am packed off to Camp Jubilee at the end of June. When I return in September, my weekends at the de Rosa's are resumed. In my happiness to be with them I spill out to Rose and John my stories about summer camp and the new school. They hear about Mr. Fox, my English teacher who makes us memorize poetry and who reads aloud to us from the tales of Edgar Allen Poe. "He invited me and another boy from the Home to his house for supper one night. We met his wife who made us spaghetti. Afterwards, we listened to a recording of "The Raven" on his record player."

Rose and John don't talk much about themselves, and they don't mention the Home either. It is almost as though none of us has had a past before we met. They ask me about the Glee Club's Christmas concert. "We have a whole morning's practice once a week. There are altos, tenors, bass', sopranos, and first sopranos. All the parts practice separately and it sounds wonderful when we sing them all together. We are already making costumes to wear for the concert!"

Other classes are not so wonderful. We are three weeks into domestic science but so far we haven't even worn our aprons. We are still learning theory, all about keeping the place clean, organizing our recipes, and cleaning up afterwards. I don't think we're ever going to touch the pots and pans. Then, finally, the teacher tells us that next week we're making cocoa.

John picks me up as usual at the Home one Saturday morning, dropping me off at the front door where Rose is waiting. He zooms off quickly to work, doing the odd Saturday shifts as a policeman. Inside, the kitchen is brimming with the smell of freshly-baked cookies. Rose has already filled several tin boxes of Danish-style butter cookies and more are about to come out of the oven.

"You got here just in time. Put on an apron and get these onto the cooling trays," Rose says handing me an oven mitt with one hand and a tray of steaming cookies with the other.

"What are they all for?" I ask as I slip my head through the loop of the full apron.

"Christmas presents for friends. It is something I can do in advance. I'll seal the lids with scotch tape and they'll stay fresh for months." Later on I transfer dozens of cookies from the cooling trays to more tins, being careful not to break or drop any.

All the while I have been watching Rose fill a bag with cookie dough and squeeze the shapes onto the trays. "Pop them in the oven as soon as there's a space," she says over her shoulder and starts on the next tray. We work side-by-side until Rose arches her back and says, "Whew, you wouldn't think making two hundred cookies was such hard work!" She hands me the bag. "Why don't you take over?"

There is nothing like a cold glass of milk to wash down half a dozen butter cookies still warm from the oven. "Rose?" I ask as I wipe the crumbs off my lips with the back of my hand. "Could you come to the Home and teach the other kids how to make cookies?"

"We'll have to arrange it with the director, but I don't mind."

On Sunday, when I take back a box of cookies and hand them out to the girls in the dorm, they disappear in a matter of minutes. My hunch was right. Everyone wants to learn how to make cookies.

The director gives us permission to set up baking lessons after school on Tuesdays from 3.30 to 5.30 p.m. in the downstairs kitchen off the dining hall so long as we can get hold of the essentials we need. We scavenge trays and spatulas from Rose's kitchen and hijack bowls and spoons from the Home's main kitchen.

I am making good use of my hand-made apron now. Rose brings in bags of flour, butter and sugar and we learn how to prepare dough mixtures. Soon we are rolling, cutting and squeezing them into shapes.

On Thursday morning we are at the ready beside our stoves in ten tiny 'kitchens' that make up the Domestic Science room. We have already learned that nothing happens fast in this class. We are not going to make 'instant' cocoa. We are going to make cocoa from scratch; that is, putting cocoa powder, water, milk and sugar into a pot, stirring the brown liquid with a wooden spoon, ensuring that no lumps form, until the swirls and eddies thicken as it begins to boil. I inhale deeply into the puffs of aromatic steam that reach my nostrils when it is mine turn to stir the pot. Making cocoa is the best thing I have ever done.

The teacher oversees our every move, maneuvering beside, behind and between us, marking our progress in her book, ticking off our hygiene, methods and finished results with her sharpened pencil. There are four of us around each stove preparing the cocoa in the same pot. When we finally sit down at the table to sip our hot drink, we enjoy it with the four flat cookies that she has provided to go with it.

By the time the bell rings for Gym, our last class before lunch, everything is washed and put away and the room looks like we have never been there. As we file out into the corridor, she hands us the recipe for next week's class on "How to Boil an Egg". Ingredients: one egg.

It has been a hot September. We are already sweating from the steamy cocoa and the rush to clean up, before we wriggle into our gym suits. There must be a hundred girls in the gym when we arrive. "You are late," the Gym teacher says. "Where have you come from?"

"Sorry. Domestic Science."

"Oh? What have you been cooking?"

"Cocoa."

"Cocoa? Nothing else?"

"We had a cookie with it."

"Okay. Hop to it. I'll give you an extra minute to get changed." She claps her hands and shouts above the din, "Girls, girls, girls!"

There is no place to stand at the back by the time we're ready.

"Come, come you late-comers. Up here. You'll fall into the benches if you go any further back. Don't worry, I won't bite your heads off." She shouts, "ATTEN...TION!"

I'm at a disadvantage in the front row, having to look sideways at the others to make sure of what to do. She has decided to perform the first inspection of which she warned us during previous classes. She starts with the first row on the left. I breathe a sigh of relief until I notice that almost everyone has a new, stiff, apple-green gym suit and sparkling white sneakers. Mine are hand-me-downs from the Home. They are only faintly green with sagging elastic around the legs, and the button on the belt dangles dangerously, while the white sneakers' toes are scuffed to gray.

"Don't you know, Missy, that you've got to IRON and WASH your gym suit before you come here?" I hear this said behind me. Sweat trickles down my back From the corner of my eye I catch a glimpse of the teacher. Her snow-white hair is coifed in waves at the front. The rest of it is done up in a bun resembling a small toilet-bowl on the top of her head. She moves down the lines, standing right in front of me. Her silver-rimmed eyeglasses glint caustically as they catch the sun from slits of windows above the lockers that line the room as her eyes peruse the green gym suits and sneakers. She wears an immaculate white blouse with lace trim running down the front and along the collar and cuffs. Like a skin fitting a sausage, her gray tweed skirt surrounds a pair of solid hips. It stops just below the kneecap. Heavy denier stockings cover the bulging calves that end in plump ankles. Stout, 'old lady' shoes support her overflowing feet.

I am suddenly alert, reminded out loud, about my loose button. Her raised eyebrows and pointing finger incriminate my dirty footwear. She signals the end of her inspection, which covered less than half the girls, with the flourish of a hand, and a promise to start at the other end of the gym next time.

"Let's get moving, girls." She puts on a record of a marching band from the beginning of the century and starts us off in an exercise routine. Without missing a beat her arms are above her head, then she's bending at the middle. And, while not quite reaching her kneecaps, shouts, "Down. Right down, girls. Touch the floor with your palms. That's it. Now, bend your knees up to your chests. Up, one, up, two." Her breath is already *chooing* like a locomotive.

I am too close to the front to get a giggling fit, but I can't help it. She is such an unlikely person to teach gym. Her iron clad undergarments constrict every movement and the friction, the *szizz, szizz, szizz* of her heavy nylon stockings rubbing together as her legs work up and down, might, I believe, set the room on fire.

She issues orders in a voice that demands compliance and respect.

"Everyone on the floor. Face down, arms supporting. Right leg, UP. Left leg, UP." She claps her hands in time to the music. "Come on you girls from domestic science," she says to us in the front row. "Get those legs up high. What's the matter, too much cocoa and cookies?"

Chapter Twenty-Five
42nd Street

"Stick close to your partners when we get out of the train. I don't want anyone getting lost in that rush-hour crowd," Mr. Lockwood, the boys' housefather, warns all twenty of us on the platform of the BMT line at Fourth Avenue. Since parking would be a problem in New York City, we're taking the subway to 42nd Street, which is only a couple of blocks from our destination.

We file out of the train at Times Square in two's like ex-inmates of Noah's Ark, and mount the stairs behind Mr. Lockwood. The station is packed with travelers and the crowds need to part to make room for us to pass by as a group. Despite people spilling around us, criss-crossing one another's paths and avoiding each other with the dexterity of a marching band, we manage to keep together. At this hour business people converge with pleasure seekers. We emerge from the subway into honking traffic onto a street thick with tourists, office secretaries, men in sharkskin suits and red-lipped women dressed for a night out. The last time I had seen so many people was about the same time last year when I went to my first Billy Graham rally at Madison Square Garden.

"Stay with your partners and don't dawdle," Mr. Lockwood pleads, sounding nervous. "We need to get to Madison Square Garden early to ensure a good seat." Thousands of followers flock to New York City to hear Billy Graham preach. As with Jesus on the Mount of Olives, they come to hear the Word of God.

"Can we stop for a packet of Life Savers at the drug store on the corner, please, Mr. Lockwood?" my partner, Valerie, asks.

"All right, but make it quick. The rest of us will wait here on the corner. Go with your partners. I can't keep counting heads." We rush to the counter and select our candy. I'm the last one in line to pay.

"Hey, wait for me," I shout to the others, handing over my money to the girl at the checkout.

A few seconds later I'm on the sidewalk, but they're gone. I'm on a street thronging with people and I don't recognize a single one of them. I can't just stand here. Which direction should I go? I choose right. Lurching into the crowd I slither between strolling couples, push

169

past doddering old men, all the while keeping pace with my speeding heartbeat. But I don't see them. I run back to the drug store thinking they may have come back for me. I ask the checkout girl if anyone was looking for a lost girl, but she shakes her head. I fly off in the other direction, panic keeping my legs moving under me.

I stop a friendly-looking person and ask the time. It's already 7.30 p.m. and getting dark. The rally is about to start. Even if I find Madison Square Garden, how would I find them among the crowds? What should I do? I can't go back to the Home. I don't have the subway fare; besides, I don't know how to get back. *Find a policeman* a voice in my head tells me. From my vigil outside the drug store there is no policeman in sight. I head towards the bright lights.

People stare at me as I walk alone on Broadway. It is quieter now. The swarms of workers have filtered away to their warm suppers and cozy parlors. Night birds settle in for the evening around Times Square. As I pass by dark alleyways between the brightly-lit theaters, stray cats zigzag in search of supper among overflowing garbage cans. Straight ahead taxi headlamps blind me. On the buildings photographs of naked women jump out at me from sex shop windows. A man crooks his finger in my direction and beckons me with a lurid smile. "See Sexy Suzy Swivel" reads the sign above his head as wheezy music slips past the flashing lights around the door and flows onto the sidewalk. I scurry past, keeping my eyes averted and quickening my pace until I reach the next corner. I tug at my skirt, conscious for the first time of its short length exposing too much of my legs in new, sheer nylon stockings.

I need to find a policeman before it gets completely dark. There's one on the corner diagonally opposite! *Be quick, he's moving away.* I leap across the wide avenue, and dance from one foot to the other as I wait for the traffic lights to change. I chase him half way down the block before I am able to throw myself in his path. "Whoa. What's up, Miss?" I'm so glad to see his friendly face I start to cry. I blubber on 42nd Street with nothing but the back of my hand to wipe my nose. "Whoa. Steady now," he says soothing me as you would a colt on the run. "What's the matter?"

I blurt out my story as we walk a block together, crossing at the end to a small 'island' in the middle of the street. He tells me he's going off duty as we enter a narrow, glassed-in cubicle, but another policeman will help me out. At one end is a tiny, sealed-off office where the other policeman sits. He tells me to wait on the bench. "Everything's under control," he says, returning a few minutes later. "Just wait here. Good luck," he adds and leaves. I open up my Life Savers and suck on a yellow, pineapple-flavored circle until it disappears to nothing. Traffic noise is muffled in my glass cage, but I have a wide view of the street and hundreds of colorful signs light up the night. Opposite me is an enormous advertisement for Camel cigarettes. It shows a man smoking a cigarette and giant smoke rings billow from a hole in his mouth. Oooo, Oooo, Oooo.

A young man in a chef's hat in a nearby Italian restaurant performs pizza acrobatics in the window as he twirls a lump of dough in his hands, throwing it up and down and all around until it stretches into a flat 'pizza pie' shape. He attracts a crowd and a few people enter the restaurant as he spreads the tomato sauce over the top. My mouth waters.

The beep of a taxi's horn close by wakes me up. The street swirls with people leaving theaters and movie houses. What time is it? What are the others doing? They must miss me by now. Do they think I have been kidnapped? Where's the policeman? I knock on the door, but there's no answer. *Don't panic, wait. That's what he said. Wait.*

I suck my way through the packet of Life Savers - lime, lemon, orange, and finally, cherry. The director is going to kill me. He'll say I'm nothing but a troublemaker and this time he'll be right. What'll Andy think when he finds out I never got to Madison Square Garden?

During the rally I attended last year, Billy Graham, exhausted from his preaching and Bible reading, said in a low voice to the audience, "Dear people," (pause), I know that out there among you (pause) are hearts wanting to give themselves up to the Lord. I say, Now is the time to do it. Give your heart to Jesus. Come upon the altar of the Lord and be saved. Count yourselves among those who have seen the Light. Leave your seats and leave behind your old selves. Be renewed in God. Give yourselves to Jesus. Those of you who have already seen the Lord, pray for your brethren who have but to say, 'Yes, I come to thee Lord,' and He will welcome you with open arms."

171

Amazing Grace played softly on the organ. There were more people in this one place than I had seen in my entire life, but I could have heard a pin drop. We held our breath and waited for the miracle to happen. Billy Graham left the platform and went down to the front of the congregation. The choir hummed. Thousands of heads bowed in prayer. One person stood up and made his way down the aisle. Then another and another. I took secretive looks in all directions, my heart skipping a beat each time someone made the commitment. Dozens of penitents took courage and heeded the call. "Ladies and gentlemen," Billy said, "the Lord is working among us in His mysterious way. Come. 'Come all ye who are heavy laden and I will give you rest.' Glory Hallelujah!"

People crowded the front of the platform and Billy put his hand on each head, moving among them swiftly. "Brothers and sisters in the Lord," he appealed to us, "Pray for those who know they are sinners, and want to be cleansed by our Lord's blood, cleansed by Him who sacrificed His life for us. For God so loved the world that He gave His only begotten Son that whosoever believeth in Him shall be saved. John, Chapter Three, Verse sixteen."

To me, it was a miracle; a miracle that if we wanted our sins to be washed away, all we had to do was to really mean it when we asked for it, and mended our ways afterwards. This took care of a lot of things. It cleaned the slate of sins I committed because I had to, like stealing for my sister, as well as the ones I did deliberately, though didn't know any better, because I was too young. That left me with the ones I committed because I wanted to get even with someone, but I realized that was wrong, too.

"My dear, dear people of God among us. I know there are many of you who are too timid, too shy to confess yourselves to our Lord up here. Do not give up hope for the Lord is near. You may silently give your hearts to Jesus and be saved right along with the others. Bow your heads in prayer and open your hearts, ready to receive our Lord."

At that first rally, I counted myself among those too timid to come forward so took the Lord into my heart at my seat. There was no going back. Billy Graham had worked his magic on me and I had my spirit renewed within me.

I have been in this cubicle for a long time. My eyes burn from lack of sleep and from staring at the blinking neon signs. I have been looking at women propped up against the walls of empty theaters and wondering what they could be doing there at this time of night. Cars drive by slowly, stopping occasionally to pick one woman up and drop another off.

Tramps in heavy overcoats, pockets bulging with belongings and bottles, pick through litter bins. I watch, fascinated, as they finish half-eaten burgers and cram cold French fries that they find among the litter into greedy mouths. I am incredulous as one of them rakes through the crumpled paper and debris for cigarette butts, collecting them in a paper cup under the watchful eye of the Camel man whose never-ending smoke-rings disappear into thin air.

Where is Billy Graham now? In bed, probably, happy to have saved so many. I wish he could save me – again.

The door swings open. "Hey, what are you doin' in here, chile?"

"I was lost. The policeman told me to wait here. It's been hours…" I tell my tear-filled story to the Negro cop who has just come on duty.

"Okay. I'll make a couple of calls and see what I can do." As he turns quickly in the confined space, the gun in his holster brushes my arm and I hear a slight creak of leather as the weapon settles into its snug case.

When he comes back he tells me he's taking me to the police station. "It's three o'clock in the morning. You shoulda' been in bed hours ago. You say you live in Brooklyn?"

The night air is cool and the streets are practically deserted. The nearest police station is several blocks away down a side street. I wait inside the entrance, opposite the night watchman who lolls on a chair behind a desk. "What's your name?" he asks me.

"Jeanne."

"How old are you, Jeanne?"

"Twelve."

He nods and hides a yawn behind his hand.

"It looks like you've been forgotten," the policeman who brought me in reports back. He shakes his head. "Them people in the Home didn't like being woke up at this hour. No one even realized you were gone. How about that? The director said he couldn't send anyone for you before morning and we're short-staffed here, too. I'm afraid you'll have to be our guest for a while longer." He settles me onto a nearby bench and turns to the man behind the desk. "Keep an eye on her, Ed. Someone's coming for her after 8 a.m. Gotta run. Bye little girl."

Mr. Lockwood arrives for me at 8.30 a.m. His hair is not its usual neat self and makes him look as though he's been dragged out of bed feet first. He drove up in the van with "Kallman Home for Children" emblazoned on the sides. Everybody hates being seen in it because it advertises where we come from. This time I don't mind.

Mr. Lockwood is a gentleman. He opens the door on my side of the van and helps me to get in. We all know that he's leaving his job at the Home after Christmas. He doesn't get on with Mr. Scott, our new director. Everybody agrees that we're going to miss him. He's the only one who cares about us.

"I don't know what's the matter with that Valerie," he says to me on the way home. "She's such a dunderhead! She should've told me you weren't there. She was your partner for Heaven's sakes! Are you all right?"

I nod and ask him about the rally. "Was it good?"

"Terrific! He is the most inspiring preacher in the whole world. So many people were saved. You wouldn't believe it."

Chapter Twenty-Six
Gleaming Tiles

We spend more time in the bathrooms than we should because we are teenagers. We have pimples to pick, eyebrows to pluck, bras, pants and nylons to wash out. But we're on a schedule, twenty minutes maximum in the mornings, half an hour at night. "Come on, girls. Chop, chop! Make room for others," Mrs. Sackella, the senior housemother who took over after Binnie retired, commands with the clap of her hands.

Sixty girls of all ages converge on two showers, two bathtubs, eight sinks and six toilets, two of which usually don't work. The house bell rings at 6 am and we shoot out of our beds like rockets - not because we love getting up, but because we have half an hour to get dressed, washed and make our beds.

Everything in the bathrooms is white - the sinks, the bathtubs, the tiles, the floor. Even the towels. When sunlight falls through the skylights above the wash basins, all that whiteness dazzles our sleepy eyes. Four sinks on each side back onto one another with long mirrors above them on the tiled, separating walls. "Hey!" Beverly shouts at a couple of smaller girls. "Get outta there. Them sinks are for us seniors!" Beverly is a big girl, and this morning her face is a mass of newly hatched pimples so she is angry, aggressive. The sinks towards the back give a bit of privacy and the older girls strip to their bras to wash.

The rule is: Washing only, in the morning. Showers and baths, at night. There is no true privacy anywhere, least of all in the bathtubs, unless we wait until everyone else is finished. But then we risk 'lights out!' and our bath time all together. There is no real chance to examine budding breasts or sprouting pubic hair in the bathroom where girls come and go as they please. Everybody else knows what we look like better than we do ourselves. Sometimes steam from the showers mercifully fogs the air long enough to lie back and relax in the tub with a washcloth over our faces, the only way to convey modesty.

I have my first cigarette in the bathroom. Geraldine, already a hardened smoker by the age of twelve, takes me into the showers. She turns on the hot faucets to full power and as the steam gathers volume, she slips a cigarette out of a squashed packet that she keeps in her bathrobe pocket. Striking the match many times before it ignites, she lights up. I watch as she pulls at the limp cigarette between tight lips. The tip glows red and alive. She lets out the smoke in a slow stream, then hands it over to me. I imitate her. Mounting steam disguises the smoke as it curls around us. Its aroma vaporizes upwards where it joins residues of soap and shampoo on the tiles and ceiling. I am half way through the blunt cigarette with the name "Camel" written on one edge when the thick steam, with nowhere else to go, swirls heavily around our legs. Geraldine disappears. My knees buckle and I fall towards her, hitting my head on the white ceramic tiles before I black out.

Mrs. Sackella comes to my rescue and so does the wrath of Almighty God. "You'll pay for this. Smoking indeed." For punishment, Geraldine and I are separated. We are not allowed to speak to one another for a week. If we do, percentages will be deducted from the seventy-five cents pocket money we earn weekly from chores. In addition, Geraldine is given the downstairs girls' toilets to clean, which is the most hated job in the Home. I have to scrub out the dorm bathrooms for a month. The second worst job.

I sprinkle the sinks and bathtubs liberally with pine-scented scouring powder and scrub away layers of greasy watermarks, proof of dozens of well-needed baths. Brushing out toilet pans clogged with wads of paper that no one bothers to flush away, I hold my breath to avoid the smell and breath in deeply between each cubicle. I make sure the empty toilet roll holders are full, polish the tiles around the sinks, and mop the floor.

Then I check and tidy the closet where the sanitary napkins and spare toilet paper are kept. I smile inwardly at my little secret. Last week I had my period, but I didn't shout it from the rooftops like everyone else does when she gets her 'friend'. I was worried it might never come.

I want to keep it private for as long as I can. No one but Mrs. Sackella knows. She won't tell anyone. We have to let her know so she won't panic when the Kotex disappears. When I spoke to her about it, I was straight and direct and slipped in that I thought I needed a bra.

She looked me over and declared, "You don't need a bra. You need a couple of Band-Aids!" And sailed away down the corridor.

I stand back and admire my job. Everything gleams. Even the tiles. It's Saturday and Geraldine and I are going to the movies after chores. Our sentence of silence will be over as soon as our jobs are checked and we are released with a half-dollar and a quarter in our possession.

The corridor, dressing rooms, dorms - everywhere is silent. The housemother has left me till last. Everyone has been checked and gone out. When I hear her footsteps pounding their way towards me, I quickly take a towel from a hook and wipe off a droplet in the sink nearest the door, then swipe a smear off the mirror.

She enters the bathroom and stands in front of me. "So. Now it's you." A muscle twitches near her upper lip. Her bosoms rise and fall in time with her breathing. Her corset is too tight again I think, then quickly hope she can't read my thoughts. I stand at attention and watch as she inspects the bathrooms. She is agile for a buxom lady of advancing years. She pushes through the swing doors of the shower room and back out again with such vigor that they have no chance of slapping her in the rear. Her face set, she storms over to the toilets and checks behind and beneath every bowl, straining down on her hands and knees for a better angle. She rises, cheeks flushed, and sails past me to the sinks. Her eyes scan faucets that sparkle. All eight sinks deny her criticism. She is about to give up. Then she remembers, whirls around, pivoting on the soles of her black leather lace-ups. "Ah, ha!" she says running her index finger along the top of the tiles where they meet the wall just above eye level. "Dust! Do it again," she sighs, waving at me the tiny mound of dust her finger scavenged. "Everything. I'm on duty all day. I'll be in my room. Call me when you've finished."

If it weren't for the seventy-five cents I'd skulk off and lay down on my bed, then call her an hour later. But she'll listen for the water, the bucket, the toilet seats banging. She'll cock an ear to the air, sharp to things out of reach. Her beady eye will swivel in her head like an ostrich, seeing everything while her neck remains still.

There's no use rushing. Geraldine will probably go to the movies without me. I don't care. I won't spend any money this week because I've got another secret. I'm saving up for college.

Chapter Twenty-Seven
Birthday Treats

This morning I woke up a teenager, at last. I had been dreaming of owning a crinoline, one full of cascading ruffles that will make my flared skirts stand out and undulate when I walk. It is 1958 and dancing is everything. Music is everything. We hip-hop in the playroom, bebop down the halls and jitterbug to the dining hall. I was asked some time ago what I might like for a birthday present and a crinoline slip was among my many wishes, but I knew better than to get my hopes up.

Mrs. Sackella is waiting for me when I get home from school to give me my birthday present. I take the large box covered in glossy dark blue paper tied with a lighter blue ribbon and thank her. "Happy Birthday, Jeanne," she says and her stern face cracks into an unfamiliar smile. All the girls in the playroom gather around and watch as I run my hands over the shiny paper, and slowly release the ribbon.

"Hurry up, girl," Margie Thomas says, nudging my elbow playfully. "We wanna know what's in there, too." From between the sheets of pleated tissue paper I pull out a full-length crinoline. Pale blue satin ribbon runs through the holes of the eyelet embroidery straps.

"It's gorgeous," Margie croons. "Put it on."

They don't have to wait long to see me in it. My flared skirt billows out so far I can hardly see my feet. "Come on, let's dance," Margie says. She selects a record and snaps it onto the turntable of the portable record player that she carries wherever she goes. *Rock Around the Clock* sends shock waves out to the walls and back. "I'll lead," Margie shouts above the blast. She grabs hold of my hand and slaps her arm around my waist.

Margie is a big girl for her age and it never seems to bother her. She is always happy even though we suspect that she has experienced many awful things. She doesn't talk about her past life in Harlem, but a dark cloud passes in front of her eyes whenever she mentions home. Her only regret in life is that after an attempted ear piercing went wrong, she has a large lump on each ear lobe. She rubs and pulls at the lumps, often wearing large clip-on earrings to hide them. "My kinky hair won't grow fast enough to cover my ears," she whines in front of the mirror, yanking down her hair at the sides then pinching at her ears.

"Leave them alone," I tell her. "From here they look like pearls to me."

Sometimes she asks me to help her straighten her hair. We meet up in the laundry room where we heat up the straightening comb on a gas ring that is usually used to make starch. I apply a special yellow pomade to her hair with my hands, slapping it on thickly and running my fingers through her hair to disperse it evenly before carefully pulling the hot comb through it. It crackles and sizzles, worrying me slightly that I might have gotten the comb too hot, but Margie's hair turns out as smooth and shiny as licorice by the time I've finished.

She is a great dancer, pulling me to her, then pushing me away, and I dance better than usual under her influence. The girls form a circle around us, clapping encouragement whenever I twirl. After all, that's what the crinoline is for. We stop, facing each other for a second to catch our breath. "You got rhythm, girl," Margie gasps and my feet hardly touch the floor until the dance is over.

It is the 30th of November, and we are finishing lunch in the dining hall. In a while we are all going up to New York City to see *Around the World in Eighty Days* in wide angle Cinemascope for the first time. Mr. Scott, the new director who has replaced Mr. Persiko after retirement, comes up behind me. He rests his hands on the top of my chair, leans heavily on it and says to the top of my head, "You've got a visitor waiting for you in the library. Go up as soon as you've finished. And tell your brother, too."

Who else could it be but Dad? It is around that time of the year. I can tell by the way Mr. Scott looks at him that he despises my father. Why not? Who wouldn't? Dad arrives half drunk and offers the director a couple of dollars to 'look after my kids'. With a wink and a nod Dad slips him of a couple of cigars, which the director takes with a smirk. I cringe inwardly, not wanting to show the director how much it upsets me to see Dad do this. I want him to think that this is no fluke, that my Dad is a caring sort of guy who shows up every year with gifts for everyone.

Andy is about as pleased as I am to hear that Dad has arrived, just as we are about to embark on our special outing to the movies, which we will, of course, have to miss. We trudge up the stairs together to meet him. Dad is standing by the library window watching some senior boys shoot a few baskets. They linger in the courtyard wanting to be sure to be the first to hop onto the bus when it arrives. In the distance, a couple of girls are working up a sweat at tetherball. The first thing that strikes me is that Dad doesn't seem as tall as he was. He is stooped over a bit and his hair barely covers his scalp at the front. His clothes look like a bigger man's, though this time, they don't smell of engine oil or of the garage. They bear no traces of gasoline or axle grease probably because he has not been working.

On hearing us approach he looks over and fixes us with the stare of a stranger. We've grown some and he doesn't recognize us. When we say "Hi, Dad", the watery eyes, red-rimmed already, fill up.

"It's my birthday today," Dad announces, smiling. We are not surprised. We have been treated to his annual birthday visit for the last two years. Andy turns twelve in three weeks' time and I've just had my thirteenth birthday, but Dad hasn't given a thought to us.

"So, how's my Jeannie-girl?" he asks, swaying towards me, listing like a rusty old ship. He has already had a few drinks to celebrate his birthday or maybe he gulped down a couple of whiskeys to drum up the courage to pay us a visit. As he nears, bending down to kiss me, my nostrils smart. He reeks of tobacco and an unwashed body. I manage a peck on his cheek, my lips tripping lightly over rough stubble.

"So, how ya' been, Andy-boy?"

"Fine."

There isn't much we have to say to him. Without his help we have begun to carve out a life for ourselves and have accepted the Home as our refuge during the past three years. We have been grateful for three meals a day, clean sheets every second week and if we keep out of trouble, pocket money and occasional outings. Dad no longer features in our lives. We share nothing with him. On top of this, we have learned what true shame is and are disgusted when we see him hand out petty bribes to a man whom we hate and who hates us. Andy and I have talked it over and agree that we can endure his short and infrequent visits, if he leaves us alone for another year. We have no idea what he does or where he lives since the eviction. Phyllis once telephoned us and told us that when Mom is occasionally released from the hospital, she stays with my Aunt Sophie. Mom isn't supposed to see Dad, but she sneaks out with him whenever my aunt and uncle go out and she is left alone. Mom has never come to see us. We can't understand why and think maybe it is because she isn't out for long enough. A couple of days after Mom gets back together with Dad, she gets sick again and needs to be in the mental hospital.

I don't say this to Andy, but I keep telling myself that it's their life. We don't need them any more. We are safe here, from them and from whatever it is that keeps sending Mom back to the hospital.

"Are they treating you good?" Dad asks.

"Yeah," we say together, only I am fighting off a flashback of the same day last year.

Dad was waiting for us in the office when we got home from school. I got there before Andy and waited for him outside the office door in the corridor. I overheard Dad talking to the director and sneaked a peek through a crack in the door. He was making a point and wagging a finger in Mr. Scott's face. The director backed away as Dad advanced. Dad held out two five dollar bills and said, "Look after my kids." Mr. Scott's hand shot out as quick as lightning and he tucked the bills into his pants pocket without looking at them. When he saw me in the doorway, he made a quick getaway.

"He's a nice man. I hope you two are behaving yourselves," Dad warned mildly.

That afternoon he wanted to take us shopping. We were excited and lead him to a string of stores. We peered into windows and pointed out things we liked and had secretly admired for ages, by-passing expensive-looking stores selling fancy things that we knew we'd never be able to afford. We wound up in Woolworth's. Dad led on and we followed him, watching curiously as he cantered along the aisles, sauntered between the counters, pointing and commenting, then moving away. Once he turned to us and winked. He was acting peculiar. We left Woolworth's without buying a thing.

We had to walk fast to keep up with him as he sped along the street in the direction of the Home. When we were nearly there, he stopped and sat down on a low brick wall and emptied out his pockets. Spread out beside him lay a packet of batteries, a pair of pliers, a model car, some hair barrettes, and a key ring. Andy and I looked at each other, too stunned to say anything.

Taking our reluctance for shyness, Dad insisted that we share out the stolen articles then and there. Five minutes after we said goodbye to him his gifts were lining the bottom of the garbage can. We agreed not to mention birthdays or shopping again.

We are hoping this isn't going to happen today and because we can't think of anything to say, I listen as Dad rambles on about cars. I run my hand along the top of the polished oak table, my fingernail tracing the grooves of the grain. I glance around the library, which has become a special place for me. No one ever comes in here. I guess nobody reads books. Mr. Scott was surprised when I asked permission to use the library. He told me to go in whenever I liked, to use it at will. It has been a hideaway for me while everyone else is out playing baseball. I pour over pictures in the National Geographic magazines of natives with bones through their noses, of rivers and jungles in strange lands and of blonde women in folk costumes hugging fat, cherub-like babies with rosy cheeks and yellow ringlets. With the mere turn of a page I can be somewhere else – Japan, Cornwall, Norway, Texas or the Sahara.

"Who reads all this stuff?" Dad asks with the sweep of an arm, breaking my train of thought.

"I've read some," I say, glad to have broken the ice, "all those and those," and point to the Bobsey Twins adventure stories and the Judy Garland mysteries.

"That's a mighty lot for a little girl!"

"Now I'm reading these," I add, and touch the shelf marked 'D' pulling out *A Tale of Two Cities*. "I've got *Great Expectations* upstairs in the dorm. It's a great story about…."

"Yeah, yeah," Dad mutters losing interest quickly.

Andy isn't talking today. He's busy running a small red car up and down the tabletop. "*Brummm, brummmm,*" he utters occasionally.

"I saw Mom," Dad says out of the blue. "She's fine. Says to say hello." Andy's car stops. Together we look up, expecting more, but Mr. Scott's secretary knocks on the door interrupting him.

"I'm sorry to disturb you, but there's someone on the telephone for Jeanne."

Before I have time to guess whom it might be, the receiver is in my hands and I hear Mom's voice spilling down the line. I can't understand what she is saying. It must be a bad connection. She is talking and crying at the same time. Something about Dad and her in the car yesterday. He beat her up, pushed her into the street, and knocked out a couple of teeth. I hear a string of swear words. More crying. She thinks she's pregnant. What can I do to help her?

I listen to this teeth-grinding news and my bones turn to steel. It hasn't taken much to carry me back to the misery of Wyckoff Avenue. She wants my advice. What am I supposed to say? But she doesn't wait for a reply. I am so angry by the time I hang up that the world appears out of focus for a couple of seconds. I can no longer pretend to care about them. I cannot be the obedient child and look after them, make decisions for them. I cannot.

As I head back to the library the nurse stops me. "Do you know where your brother is?" I nod. "Send him along to the infirmary immediately. The doctor is here and needs to treat Andy's verrucas."

Dad and I are alone. My brain has reached boiling point and the bubbles churn around and around. *Say something. Say nothing. Say something. Say nothing.* Dad sighs restlessly by the window. "What's all the commotion out there?" We peer out together, shoulders touching.

"They are lining up to go to the movies. The bus is just arriving."

He turns away, bored already with the routines that make up our lives and looks me up and down, as though he were looking at me for the first time. I am conscious of my height - five-foot-six inches tall – four inches shorter than Dad is. From the corner of my eye, I see his arm move towards me, and before I have a chance to react, his fingers tweak my left breast. "You're getting titties," he laughs.

The *zinging* in my head intensifies. I stiffen and step back. Then the words tumble out brittle, sharp as knives. "Don't you ever touch me again, you hear?" Everything I have ever wanted to say to him rises to the tip of my tongue. "You're disgusting. I hate you. You've ruined my life. If you only knew how your cheap cigars and handouts make it worse for us. Do you think the director gives a damn about you or treats us any better when you've gone? He despises you and laughs at you behind your back! That was Mom on the telephone. She told me how you beat her up."

Dad steps forward to say something, but I put my hand up and stave him off. "Stop! Don't come near me or I'll scream blue murder! Don't bother to come and see us any more. Why should we celebrate your birthday? We have birthdays, too, you know. We're better off without you. Better off on our own. I hate you and never want to see you again. I wish you were dead!"

Andy is standing in the doorway and I push past him to get out. At the end of the corridor I turn before going upstairs. Andy is headed in the other direction for the boys' side, limping badly to one side because of his verruca treatment. His head is down, his shoulders are slumped and my heart bleeds.

Chapter Twenty-Eight
Why Run Away?

We come in all shapes and sizes at The Kallman Home for Children. And we come from diverse backgrounds. Our skin tones range from pale pink to dark brown, our hair textures from corn silk to wire wool, and our names from Rodrigues to Kliarsky. Yet, in the midst of this muddle of similarities and differences, we learn to get along with one another. There are no physically handicapped children among us, but handicaps such as buck teeth, stick-um-out ears, eye-glasses and weight problems run you the risk of being labeled Bugs Bunny, Dumbo, Four Eyes, or like myself, Pear Shape. Even my brother, Andy, who appears normal enough, is re-named Andy Pandy, because of the dark circles perpetually around his eyes, due to the lack of a proper diet in the past.

When a newcomer settles among us, it isn't long before some clever upstart coins a nickname that the boy or girl will have to put up with until they leave the Home for good. This form of bullying is tolerated and rarely gets out of hand. Among us there are unspoken rules of etiquette. None of us is perfect, but we still throw stones, albeit, small ones. After all, nicknames are the handles of our worst fears. No one wants to have large ears, protruding teeth or thick eyeglasses, but most of all, no one wants to be fat, or skinny.

Efforts are made to fatten up the 'skinnies'. The nurse leads the campaign. Every afternoon at 4 o'clock on the dot they line up in the dining hall for milkshakes, which are a combination of carnation milk, sugar, cocoa and a whole egg whipped together. The milkshakes are designed to pump extra calories into the undernourished. They must be consumed under the watchful eye of a houseparent. It is a punishment to the kids who would do anything not to be skinny, except drink those milkshakes, while the 'fatties' wait for them outside the dining hall, salivating at the thought of a thick chocolate shake sliding down someone else's throat.

Things get tense in the Home when a Norwegian girl from our school called Linda Walenska, who is also known as Linda the Whale, comes to live with us. At ten years old, she is probably the fattest girl anyone has ever seen. She has very white skin and pale yellow braids that snake down her back as far as her waist. Linda has no friends. She walks to school alone and reads a book by herself seated on a bench in the playground at lunchtime. Her desk is already too small for her and during lessons, she sits at it with her head down and her eyes concentrating on a speck in front of her. Her China-blue eyes avoid contact with everyone and everything.

Linda was living with her grandmother until the old lady got sick and had to be sent away. Nobody knew this until Linda arrived in our dormitory one Saturday morning with a suitcase in each hand. You could have cut the hush of the fifteen of us all talking at once with a knife. Everybody knew about Linda the Whale. Even the kids who were already in junior high and high school. She was a legend.

I can tell that Linda's size disgusts people. But I can't help thinking to myself that we could all be fat like Linda if we keep eating or that there could have been something wrong with her glands. She never smiles or thanks you, even if you try to help her, as I did, that first day. I found clean sheets for her, sorted out an empty drawer, and showed her around the Home. After that, I left her to it, keeping out of her way, letting her find her own feet.

At first it was terrible to watch everyone, especially the boys, staring at her, making snide remarks behind their hands, to each other and out loud. Linda silently sailed by them in a world of her own. Occasionally her pale cheeks flashed scarlet patches and her lips moved with unvoiced utterances. After a while, because she didn't rise to their bait, things settled and Linda began to blend into the background.

But it is clear to me that Linda has never wanted to make friends. Being fat and hated for it must have affected her personality. She prefers her own company and keeps to herself. No one picks on her any more, but neither is anyone nice to her.

Everyone in the dorm rushes around trying to get ready for bed before lights out. Linda comes into the room at the same time that Valerie is leaving the room. Linda fills the doorway and can't move out of the way fast enough so they wind up bumping into each other. "Get outta my way you fat lump!" Valerie says. Linda freezes. "Move, you big lump of lard!"

I am behind Valerie. "Come on, Val. Stop picking on her."

"Why shouldn't I? She oughta move outta the way!" Linda is still standing there, blocking the passage. Waiting. "Move," Valerie repeats, throwing her puny weight at Linda in an effort to shove her aside. Linda's eyes widen. I put my hand on Valerie's shoulder and pull her towards me, leaving room for Linda to pass through. "Get your filthy hands offa me!" she says, shrugging herself away while throwing her right arm out, hitting me across the shoulders.

"What's the matter with you?"

"Nothin'. What's wrong with you?" She shouts and aiming better, hits me in the head. We both drop our towels and toothbrushes and start pushing and slapping each other. From the corner of my eye, I see Linda scurry away to her bed before the other girls crowd around.

We are having a full-blown fist fight and have got hold of each other's hair when the elastic on my pajama bottoms pings and they start to slide down. I release my grip on Valerie's blonde pigtails for the sake of modesty and grab for my bottoms when she takes advantage and knocks me over. I'm on the floor desperately trying to keep my pajamas up as she attacks me with punches and slaps. To hell with it, I think, letting go of my pajamas and get in a couple of good punches before my hips and buttocks are exposed and the housemother arrives and breaks it up.

For punishment Valerie and I are grounded the following Saturday. Everyone else, including Linda, is going to the movies to see *South Pacific*. We are restricted to the playroom and sit down as far away from each other as possible. After half an hour of sheer and utter boredom Valerie clears her throat and says, "Feel like a game of checkers?"

"Yeah. Why not?" I answer, feigning indifference with a shrug, but secretly glad she has broken the ice because it was going to be a long afternoon. That day Valerie and I get to know each other and begin a friendship that lasts for many years.

Our squabbles may be many and diverse, but we have a common bond - we all hate the director, Mr. Scott. Our loyalty to each other is stretched to the limit during the 'sessions' in his office when he expects us to snitch on each other. Fortunately, there are no turncoats and we frustrate his attempts to undermine our solidarity. If we misbehave, it is only petty crimes that we commit around the Home like stealing sanitary towels by the packet that are usually doled out one by one. We might break into and raid the walk-in refrigerator for midnight snacks. We don't rob or vandalize on the outside. Our insolence is directed at the houseparents or the director and our punishments are dealt with internally. There is only one serious misdemeanor committed and that is when someone runs away.

"Nobody is stupid enough to run away on their own," Tina Manley tells me in the washroom, spitting toothpaste into the sink. We brush for a while without saying anything. "There's safety in numbers. Last time there were two."

"Did they get caught? Did they come back?" I am curious to know what might happen to the three girls I overheard this morning who are planning to run away.

"They were gone for a week and were brought back here. A couple of days later they were sent away and we never heard from them again."

We all know what they are planning to do but are sworn to secrecy. There is no way that 20 girls sharing a dormitory are not going to know what is going on. We promise to keep it a secret from everyone else.

Getting away from the Home is not the problem. We are free to come and go, within reason. We only need to walk down the hill and keep walking. It is true that there are grills on the downstairs windows and a black spiky iron fence surrounding the property, and the doors are locked at night, but these measures are taken so that others don't get in, they are not designed so that we cannot get out. We do have a curfew restriction to be on the premises by 6 p.m., and no strangers or visitors are allowed in the dorms without permission. Otherwise, we can go to school, to part-time jobs, or visit friends or relatives, with permission. Our whereabouts is always written up in a book. Running away from The Kallman Home for Children is not so much a physical problem as it is a psychological one.

I personally don't understand why anyone wants to run away. We have all gotten into trouble with the director, but that doesn't make us want to run away. We have everything we need here. Besides, where would we go?

"They want real freedom," Tina says, "without all the rules. They want to be able to go out after 6 o'clock at night. Wouldn't it be nice to lay on your bed when you wanted to, instead of between this hour and that? Not to have permission for everything you do. Or to eat something, something really bad, like a packet of Twinkies, whenever you felt like it?"

"I hadn't thought of it like that," I admit.

The three conspirators whisper in a corner. They have been planning to run away for a month, ever since they were grounded for stealing bread and baloney from the walk-in refrigerator to make sandwiches for everyone in our dorm one night. Mr. Lockwood, the boys' housefather, had trusted them. He had given them his keys when they volunteered to put away a weekend milk delivery while he was overseeing the after-school woodworking class. But it was Mr. Scott, the director, who doled out the punishment.

"We're going to get even with Mr. Scott," one of them vowed.

"This place stinks. We don't need it anymore," another said.

"I'm with you guys," the third agreed.

I watch them. When they are together they laugh and joke. On their own, they are glum and quiet. Everyone in our room is involved in their plan because you need a lot of things if you want to run away, like money, extra clothes, food and maybe friends who will put you up for the night. We contribute what we can. The runaways don't tell us in which direction they plan to go so that if we are questioned, we couldn't say where they were if we wanted to.

Tension mounts among us until the day they leave. They plan to go to school like any other day only their school bags will bulge with food and spare clothes instead of books. The girls are all under fifteen years old and once it is discovered that they are gone, the police will have to be informed and a search party sent out. This is all that is definite. The rest is up to chance and luck.

We wave them good-bye at the bus stop and try to forget about it immediately. Their absence will probably not be noticed until suppertime at 6 p.m.

When I get home from school I look around for the runaways just in case they changed their minds and chickened-out, but they haven't. I rehearse saying, "I don't know", in a surprised, but nonchalant

189

manner, under my breath because, sure as lightning, I'll be asked where they are. As predicted, at the dining table the housemother looks at the empty places and asks us where the three girls are. Everyone looks surprised. We shake our heads and consult our neighbors. "I don't know where they are? Do you?"

Mr. Scott appears in the doorway of our room when we are in the middle of our homework. "Pens and pencils down, everyone. I want your attention." Only our hands move. I am frozen to the core with fear. I find it hard, and don't like keeping secrets, especially someone else's.

"Three girls did not appear in the dining hall tonight. Does anyone have any idea where they might be? Did they leave for school together? Were they going to meet anyone?" He looks around and no one budges or looks at him. "I see. Well, I will have to consider this most serious and inform the police immediately. You mustn't keep anything you might know to yourselves. They could be in danger, real danger. If you change your minds and have something to tell me, I'll be in my office."

When he leaves I realize that I'd held my breath the whole time he was there. "Ha, ha," Margie says, rolling her eyes up to the ceiling. "He's gonna go on some wild goose chase now."

"Shut your mouth," Tina snaps. "We don't know nothin', you remember that! You just better pray they're all right." She grips tightly onto her pencil, which is still poised in the air and wipes a tear from the corner of her left eye. I wonder, then, if she had wanted to go with them.

They've been gone for three days. A policewoman came to the dorms and went through their stuff. She took away autograph books and a picture album. How far have they gotten, we wonder. "I'd've hitch-hiked to California by now. They're probably miles and miles away already," Tina says with spirit. "Just think, no school, stay out late, have a boyfriend, drink beer if you want to...."

I can't picture any of this. I wouldn't have anywhere to go, wouldn't have a clue how to get there if I did. I wouldn't run away. Freedom's got to be more than doing what you want, when you want, regardless of the consequences. What happens if they run out of money, food or clean clothes? Would they beg or steal for it? I worry about all the bad people out there, too. What if someone kidnaps them? Where do they sleep at night or go to the toilet, for that matter? Did they remember to pack toilet paper? I keep my questions and my fears to myself.

Mr. Scott hasn't done his usual 'rounds' of the premises ever since they left. We haven't bumped into him skulking around corners, or tip-toeing into the laundry room when we are working, trying to catch us at something we aren't supposed to be doing. He has been too busy sticking close to the telephone in case there is any news. He doesn't fool us, though. We know that he isn't really worried about the girls. He is worried about how their running away reflects on him. And he is probably dreaming up new and dire punishments for their return.

On the tenth day of their absence, he comes into the dining room at breakfast time looking triumphant, even though his shirttails are hanging out of the back of his pants top. He surveys the room with his hands on his hips, directing a long gaze at our table and leaves. I hear the news as we clear away the dishes – they are back!

I catch up with Tina at the top of the stairs. "What's going to happen to them?"

"Wait here for me. Behind the door," she says. "I'm gonna try and see if I can see them. They'll be in his office or in the infirmary."

"Why the infirmary?" I ask, scared they might be hurt.

"I'll tell you later," she says hurrying down the hall. I don't have long to wait. Her hand trembles as we walk upstairs to get our books and coats for school. "They look awful," she says looking into my eyes. "They are filthy. Must've slept like a bunch of rats."

"Is that why they are in the infirmary?"

"Of course not! Whenever girls run away and are brought back, they have to be examined by the doctor for...you know, sex. They automatically assume that girls run away just to have it off with boys."

On the way down the hill to catch our bus to McKinley Junior High School, a 20-minute ride away, the doctor's black car speeds up the hill. The sight of him makes us cringe. Every single girl who had been examined by him said he touched her in certain places and in certain ways that wasn't normal. It was the same with me when I was sent to him because of bad stomach aches. He gave me an internal examination through my vagina and said, "Nothing wrong with you.

You're just about to get your period, I'd say." He was wrong. I didn't get it until two years later.

Tina tells me on the bus that it will be like that and worse. I shut my eyes to blot out the memory, too upset to ask what would happen if it is discovered that they had been with boys. I feel sorry for the girls and the ordeal they are about to face.

Their story unfolds slowly. They tell us later that they had been befriended by boys, helpful boys who found them a place to sleep in a warm basement and brought them food. They hadn't gotten very far away because they didn't realize how much money food would cost for three. They always seemed to be hungry. They hid during the daytime frightened that the police might be after them. At first it was a laugh and they were thrilled that they had actually run away. But after a couple of days, it got boring because the friends they had made were in school during the day and they only had company for a few hours in the evening. There was nowhere to wash.

How did the police find them? Someone in the building where they had been hiding telephoned the police to say that they had seen a bunch of dirty and suspicious girls hanging around.

The doctor must have found nothing wrong with them because they got their old beds back in the dorm and carried on like normal. Their adventure didn't amount to much and they wove themselves back into the fabric of Home life without too much difficulty.

If they had gotten away with it, traveled far away and had brand new lives, or sent us a postcard from an exotic place, perhaps they would have become our heroes.

Chapter Twenty-Nine
Insubordination

"What do you have to tell me?" the director of the Home asks abruptly, his voice a shutter clicking me back to consciousness after intense concentration on inanimate objects which fill up his office like filing cabinets and waste paper bins.

"Nothing," I say to the top of my shoe, knowing that this is not what he wants to hear.

"Look at me when you speak."

I raise my eyes level with his and look through the horn-rimmed glasses at magnified eyes and stare. I remember what my father had told me. Whenever anyone tries to scare you, he said, you look them in the eye. Lock into them hard until they back down. I'm right. You'll see.

The eyes of Quentin D. Scott, whose name gleams on a brass plaque in front of me, are yellow and speckled. They fare badly in the showdown. He coughs into his hand and shifts his feet as my brown eyes narrow, darkening like slits in an almond shell. My heart bangs, but the sense of power I feel as he shuffles papers on his desk and rearranges himself, crossing his legs, first one way then another, burns warm inside me.

"Why don't you tell me who stole the doughnuts," he presses. "It's no good keeping quiet. I'll find out sooner or later." He leans back in his chair so sure I'll talk.

I relax my shoulders and let my eyes roam the room. They land on the hateful clock. It looks like an ordinary white-faced electric clock with black numbers until you look closely at it. The red second hand swings counterclockwise and the numbers are printed in reverse order. My eyes follow its rise and fall. Am I going back in time? I try to look away, but am mesmerized by its stubborn backward journey. I blink against its hypnotic pull and listen for sounds that will release me from this mind-bending exercise.

I hear the wheels of the supper trolley squeak towards the dumbwaiter, indicating that the evening meal is about to be sent downstairs. He'll have to let me go when the supper bell rings. I watch him pick up a pencil and twirl it between his fingers. His too-long fingernails tap against the sides and his fat-cushioned fingertips do press-ups along its flat ridges. His hands are nothing like my father's car mechanic's hands with their permanently grease-caked nails and callused palms.

He pops the yellow pencil into the Moroccan leather holder and says, "Go down to supper. But report to me as soon as you've finished. I'll expect some answers by then. You are dismissed."

Standing in line outside the dining hall, I look over my shoulder every once in a while. I've been dismissed, but that won't stop him from walking along the line and singling me out, picking on me in front of everyone, calling attention to my faults. "Tuck your shirt in. Wipe that smile off your face. Get to the back of the line for talking."

He has the freedom of the building and uses it. Our houseparents have been relieved of their authority to give us permission for routine things. We have to go to him for everything. But we can never find him - he's never where he's supposed to be.

We obeyed our houseparents, but many have left and have not been replaced. Their presence in the dorms at night is what kept us in bed. We were used to them taking up space on a bench in the playrooms and so didn't bully anyone or get rowdy and disturb homework or games. Without them we goof off at bedtime and decibel levels reach new heights on transistor radios.

We feel the weight of his unease among us. His striped woolen suit, light shirt, open-necked at times, but stiffly starched, intrudes on a piano duet in the playroom. Rose's fingers fumble and fail to reach the octave as I turn the page. I look up. Is he after me? We are summoned to his office one by one for 'consultations', but all he wants us to do is to tell on each other like spies. What do we have to say to get him off our backs? We don't want any more grief than we've already got. We want to throw a few baskets in the playground, flirt with the boys, steal something from the supplies that we don't need, lie to the housemother, skive off our chores, read a book after lights out, eat something out of the dining hall, skip religion. What's his problem? His problem is that he will never be liked and he knows it.

When Mr. and Mrs. Scott took over from Mr. and Mrs. Persiko, we marveled that someone could have a name beginning with a Q. Quentin D. Scott – the name outside the Director's quarters was replaced immediately. The Persikos had earned their retirement to the countryside. We intended to love the Scotts as we did the Persikos who had run the home for twenty years. But Mr. Persiko's arm around your shoulder and firm but kind words had been replaced by Mr. Scott's distant and dictatorial approach and the whole atmosphere in the place had altered.

I had only been living here for a couple of months and it was All Change. The kids who were here longer than me had a hard time adjusting. Mr. Scott's disciplinary routines turned them sour and they wrote letters to Mr. Persiko complaining about the situation. Their letters were received with kindness, but he couldn't do anything, he wrote back. It was hard finding people to work in children's homes these days. We had to be grateful for what we got.

It was a whole year before I spoke with Mrs. Scott, a small blonde woman, efficient-looking and neat, who bustled busily in and out of their quarters *shushing* their two small children out of the path of any of us riffraff, which was fine by us. I still had my memory of Mrs. Persiko with her dark, curly hair sprinkled with gray, her head bent close to mine as she explained the routines and selected brand new underwear and pajamas for me on my first day in the Home.

I might be enjoying my hot-dogs and mashed potatoes over supper and suddenly feel the presence of the director. He is always lurking in the background. I pretend to have an itch and quickly glance around the room. It is hard to be at ease when he suddenly appears in doorways or hovers behind our dining hall chairs. We don't like to think a grown man is listening to our conversations, but he is. His crepe-soled shoes buoy him soundlessly along the corridors and we brace ourselves for an unexpected encounter.

"Jeanne Kliarsky," I hear him say from his post at the bottom of the stairs that I'm flying down, "what were you doing in the dorms?

"I was just…."

"I don't care what you were doing. The rule is nobody goes to the dorms during the day. Is that clear?"

"I only wanted to get a pencil…for my homework…"

"Enough!" He bellows and I cringe. "Any more back talk and insubordination from you and I'll have your privileges taken away." He doesn't move to let me pass and to avoid turning my back on him, I feel for the rounded edge of the banister behind me and use it to guide me towards the flight of stairs down.

He will be expecting me back, I say to myself, as my lemon Jell-O slides slowly down my throat. I can't stall the moment any longer. I see, from outside his office, that he is already in there and waiting for me, because the sharp fluorescent light bounces into the darkening corridor through the frosted glass on his half-glazed door. I knock. He says to come in and sit down, motioning to a chair in front of his desk. He has changed my chair! It is lower than the usual one and to face him I have to look up. "I see from your file that your disobedience and insubordination has cost you loss of privileges and pocket money," he says flipping the loose pages in a manila file.

He stresses the word "insubordination". When he shouts this out around the Home his body goes rigid like an exclamation mark. Sweat forms on the puffy mounds under his eyes where the edges of his glasses rest. His pasty face quivers when he utters these six syllables. Whenever the airwaves carry, "I'll have none of your insubordination," to our ears, we hide our heads in our lockers, our noses in a book. With sly smiles safely tucked away, we wonder who is in for it now? Who will get the better of whom?

My own heart leaps, soaring to a throat that quickly dries up as he beats a path towards me.

Insubordinate, disobedient, rebellious.

His words describe me and I become them.

Over the months, I try to avoid confrontations with him, realizing the uselessness of arguing, and that I can never win. I keep my head down and avoid his gaze for fear of being accused of *defiance*. I show rapt attention at religious meetings in the auditorium because I feel him watching me and I don't want to be accused of *indifference*. I give out the hymnals, collect them and put away the chairs in case I am labeled *lazy*. I am diligent to the extent of putting in extra hours in the ironing room. I keep a smooth bed and orderly drawers. I do anything to avoid his wrath and the endless, mind-bending 'sessions' in his office, but I still wind up there.

"One of these days you are going to wise up and tell me what I want to know."

I purse my lips closer together. If it's the stolen doughnuts that he's on about again, he's wasting his time. Even if I knew who did it, I wouldn't tell. They've been eaten and digested long ago. It would be useless to bring that up again. But he does – over and over again. He is talking, but I am not listening. I sneak a look and notice that his hair is loose and wavy at the front, not it's usual pristine side parting and comb-over to the right "…and so I thought you might like to help out," I suddenly catch the last few words, and tune in to a change in his tone of voice.

In his most ingratiating voice Mr. Scott says that he has decided to give me another chance. He wants me to help out at the next Board of Directors' dinner; you know, serve at table, clear up, wash the dishes. And by the way, would I mind performing a little something on the piano for them just before the meeting?

Chapter Thirty
A Helping Hand

Over the next few years Mr. Scott manages to make use of me. Even though I would rather watch television or curl my hair in my free time outside of school, I help with extra duties whenever asked.

At the time I arrived, the Home was governed by a large Board of Directors of whom Gustav Kallman, its founder, was one of the first. The Home was originally established for Norwegian children whose parents were single, ill or dead and couldn't look after them. But they extended this to include north European children, and, as time went by, all children, including Negroes and Puerto Ricans. Everybody came from broken homes.

The Board's main fund-raising activity was a grand Bazaar and a sumptuous Smörgasbord. This wonderful affair took place on the premises, which, overnight, became a hive of activity. Every corner was swept and dusted. Extra tables were brought in and cars loaded with raffle prizes struggled up the steep drive. All of us were roped in to help. I unpacked Hardanger linens, crocheted doilies, embroidered pillowcases and handmade aprons. We emptied the auditorium of chairs and it became a market for Scandinavian handicrafts, with long tables lining the walls laden with Christmas ornaments and toys. Everything was for sale. A giant Christmas tree filled most of the stage at one end and the library room adjacent was transformed into Santa Claus' grotto. A Lucky Dip was set up by the entrance and I had my dime at the ready in my pocket.

My job was waiting on tables in the dining hall, which had become nothing short of a real-live Smörgasbord restaurant. There were thirty tables covered in powder pink tablecloths and matching napkins on the plates done up in a cone shape. Our long dining tables were pushed together at the far end of the room and every inch was taken up with platters of food. Dishes were served up that we had never seen, like herrings, smoked salmon and cucumber salad.

When they opened the doors, people flooded in from all over the neighborhood and the dining hall filled quickly. I wore a pink and white waitress' uniform and looked older than my 11 years. My job was to collect the meal tickets as people sat down, as well as to keep the tables cleared of dirty dishes. People served themselves and piled their plates high, taking any amount of food for one price. From midday until 7.30 p.m. I ran to the kitchen with trays of dirty dishes. There, a couple of the boys emptied them straight into the dishwashers. People were kind to the waitresses, occasionally slipping us a tip. After we finished, and the Bazaar was over for another year, my tired feet throbbed and felt like they were on fire.

Whenever I wait on the Board of Directors' dinners, the men remember me from the Bazaar and greet me as though I were a waitress by trade. But I don't mind. They are white-haired and doddery and becoming fewer in numbers all the time. They cannot be expected to remember that during the last dinner, as an exemplary child from the Home, I had recited the poem *Annabel Lee* by Edgar Allan Poe. They may clap after I play my first tune in waltz time, but forget who I am by the time the door closes behind me.

All the children in the Home are required to learn a musical instrument. We have our own brass band, run by a former boy from the Home that has become so proficient that he plays with the Salvation Army Band. He is good on trumpet, coronet and tuba and practices the French horn after giving us lessons in the dining hall. I tried to play the trumpet, but split my lip and did not want to continue. Mr. Scott agreed in the end to pay for piano lessons instead, provided I perform once in a while before the Board. I made terrific progress and glided effortlessly through the pages of scales and exercises. But, in a fit of pique during a session in Mr. Scott's office, as a punishment for insubordination, he rescinded my lessons. In one stroke he took away my prize.

Since then I have learned to mask my true feelings and not let anyone see when I am in love – with music, with books, with people or with life.

The Boardroom meals are served from the Main Kitchen. But by the time the directors are finished eating and I clear the table, the kitchen staff has left to go home for the day. All the refrigerators, pantries, closets and machines are tightly locked up and the keys hidden away, so I have to wash the dishes by hand.

I stand at the sink under a lone fluorescent light that illuminates a few square feet around me in my black uniform with the white organza apron and cap. I let my ramrod table-waiting posture go, and slump heavily against the sink, tired and ready for my bed. Through the kitchen window, I can look up and see the girls' dormitory. Everyone is asleep. Lights out was a long time ago.

I throw a handful of powder into the sink and run the hot water. Glasses first, Mrs. Scott had said while training me for the job. One by one I slide the glasses into the rising foam. In the distance I hear Mr. Scott call to me for a cloth, fast. I quickly run to the Boardroom. One of the men has knocked over his coffee cup. "Would I clean it up?" Mr. Scott asks me sweetly in front of everyone.

When I return to the sink the faucet is still running. I quickly shut it, catching it before it overflows. I plunge my hands into the water without realizing that the extreme heat had shattered all the glasses. It is a couple of seconds before the pain tells me I burned my hands, then cut them on the slithers of glass hidden beneath the bubbles.

The water is blood red and my dripping hands splatter the floor with large blotches of red and white bubbles. I wrap them around my pretty little apron, and running, hesitate outside the Boardroom door realizing that I can't interrupt the meeting. Is everyone else in the building asleep? The nurse isn't here at night unless someone is in the infirmary with chickenpox or measles.

I race to the top floor. There's a chink of light under Mrs. Sackella's bedroom door. I knock. "Who is it?" she asks warily. I try to speak in a loud whisper, but my mouth is so dry, the words get stuck. "It had better be good. You better not get me out of bed for nothing."

Before I can say anything, she is a giant silhouette in the open doorway. "Good Heavens, child. What have you been up to?" Maybe it is the loss and sight of blood, or perhaps the shock of seeing her, corsets undone, hair caught up in a net, and in a floor-length night gown, I don't know, but I can't speak. "Never mind trying to explain. Come along."

That night I am grateful for the care Mrs. Sackella gives me. She gently unwinds the apron from around my bleeding hands and bathes them in lukewarm water. Then she pats them dry with a clean towel. Holding them under a strong light, she examines them for shards. She unwinds a roll of sterilized gauze and wraps it around my fingers and palms. "There you go," she says and looks at me. "Don't worry so much. You'll live. It looks worse than it is. The cuts are small and I am sure there's no glass in them. Now get yourself off to bed."

Chapter Thirty-One
Fire!

The excitement is over by the time I arrive on Sunday night. I had been away at my weekend baby-sitting job since Friday night. As I haul myself up the steep drive, the last stretch of a two-hour journey back to the Home, Andy is waiting for me.

"There was a fire in the girls' dorm last night. But it's okay. I've saved some of your stuff." My eyes slide upwards as his words tumble out. The red bricks around the windows are as scorched and black as burnt toast and plywood boards cover a gaping hole where the glass used to be. "Smoke was coming out of the windows so I ran over in case your wardrobe was on fire. There were no big flames so I went in and...."

"You shouldn't have. You could have gotten killed."

"...and the draws weren't touched, so I grabbed up armloads and threw everything out of the window."

"Andy, you're nuts."

"I was out of there before Mr. Scott came up. A couple of guys helped me load your things into two milk crates we borrowed from the walk-in refrigerator. Three of your records got smashed, but everything else is okay. It's all in my locker for now."

"What about the rest of my clothes? You know, coats, dresses, suits, blouses?"

He looks down at his shoes. "By the time I got downstairs, the flames were coming out of the windows. Everything on hangers got burned." He fills my silence with more details. "The fire bells went off and it was more exciting than a silly old fire drill."

"Thanks for doing that, Andy" I say patting him on the shoulder, grateful he didn't get killed on my account.

The girls' dorm resembles a campsite after a hurricane. Beds and belongings line the corridors. Shoes and boxes of oddments are scattered helter-skelter. A large area is sealed off with yellow tape. "You're not allowed in there. That's where the fire was," Valerie says pointing to the dressing rooms, and the bedroom that was damaged by the smoke. "We have to sleep out here for two weeks," she continues, sitting down carefully on her tightly made bed, under which she has neatly stacked her personal treasures including her jewelry box, white gloves and movie magazines. Last year she won the prize for having the 'neatest drawers' and it looks like she plans to keep the prize forever.

Ignoring her warning, I step over the yellow tape and flick on the light switch in the dressing room. Charred ruins jump out at me. The sight of my junior high school graduation dress consumed by flames up to the bodice and dangling like a dead thing on the blackened hanger curdles my stomach. What has taken me years of baby-sitting hours to accumulate has been devoured in a flash.

"Your brother saved a mess o' your stuff. He threw it out the window. I saw it myself," Margie says behind me. "Your records, too. You missed all the fun. You shoulda' seen Mr. Scott's face. He's mad all right."

My shoulders have taken the brunt of her words. Without turning around I ask, suddenly very tired, "Where's my bed?"

"You're the last one back from the weekend. They're all taken. I'll go ask the housemother," Margie says hopping away between the sooty patches on the floor. "They are gonna clear away the rest of the burned things tomorrow, Mr. Scott said, because the insurance man already came today," she says over her shoulder.

A final look at the black hole that was my wardrobe and I tally that I had ten skirts, fifteen blouses, two coats and five pairs of pants hanging in there. Plus the white graduation dress and shoes. And new loafers and my black high heels.

"You are sleeping in the infirmary 'cause there's no beds left up here," Margie says when she gets back. Then in a hasty whisper she adds, "Quick. Get outta there. The housemother's comin'."

"You'll have to make do with these," the housemother says handing me three dark, woolen skirts. "The fire started in your wardrobe and spread to the one next to it. It looks worse than it is. The smoke and water from the firemen's hoses made most of the mess."

"What am I supposed to wear to school tomorrow?" I ask, keeping my tone of voice steady, unequal to the sense of loss I am feeling.

"Wear what you wore on Friday. You're good with a needle. By tomorrow, you'll have those skirts ready. They only need hemming and a button or two. Borrow a blouse from someone." Moving down the corridor in the direction of the juniors' room she raises her voice. "Lights out in five minutes, girls."

The dress I wore to school, my pajamas, and a pair of blue jeans and cotton blouse that I wore while baby-sitting are all that I have left. Then I remember. *Don't forget about what Andy saved for you.* Andy's locker is jam-packed with my underpants, bras, slips, socks, gloves, stockings, shirts, shorts, 45 rpm's and a pair of slacks. At the sight of all this, the dragging sensation at the pit of my stomach lessens.

"Everyone around here thinks that the new housemother did it," he says. "She chain smokes and was probably having a sneaky fag and flung the butt in the closet when she heard someone coming. She might've heard Scoot doing the rounds, coming around the corner, you know, like he does."

"Could be," I agree, picturing it vividly. As I sift through the pile and select some clothes to take upstairs, Andy mentions that the woman has already been fired. There had been an argument on Sunday morning between her and Mr. Scott and she packed her bags and left straight after. The houseparents we have had lately have been useless. It is obvious to us that they know nothing about looking after kids in a Home. They are just any old body that needs a job and a place to stay, not like in the old days, when some of them had been trained nurses. "He probably gets them on the cheap," one of the senior girls guesses out loud when we talk about it. The staff has been replaced so often that if I go away for a weekend, there can be a new housemother when I get back. When I first arrived in the Home, the staff members only left when they were due to retire.

Andy understands why I get upset over losing things. Ever since Phyllis told us how the neighbors helped themselves to the contents of our apartment after Dad's eviction from Wyckoff Avenue, I like to hold on to what I own. Andy has seen me slowly stockpile a wardrobe full of clothes.

Everything I owned I bought with the money I had earned. My shoe shining apprenticeship of long ago taught me to watch out for moneymaking opportunities. My first baby-sitting job at twelve years old led to a weekend job as a mother's helper. Now I work from Saturday morning to Sunday night for $6. If I go straight from school on Friday night, I make $9. By the time I was thirteen years old I was let off going to summer camp and instead of horse riding, archery and swimming, I worked during my summer vacations as a live-in mother's helper for $20 a week. I kept $5 a week to spend on my days off and banked the rest. By the end of the summer I had saved $150.

I like being a mother's helper even though the work is hard and hours are long. I get up before everyone else at around 6 a.m. and make the breakfast. After I dress and feed the children, I vacuum around, do a bit of ironing, walk the dog, wash the dishes, play with the kids, prepare them some supper and baby-sit in the evenings. The people are nice to me and treat me like a member of the family.

Each Fall before school starts, I spend some money and shop for new clothes. It is either that or I am at the mercy of the grab bag, the slowly-getting-more-shabby-by-the-week pile of second-hand clothes available for kids whose families cannot afford to buy them anything. I am already fifteen years old and don't want to be labeled as 'a Home kid' because of my threadbare clothes. No one from school suspects I live in the Kallman Home for Children and to avoid their prejudice, I want to keep it that way. Andy likes to shop with me and I often let him choose something for himself. My wardrobe had gradually built up over the years.

Luckily the infirmary door is ajar when I fall through it with my weekend case and some of the things from Andy's locker. The bitter odor of aspirins mixed with antiseptic and clean sheets that greets me is marginally better than the scorched one of the dorms. I drop everything at the foot of one of the beds. It is so quiet in here compared with the hustle and bustle of the dormitories. Noise from the building doesn't reach the infirmary, which is tucked away at the far corner of the building between the main kitchen and a large storage closet. Silence is something I am not used to, spending my evenings in the company of fifty-odd other girls who talk, curl their hair, read comics, watch t. v., listen to records and the radio - all at the same time.

I hear someone moving around in the kitchen and peer around the door. The lights are on and I hear the faint chink of cutlery. "Well, Jeanne. You're back," Mr. Scott creeps out of the shadows behind me, making me stiffen. "Come on in." Our footsteps echo down the long entranceway to the kitchen. Mrs. Scott has laid out coffee on the table. Her husband helps himself. "Yes," he says, not looking up. "What can we do for you?"

"I'm...uh...I've been told to sleep in the infirmary. There aren't enough beds upstairs," I say, justifying my presence on the main floor at night.

"Yes. Quite right. Jeanne, about that fire. Did you have anything flammable in your closet, like lighter fluid or matches?" Mr. Scott asks me without any preamble, as he sits down and sifts through a pile of documents on the table in front of him. "I have to make certain in my report that we are not liable for the fire."

"No, I didn't. Why would I...?"

"I'm asking the questions. What about a hairdryer or other appliance that might heat up? You didn't leave anything plugged in or on like an iron?"

"No," I say with mounting indignation and the suspicion that I am being accused of something. "What caused the fire, anyway?" I ask, deflecting his line of questioning.

"We aren't sure. That's what we're trying to ascertain. Did you leave for your baby-sitting job on Friday night or Saturday morning?"

"Friday, straight after school. Ask the housemother, or you can call the lady up if you want to. I have the number..." A snarl creeps into my voice.

"No need for back talk! I've got enough on my plate without your insolence. Dismissed." He looks down at his papers and flicks his hand in my direction as though he were whisking away a pesky fly. I don't move. "Well?"

"Am I going to get any insurance money for the clothes I lost?"

Mr. Scott acts like he hasn't heard me.

"All my clothes, except for some underwear and shirts have been burned," I blurt out. "I bought everything with my own money."

"How dare you ask for money when I am looking at thousands of dollars worth of repairs to the building?"

"Can't I fill out a report? I know about how much everything cost," I start to say, but can't finish because he is already on his feet, his anger bearing down at me like a ton of bricks.

"What makes you think I owe you anything? You can get your clothes from the grab bag like everyone else. You're too high and mighty anyway. Let this bring you down a peg or two. You'll not get anything!" His teeth are clenched like his fists, his body stiff and leaning towards me.

"I only want to be able to put in a claim." I am trying to be calm. I need to get my point across now or it will be shelved forever. "It was my closet that burned down!" I hear myself say in a tone that has been gathering force like a summer storm ever since I stepped into the courtyard and saw my brother waiting for me.

The slap across my face echoes loudly in my ears before it begins to smart and have a heartbeat of its own. His back-hander makes my head jerk to the right. "Quentin!" Mrs. Scott gasps, rising to her feet and looking down the entrance way to make sure that no one is coming.

"It is my Home that burned down! We don't even know if the insurance company is going to pay up. As far as I'm concerned, there will be nothing coming to you. Your clothes are the least of my worries. Now get to bed."

By the time my feelings of hatred and disappointment simmer down I am lying on the high and narrow hospital bed under the white sheets with nothing to stare at but the blank white walls and white ceiling. Pricking behind my eyelids are the tears that I didn't want to shed in front of him. Only my anger holds them back. One part of me feels that I shouldn't get so worked over a bunch of silly old clothes, while another part insists on reminding me that for every step I take forward, I am taking two steps backwards. Since there's no company in the infirmary, I argue with myself. It's not fair! *Fair? What's fair?* Hot tears aren't fair, or the blocked nose, or the hiccups, or the snot dripping down past my lips and chin that lands on my chest. *Go ahead, no one can hear you. Howl, go on.* I reach for the white tissues in a white box on the white bedside cabinet next to the white lamp, helping myself to a bunch, and hoping I don't catch the chicken pox or the measles from the last person that picked a tissue out from it.

No matter what I do, I can't sleep so I get up and walk around the room. Rearranging some of my things on the bed next to me, I pick up a brand new box of nylon stockings and look inside. Beneath the pale pink lid a paper ring with a seal surrounds the tissue paper protecting the nylons. I bought them in a tiny store, not much bigger than a couple of double beds pushed together, where only nylon stockings are sold. The saleswoman wanted to know my shoe size and what denier I preferred, what color, should they be long or short, seamed or plain? I looked at the models of legs displayed on the counter and in the tiny window. Along the back of the calf on a pair of legs suspended in mid-air were butterflies with diamonds on their wing tips. I said I needed plain beige ones, long and sheer and the saleslady reached for a slim box from stacks of boxes filling the shelves behind her that stretched nearly to the ceiling. She placed it on the glass countertop and slid off the lid. She gently broke the seal, flipped up the tissue paper on one side then the other and slipped her hand into the top of a stocking to model the color and sheerness. When I nodded and said, "Fine. I'll take six pairs, please," she pushed the box aside and selected a brand new box and asked, "Will that be all?"

The three woolen skirts that the housemother gave me are slumped upon the white bedspread nearby like old dead carcasses. I switch on a couple of bedside lamps for extra light and inspect them carefully. Two of them need to be hemmed up by six inches as they practically hang to my ankles. *What century are they from?* The third one is riddled with moth holes and needs a button at the waist. The tiny holes can't be mended, but you would need to look really closely to see them. It will have to do.

During the night, instead of sleeping, I carefully stitch around the circumference of the old skirts, hemming them up into a new era along with my heavy sighs.

Chapter Thirty-Two
Pink Organdie In The Toilets

You would think that we wanted a dollar fifty the way Mr. Scott takes it when we approach him and ask him to raise our pocket money by fifteen cents a week.

"I want all the ringleaders in my office at once," he snarls. Then, pointing at us each in turn, he says, "That's you, you, you, you and you."

He's crept up to the dormitory just before lights out and has us at a disadvantage as we're already in our pajamas, cold cream-faced and trussed up in curlers for the night. We're not a pretty sight. Our boxy flannelette pajamas are faded and in most cases, the tops don't match the bottoms. Buttons are missing and the elastic has gone in Chiquita Manley's bottoms so she's holding them bunched up in her fist. Covering our freshly washed hair, assorted floral headscarves firmly hold our wide pink rollers in place. We must look like Martians evacuating a spaceship as we are made to file down the stairs to his office, bed-weary, disheveled and disgruntled for yet another telling off.

"You'll be punished more than the rest of them," he tells me after the others have been dismissed, "because you ought to know better. They are only following your lead."

"It wasn't even my idea. They asked me to ask you for a raise."

"Then you're dumber than I thought. You're dismissed."

The number of kids in the Home has gradually gone down from a hundred and twenty to a mere fifty at this stage. Those who run the Home, our houseparents, kitchen workers and cleaning staff, is down to a just a few people. Each month when the chore list goes up, we are given additional jobs to do but we still get the same pocket money. Morale drops lower and lower. Everyone is sick of it. The big boys, agitated, congregate in the playground to decide on a plan of action. Some of them are talking about going on strike or running away and getting a job where they will at least get the minimum wage. In the playroom on the girls' side, we decide to go for democracy and ask for a raise from seventy-five cents a week to ninety-cents. It sounds reasonable to me and before I know it, I'm chosen to be the spokesman.

"Impertinence! Gall and impertinence!" is Mr. Scott's reaction.

We rebel the following week by keeping the television on after lights out. How does Mr. Scott find out about this? By spying on us, by keeping tabs on the girls' dormitory windows. The shades are fully drawn, but the blue glow of the t.v. screen gives us away where the shades don't quite reach the windowsill. We're in our beds watching the Million-Dollar Movie for the fifth time that week when all six light switches by the door are flipped on at once.

"That's done it. Since you can't be trusted, I'm pulling the main light switch on you from now on!" He turns off the lights and disappears as quietly as he came. It is frightening to know that he strode down our long corridor without being discovered. We always kept a lookout when a housemother lived on the floor. We'd gotten lax lately.

After this Mr. Quentin D. Scott makes it clear what he means by lights out. Somewhere in the depths of the building he pulls a master switch and, quick as a slap in the face, we're plunged into darkness. The television screen sizzles off and we watch in amazement as the white dot in the center slowly disappears. The record player drones to a halt. "What's that man got buggin' him? Shoot, man. He needs to see a psychiatrist or somethin'," Margie Thomas says, groping in the dark for her records. "He needs his head examinin'." There's a loud clatter and Margie shouts, "Shit! I dropped it! It's broken. I hate that goddam son-of-a bitch. NO mistake."

My eyes adjust to the only light we have in the room, which is the small red globe above the door by the exit sign. The silhouette of twenty beds and the lump of a body in each one gradually takes shape. Margie is right. Mr. Scott has a thing about switching off lights, but more likely, it's to do with keeping people in the dark.

Not long ago I got into trouble over a lamp. My brother fixed one up that he'd found in a garbage can. "You can use it to read in bed when everyone is asleep," he told me. "I painted it myself, in woodworking. The bulb," he added, "I stole from the boys' toilet."

After everyone had settled, I turned on my blue, shadeless lamp and read under the covers for about an hour. No one seemed to know or care about what I was doing. One night as I was happily reading away, my sheet and blankets were ripped off the bed in one swift motion. I was instantly blinded by the glare of a flashlight held three inches away from my face.

"Caught you in the act!" Mr. Scott's voice boomed triumphantly. The room ignited into a mass of screams and cries. He turned around and growled at the girls to shut up. In the pin-dropping silence that followed, he told me to turn off the lamp. "Give it to me, and get out of that bed!" He pushed me towards the door. "You can stand out in the corridor for an hour since you are so keen to stay awake."

Now each night when the light-killing switch is pulled, I lay with my hands under my head and ask myself, How can we get over this one? It isn't long before an idea comes to me.

On the way home from school the next day I stop by Woolworth's and buy a gadget. Just before lights out I round everyone up. "I know how we can beat him this time," I say, "but you've gotta promise, solemnly swear, that no one is going to snitch on me." Swearing out loud and crossing of hearts over, I show them the electrical socket I bought. "We take out the red bulb over the exit sign and screw this in its place. Then we plug the television in." No one utters a word. "Don't you get it? That light stays on all the time because it's the law. He's not allowed to turn it off!"

We post a guard by the door and roll up our bath towels and stuff them along the windowsills to keep the blue light from spilling out. Once more we are watching television after hours. I would rather read a book, but I join the others in a circle on the floor because it gives me so much satisfaction to think that we have out-smarted him again. Even if we get caught and the finger is pointed at me, my punishment would be worth it just to see his face.

Apart from the usual 'bigger girls' Saturday afternoon laundry room duties, which consist of washing, wringing out and drying the laundry and ironing the younger girls' clothes, we now have at least two other jobs. We do them on a monthly basis, changing jobs regularly so that in the end, we know and have cleaned every square inch of that enormous building. The main office, which used to be cleaned exclusively by paid staff as none of us could be trusted in there, has been assigned to me because the director says he wants to keep a close eye on me. I have also been given the girls' downstairs toilets to clean, which everyone positively hates.

The office cleaning has to be done in the mornings which means rushing out before breakfast is finished to get it all done in time. Before I dash off for school I run a duster over the tops of the desks, empty the wastepaper baskets and pencil sharpener, water the plants and dust the windowsills. On Saturdays, I do a more thorough job, including washing the inside of the windows and mopping the floors. I hate working in the office because I continually have the feeling that someone is watching me, that I am doing something wrong and am guilty. Guilty of what? Anything. Everything. Mr. Scott never shows himself before 9 o'clock, it's a fact and since it's only a quarter past eight, I should have nothing to worry about. But I still have a creepy feeling coming over being so close to his quarters which are directly across the hall, so rush the job to get out quick. After the first week I begin to notice that there are a lot more papers on his desk. It becomes harder to dust and takes more time.

One morning around 8.15 am, as I am putting his papers into a pile and straightening them, the door swings open and he says in a rush, making me jump out of my skin, "What are you doing with those papers on my desk?"

"I…"

"You were reading them, weren't you? Don't deny it. I saw you. Were you reading them?"

"No. I might have looked at them."

"So if you looked at them and they have words on them, you were reading them?"

"No, I wasn't, I wasn't."

"Don't you ever do it again, do you understand? I consider it a very serious offense."

"Yes."

"Yes, what?"

"Yes, Mr. Scott."

I'm jumpy after that. He's watching me. I'm under the spotlight in the office. Under his scrutiny. Under his thumb. Under. Under. Under.

My other job, the one in the girls' downstairs toilets, is a disgusting one – the most hated by everyone. The toilet bowls, all six of them, are usually clogged up, mainly by girls too lazy to flush when they are finished. Soggy toilet rolls, which never make it to the roll holders, sag in corners where the toilets have overflowed and spilled over. The wastepaper basket is stuffed with soda bottles, used sanitary towels, broken toys and wilted comic books. Faucets are left dripping and sink drains are blocked with bubble gum. Paper towels, used and unused, cover the floor like a carpet.

Determined that the downstairs toilets are not going to get to me, I clean the place with a fury, using Lysol and Ajax like it was going out of style. But by the next afternoon, it is practically back to where it was. Someone had vomited in the corner cubicle and stepped in it, leaving a trail of regurgitated food through the toilets and out into the hallway. I decide that I am going to hang out in there and bring in a chair from the playroom to sit on. I greet girls as they come in, get them to wash their hands, then put the towels in the wastepaper baskets on the way out. I remind them to flush the toilets after themselves. Sometimes the girls stay a while and chat, like you do in toilets in restaurants or the movies where there's a cleaning lady who loiters behind a saucer full of coins. Each day the toilets are left a little cleaner and my job gets easier.

By the end of the month I have had enough of nagging and toilet flushing and look forward to changing to a different job, something easy like setting and clearing tables in the dining hall. I read down the list posted on the back of the playroom door.

Jeanne Kliarsky – Laundry Room, Main Office, Downstairs Toilets.

"I don't believe it, you've got toilets again, Jeanne," Valerie says, and runs off, grateful it's not her.

The next month it's the same. "Toilets for you, again," Margie comments. "Man, he's got it in for you, girl. Better you than me. Tell you what, if you behave, I'll come and keep you company after school tomorrow."

I spend more time in the toilets than I do in the playroom. If anyone wants me, she knows where to find me. When I'm in there, the girls don't fall back into their old habits. I drag in another chair to rest my feet on and read a book or do my homework while I keep a watchful eye. "Hi, Jeanne. Can I come and sit, too?"

"Lug a chair in here," I say agreeable to some company. A kind of clubroom begins to form. Opposite the sinks six chairs now line the wall. After school I go straight in there, clean up, just a bit, because only the waste paper basket needs emptying and I give the sinks the once-over with scouring powder, polishing them and the faucets dry with paper towels. I am beginning to like the place with its fresh aroma of bleach. I am aware of its seclusion, how it is tucked away from the prying eyes of houseparents or the director. "I have a mind to jazz this place up, make it a real clubroom. What do you think, Valerie?" She looks at me like I'm crazy, then nods tentatively. With several weeks' worth of my seventy-five cents' pocket money saved up, I figure I can smarten the place up somehow.

There are six toilets at the back of the room and four sinks line a dividing wall near the entrance. Above the sinks, instead of mirrors, are three frosted-glass windows. Natural light filters through the windows above the toilets on a sunny day and passes through to the sink area. In my mind's eye, I picture curtains on the frosted windows above the sinks, even though I don't know a thing about making curtains. With my wooden school ruler I measure them, standing on a chair to get to the top. In the five-and-dime store, a bolt of pink organdie catches my eye. With the help of the man at the counter, we work it out that I can do the whole job for $3.75. I ask him then and there to cut the fabric into three equal parts, then in half again.

Sitting opposite the sinks, I sew three wide hems on the bottoms and three narrow ones on the top for a string to run through. Andy borrows a hammer from woodworking for me. I keep guard while he sneaks over to the girls' side after supper and slips into the toilets. He quickly bangs in the six nails he also 'borrowed' and helps me hang the pink organdie curtains up. When it's done, everyone comes to have a look. The pink organdie strikes a feminine chord among the girls, so unlike the rest of the stark utilitarian décor we are accustomed to. They become proud of their toilets, respecting their use, nagging one another to keep the place nice. If I'm out, someone else volunteers to stand guard. No one throws paper towels on the floor or spits gum into the sinks. Valerie even wanted to know if I would like to swap jobs, which greatly surprised me as her sense of order and tidiness far outweighs mine. A person could stumble into her closet or drawers at any time of the night or day and everything would be prissy, pin-clean. Not like mine, one rushed rummage for a scarf or a pair of gloves and everything is topsy-turvy for ages.

I have been cleaning the toilets for over six months. I almost feel like I own them. Five of us hang out in there after school. Munching our way through a shared bag of potato chips, we talk about records, boys, and whatever's bugging us, which usually boils down to Mr. Scott. Since I've been on toilets, I have managed to avoid his attention. I have perfected my office cleaning eyes to looking without seeing, and on the odd occasion when he does show himself, I am usually on my way out. I guessed he was trying to see if having to clean the toilets for so long had finally gotten to me, so looked away when he tried to lock into me. Maybe the triumph in my heart showed in my face. Somehow or other he finds out about how I've spruced up the toilets and how they have become our lovely clubhouse.

One afternoon we are having a particularly loud discussion about how much we can't stand him. We are laughing, getting our frustrations off of our chests, when he suddenly storms in on us. We are so taken aback that he dared to come into the girls' toilets that we didn't have a chance to wonder if he had been listening outside the door for a long time. We felt so safe in our clubhouse. We had been stalked, jumped up upon, 'caught in the act' by him so many times before in the dining hall, the dormitories, along the corridors, in the playroom, but never, never in the toilets. We didn't have it in our vocabulary of understanding that he would barge in the one place we thought sacrosanct from his prying eyes and ears.

One look at his face and his uncontrolled anger scares us so much we scatter and run for cover to the cubicles. But he's not after them. He's after me. Calling their names, calmly, one by one, he orders them out. We are alone and face one another. "This is the final straw. You've gone too far this time. We'll get rid of those ridiculous curtains, right now." He lunges forward to make a grab for them and I stand in his way.

"They're mine. They're nothing to do with you!"

"Right. I'll deal with you first."

Realizing that he's lost control and not knowing what he's capable of, I turn and run for the cubicles since he is blocking the passage to the door out. A split second later he has me by the hair and pulls me back to the sinks. I try to wrestle out of his grip, my hair roots screaming with pain, but he's strong and pushes me to the floor. My barrette has broken and my hair is loose around my shoulders and flowing down my back. His pudgy fingers wrap themselves around it as he drags me through the door like a caveman. The crowd of children outside fans out in a silent arc of disbelief.

One look at their faces and it floods back to me. He came into the toilets. I thought we were safe, that he couldn't, wouldn't step over the barrier. After he releases my hair, I scream, "You had no right to come into the girls' toilets!" and go beyond a barrier myself. His first slap stops me from going any further. The next day there is a notice pinned up on the playroom door:

ATTENTION ALL GIRLS

Due to increased incidents of nits, you will be advised that all girls with long hair are required to have it cut short. A volunteer from a hairdressing school will be waiting in the laundry room from 4.00 p.m. to 4.30 p.m. Report there immediately after school.

No exemptions allowed.

By order of - QUENTIN D. SCOTT, Director

Only two girls in the Home at this time have long hair - an 8-year old girl and myself – and neither of us has nits. As my hair falls to the laundry room floor, turning the green tiles brown, I think it is a high price to pay for pink organdie in the toilets. Only I don't know if I'd have done anything differently if I'd had the chance to do it again. Even taking a wild guess I wouldn't have thought that years later when I wear my first floor-length gown at the senior prom, I am swathed in yards and yards of pink organdie.

Chapter Thirty-Three
The Laundry Room

Watery sunlight leaks through the opaque windows of the laundry room illuminating its high ceiling and stained walls like a domed cathedral. We slip by this splendor, passing the sinks and washing machines, to the gloominess of the ironing room at the back where a stack of ironing, tall as a man, is waiting for us. With the volume turned down low on the transistor radio as we work, each one of the older girls puts in three hours of ironing per week after school. The ironing rule has been in place for many years.

Once staff worked the washing machines, wringer and dryer, but since they have become a thing of the past, we operate the machinery ourselves. There are only twenty girls left in the home; if I count the boys, the total number of kids rises to thirty-five. Each week an overstuffed, raggedy suitcase finds its way to the hall outside the main office. This means that one more child has been placed elsewhere. It could be to go back home, or to live with relatives, or to wind up in another institution. The children have left, but there will always be laundry and ironing.

My brother, Andy, has left, too. He wasn't yet sixteen years old when he packed a couple of brown paper shopping bags, got on the bus to New Jersey and went to live with our sister Phyllis. We'd been to stay the weekend with her several times. She and a friend rented a spacious apartment in Newark on the top floor of a doctor's house down a tree-lined street in a quiet suburb. I remember how in autumn the leaves on the ground were so plentiful it was like wading through floodwaters to get to the bus stop.

My relationship with Phyllis has always been like oil and water. We don't mix for long. When we don't see eye to eye, she bullies me, having the advantage of age, size and weight over me. She is moody, and too often instigates fights over nothing. She doesn't like the way I move my head, or the way I say something, or smile. I am never sure if I should agree or disagree with whatever she might say. She works in a factory and wants to better herself. She asks me what she should do. When I offer a suggestion, she gets enthusiastic over it. However, when it fails, it's my fault and her problems continue to be my responsibility. She asks me why I am always succeeding. She wants to better herself. But when I try to talk her through the steps of reaching her goals, she doesn't want to go that way and says it's not easy enough for her. Everything I suggest is too complicated, too hard for her to do. She is so mixed up.

One night she threw me out of her apartment after a fight. She was complaining again about being sick of working in the factory even though she was already a foreman. She wanted to be like me, she said. She wanted to go to secretarial school so she could work in an office. How could she become a secretary? I tried to advise her to go back to school. She resisted this and argued every case in the book saying how impossible it was. Why did I think I was so smart? She wanted to know. "You don't know what the hell you're talking about. You stupid idiot," she said, getting worked up into a frenzy. "You listen to me, you hear? I'm older than you and know more about life than you'll ever know. You stupid little ignorant bitch. You're too young to know about anything. Now get outta here. Pack your bags and get out. You're just a baby and don't know nothin' about nothin'!"

I was getting tired of this going around in circles, winding up back to nowhere. It had to stop. "Why do you keep asking me how to succeed then?"

"Because you act like you know something."

"I know more than you think I do, for your information."

"Yeah?" she laughed. "What's that?"

"You might be older than I am, but for the rest of your life you'll never be as young as I am," I retorted. One smart-ass thing was all I said to keep her from going on and on. I was desperate for her to stop her line of questioning, her building up to a crescendo, then to a pinnacle of failure and defeat before she got off the ground.

Violence was what she always resorted to. I should have kept my mouth shut. I knew what was coming. She grabbed me by the hair and slapped my face until my nose bled. Then she shoved me towards the stairs and threw my overnight case and pajamas down after me. I wandered around the streets until daylight and took the first bus that came by that would bring me back to Brooklyn and to the safety of the Home.

Phyllis had been in a vile temper all day and had already vented her anger on a dozen glasses that she smashed one by one on the kitchen floor. I had swept it up trembling on the inside. No matter what I said when she asked me anything, it was going to be the wrong thing to say. I knew the day would end badly, but I couldn't turn against the tide. I gave up. I was sixteen years old, too big to be beaten up by my older sister of twenty-one years. After this, I knew we could never be friends again.

Andy came back on his own on Sunday night. He told me he couldn't understand why I went back to the Home and why I couldn't get along with my own sister. Before we parted, he said Phyllis had asked him to go and live with her and he agreed. I begged him to wait and think about it. In the hope of quitting one intolerable situation, Andy sped headlong into another. He went straight to the director and told him that Phyllis was willing to look after him, despite my protest that it was the worst thing he could do. The director was emptying the Home of children as fast as he could. He acted on Andy's news immediately and before long my brother was gone.

The director's opinion is that I should move in with my sister and brother. I wouldn't be a financial burden. Phyllis would receive welfare checks for each of us and he urged me to join them. There didn't seem to be any looking into the arrangements for Andy. He was still a child and my sister, though willing, wasn't necessarily the best thing for him at the time. He was also going into another State and once he crossed the boundary, no one in New York State would be responsible for him. It was the main reason I was able to resist the director's pressure. My high school is in Manhattan and I can't cross the state line to go to school. I told him it was impossible. In a year and a half I'll be graduating, but I don't know how long the Home would continue to operate with so few children. It seems that Mr. Scott is hell-bent on closing the place down. He did say once, a couple of years ago, "I'm not accepting any new children from now on." Since an allowance is allotted by the government for each child, the fewer children there are, the lower the income. Those of us who are left do most of the work that it takes to run the place. We do it because we have nowhere else to go.

Today it's George Washington's birthday and there's no school. Before I settle to a good book or think about going out, I turn my attention to the mountain of dirty clothes on the floor in the middle of the laundry room. I begin by separating the lights from the darks and stuff the two six-foot-high industrial-size washing machines to capacity before I turn them on. While they belch and slosh, taking in water and expelling it, I sweep the floor and straighten up the place. I scrape off the filter from the dryer which is clogged tight with fluff and fish out the three shirt buttons that jangle at the bottom of the wringer.

I think of the dorms as the heart of the place. Whereas, the laundry room I think of as the lungs with the wheezing dryer, the hiss of spit-tested irons and warm steam rising above the boiler. Everything in here is in constant motion. We breeze in and out to bleach our underwear in the deep sinks or make starch on the gas ring. During the craze of circular skirts, we boiled sugar and water in a large metal pot to sugar starch our nylon crinolines until they stood out bigger than open umbrellas. We even sugar starched our hair, which enabled us to style it into *bouffant* and elaborate French twists. Our hair-do's were stiff enough to rest a plate on and guaranteed to remain in place for a week. We stopped it only when we read in a magazine that someone left her sugar-starched hair untouched for a year and cockroaches nested in it and fed on the sugar.

My broom clanks against the metal starching pot, dented and crusty with age. Its purpose served, it catches drips from a leaky pipe nowadays. The gas ring looks sad, too. The rubber hose, dangling limply from the nozzle, has disintegrated and could be mistaken for a piece of red licorice that got run over by a car. I stood for hours over the gas ring waiting for the straightening comb to heat up. Margie was the first girl to let me straighten her hair. I got quite good at it and wanted to experiment on some of the younger girls' hair, but they preferred me to braid theirs, and to tip each little spike with colored ribbons.

The washing machines only wash and drain the clothes. Then they need to be transferred soaking wet to the wringer. Operating the wringer is like running a ride at an amusement park. You've got to fill it up, clamp the top down, get it started with the foot pedal, press the electric button and away it goes. You can't get distracted or forget

220

about it because if you do, the centrifugal force of the machine is so great that the wringer permanent pleats everything inside it.

As the dryer rotates, the clothes tumble down like a fabric waterfall. To its hum is added the tinkling of buckles and metal buttons that free fall rhythmically onto the sides of the drum. I sort the ironing into categories - shirts and blouses together, pants and dresses in another pile, then shorts. The four ironing boards are built into the wall so that we have to stand one behind the other to iron. When there's more than one of us ironing, we keep our heads down and speak over our shoulders or to someone's back. We gossip and complain, making ripples in our lives while we smooth out the wrinkles in our clothes.

When the Kallman Home for Children was in full swing, bed sheets and linens were sent out weekly to a laundry service. Every Wednesday we stripped our beds as soon as we got up. Our bottom sheet, our pillowcase and our towel was exchanged each week. The top sheet became the bottom sheet and the clean one went on top. The dirty sheets were stuffed into large bags and the bundles were left on the floor in the middle of the laundry room to be collected the next morning by the laundry service.

The laundry room, like the playrooms, isn't a restricted area, and since we often have last-minute ironing to do, it isn't locked at night. But it is situated in a dark and quiet corner of the building and in the past, for some children, the temptation to sneak in there and do things that you're not supposed to was very great. I had known for some time that my friend, Geraldine, had been meeting one of the boys in the laundry room on Wednesday nights. "Be careful," I told her. "You don't know what Mr. Scott might do if you get caught."

"It's just a laugh. Don't worry. We're not down there long enough for anyone to notice we're missing," she said. But she was wrong.

Mr. Scott took the telephone call from the laundry service himself. They reported that the man making Thursday morning collections complained that the laundry bags were scattered all over the place. That Wednesday night the director made a surprise inspection. He hid in the shadows outside and waited for something to happen. Some time after he saw several kids slip through the heavy doors and pull them quietly shut, he barged in and switched on the lights. He caught four couples embracing on top of the bags. He promptly ordered a huge padlock to be put on the laundry room door where a latch had sufficed for so many years.

I miss Geraldine. She quit school and left the Home the day she turned sixteen. We'd been friends since we met in the temporary shelter. The small fact that we knew each other beforehand was enough to cement our relationship on my arrival. We stuck together like glue from the start. But as we grew up, our differences got larger. One of our favorite games was to stand in front of the large mirror in the playroom at the start of each month and compare our heights. One month she would be a bit taller, another time it would be me. It all stopped one day when I said, "Look! I'm taller!" She turned on me and scowled. "Well, bully for you! Who wants to be a giant? I'd rather be small anyway." She stomped out and left me standing there asking myself why I had to grow up.

After that things weren't the same. Our bodies had begun to change and Geraldine's proportions were far more alluring than mine. She showed her curves off to advantage with tight sweaters and short skirts, while I, more self-conscious of the changes going on in my body, went the opposite way, selecting my sweaters looser and my skirts longer. Unwilling to draw attention to myself as she did, we conflicted often. Physical differences didn't matter to me as much as they did to her and I still liked her. But I had the feeling that sometimes she was ashamed to have me around because she didn't approve of my dress sense or hair style. Other times, if I became the center of attention because of something witty I might have said, she would view me as her competitor and get angry with me. In the end, we grew away from one another naturally.

Geraldine is pregnant now and will have her baby before she turns seventeen. When I went to see her last week, she didn't look well. She was chain-smoking and constantly ran her fingers through her new, and shorter, hair style. I noticed that she'd been biting her nails. Her maternity dress was designed like a sailor's suit, white with a navy blue trim. I couldn't take my eyes off the blue tie that flopped from one side of her bulging belly to the other as she waddled around the small kitchen. She was happy to see me, she said, hadn't seen anyone for ages, and made me a cup of instant coffee, serving it up as though she'd done it all her life from that small space of a kitchen.

"I've got everything ready for the baby. Come and see," Geraldine said leading me to the bedroom. I followed her into a small room dominated by a large double bed. A small crib sat waiting in the corner. She opened a drawer full of tiny undershirts, booties and matinee coats. "My boyfriend's mother gave me those and these," she said, patting the top of a pile of diapers.

"That's nice," was all I could manage before my throat seized up. The plug had finally been pulled on our dreams of going to college, having careers, money and clothes. My ears roared with the gurgle and suck of our joint hopes spinning down the drain like unwanted dirty water. The elastic of our friendship had already been stretched to the limit before she left the Home. With a small ping within me it snapped that day, and Geraldine drifted away for good.

"So, what's new at the Home?" She asked me back in the kitchen while she rinsed out the cups and saucers.

"Not much."

"How many kids are left?"

"Not many."

"Are you still running the laundry room?"

"Not really."

Chapter Thirty-Four
The Burden Of Letters

9 April, 1962

Dear Jeanne,

How are you? I hope you feel much better than I do. Phyllis has been getting me sick. Ever since you left, she has been bugging my ass for no reason. She keeps on bringing up the same thing, "Just because Jeannie was arguing with me didn't mean you should have butted in."

She has really gone ape shit with her anger fits. You should really see her. She always says I never get out of the house, when I try to go with my friends, she always makes an excuse so I can't go, she really drives you to drink. (Booz)

Like this past weekend, my friend, Dennis wanted me to go down the shore this weekend, at Long Branch. Don't you think she would make up an excuse? She would, but she couldn't, so she got up like usual on weekends and started off bad so I couldn't go. She said get out of the house and don't come back, I said I wouldn't.

That all took place after she started hitting me with her hands, I kept on putting up my hands to block myself. Then she went and got the mop stick. It had an iron piece on the end. After beating me with that for a while she got an extension cord, folded it up and used it as a whip. I had some nice marks on me, but now they're almost all gone. After I stayed at my friend's house, she probably got worried. I didn't even have a coat and it was pouring cats and dogs. My friend Bobby gave me a sweatshirt with a hood.

When I came home around 9 o'clock, she really blew a gut. After hitting me she took my transistor radio and threw it against the wall, after the case was broken up, she stepped on the radio and broke the whole damn thing. She still wasn't satisfied. She took scissors and cut all the wires, she also tore up the speaker by stabbing it with the scissors. She said the record player and records were next.

I told her I think I'll tell Mommy where her $10 she gave me went, "into pieces". Then she started hitting me and said there's my pay check take $10 and bring it to your drunk no good fucken lazy mother.

Let that drunk bastard take care of you. I said maybe I will. After she started once more, I said, I wish Aunt Helen and some other people could see this. She said when I lived with Aunt Helen I never was like you. I said, not what I heard. And she tried to beat it out of me. She keeps on calling you a nigger bastard and Blackie. She must really hate you, she's just jealous. She needs a reason to keep me in the house now she's got one. For the whole month of April. After school I have to go home and scrub out the bathroom, nice hobby isn't it. The kids at school must think I'm some kind of a GOOK! When they call me up to go out on the weekend, I never can go. I had more freedom in the home. And to think I used to call it a Jail. It's like a paradise compared to here.

She's got a new one now, she don't call me winky anymore, she calls me Chink and Lard Ass. She really thinks of them. Every time I do the least thing wrong she says, "Brains don't mention it". That's all I ever hear. Oh, she calls me club feet. She rubbed my face against the bathroom wall because she says it was dirty. And the way my hair gets pulled, I think I'll be bald in a year. If I live that long. I really don't know what I'm going to do. Because something's going to happen sooner or later. She says she can't take it any longer, I'm the one that can't take it.

How is everything at the home? She still makes me wear that red winter coat in 75 weather. Have you gotten a new spring coat? Did you hear anything about getting Easter clothes this year? I'm not getting any. Maybe this Easter vacation I could come to see you. She's always complaining about how Mommy's complaining. She said to write to her and tell her to stop writing to her. I know how Mommy will feel when she reads it. She always says that she don't ever want to see you in the house again. Phyllis don't know I'm writing this letter. So when you write back make like you never got it. So I can be sure you got it, make an * in the corner of the letter you send me. Tell Valerie I said hello, and tell the other kids. Did you find out if I could come back to the home? I really mean it. Guess I'll sign off now.

Love, Andy

P.S. I don't think I'll be around long.

* * *

11 April, 1962

STATE OF NEW JERSEY
Board of Child Welfare
163 West Hanover Street
Trenton 25, New Jersey

Dear Sirs:

At present, there is a young boy very much in need of your help. This boy is my brother, Andrew Kliarsky.

My brother and I had been living together in a children's home in Brooklyn, New York, called Kallman Home for Children, for the past 5½ years, ending July 1, 1961. At this time he left the home to live with my sister Phyllis in Newark, New Jersey. It has now been 9 months since he has gone.

Being Andrew's other sister, I am very much concerned with his welfare. My sister is 20 years of age, my brother is 15, and I am 16. I suppose at first my sister had nothing but good intentions. Now, either she does not desire the responsibility of caring for him, or is not capable of handling him in such a way that I would not have to be writing what I am now.

Andy is not a happy boy, and I have become a nervous wreck worrying about him. I have visited my sister's house, but my visits have been very short and far apart. The reason for this is on the same basis for my appealing to you.

I am enclosing a letter which I have recently received from Andy. In it he states certain events which have occurred during his recent stay there. I, too, have witnessed previous incidents of the same nature. This is not what I can exactly call, "being brought up." Undoubtedly you have already noticed the atrocious, profane language used to describe the scenes. I have also witnessed this! Surely a person of ordinary surroundings would not write his sister a letter containing such vulgar verbiage unless he had been accustomed to such vulgarity.

Does a boy his age have to live amongst such poor examples of human relationships? Andy's presence in that house has brought

226

nothing but sorrow and almost hatred. My sister has high blood pressure now, and claims that Andrew has caused it. Andy has been blinking his eyes constantly the last few times I had been to see him. This was, no doubt, due to tension and nervousness. My sister is absolutely miserable and sorry that she had ever taken him "home."

Phyllis despises me because I tried to explain that things were not going as well as they should. But, my main concern is Andy. Is there any possible way of having him removed from his present environment? Please help me. I want the best for both my sister and my brother, and only you can help me. As I am where I am and only of the age of 16, it is quite difficult for me as my hands are tied.

Being that Andy is now a resident of New Jersey, is it altogether impossible for him to return here to Brooklyn? I am sure that even a children's home in New Jersey would be a place where he would be given considerable understanding.

As I said before, I want only what I seem would be the best for both sides. But, without doubt, Andrew will not be strong enough to resist the daily conflicts with which he is so unfairly faced.

Will you please notify me if any kind of action is introduced into this situation? I am deeply indebted to you if a feasible solution is sought out soon.

Very sincerely yours,

Jeanne Kliarsky
Enclosure

STATE OF NEW JERSEY
BOARD OF CHILD WELFARE
Joseph E. Alloway, Executive Director
163 West Hanover Street
Trenton 25

April 19, 1962

Miss Jeanne Kliarsky
Kallman Home for Children
8515 Ridge Boulevard
Brooklyn 9, New York

Dear Miss Kliarsky:

This is in reply to your letter of April 11, 1962. We can certainly understand your anxiety about your brother. It sounds as though he is having a difficult time. Unfortunately, there is not anything that our agency can do for the present. It seems to us that the first thing you could do would be to talk to your caseworker about this problem. Perhaps, the Home could take some steps to help you and your brother. They would know, for example, how the arrangements were made for him to go to live with your older sister. They would know if there was another agency in New York City which was involved in this decision and, if so, whether that agency would be able to do something.

If after you talk with your caseworker the Home wants to write to us, we would be glad to see it there is any action we might take.

We realize that this may be disappointing to you, but we think that this would be the best way for you to get started on this matter.

Very truly yours,

G. Thomas Riti, Acting Executive Director

The tears that I've shed for Andy and his predicament have dried up, but the burden of these letters lays heavily on me. A sharpness stabs me in the chest whenever I breathe in and I sigh heavily when I exhale. My arms and my legs are like rubber. I can't eat. When I pick up my fork and put it to my mouth, my lips won't part. I don't speak to anyone because I am afraid that the effort needed might break me up into little pieces. I don't go to school. What's the use?

The nurse lets me stay by myself in the infirmary for a couple of days, even though she insists that there's nothing wrong with me. My hands fumble with the buttons of my blouse so badly that I don't bother to get dressed and lay in my pajamas in the narrow hospital-like bed. I'm so weak that I can't even make a fist or comb my hair.

"I think she's suffering from a nervous...," I hear the nurse whisper through the thin walls of the infirmary before her voice drops away to nothing.

"Keep her off school for a couple of weeks," I hear the director say. "She can stay in the dorms. Whatever it is, she'll get over it sooner or later."

I had forgotten how quiet it could be in the Home without the shuffle of feet along the corridors, the slap and bang of the wardrobes and drawers, the shouts above the bathroom faucets and the flushing of toilets. I lay in bed for days and watch dust particles dance in a ray of sunshine. When rain patters on the windowpanes, I watch it fill up the dry spaces. Then I find myself outside on a nice day.

"Look at her! She's not allowed! No one's allowed on the lawn," I hear Anita say from the open door.

"They said she could. She's sick remember," Margie snaps back.

When my mind clears, I re-read the letters. What the New Jersey Board of Child Welfare writes is correct. I should be able to talk to the social worker, the director, a caseworker. But how do I tell them what they already know, that it was the 'Home' that encouraged Andy to leave in order to empty the place? I have no power to explain their objectives for getting rid of everyone. The Home's social worker backs up the director. He does what he is told. If confronted, they would back each other up. It is useless going to him. He would never agree to getting Andy out of the situation that the social worker pushed him into. I should have known that I was wasting my time writing letters.

Andy came to see me over Easter vacation. He admired my new suit, a pale green woolen skirt and jacket that I now wear to school and to work afterwards. He still regrets leaving because he has outgrown his clothes and looks silly in his too-short pants and too-tight shirt. He said that things have settled down between him and Phyllis, but I noticed bruises on his face and neck. His nervous eye twitch was worse than ever. As he cracked his knuckles one by one, over and over again, I saw that his fingernails were bitten down to the bone.

We talked about long ago when we lived at home and he reminded me about the time I smashed his finger in the bathroom door. "I didn't do it on purpose. It was an accident," I said, defending myself. He held up his crooked finger. And I held up mine. They matched. We hooked them together like you do when you make a secret wish, and we could laugh now at what we'd been through. At the time my finger was damaged, I thought back to Andy's injury and though maybe it was just punishment for what I'd done to him.

It happened a while back when there were still lots of kids in the Home. We were playing volleyball in the courtyard. Being tall, I had a position close to the net. I raised my arms to block the ball and it caught my small left finger. I heard a crunch and cupped my hand close to me as the stars I saw flashed and winked even though my eyes were shut. The pain was excruciating. Within minutes the finger had swollen to double its size. The housefather refereeing the game said I should report it to the Director who would run me to the hospital, as it was Saturday and nurse wasn't on duty.

"What's the matter now?" he asked as I entered his office. I quickly explained what happened and showed him my finger. He glanced at it from over his desk and laughed. "Nothing wrong with that. Get back to the game and stop wasting my time." I took myself and my pain away in silence.

When the swelling and discoloring went away and the pain subsided, the finger was bent out of shape in two places. It was apparent that I'd broken it. It is funny how things turn out and how it resembled Andy's finger. The pain was bad, but nothing like the pain I felt when I was unable to help him when he needed me.

Mom writes that she has been temporarily released from the Kings Park State Hospital and is working in a nearby hospital as an aid. She is still under the mental home's care, however. She keeps in touch with Andy, sending him a letter once in a while, and some money to cheer him up, but that doesn't mean that she's able to look after him yet.

Chapter Thirty-Five
Flight

If I had someone to write home to I would say that junior high school was great, cool, groovy. Since I don't, I keep my feelings locked up. But there's so much I want to tell and it's almost bursting out so I start a diary. *Dear Diary,* I write, *The boy who sits behind me in English class keeps pulling my braid when I'm not looking. He calls me "Wang Lung". That's the name of the man in THE GOOD EARTH, the book we are reading. He also has a single braid, but cuts it off. I think he likes me.*

I stop there, too embarrassed to write this even in a secret diary. I am also scared that I can't keep it a secret in the Home. Someone is sure to find my diary and then the whole world would know everything about me. I tear out the page and rip it up into tiny pieces, chucking them and the diary into the garbage can. I tell myself it's a stupid idea anyhow.

I take a public bus to The William McKinley Junior High School #259 in Brooklyn. It's far enough away from the Home that I feel like I can become a whole new person there. Hardly anyone knows me and I fit in with the crowd like everybody else. I don't stand out as a 'Home' child like in elementary school. There it was obvious who the Home kids were because we lived across the street and they saw us coming in and out of there at lunchtime. But we have a cafeteria at McKinley and stay in the building at lunchtime, so I've made a lot of friends. We've got dancing in the playground over lunch hour. The gym teacher puts records on over the loudspeaker. Only the girls dance, though.

The teachers treat us like grown-ups. My 7th grade home teacher, Mr. John J. Fox, is also my English teacher. He's really nice. He knows that I'm in the Home, because of the social worker's signature on my report card, but hasn't let the cat out of the bag. I went to his house for supper once with another boy from the Home and his wife made us spaghetti and meatballs. Afterwards we listened to a recording of poetry and short stories by Edgar Allen Poe – *The Raven, The Pit and the Pendulum, Annabel Lee.* Mr. Fox encourages me to read poetry aloud to the class. He has put my name forward for the

Public Speaking Contest. I am not too sure about this, but he assures me I can do it. I am reading *Matilda*, a humorous poem, but would have preferred something more serious like Julius Caesar's speech.

I'm on the Honor Roll! Being in junior high school is wonderful. The work is easy and the teachers have given me good grades. I can't wait to get home every afternoon and start my homework. Everything is so interesting! I don't like missing classes when we have Glee Club rehearsals, but it is such fun being in the school choir. We've put on a few shows and I've been a 1920's flapper. I made the dress myself in Home Economics and there's even a picture of the four of us dancing the Charleston in the yearbook.

We have 'Options' and I've taken up typewriting and French. I'm so busy at school that I hardly have time to worry about the Home. Mr. Mark Smolinsky, my 9th grade home teacher, has congratulated me on getting on the Honor Roll again, and this time with a star. For the graduating class yearbook, THE MCKINLEYAN 1960, my achievements have been listed: Cafeteria Squad, Office Monitor, Class President, Class Vice-President, Glee Club. Mr. Smolinsky says I should consider going to Fort Hamilton High School in Bay Ridge to do academic studies, so I put that down, too, but I probably won't go there. For a start, it's too close to the Home!

It must have snowed during the night. There's a thick layer of frost on my window and though I have scraped it off the inside, I still can't see out. It's freezing in the dorm and the radiators are barely warm. I put so many heavy blankets on my bed last night that I could hardly turn over during the night. I can always tell when there's been a lot of snow because the outside sounds are muffled. The window by my bed is frozen shut, but I blow my hot breath on a small spot for a while and melt a view of the street. Was there a blizzard while we slept? "Snow's coming down, fine, like white rain," I announce to the others still warmly tucked up. No one seems to care.

"Yippee! No school!" one of the juniors shouts running barefoot down the corridor in her underpants.

"Get your clothes on," I tell her. "You'll catch your death!"

"I don't care," she shouts over her shoulder.

"You will when you're dead," I say chasing her into the room.

233

Will there or won't there be school? The young girls only need to cross the street, but the junior high school pupils need to take the bus. Will there be one? After breakfast I wrap up like an Eskimo and head for the bus stop across the street. My booted feet sink into snow clear up to their tops. I wade past snowdrifts with peaks as stiff as whipped egg whites. The snow beats against my face, stinging it in a million places. It's hard to see ahead of me. Luckily, there is no traffic yet on the unplowed streets, but curbs and steps, gutters and hydrants are hidden and I walk where I should step and step where I should walk. I am the only person out and except for a faint whistle in the wind, all is silent. Then, through snow thick as a gauze curtain, I see a bus. It gambols towards me like a white elephant. My heart skips a beat as I get on because I won't have missed one single day of school.

I didn't think junior high school days would ever end, but they did. I graduated last week and was sad to say good-bye to my friends. We cried, but we laughed, too, because we were happy. We discarded our bobby socks and baggy sweaters, saddle shoes and straight skirts for graduation dresses, high-heeled shoes and white gloves. My friends were getting fancy white dresses – they talked of nothing else since Easter. I was determined to have one too, and saved up hard for mine by going for every baby-sitting job I could get and sacrificing candy and chewing gum. I had seen this advertisement in the back of the yearbook:

JAY DEEN TEEN SHOP
HEADQUARTERS FOR ALL TEEN APPAREL –
DRESSES. COATS. LINGERIE. SUITS.SPORTSWEAR.HOSE
SIZES 6-14, 7-15
We also carry trim teen sizes 8 1/2 – 16 1/2
COME IN AND SEE US FOR YOUR GRADUATION DRESSES
7302 5TH AVENUE, BROOKLYN, N.Y.

The store was easy to find and once inside, it didn't take me long to choose a dress. I was used to making quick decisions, too afraid that if I hesitated, it might never happen. The saleslady helped me select a pair of white cotton gloves to go with the sparkling white organdie dress with the tulle crinoline under slip. The next day I bought a pair of shoes to complete the outfit. It took a lot of concentration to walk without wobbling in the 4-inch-high white stilettos, but worth it because at the graduation ceremony, everyone else was wearing similar shoes.

Only a few of my classmates knew that I lived in the Home and I wanted to keep it that way. I made excuses when anyone asked me where my parents were. I had half-hoped that my sister, Phyllis, would come. She promised to when she came to see me at the Home last Christmas, but that was six months ago, and she probably forgot. It would have been nice, though. Phyllis is our most loyal visitor, the only one Andy and I could call 'family'. She tries to be mother, father and sister to us, but she winds up being so bossy that we usually ended up arguing.

After Andy and I moved into the Kallman Home for Children, it was nearly two years before we set eyes on Phyllis. She had written us a couple of short letters just before and after she left Aunt Helen's, telling us that with the new baby our aunt couldn't cope with looking after her, too. She was too old to join us because you have to be no more than 12 years old to get taken into a children's home. She was sent to a convent in Albany. She wrote that she hated it and the nuns. It was like a prison and the only way to get out was to quit school at age sixteen and get a job. We didn't hear from her for a long time after that. Then one evening she showed up. We didn't recognize her until she spoke. "So, what've you kids been up to?" She looked taller than 5'10" because she had lost weight. Her straight black hair was bleached blonde, almost white, and it fell to her shoulders in thick curls. She wore heavy black eye make-up that was smeared from squinting into the wind on the motor bike she roared up in. Her black leather trousers and jacket squeaked when she walked. She didn't stay long, and promised to come back soon. Every once in a while she took us out for the weekend, but with her busy life she didn't have too much time for us.

Exactly a week after my graduation she rang up. When someone shouted, "Jeanne, there's a telephone call from your sister," I stood up proud, hoping that everybody heard. There is an advantage in a children's home to having family. No matter how much you might love

235

or hate them, having some family is a status symbol. If nothing else, it means if there is a problem, you have someone to stand up for you. Orphans are pitied and farmed out to strangers at Christmas, and while the others wait with excitement in the entrance hall to be picked up by relatives, they hang back wrapping presents for people they have never met. All the staff, even the janitor, has family to go home to at Christmas when the Home shuts down for a week. Andy and I aren't orphans, but when no one comes for us, we know what the routines are.

All our phone calls come in at the office. "Hello," I say into the receiver, hoping no one else is listening nearby.

"Hi, it's me. I guess I missed your graduation. I had to do an extra shift at the factory. Was it good?"

"Yeah, great."

"Did you get that dress you wanted?"

"Yup."

"So, when are you coming to see me?"

"Well, I'm not baby-sitting this weekend, because Mrs…"

"Good, then come around lunchtime on Sunday. We'll get a take-out and you can tell me all about it."

"All right."

"Wear your graduation dress so I can take some pictures of you for my album."

"But if I take the subway it might get dirty."

"It'll be fine. I want to see you dressed up."

Phyllis has a new apartment in Manhattan. She sounds like she's in a good mood. Maybe this time it will be all right. Being with her lately has been like walking through a minefield. Everything is going fine, then puff! an explosion occurs. She scares people, even the ones she works with at the factory. It must be a nightmare working under her. She told us she was made a foreman because of her reputation for being tough. "You ought to see 'em run whenever I come around the corner. I tell 'em, 'Get back to work, you slobs, or, What'er you lookin' at, four eyes?' Ha, ha."

It was great having a sister like that when I was little. She was the powerful queen of the neighborhood. I hid behind her blue jeans and sneakers as she huffed her way up and down the streets like a genie released from a too-small bottle. I benefited from her power, but always paid for it. Phyllis expected loyalty and obedience, no matter what. Now she has me dressing up and going on the subway in my graduation dress. If I don't do as she says, she'll hold it against me and get back at me somehow. She's so temperamental. She contradicts herself so much. All of this puts me off balance.

I don't need any excuses to go to my closet and admire my graduation dress. I've only worn it once and felt wonderful the whole time, like a dream come true. The housemother says I keep the neatest closet in the dorms. Skirts and slacks are on the left, dresses and blouses on the right. In the corner, separate from all the rest so it won't get crushed, is the white dress.

With Phyllis' anxious face in the forefront of my mind on Sunday morning, I make sure that everything is exactly as it was last week. The organdie fabric with the satin trim around the scooped neckline is very white against my tanned skin. The bodice hugs the contours of my developing bustline. The short, puffy sleeves and flared skirt make my waist look small. The housemother comes up behind me and coos, "You do look marvelous, if I must say so myself." As a graduation present she had given me a finely embroidered handkerchief which I wore pinned to the satin sash at my waist. When I lifted it from its tissue paper wrapping, it carried with it the scent of her room and of violets.

Being the end of June, it is already hot outside and for once I am glad of the subway's cool drafts. Sundays are quiet down here. Most of the passengers are dozing or reading the Sunday papers. One or two slide admiring glances at me, but I look the other way, not wanting to encourage anyone.

Phyllis' new address is on Bleecker Street in Greenwich Village and when I emerge from the subway, I'm not sure which way to go. It's nearly midday and the humidity must be in the 90's. I rush to the corner to read the street signs. Within minutes there's a river of sweat running down my back. I wish I hadn't worn the dress. I should have resisted her demands. The dress is sticking to my back. It'll be ruined. I make a wrong turn and have to retrace my footsteps. I'm running now, speeding past bars and night-clubs, holding my breath against their promise of sour smells like stale tobacco and beer-polished tables. The strip joints are shut. I clatter past them and their meowing cats that seek shade outside their sun-tight doors. I mustn't be late. Nothing riles Phyllis more than being late.

I buzz. Phyllis opens the door quickly. "You're here! Well, look at you. Miss Glamorous! Come and sit by the fan. You hot? Wanna drink?" she asks in a rush.

We sit in the kitchen sipping Coca Colas and I listen as Phyllis chatters. It's mostly small talk. I hear a door shut behind me and suddenly remember that I forgot about my sister's friend, Max, short for Mary Craddock, from Ohio. I turn around and nod to her. Her hair is shorter than a boy's and when she smokes, she cups the cigarette in her hand between puffs. She never says much. She sits with her head sunk in the newspapers reading boring things like the sports and racing results. She nods at me, looks at Phyllis and plops herself down in front of boxing on the television.

Phyllis admires my dress, gloves and shoes one by one, running her fingers over the dainty lace handkerchief. "Nice. Very nice," she says. "I had no graduation dress. I skipped school that day. I hated it. I quit after that."

"But you're a foreman now," I say in her defense.

"Yeah. Couldn't get into a dress like that now. Too heavy."

I don't want to stare because I know how sensitive she is, but I notice that Phyllis is letting herself go. She's wearing a shapeless shift. Her bare arms, as big as hams, swing outwards instead of hanging at her sides.

"I'm starting a diet next week. Can't let myself get over 300 pounds, can I?" she says, laughing with a hiccup. "That reminds me. Hey, Max, how about going out for that pizza?"

"What'll it be?" Max asks without enthusiasm.

"Family size with the works."

Max rises to go. I watch her and just before she shuts the front door behind her I notice her shoes. She's wearing men's black lace-ups.

"That dress makes you look so grown up. You're even getting a bit of a shape, too. How do you get your hair in a bun like that, so round?" Phyllis says eyeing me up and down.

"There's a 'rat' inside."

"Lemme see."

I take out the pins and my hair falls down around my shoulders and half way down my back. "See, it's made of plastic strands and it's round like a doughnut. You put a ponytail in the middle, then spread it around and quickly pin everything into place. It's easy."

"Let me comb your hair," she says with her hand already on my head.

"It's okay. I can manage."

"I want to. Sit down over here." Phyllis sounds edgy so I obey her - anything to keep the peace - and let her run the comb through my hair.

"Ouch!" I say as she yanks at my head.

"Just a knot." I close my eyes and let the revolving fan blow cool air over me wishing Max would return with that pizza.

I only hear the second *Snip!* But by then, it's already too late. Phyllis has taken a pair of scissors and cut my hair off. I feel the perspiration on my naked neck cool to icicles before I leap out of the chair and head for the door. I crash through it unable to speak and slam into Max on the front stoop. The pizza box she's holding flies open and the pizza slides down the front of my dress landing on her shoes.

"Hey, you!" I hear her say, but I am already half a block away. The broiling heat has reached fever pitch. Black clouds threaten overhead and thunder is heaping up behind. Fat splotches of rain smack my cheeks and bounce off sizzling car hoods. My stilettos spark over granite pavements and sink into the melting tarmac streets. I make for the subway at breakneck speed. Just before I reach the staircase the skies open. I stop, tilting my head upwards, letting the rain roll right over me, soaking it up as the clouds empty, wanting to be brought to my senses. In no time my organdie graduation dress and its stiff tulle under slip are as limp as old lettuce.

On the dark platform I try to wipe off the tomato sauce with the handkerchief but only smear it further. As the train pulls in, I stare at the multiple images of the person reflected in its windows. I am ashamed of her and shocked by her stricken face. Her wet hair is unruly and sticks out in all directions. Her soggy dress hangs from her like a lifeless old dishrag.

The motion of the train lulls my dulled brain. In the swirl of jumbled emotions, I keep coming back to thinking how it is such a short way from flying high at the top to dropping low on the bottom. I shiver, hugging myself, rubbing my hands up and down the goose pimples on my arms.

Unconnected words slither around my brain, words that sound like what they mean. *Wretched: a., miserable, unhappy; of poor quality; contemptible, displeasing.*

As the train rolls along carrying me towards my future, I brighten, a little, and look forward to returning to the Home, where, whether I have family or not, at least I can be safe.

Chapter Thirty-Six
Central Commercial High School

Everyone, including myself, thought that I was going to go to Fort Hamilton High School, a short walk away from the Home. Middle class kids go there because the academic program is guaranteed to launch them into colleges and universities all over America. This is exactly what I want, but given the chance I graduated, what then? Where would I get the money to go to college? I needed to re-think my acceptance into Fort Hamilton High, even if it meant relinquishing my aspirations for the purely practical. To get from one step to another I needed to have short-term plans that included learning a skill or trade that could earn me better money than baby-sitting did.

There are schools where I can learn hairdressing, tailoring or bookkeeping. I ask Alice Marie Reed, a girl in the Home to tell me about Central Commercial High School in Manhattan. She is taking shorthand and typing there and said that the school has 2,500 students who come from every borough of the city except Staten Island, as well as 119 teachers. The tenth graders attend from 1 p.m. to 6 p.m., and the eleventh and twelfth graders from 8 a.m. to 1 p.m. These split sessions allow the students to work part time. It's a co-ed school with girls making up most of the student body. The idea of learning and earning at the same time appeals to me.

On the day of my interview, it takes more than an hour to get to 214 E. 42nd Street on the corner of 3rd Avenue, where the school, an old-fashioned, Gothic-style brick building, is tucked in among, and dwarfed by, glass and steel skyscrapers. When I see this, I am convinced that it's the school for me because the world around it throbs with life.

Alice is excited that I'll be going to Central even though she's graduating. I have known her since I arrived in the Home nearly six years ago. Her sister Jean is my age and joining Central, too, but she's leaving the Home this summer. Their brother Gilbert goes to a technical school. I ask Alice where her family get their almond-shaped eyes, high cheekbones and perfect skin.

"We're part Negro and part Cherokee Indian," Alice says smiling, a little self-consciously, before covering her laughing face with slender hands and long, freshly manicured fingernails.

From a distance I have always admired her poise and how she dresses better than most high school girls. "When you work in the City you've got to look good. We are not the 'collegiate' type. We're 'career kids'. We dress for business at Central." This may be true, but I believe Alice has natural class and style.

My guidance counselor, Miss Gelshenen, says, looking over my records, that I should be in the college program. "It's heavy, combining the commercial course with the academic, but others have done it. Over the next three years you'll take English, French, Biology, Mathematics and History, as well as Shorthand, Bookkeeping, Business Law and Typing." I haven't mentioned to her yet the small problem that I live in a Home and will have no financial support after I graduate. I tell myself, *One small step at a time.*

All my routines change. It's dark outside when I finish school at 6 o'clock. Not leaving for school until 11.30. means I have the mornings to myself. I'm not used to the quiet. Dormitory life means that the radio competes with the record player, and the record player competes with the television. Everyone's always talking, arguing and laughing at the same time – it's a wonder any homework gets done. I am used to screening out noises but the quietness of the mornings will take some adjusting to. Right now I wish I had someone to talk to. I have two hours before I leave for school. Last week I cleaned out my closet, drawers and locker. Maybe I'll comb my hair again.

Going up to Manhattan to school every day has given me the confidence to travel around New York City, and I love it. I visit museums on Sundays taking in the Metropolitan Museum of Art, the Guggenheim, the Museum of Modern Art, the Cloisters and wander among the Egyptian treasures of the Brooklyn Museum. I discover Matisse, Van Gogh, Pollock and ancient civilizations.

Looking at art makes me want to explore the outlines of myself. When I am totally alone in the dorms I sit before a mirror and attempt a self-portrait, carefully forming the oval of a face, adding the deep-set eyes above the high-cheekbones, having trouble with the up-turned nose, and not being happy about the full mouth.

I screw up my paper portraits, one after the other. I can't make a self-portrait because I'm only putting down what I see on the outside. I try smiling, but fail at that because everything alters and I look silly grinning at myself. Whatever I turn out like in my portrait isn't what I feel like. The pictures show a very serious almost sullen young woman with a faraway look in her eyes. They don't show that I've got guts, can stand up for myself or my determination. I abandon drawing until I am can capture what is behind my face.

Through experimenting I learn about make-up, drawing thick, black Cleopatra-style eyebrows over my sparse ones, only to be discreetly told by Miss Lanier, my stately English teacher, that my originals were better. I try to copy girls with elegant hands but after an evening of meticulously gluing on false fingernails I lose them the next day between the typewriter keys in Typing 101.

I am learning to accept myself as well as to admire the best in other people. My best friend Monika is tall and wafer-thin like a fashion model. She wears designer clothes that her parents buy her in Europe. "They spoil me because I'm an only child," she admits. I am glad when she's in the school fashion show, leading the others with natural grace and ease. It no longer worries me that I will never be like her because I have found my own niche. "I wish I could be like you, Jeanne," Monika admits, to my surprise, when I am appointed class monitor or when my French teacher awards me the *Prix d'Honneur*, or when I become editor-in-chief of THE HOURGLASS, our school yearbook.

During my three years at Central, Monika and I support each other in all things and grow close. I now dress better and she has lost some of her reticence. I am no longer ashamed to let people know I come from the Home and Monika, making up for a childhood of selfish oneness, throws a surprise birthday party for me on my sixteenth birthday, inviting Carol, Rosemary, Joanne, and Anna, our friends from Central High.

Discipline problems are few at Central because we work so hard. The sound of twenty manual typewriters going at the same time is so deafening that you couldn't talk out of turn or act up if you wanted to. Heads are down during shorthand dictation and it is so quiet you can hear a pin drop. We might shout across the crowded narrow corridors during class changes but are soon concentrating on our bookkeeping accounts or algebra. We don't get much of a chance to misbehave. As soon as school is out, we head for our jobs in lawyers' offices, accountants' firms or in the courts.

And there is more to be learned in school than you can get out of books. Monika and I are leaving school one afternoon when we bump into Mr. Buckley, the accountancy teacher. He talks to us a while, but as I am anxious to get my lunch and head for work, I urge Monika,

"Come on, let's go and have our cup of coffee at the Horn & Hardart."

"Listen to her," he says looking at Monika but pointing at me.

"What do you mean?" I ask. He's got my attention now.

"Cawfee! Let's have a cuppa cawfee!" he mimics me.

"What's wrong with that?"

"You need elocution lessons. You sound like something the cat dragged in. Cawfee, indeed."

So, I talk like a New Yorker! That's news? I should do, I come from Brooklyn, don't I? He makes me so mad I could spit! But after listening to myself for a while I realize that he's right, and that he's done me a favor. I realize then that I need to do something about my terrible New York accent.

I work hard at all my subjects and my report cards sing with high grades averaging in the 90's. I take to typing and shorthand like a duck does to water. My fingers and hands go like the wind. I love everything about office work, its orderliness, the smell of clean paper, even office machines with their way of getting under your skin when they don't cooperate. I can work any type of switchboard between old-style and monitor. My brain is in full gear and I am in top form.

However, there is an area in my life where I still can't strike a balance – in the Home. The more praise I get at school, the more I am ignored in the Home. Since junior high school days, no matter how well I do, it doesn't change things. I am worse off than before because the director now considers me a 'smart-ass' and 'a know-it-all'. I would be lying if I said it doesn't bother me. It bothers me a lot. My instincts tell me to ignore him and to become more determined to succeed than ever. *Don't be undermined. He's trying to get at you in another way.* All my report cards are signed by the social worker or the director and returned by way of the housemother without comment. I guess they know as well as I do that I am working for myself and not for their praise. At the end of each school year their signature is not required. I keep all my report cards, stowing them in my bedroom drawer.

It's February, 1961 and Manhattan's streets are piled high with snow turned a dirty gray by the traffic. I'm cold and hungry when I finally get home around 7.30 p.m. Ever since I started split-session school my supper has been saved on the stove in the main kitchen because the downstairs dining hall has been cleared away and locked long ago. As I am stuffing a forkful of cold mashed potatoes into my mouth and going over a page of intermediate algebra equations, I hear Mr. Scott creeping down the long entryway. His crepe-soled shoes squeak on the waxed linoleum tiles forewarning me. My potatoes are still on my tongue as he pulls himself up. Obvious that it's me he's seeking, as I am the sole occupant of the room, I raise my eyes and wipe my mouth with my napkin.

"I have some bad news for you," he says staring hard at me to take in the full impact of my reaction to what he is about to say.

"Umpf?" I say, the potatoes still in my mouth, weighing down my tongue.

"Your father is in the hospital. He's dying. You're to go and see him tomorrow morning. Your brother knows already. Take him with you." The yellow-speckled eyes pierce my confusion and unhappiness. In memory of my father I do not let my gaze waver, either. Only I have had no success in swallowing the mashed potatoes. They won't budge, won't go passed the lump in my throat. Tears of pain form in my eyes. "Okay," I say in a grunt and pretend to cough into my napkin. He's gone when I look up.

I take my plate over to the garbage can and scrape everything into it, spitting out the mashed potatoes on top. The rest is automatic - washing and drying the dishes and cutlery, wiping the table, turning out the lights and going upstairs. All the while I am thinking of one word that he said, "Dying". I haven't seen Dad since the day he came to celebrate his birthday two years ago, when I told him I wish he was dead and that I didn't want to see him again. He never came back.

Two more birthdays, celebrated who knows how without us, and now my wish has come true

Andy and I find out that Dad was admitted to ward A4 at Bellevue Hospital on January 30th, a full eight days before. After visiting Mom in the mental home we both hate hospitals - the smell of antiseptic and bandages, injections and coughing old people, gives us the shivers. Following our feet to the assigned place we find ourselves at the bottom of his bed. A wizened, yellow-faced man with almost no hair writhes under a white sheet. His skin is dry, resembling parchment. His mouth gapes open like a guppy struggling for breath at the top of a fishbowl. We don't know what to say. Was this the man I feared? The father whose hand's strength sent a kid flying across the room in a single swipe? The stare in his eyes is gone. Where is the fixating hold of a soul tormented between right and wrong, between beauty and ugliness, and love and sentimentality?

The fingers on Dad's left arm move. Is he beckoning us to come closer? "He's going in an out of consciousness at the moment," a male nurse says behind us. Andy turns to the man and I walk to the head of the bed. My father's eyes open and suddenly he grabs my hand. The grip is brittle and feverish. "Jeannie," he says. "Jeannie." Before his eyes close again, I notice that even his eyeballs are yellow.

The nurse picks up and reads the clipboard at the bottom of Dad's bed. He shakes his head occasionally as he turns the pages. While we wait for him to say something I look around the ward that's full of dying, old men. They cough and spit, they twist and turn under the covers and it reverberates in my ears, ping-pongs against the side of my head and I want to run out. "He has cirrhosis of the liver," the nurse says. We hear Dad's full story from the ward doctor.

"He was picked up unconscious in the Bowery."

Dad, you have sunken low. Facing a harsh winter, you searched for warmth among those bodies in the Bowery that are no better than corpses. What were you thinking of?

"He has an address, but doesn't appear to have been living there."

Was it your loneliness that drove you there? No one to hear your snores, to prod you awake?

"He's in the final stages now. His liver's gone. Wood alcohol is what they drink when they can't afford real liquor."

246

Nothing but filthy derelicts sharing rotten booze down at the Bowery. Did you trade your responsibilities for that?

"I'm afraid his prognosis isn't good."

Adieu, written on bitter yellow parchment.

Gall fills my mouth and I hurtle out of the ward in search of a sink. Andy chases behind me. "Jeanne, wait!"

"What's going on?" he asks outside the toilets. "What are you crying for? I thought you hated him like I do? Why are you crying, Jeanne? Aren't you glad he's dying like I am?"

"I don't know. I can't help it. It's useless. That's all. The whole rotten world is so damned useless! He's dying, Andy, dying. Does it have to end up like that, one great big nothing?"

"But we hate him, we hate him, we hate him. Look at how many times he tried to kill Mommy! How he ruined our lives. I can't understand you. One minute you hate him and the next minute you're crying because he's dying."

"I know. I'm sorry. I can't help it. I'm not crying for him, I'm just crying."

I look up *wood alcohol* in the dictionary. *n. another name for methanol, a colorless volatile poisonous liquid compound used as a solvent and fuel, also called methyl alcohol.*

Two days later Mr. Scott comes down to breakfast and calls me out into the corridor. "Your father died last night. There won't be a funeral. He's being buried by the State in potter's field."

I drag out my dictionary again.

potter's field n. 1. a cemetery where the poor or unidentified are buried at the public expense. 2. New Testament. The land bought by the Sanhedrin with the money paid for the betrayal of Jesus (which Judas had returned to them) to be used as a burial place for strangers and the friendless poor (Acts 1:19; Matthew 27:7).

247

Chapter Thirty-Seven
"You Want Miz Johnson?"

Today I'm crossing over to the other side of the tracks. To get to where I am going I have to cross Queens Boulevard, walk through Forest Hills village, pass under the brick archway into Forest Hills Gardens, side-step the Forest Hills Tennis Courts and make my way along Greenway South. I set out early and my round overnight bag bangs against my knee as I stride away from the sign saying BROOKLYN HOME FOR CHILDREN. The funny thing is, the home isn't in Brooklyn any more. It moved years ago – lock, stock and barrel - to Forest Hills in Queens.

At the end of my road, I glance backwards. Parallel rows of elm trees lead up to the entrance of the Home which is made up of four brick-built cottages surrounding an administration building, all snugly set in a stretch of green lawn. It's a good place. I like it, even though I had what you'd call 'a bad start' there.

Mr. Quentin D. Scott was adamant that the Kallman Home for Children would close down by the end of June 1962 and told me I'd better think of packing my bags, get a job and make something of myself. "But I can't drop out of school now that I am doing so well. I've got just one more year to finish. Can't I stay on here? I've got nowhere else to go," I told him.

"What about your sister? Why don't you stay with her?"

"No. Impossible," I said, shaking my head. "Besides, she's living in New Jersey now and I couldn't go to school from there."

"There's a place in New York City on 14th Street, The Wayward Girls Home, that takes girls your age. It's not free, though. You'll have to pay $40 a week for your room and board. If you use your secretarial skills, you can work during the day and go to night school," he said, sewing up all the details nicely.

"I'm supposed to graduate with my class next June!"

"It's tough, I know."

"What about another Home?

"Out of the question. Once you've turned 13 you can't be considered for a place in a children's home. Sorry. Too bad you can't get along with your sister. Why don't you go and see that place in the City?"

After she left the convent in Albany, Phyllis stayed at a place similar to the one Mr. Scott recommended. She brought Andy and me over there quite a few times. It wasn't bad. The other girls were all right, but they were all working girls. Not a single one was going to school. She made quite a few friends, I remember. She even had a nice room where you could look out on the back yard from her window. It was about the time when she bleaching her hair, wearing lots of jewelry like jangly bracelets, earrings that looked like sunbursts and flowers, and colorful, beaded necklaces. She had small baskets on her dresser full of lipsticks, Coral Sea, Luscious Pink, Ruby Red, and let me try some on for the first time. Another basket overflowed with eyebrow pencils, Maybelline mascara (the kind where you spat on the small brush and rubbed it on the block of black and then applied it to your lashes) and there was Peacock Blue, Emerald Green and Gold eye shadow in separate plastic cups with lids.

With these memories I began to get my hopes up and wondered if my savings would hold out long enough for me to finish school. My after-school job money could go towards my toiletries, books, carfare, clothes; well, it would pay for some of it. Maybe one year? But two? If my calculations were right, it wouldn't last that long. I decided to give it a stab as it was my last resort. Maybe the person in charge would be understanding, give me a loan which I could pay back later. When? What about college?

I took the subway to Canal Street station the following Saturday morning. As I got off the train I saw a couple of tramps in dirty overcoats sleeping on the platform. I ran up the stairs to the street two at a time and took a deep breath outside as my nerves were getting the better of me. I only had to walk two blocks, but before I was halfway there wolf whistles rang out from a gang of youths across the street. I quickly looked away, stumbling over my own feet, and breaking out in a sweat. I climbed the granite stoop at the address on my piece of paper and rang the doorbell. I caught a glimpse of several women sitting in the front parlor by the window. Their faces were heavily made up and it was only 9.30 in the morning. They were smoking on the sofas in their dressing gowns. A black-haired lady with red lips and gray eyes the color of bullets interviewed me. "We don't put up with men in the house and curfew is at 10 o'clock. We expect your rent on time. There's no loud music in the rooms. Someone will show you around. Come back afterwards and we can make arrangements. Have you got a deposit?" I took in her questions and comments like a dartboard takes in darts. "Sylvie, show her around, will you?" she said to a tall girl passing by her office.

Sylvie gathered her kimono around her long legs and smirked, yanking her head for me to follow her. "Parlor," she said and opened the door. Inside the parlor I murmured a small "hello" to the women, but they looked right through me. Upstairs she showed me the toilets and bathroom. "Bogs," she managed to say and lit up another cigarette, throwing the butt end of the other into the toilet bowl. She was about to make her final utterance, "Bedroom" probably, but I didn't wait. I turned and ran out into the street without a goodbye or a thank you.

I don't think anyone living there was going to school. I couldn't visualize myself moving in with those women or living in that neighborhood. I wasn't ready for that yet.

My school guidance counselor confirmed that I would have to leave Central Commercial High School and go to night school if I had a full-time job during the day. Doing it that way it would take me at least two years to finish school and it wouldn't be the same. I wouldn't know any of the teachers or students. Feeling desperate, I tried one more time to appeal to Mr. Scott. "Sooner or later you'll have to find out the facts of life," he said to me, a grin twitching up at the corners of his red, full mouth. "It's been easy for you so far. You'll have to find out what it's like to fend for yourself."

"Couldn't you at least try to find out if any other Home would take me?" I pleaded. I hated begging him, knowing that he was loving it, but I had too much at stake to let my pride get in the way. The time for games of wit were over.

"I've already told you. It's out of the question," he replied, losing his temper slightly.

"Can't you ask them to make an exception? You've got to do something…"

"Why should I do anything? After your insolent behavior over the past years you don't deserve any special treatment."

"What am I going to do? Where can I go? I've got to finish school. I've got to. You've got to do something!"

"I don't have to do anything. For all I care you can walk the streets for a living. Let's see what other talent's you've got. It's none of my concern anymore. Now leave me alone. I have other things to worry about."

On the seesaw of events, I had reached my lowest point at the Kallman Home for Children. While at school, I soared to dizzying heights, receiving the accolade of my teachers and getting over 90% in almost all of my subjects. I was beginning to think I was suffering from a split personality. What else would explain the difference in the two very different lives I was leading? On the one hand, I could do nothing right. On the other, I could do no wrong. But I couldn't afford to linger on these questions. I had to find a solution to my problem, and fast. Time was running out and it was obvious that it was up to me to do something.

I racked my brain for a solution. All I could think of was to write a begging letter to all the children's homes that I could think of in Brooklyn, Manhattan and Queens, explaining my situation, leaving myself at their mercy. Of the replies I had, they were sorry about my plight, but they couldn't do anything, their hands were tied, but they wished me luck. Only one reply was positive. Margaret A. Milne, founder and administrator of the Brooklyn Home for Children, Forest Hills 75, New York, replied that I could move into the senior girls' cottage from June, 1962 to June, 1963.

I was so relieved I became immediately engrossed in studying for my final exams. Memories of my last days in the Kallman Home for Children blur and wobble like a mirage. I rose early, left for school at 6.30 am, worked after school and studied at night. On the weekends I sorted through my belongings, packing away birthday cards and souvenirs, throwing away letters and old term papers. There were five, four, then three of us left to rattle around in the old place. Dust gathered in corners, beds lay silent, their sheets and spreads gone and their mattresses rolled up like herrings. We had all the sinks we wanted in the morning and took a bath whenever we liked. There was no one fighting over the last towel, or whose turn it was to have a shower. But when I opened my eyes each morning, the sun still shone through the windows as it always had, projecting a yellow rectangle on the polished wood floors – and probably always will.

It was rumored that Mr. Scott was going to turn the place into a home for the blind. How we laughed at that! At least they wouldn't be able to see what a creep he was, we all agreed. We needed that laugh at the end. It was the only way we could go and never look back.

Valerie and I were the very last to depart. We brought our bags out into the hall, autographed each other's albums and yearbooks - *Roses are red, violets are blue, Don't forget me, I won't forget you* - and promised to keep in touch. My eyes blurred over when I thought of our various futures spun out before us. Would they be rosy, like pink cotton candy from Coney Island, once a handful of sugar, to expand and broaden into something completely different and wonderful?

My report card was the best ever so far. I was voted Honor Society President and appointed Editor-in-Chief for the Senior Class Yearbook. Most important of all, I was accepted for full-time summer employment by my part-time employer at the lawyer's office. He was raising my pay from $63 to $85 per week and wanted me to work with other lawyers renting his offices. I was on top of the world and looking forward to a fresh start at the new Home. But as fate would have it, things didn't go forward, they rolled backwards. Nothing could have prepared me for the reception I got on arrival. I was foolish to believe that leaving the Kallman Home for Children meant leaving troubles behind. Mr. Scott turned out to be too vindictive for that. I should have suspected something when I showed him my letter of acceptance into the new Home. He went quiet and after clearing his throat a couple of times, said he would send my files ahead in the mail. I wasn't expecting handshakes or good luck wishes, but I also wasn't expecting him to do what he did.

"Welcome to the Brooklyn Home for Children, Jeanne," Miss Milne, the director, said motioning me to sit down near her desk. Her hair was pure white and done up loosely in a French twist. Trailing, end-of-the-day wisps of hair caught the light from the window behind her casting a glow about her head like a halo. I looked up at her beatific smile.

"Thank you, Miss Milne," I said politely, hoping to make a good impression. But she turned away from me and spread her hands over a manila file lying in front of her on the polished desk. She removed her eyeglasses and closed her eyes for a couple of seconds and drew in a powerful breath through her nostrils. Her eyelids trembled like a blind person's, but stayed shut.

"I have before me your file from the Kallman Home for Children." In the long pause that followed before she opened her fluttering eye lids, somewhere deep in the heart of me a tremble started. I tried to concentrate on the kids I could hear playing a game outside. "When I accepted you, I took you at your word. I trusted you. I believed that you truly needed a place to stay until you finished your studies..."

"Yes, that's...."

"Don't interrupt me!" she said loudly, slamming her hands down on top of the file. "I have read the complete report on you from Mr. Scott so don't think you can pull the wool over my eyes! I am a woman of my word and if I said I would let you stay here, I will. But, by God, if you step one foot out of order, you're out of here."

"Miss Milne, I don't know...."

"I know exactly what kind of a girl you are, so don't think you can fool me. I've seen a lot of liars come and go, but you take the cake! No, don't try to talk your way out of this one," she continued, shielding herself with her hands as though a word from me would X-ray zap her from the universe. "It's obvious you can't be trusted. Don't worry. We'll be watching you."

I sat still in the chair, mute, staring down at my hands, the fingers twisted together, the thumb muscles working, working.

"Report to the social worker for a psychology test before you see Mrs. Fraser at the cottage."

By the time I was assigned a bed and unpacked my suitcase, the word was out that I was a troublemaker. The housemother, Mrs. Cortwright, or 'Cortie' as the girls affectionately called her, gave me a towel and showed me to a seat in the dining room as though I were a leper. None of the girls showed signs of wanting to talk to me so I kept silent. I knew if I tried to defend myself, it would make a liar out of me. I recognized a few of the girls from summer camp. We were friends once, but now we roomed in silence.

Luckily, this didn't last long. A week later, the girls went off to camp or summer jobs and I was left completely on my own. It was made clear from the start that I was allowed to go to work; otherwise, I was grounded and kept under surveillance. "We know you're going out with men. It will have to stop," Mrs. Fraser told me. "One of them called up the other night. We know what you are up to." The blood rose to my cheeks when I heard this. Where did they get that from, I wondered. But the more they chided me, the more I pressed my lips together in silence. I tried my best to look pleasant and not miserable, but not too pleasant which might have been thought of as a form of triumph in having one over on them.

As soon as I'd heard the good news that I'd gotten a place in a children's home, I gave the telephone number to Andy. He was probably trying to reach me. I didn't have a boyfriend. When would I have time for one? I knew plenty of boys who were friends, at school, in the other Home, and once a Puerto Rican boy had tried to French kiss me in the Spook House ride in Coney Island three years ago, but "Men?" Why accuse me of that? I was tired of being an outcast and guilty until proven innocent, but at the moment it was my only means of survival. Miss Milne was acting on what she considered was the truth from someone in authority. She wasn't to blame. I was back where I started – it was Mr. Scott's word against mine.

As summer went by, Miss Milne went away and so did Mrs. Fraser, the senior housemother. Cortie and I shared the cottage. She was polite but kept her distance, and I, lulled by the silence and the lovely summer, spent my spare time in the grounds and read for hours in the rose garden. At work I typed like the wind. My boss was so impressed that he let me use the executive typewriter. I typed long legal briefs (one original and five copies). I transcribed straight onto the typewriter after three hours' dictation. When I finished my work, I was lent out to the other lawyers. I only stopped to go to the toilet and to take a half-hour lunch break. I spent all summer in the air-conditioned offices at 42nd Street and Avenue of the Americas. Each evening I joined other secretaries rushing home. Our stilettos clicked upon the sidewalks together. I returned to streets of rustling leaves, where, in the empty Home, my dinner was waiting for me on a plate on the edge of the kitchen stove.

Monika and I hadn't talked much about the children's home and she'd never been to see it. We spent too much time painting our fingernails and talking about school when I spent the weekends at her place. When I explained to her that I was grounded, she didn't bat an eye lid, just nodded at what I said and came to Forest Hills and spent Saturdays with me at the Home. It was remarkable how her friendship stretched to all things.

I had to learn new routines when school started. On Monday nights, we had 'religion'. The other kids were not allowed to attend the local church and Sunday school because they played up and the old ladies didn't like it. So a woman came to us from 7.30 to 9.30 p.m. to read from the Bible and play hymns on the piano. During the summer I had gone to church and Sunday school and continued to do so on my own. I explained to Mrs. Fraser that I didn't need to go to Monday night religion because I'd already been to church.

"I don't care. The rule is EVERYONE goes to religion on Monday nights, and that's FINAL. Now GET DOWN THERE!"

"When can I do my homework? It's due in tomorrow," I said in my smallest voice, trying to counteract her crescendo.

"Just do as you are told."

I wanted to protest, but didn't want to jeopardize my chance of being allowed to stay there, so went downstairs with the others. *Why don't they let me do my homework? I'm not asking a lot. I've already been to church and Sunday school.* These thoughts went round and round my head. I had a lot of homework. I slumped down in a chair at the back of the room shutting my eyes and ears to everything except the phrases ringing in my head. Afterwards the lady singled me out." Is something wrong, Jeanne?" Her voice was so sympathetic and kind that my story spilled out in a rush. "You sound very busy. Can you write down your timetable for me? Don't you worry one little bit. I'll talk to Mrs. Fraser about this," she assured me. I jotted down an outline of my day and gave her the slip of paper.

TIMETABLE

5.30 a.m. Get up
6.30 a.m. Leave for School
7.30 a.m. Arrive in Manhattan
7.30 – 8.00 School Door Guard
8.00 a.m. School Starts
1.00 p.m. School Finishes
1 – 1.45 Lunch with Monika
1.45 Leave for Work
2 – 5 p.m. Work in lawyer's office
5 p.m. Leave for Home
6 p.m. Arrive Home
6 – 6.30 p.m. Dinner
7 p.m. – 10.00 Homework

Her name was Mrs. Johnson. She fixed it with Mrs. Fraser to let me off religion on Monday nights because with lights out at 10 o'clock, she told her, I couldn't possibly finish my homework. "After all," I heard her say sweetly, "she has English, Social Studies, Biology, Mathematics, French, Stenography, Typing, Bookkeeping and Business Law, you know."

"Does she?" Mrs. Fraser said, her eyebrows rising to her hairline.

The following Monday night, I stopped my homework for a minute to sneak a look through the banister rails at Mrs. Johnson as she played the piano. I had been so upset that I hadn't noticed much about the lady who helped me. She was tall and strong-looking with a head of curly hair the color of spun gold. It was short and framed her face at the front but pinned up in a French twist at the back. She wore an opal ring with a stone the size of a quail's egg and it was surrounded by diamonds. I noticed it because the opal is my birthstone. I found out later that her birthday is a few days after mine in October. As she played the piano, she turned to face the girls and mouthed the words to the hymns, a bit in advance, for them. The whole time they never took their eyes off her and I envied the time they spent with her, but we can't have everything, can we?

Before leaving she came up to my room as I worked at my desk. "I've never seen anyone sit so still for so long. I have a daughter nearly your age," she said. "I wish she could do that. How would you like to come over for the weekend and meet her?"

"I'd love to, only... I'm grounded on the weekends."

"We'll see about that!" she said and went downstairs.

I waited a few minutes before curiosity got the better of me and dropped my pen and followed her. She was talking in quiet tones to Mrs. Fraser in the downstairs hallway. I rushed back and sat down quickly.

"It's all set," she said coming back. I stood up and faced her. As she spoke, her hands came up to flatten the collar of my blouse. All the while her eyes drove straight into mine. I couldn't help it. I was smiling. Had she come at last, I was thinking? Was she the guardian angel I had been waiting for? The one who will see me as a whole person, one worthy enough to be cared for, the one who will watch over me?

"You're coming over to my house on Saturday morning for the weekend. Here's my address," she said giving me her card. It read: "Mrs. Margaret Johnson, 53 Greenway South, Forest Hills 75, New York. Telephone – Boulevard 8-2822". It smelled of her cologne when I put it to my lips before going to sleep.

That's where I'm going now, to Forest Hills Gardens on the other side of Queens Boulevard, under the brick archway, past the famous tennis courts, along a winding street of magnificent houses, each one different and more splendid than the other. Hers is a corner house, a large red brick one with white woodwork and white pillars beside the widest front door I have ever seen. The grass on the lawn is thick and flatter than a man's crew cut, and as tight and tufted as a bright green carpet.

I press the bell and a *ding-dong* chime rings inside. For a second I feel self-conscious in my slacks and sweater and think that maybe I should have dressed up in a suit and heels. I hear faint footsteps, muffled voices and smooth back my long hair. The door opens warily and a very small Negro maid in a pale pink uniform pops her head around the door. She asks in a high-pitched, squeaky voice, "Yes?"

I'm nonplussed and not expecting a maid to answer the door. I've only seen servants in the movies and have never met one face to face.

"I'm from the Brooklyn Home for Children and I..." I begin, almost stammering.

"You want Miz Johnson?" she asks, instantly impatient with me. I nod. "Well, why didn't you say so? Don't stand out there all day. Come in. Miz Johnson," she shouts out loud in the direction of the back of the house. "There's someone here to see you!" Turning to me she says, "Wait here," and goes through a swinging door off the dining room.

I knew what crystal chandeliers were, and Persian carpets, and I'd seen gilt mirrors and grand pianos, but I'd never been in a real live home where they were dusted every day. My eyes flitted over the black and gold Chinese credenza and the black and white marble floors of the entrance hall. They wandered around the elegant curved staircase leading to floors above. Through the French doors on my right was an elegant parlor with a large porcelain lamp on top of a grand piano; original oil paintings, not prints were on the walls.

Mrs. Johnson was in the kitchen making lunch - hamburgers and iced tea. She wipes her hands on her apron and introduces me to her youngest daughter, Claudia. After lunch, Claudia takes me with her to her friend Bob's house where they are having a get together with other high school friends.

I figure out that they must go to the same private school and dress, more or less, the same. I'd call it 'collegiate'. The girls wear pastel-colored twin-set sweaters, kilts of varying plaids, matching knee-high socks inside brown penny loafers, with pennies that look brand new. They are friendly and normal and I almost forget to ask myself: *What must they think of me in my tight white slacks, fuzzy pink angora sweater, pearl-white nail polish, black patent leather shoes and thick purple eye shadow below my carefully pencilled-in Cleopatra-style eyebrows?*

Chapter Thirty-Eight
All The Buoys

It's as though someone has switched channels on the television. On one channel, everything is going wrong. On another, the facts of the story are revealed and great changes are taking place. It has to do with the first report card I brought home before Christmas. Up till then I was the 'You'd-better-behave-yourself-and-watch-your-step-or-else' girl that everyone had to tolerate until I left school the following June. Miss Milne smiled a genuine smile at me when I was called over to the administration block to pick up my signed report card. Her fingers lingered longer than necessary on her edge of the card before she released it. I got the heck out of there in case there was something else I had done and didn't know about, something that might have met with her disapproval.

I took a quick look at it to check the signature when I got outside. This time my overall average was 93%, nothing unusual, except Mrs. Munter, my shorthand/typing teacher's grade, 99%. That's the highest percentage I ever got in my whole life. When I first saw that I laughed out loud. Mrs. Munter is our most frightening and feared teacher at Central Commercial. In her classes she tolerates absolutely NO NONSENSE! She is a female version of Charles Laughton and one bellow from her area of the room and we are scared as mice. She dictates the most difficult letters and passages that she can find to test our nerves along with our skills. Then she stalks up and down the aisles while we transcribe our notes on our typewriters, trying not to tremble as her shadow passes over our work. Fraternizing with the students is out of the question. Her method for getting results is to treat everyone with equal businesslike efficiency. "I think she likes you," Monica teases because the idea of Mrs. Munter liking anyone is preposterous.

I am surprised to see Mrs. Fraser waiting for me in the kitchen when I get home that night. "Hello, Jeanne," she says, handing me my supper plate which has been warming on the stove as usual. This is the first time she has ever done this for me, the outcast, the girl who is to be avoided at all costs. After this I notice a definite thawing in the general attitude towards me. Cortie manages a smile when she gives me my clean sheets and towels. I can only think it's because I have been to Mrs. Johnson's house on the weekends. She's invited me back every weekend since the first time. I am cautious, but enjoying the easier atmosphere when Miss Milne telephones for me at the cottage one Saturday morning. A chill of fear spreads through my veins. What have I done?

Sitting beside her desk, I fiddle with the edges of my skirt waiting for her to speak. A quick glance tells me there is no dreaded file on her desk. "Well, Jeanne, dear, how are you doing?"

"Fine." I say and fix her with a tiny smile making sure I don't look cocky. She tells me how happy everyone is with my latest report card and that staying in the Home is obviously doing me good. I nod in relief, and the little smile I'm trying to hold is fast becoming a smirk.

"We've had a meeting of our Ladies' Auxiliary, you know, our group of women who run charitable affairs to raise funds for needy children. Well, they would like to buy you something. Is there anything you need? Some clothes, perhaps?" Electric light bulbs are lighting up in my head, in the room, everywhere.

"I, uh, do need a winter coat," I say tentatively, thinking about my black fake fur coat which is nearly bald. "But it wouldn't be right," I quickly slip in, "My roommate Laura's is worse than mine. Maybe they ought to get one for her instead."

"Leave it with me," Miss Milne says winding things up. "You just keep up those good grades. We are proud to have such a hard-working child among us. Now run along."

The following week Miss Milne, Laura and I are in New York City at Bergdorf Goodman's choosing winter coats. The first few I try on Miss Milne shakes her head and says, "No, not good enough." In the end, we select a double-breasted, black woolen coat, with a price tag of $150. It has a thick satin lining and the weave is so tight it feels like felt. It seems that I have crossed many rivers and gone many miles since Aunt Sophie and I bought a winter coat together.

Laura swings around in front of the mirror. She's in love with her black, flared coat with the stand-up velvet collar. Miss Milne signals the woman to throw away our old ones which she discreetly deposits under the counter. We smile all the way home. I'm still smiling when

Laura says good night and turns out the lights. A few minutes later she says quietly, "Without you I never would have gotten anything."

Laura and I are the only high school seniors and are privileged to share a large room next to Cortie's, opposite the linen closet. Staying in the cottage is the closest I have ever been to living in a house. The four cottages are divided into boys' and girls' cottages, one each for juniors and one each for seniors. Our cottage has a large parlor furnished with cheerful curtains and matching sofas and windows all around that open onto the grounds. The small library where Mrs. Johnson teaches on Monday nights has a piano in it, and there's a large dining room with kitchen off to one side. We are expected to help out at table and to keep our rooms clean, but the cottages are kept spotless by cleaners and not by the girls. A large administration building separates the boys' and girls' cottages. The offices of the director, social worker, psychologist and secretaries are on the ground floor. Miss Milne lives in an apartment above, sharing it with her mother whom I have met several times when I have been called to 'take tea' with them in the afternoons. She is a kind, white-haired lady already bound to a wheelchair, but company for Miss Milne who calls her 'Mother'. Her mother, in turn, calls her daughter 'Margaret', not 'Meg' or 'Maggie", all of which I think is terribly formal. Miss Milne is such a formidable lady herself that it tickles me pink when I hear her mother scold her in front of me. "That's not the way to pour tea, Margaret."

Like me, Laura goes to school in New York City and is studying bookkeeping. She's a pretty girl, quite smart, but rather dreamy and unmotivated. When she saw me getting up each morning so early, she began to do the same and we left for the city together. She had an hour to spare before classes started and sat in a coffee shop and studied. By the time she graduated, she went from just passing to getting top marks. She told me she didn't think she could ever do it and that I had inspired her to work harder.

Ever since I joined Central Commercial High School I have been aware of a very special teacher, Miss Alice Lanier. The first time I heard her speak in assembly, I perked up. She had such a clear way of getting her message across that it made everyone want to sit up and

261

listen. By the time I'm a senior, she is my English teacher, Senior Guidance Counsellor and College Advisor – my mentor, for short.

I met her when I joined the college program. After she interviewed me, asking poignant questions, but without prying, she learned enough about me to mark my case special. She made it her business to do everything in her power to push me forward, to pave the way for my entry into university and for launching me into life as an adult.

She helped me in the things that mattered, big and small. When I thought I needed bigger eyebrows and pencilled in thick, black ones like Elizabeth Taylor's, it was she who suggested that I try a more natural look. And, while she was on the subject, could she suggest that I exchange my black stockings for brown ones, and maybe I ought to get rid of my chewing gum.

A small woman, not quite five feet tall in high heels, she needs a little wooden stool to reach the top of the blackboard in English Class. But she is big on vocabulary, picking out words in our texts that she believes we should know and absorb as our own, words that will elevate us to higher planes of understanding by knowing their every meaning.

Buoy, she writes in copperplate script. *v. t. Keep afloat, hearten, sustain. The ability to recover quickly after setbacks, resilience.* She closes the dictionary and dusts off her hands. "Jeanne," she says to me, "Can you give me an example, in a sentence, please, of how to use this word?"

"Where are all the buoys?" I say, unable to resist the pun. She laughs with us because, by coincidence, we haven't any boys in our English class and she often remarks on it.

This petite lady of sixty-three years, who is so passionate in her educational beliefs, and who wears embroidered silk blouses and pale gray tweed suits, buoys me up whenever the going gets rough. "You have it in you to do great things," she says encouraging me to believe in myself.

As my college advisor she has collected teachers' commendations, both academic and personal, for my college and scholarship applications. She doesn't think small, and prepares me for my interviews at Hunter College, New York University and the State University of New York at Albany. Without her I never could have received the Mayor's Committee Citation for Scholastic Achievement, or the $500 scholarship as Future Teacher of the Year.

In the 1962 school yearbook, in answer to the question, "What do you consider your greatest problem in college advising? She wrote the following:

"My greatest problem is the superior student who has not yet come to realize the value of a good education. He may have financial worries, be lured by speedy gains in a well-paying first job, or just lack interest in improving himself. Such a pupil presents the greatest challenge to the college advisor...Do not be afraid of challenges. All human beings are equipped by Divine Providence for every problem that comes their way. Grow through your problems."

When I read this, I knew she was writing from the heart.

As I am preparing to step out into the world and make my way, I receive a letter from my mother. Mom has spent the past ten years in and out of the mental home, during which time I have had almost no contact with her. Trained as a nurse's aid, she works outside the mental home, but is still under its supervision. She had so many setbacks when Dad was still alive and still isn't self-supporting. She stays with Phyllis and Andy sometimes, and I see her there, but only briefly as she and Phyllis are at each other's throats in no time. She mentions in the letter that now I'm leaving high school, perhaps I'll get a job and she can move in with me.

This reminder of my duty as a daughter drives the knife in up to the hilt. It brings into question my worth and feelings as a child who was left to fend for herself. What my mother does not realize is that I have become a person with a life of my own. She needs to respect that. I respected hers. I never once approached the complicated issues of guilt and neglect that hovered between us. What she wants me to do, maybe I should, but I don't want to. I don't know what to say or how to say it.

Conflicting arguments preoccupy me, keep me awake at night, gnaw at my conscience until I decide to tell Miss Lanier that I'll have to decline my acceptance at university. She takes it all in, as if she half-expected it, and explains to me that looking after my mother is not my responsibility. "The best thing you can do for everyone, and that includes your mother, is to make your own way in this world. Don't be like me, Jeanne. I have looked after my mother all my grown up life; and she's been good to me. I'm retiring in a couple of years and she's still with me. I haven't had much of a life of my own. Mark my words, I am right in this."

Miss Milne offers me similar advice. "Jeanne, dear, you've seen my mother upstairs in her wheelchair. She'll be 93 years old soon, and dear as she is and has been, life would have been very different for me. There might have been love, excitement, world travel. But you see how I couldn't. Your teacher is right. You have got to have a life for yourself. Don't look so glum. You have a bright future ahead of you. You know that the whole Ladies' Auxiliary and I are behind you 100%. Now you just go and get on with your studies. Everything else will take care of itself." Despite my misgivings, I accept the words of these wise women who have been honest with me.

When I think back, there have been many faceless, nameless, single people and families who have taken me in, among them strangers, teachers, houseparents and parents of friends, who sustained me from one time to the next. One in a crowd of youngsters, I shared their lives and learned to love them, even lost them. At twelve years old I had Rose de Rosa looking after me. But she left me. Left her husband, too. She left this world entirely. Mr. Scott informed me of her death at a time when our relations were at an all-time low. With triumph creeping into his voice he said, "You won't be seeing Rose de Rosa anymore," as I headed out the door for school one morning. "She died last week."

She hadn't called for ages, but often skipped weekends, when I'd baby-sit instead. Rose and her husband had recently moved to a smaller apartment. During that time, I didn't see her for a couple for months. They were still fixing up the new place. I kept remembering the last time we were together when she stayed up with me to watch a horror movie, "The Mummy's Tomb", and we clung to each other with fright every time the monster appeared. I didn't even know she was sick.

I saw her husband later on in the middle of winter. A light snow was falling. We were the only ones on the street and walking towards each other. He had lost a lot of weight and hadn't shaved recently. His hat was pulled down tight over his forehead and his collar was turned up against the weather, but I recognized him. I was stuck for words, and thought I would start with 'hello', but he walked right by me without stopping. I stood stock still in my tracks a while, my unuttered 'hello' echoing in hollow places in my chest, and watched his footprints fill up with snow.

Chapter Thirty-Nine
A Date At Carnegie Hall

Today we received our invitations for the Graduation Ceremony at Carnegie Hall.

**The Principal, Mrs. Gertrude M. Kufal, the Teachers and the
Graduating Class of
1963
Cordially Invite you to Attend the Graduation Ceremony of
Central Commercial High School at
CARNEGIE HALL
On Friday 21st June, 1963
At 10 o'clock
At 7th Avenue & 57th Street
New York City**

The reality of finishing high school looms up large and scary for me. It will be the end of one life and the beginning of another. I've thought of nothing but school for the past couple of months. Deadlines are galloping up faster than I can say 'jack rabbit'. Being editor-in-chief of THE HOURGLASS, 1963, has put on extra pressure and the other editors and I are frantic to get it ready for the printers by the Easter deadline. It hasn't been all slog. Mrs. Saper, the staff editor, has made it fun putting it together. Being our French teacher as well, while we cut and paste she entertains us with personal anecdotes about her experiences in Paris and with the French. "You are going to love France, Jeanne," she says to me. I look at her, my eyebrows forming two question marks above doubting eyes. But she assures me, "Oh, you'll get there one day. I know you will, *ma cherie.*"

Just before graduation she asks me to stay behind after our last French Class. "I want you to have this, my darling Jeannie. It has been so wonderful having you as my editor-in-chief," and places a small velvet box in my hands, urging me to open it. Nestled inside two pieces of pink cotton is a gold charm on a chain. "It's a tiny graduation cap! I wanted you to have that as a souvenir from me."

"Mrs. Saper, it's lovely. But I..." My voice gives out, the muscles working on thin air.

Taking it out of the box and slipping it around my neck, she whispers, "You deserve this and so much more, my darling, Jeannie."

"Thank you," I say and finger the tiny jewel.

"I'm going to miss you. Let's say *Au Revoir,* not good-bye," and she kisses me on both cheeks like they do in France.

Miss Lanier has been helping the Valedictorian and Salutatorian to prepare their speeches. The rest of us are learning the closing ceremony music. The music teacher says that Miss Lanier wrote the words to our school anthem that are sung to the theme of Beethoven's 8th Symphony: *"Central High your spirit will guide us over the highways of the world, Your proud banner close beside us ever gallantly unfurled."* Monika and I next to each other during singing practice, manage to miss out more notes than we sing when we get to these words. We are overcome with emotion, knowing that the stresses and strains, laughter and tears, shared by ourselves and our friends will soon be over, never to be repeated again.

On the big day we wear white caps and gowns hired for the occasion. Our robes flutter among the crowd of well wishers like wild daisies in a dark field as we gather under a summer sun outside Carnegie Hall. The signal comes from Miss Butler to form a line. She had been my 10th grade home teacher and the first of many to show me how to achieve my full potential. She wears a stylish brown shot silk dress and a large hat with flowers resting on the brim. Her large eyes show distress at performing this, her last, service for us. As she fusses along the line, straightening our caps and smoothing our gowns, she puts on a brave face, biting her lower lip not to cry. My heart swells.

Our Class of 1963 solemnly walks behind its teachers for the last time as the sound of *Pomp and Circumstance* wafts out into the street. They continue to their seats behind the podium facing the audience, while we take our places at the front of the Hall.

Unlike my junior high school graduation, where I was on my own, this time family members and friends are here to celebrate with me. Mom and Andy are in the audience. A few days ago my brother telephoned and told me he got my graduation announcement a few

267

weeks back. "We're coming. Mommy and me. Phyllis has to work," he said, and I was glad because I hadn't seen them for a long time. Mom had finally been released from Kings Park State Hospital. She'd moved in with Phyllis and Andy in New Jersey. I'd spoken to Andy soon afterwards and he said it was touch and go with Mom and Phyllis arguing all the time and that he and Mom were probably moving out and getting an apartment together now that he was working as a security guard.

It's funny but I don't recognize either one of them, my own family, at first. I walk right past them as I'm going down the aisle, even though I'm looking out for them. It isn't until I turn and look back that I recognize Andy's smile. He waves his hand shyly. Andy has changed so much. He's dyed his hair black and the gray, shiny suit he's wearing clashes with his fake tan that's turned yellowish. Mom is on his right, a scrawny shadow of her former self in a neat navy-blue dress and matching hat. Had she been ill to lose so much weight?

When the prizes and awards are given out, and I am summoned to the podium five times, I see Margaret Johnson and Miss Milne together at the back of the hall. Their faces lit up and punch-proud, they clap wildly as I quickly return to my seat. I'm flustered and surprised at the unexpected prizes, smiling down at my feet, afraid to lift my eyes for fear of losing my grip. What a fanciful team of supporters they make, rooting for me all the way to the end when Mrs. Johnson gives out a "Whoop! That's my Jeannie!" as I'm called to collect the prize for English, her favorite subject.

Both of these women are on the committee of the Ladies' Auxiliary of the Brooklyn Home for Children and I wonder how much influence they exerted on my behalf. The day Miss Milne told me that the Ladies' Auxiliary would finance my room and board at the State University of New York at Albany, I felt like the cavalry was rescuing me at the crucial moment. What with scholarships, grants and my savings and part-time work to pay for books, travel and personal things, it looks like I'll be going to college after all.

Miss Lanier put me in touch with Albany State. She said that even though Hunter College and NYU accepted me, it meant joining a work/study program that would take years to finish, if I ever did. She looked dreamy when she told me about life on campus and how I would be a part of the student life, go to concerts, plays, commune with intellectuals. Miss Lanier had such hopes for me, that if I didn't trust her so much, I wouldn't have believed a word of it. "Write," she would say. "You ought to be a writer. It's what I wanted to be. When I retire that's all I am going to do."

Miss Lanier wasn't exactly a mystic, though she believed in Spiritualism. She had a way of being right about the future even though it sounded utterly absurd at the time. "I can see you hosting cultural and literary soirées and moving in intellectual circles in foreign countries." This seemed a far cry from a girl who couldn't afford a trunk to pack her belongings for college. But I listened to her, shelving her words and ideas for another time when my life would be ripe and ready for anything.

She thought I was setting my sights too low when I applied for the business program within the teacher's curriculum. "You ought to study English Literature," she said, but quickly added, "however, I trust your judgement. You'll discover what to do in the end."

With graduation over, it is time to wind up things at the Brooklyn Home for Children, and prepare to leave after my year of grace. Miss Milne and Mrs. Fraser have organized a tea party for the graduates, Laura and me, and the committee of the Ladies' Auxiliary are there. Miss Milne heads a table piled high with sandwiches and cakes and has Laura and me sit next to her. Before we are allowed to return to our packing, Dot Relyea, the treasurer of the committee gives a little speech about how proud they are of our reaching graduation, considering the circumstances, and that they wish me luck at university and Laura the same at her bookkeeping job.

We stand up to thank them, but Dot shushes us, telling us to sit down. "We've a few small gifts for you to help you on your way." The dining room table and floor is afloat with wads of wrapping paper and cards as we unwrap the many presents the ladies have bought us. I don't know about Laura, but for me it was a whole lot of birthdays and Christmases wrapped into one. Among my presents are two pieces of American Tourister luggage, an iron and a portable Smith-Corona typewriter. "Jeanne," Dot says above the din of excitement, "I wanted to make sure you typed us a letter once in a while...and your term papers, too!"

It is hard to remember later on what I say or how I thank them. But I do remember while unwrapping the gifts, looking at their faces, soaking in the sheer delight they had in giving, wanting so much to please. How many times in the past had I seen this kind of giving? Once? Twice? Maybe it was in my grandfather's chuckle when he brought us yesterday's cakes from his friend's bakery or in my Aunt Helen's face when she celebrated our first birthdays.

I am upstairs packing my suitcases again, thinking about this, regretting not having the rest of my relatives to share in some of our better moments in life. My cousins Alex and Eddie have kept in touch, and we've gone out for the day together. But not a single solitary one of my relatives, aside from my sister and father has ever come to see me in the children's home during the past eight years. There have been no telephone calls, either, birthday or Christmas cards. It is almost as though we were dead.

I find an extra luggage label, fill it in and attach it to the handle of my new typewriter. I think it might have been the letter Andy and I typed when we felt lonely and abandoned after we were installed in the Kallman Home for Children that turned them against us. Ever since the traumas of the Shelter and the loneliness of the Home, we felt badly let down. We toyed with a broken down old machine and picked out enough words with two fingers to write a letter to our aunts and tell them how horrible we thought they were to send us away without a word of warning or good-bye. Did we ever get a stamp and send that letter, I wonder? Could whatever it was we felt and tried to say as 9 and 10 year-olds be the reason for the family abandonment? It doesn't matter now. The fact is, writing that letter made us feel better afterwards. It consoled us to think that such a large loose end had finally been dealt with in our own way.

My bags are ready by the front door. I'm waiting for Travis, Mrs. Johnson's husband, to pick me up in his light blue Cadillac. I have to pinch myself sometimes to remember that I'm going to live in their house over the summer. After spending so many weekends and vacations with them this past year, I'm not too worried about how to behave. No one will be around anyhow. The family is traveling to

270

Texas to visit their relatives and will be away for July and August. Margaret said I would be doing them a favor if I stayed at the house and kept their maid, Lena, company.

"We's gonna have some fun, ain't we, Jeannie?" Lena declares, smiling. "I'm okay when you're out workin' in that office durin' the day, but come night-time I get the spooks if'n I'm by myself." I know this to be a fact. When we are alone at night she watches television with a carving knife by her side.

Lena's quarters, her bedroom, parlor and bathroom are above the kitchen at the back of the house. Picture postcards and photographs of her family are propped up along the top of her dresser. Stacks of children's clothes, toys, even a transistor radio are carefully stacked in a corner. These are the things she puts by for when "I goes home to my folks" once a year at Christmas. A diminutive woman of not quite five feet tall, a proud grandmother of advancing years, she keeps faith with her family by working in New York City and sending them most of her earnings. Her suitcases and cardboard boxes are full to overflowing with things she's bought during the year when she carries them down South on her annual vacation.

Having poured over her photograph albums together to pass the long summer evenings, I can easily picture the surprised smiles and grins on the faces of her children and grandchildren when she passes around their presents.

She's a strong-willed woman considering her age and size and bosses me around no end of times. On Saturdays she insists that I go with her to the grocery store to help her decide what to cook for us next week. We eat the same food and sit together at the enamel table in the kitchen, the formalities of the dining room having been abandoned over the summer break.

"What about pork?" she asks. And when she gets no answer she says, "What's the matter? Cat got your tongue, girl? Make up your mind. Travis likes a nice piece of steak. Come on. Help me with those brains of yours. How about southern fried chicken, Claudia's favorite? We can have peach cobbler afterwards. Mine's better than Margaret's, but don't you go tellin' her I said so, you hear?" She stops for a breath, scratches her head, rolls her eyes up high into her head then says, "I know! Meat loaf. Everybody likes it. Well, come on, don't dawdle.

Make up your mind!" All the time she's talking, our basket is filling up and I follow behind her, pushing it along, feeling like a silly puppy dog.

Oh, precious Lena, I'm thinking, how many times have I dreamed of being asked what I would like to eat? Being told, "Your plate's on the stove, don't you want it?" is the closest I have come to making a choice, on a strictly 'yes or no' basis. How many times have I shut my eyes as I held my plate over a steaming 'hot table' of cafeteria-style boiled cabbage and mashed potatoes or the dreaded 'soles-of-my-shoes' liver to receive a dollop. Don't be too hard on me. I've still got a lot to learn.

Chapter Forty
Gaps In My Album

I have begun a picture album, filling it in as I do the late summer evenings, in a soft-edged languid sort of way. The cover is padded, thick enough to protect the people inside. I can't afford corners so Elmer's glue holds them permanently in place. In it are pictures of friends from the Kallman Home and the Brooklyn Home and their faces laugh between its black pages.

I have hoarded my scraps of photographs over the years in a sweet-smelling box I once received scented soap in. Staying at the Johnson's luxurious home has been as good as a vacation, and I have had time to work on my album, especially since my greatest worry at the moment is deciding what I want for supper.

I can't decide whether to cut up the strip of four pictures that Phyllis, Andy and I took in a booth at Coney Island. My sister is squashed up in the middle and my brother and I bend towards her. By the fourth frame we are hysterical with struggling to keep in front of the camera in a tiny booth designed for one person, not three. Our mouths are wide open beneath eyes squeezed shut as the flash goes. Phyllis is blonde, a pretty 18-year-old. I've my usual brown long hair and ragged bangs I cut myself with blunt-tipped school scissors. I'm thirteen and wearing make-up for the first time - my sister's make-up, her idea. In black Maybelline she has penciled doe eyes along my almond-shaped lids, and ran creamy Coral Sea lipstick over my mouth. Andy's hair stands on end as if he's frightened, it having grown out in bristles after the 'baldy' haircut he got before he went to summer camp.

Judging from when my collection of pictures starts you'd think I began life as a ten-year old, at about the time I entered the Home. That's because I have no record of my babyhood. Whatever pictures we had went missing when Dad was evicted; but even then, as far as we knew, no pictures of me and Andy as babies ever existed. We saw the dozens of black and white images of my sister wearing one new dress after another that filled a whole album which Mom kept in her bureau drawers. Dad took all of those pictures. He developed them, too. But he lost interest in photography and stashed his equipment in the closet for good after I was born. Andy and I always said that we'd make up for our lack of pictures of us later on when we had a camera of our own. We didn't think about not being able to go back and become babies again, though.

My album is filling up and taking shape. It shows my friendships and important events and how I have grown up.

Forest Hills doesn't escape the city's heat. I sleep fitfully, and dream about photographs, about albums filled with faces and places that float by me but are forever a hand's length out of reach. Aunt Helen glides by, smiling at the camera, in her wedding dress. She starts laughing, her voice tinkling like a bell. She's holding out a picture for me to take. I'm laughing, too, and just as I take it, she disappears.

I look down at the picture in my hand. It is lovely one of my whole family at my brother's christening at the time of my very first memory. I run my fingers along the deckled edges of the square black and white photograph re-living the story of the moment it was taken. There's a breeze. Dad's hat is firmly on his head with the brim pulled down against the glare of the sun. Mom's polka dot dress with the fake flower corsage at the shoulder flutters gently and the breeze presses the silky fabric against her thighs. She holds my brother in her arms and the hem of his long gown mingles with hers. My sister leans forward, her arms protectively engulfing me, but I don't seem too sure about any of this as I squint uncertainly into the lens.

What should I do with this picture? If I put it in the album, it will be out of place. The gap of so many years in between is too great. I'm not going to include it. I have looked deep into it with all the questions in the world, so deep that tears blur the figures. Why, they could be anyone. It was so long ago. They probably are somebody else.